STAGE STRUCK

"You are fascinating, Rachel," Howard said. "Fascinating, talented, and puzzling . . ." He brushed a wisp of hair from her temple. "I guess I'm trying to decide whether to put you in a taxi and send you home, or"—he hesitated, seeming to search Rachel's face for a sign of encouragement or rebuff—"or whether I should pour us another drink and run the risk of making a fool of myself if you stay."

"I . . . I don't think you'd be . . . making a fool of yourself, Howard," she said slowly, surprising herself. Only then did she look directly into his eyes. The gin had warmed her, relaxed her, and her cheeks were flushed. But she wasn't drunk, and this wasn't the gin speaking. "I don't want anything to interfere with our professional relationship," she said. She walked over to the French doors, opened them, and stepped out onto the terrace. She was unaware that Howard had joined her there until she felt his breath on the back of her neck and his tanned hands on her bare shoulders. He ran his palms lightly back and forth, causing a pleasant chill wherever his fingers lingered. Rachel closed her eyes, and Howard bent to kiss her shoulder. His hands felt so warm, and Rachel wanted suddenly to be held, to be needed, to be loved . . .

CATCH UP ON THE BEST IN CONTEMPORARY FICTION FROM ZEBRA BOOKS!

LOVE AFFAIR   (2181, $4.50)
by Syrell Rogovin Leahy
A poignant, supremely romantic story of an innocent young woman with a tragic past on her own in New York, and the seasoned newspaper reporter who vows to protect her from the harsh truths of the big city with his experience — and his love.

ROOMMATES   (2156, $4.50)
by Katherine Stone
No one could have prepared Carrie for the monumental changes she would face when she met her new circle of friends at Stanford University. For once their lives intertwined and became woven into the tapestry of the times, they would never be the same.

MARITAL AFFAIRS   (2033, $4.50)
by Sharleen Cooper Cohen
Everything the golden couple Liza and Jason Greene touched was charmed — except their marriage. And when Jason's thirst for glory led him to infidelity, Liza struck back in the only way possible.

RICH IS BEST   (1924, $4.50)
by Julie Ellis
From Palm Springs to Paris, from Monte Carlo to New York City, wealthy and powerful Diane Carstairs plays a ruthless game, living a life on the edge between danger and decadence. But when caught in a battle for the unobtainable, she gambles with the only thing she owns that she cannot control — her heart.

THE FLOWER GARDEN   (1396, $3.95)
by Margaret Pemberton
Born and bred in the opulent world of political high society, Nancy Leigh flees from her politician husband to the exotic island of Madeira. Irresistibly drawn to the arms of Ramon Sanford, the son of her father's deadliest enemy, Nancy is forced to make a dangerous choice between her family's honor and her heart's most fervent desire!

Available wherever paperbacks are sold, or order direct from the Publisher. Send cover price plus 50¢ per copy for mailing and handling to Zebra Books, Dept. 2399, 475 Park Avenue South, New York, N.Y. 10016. Residents of New York, New Jersey and Pennsylvania must include sales tax. DO NOT SEND CASH.

APPEARANCES

ROBIN
ST. THOMAS

ZEBRA BOOKS
KENSINGTON PUBLISHING CORP.

ZEBRA BOOKS

are published by

Kensington Publishing Corp.
475 Park Avenue South
New York, NY 10016

First printing: July, 1988

Printed in the United States of America

*For Bruce and Charles
and to the memory of Annie Singer*

BOOK ONE

Chapter One

April 1968

Dusk was settling over the city as the bus rolled into the Port Authority Terminal on Manhattan's West Side. A pelting rain washed the grimy surface of the area surrounding Forty-second Street and Ninth Avenue. Sidewalk vendors hastily packed away their plastic Statues of Liberty and replicas of the Empire State Building and took shelter under the flapping awnings of vegetable markets and fish stores. Cars were gridlocked in the evening rush hour traffic, and horns blared in every key of the musical scale.

Rachel watched, fascinated, as two truck drivers left their cabs to stand menacingly in the downpour and shake their fists at one another; their shouting, which was inaudible through the closed windows of the bus, created a Midtown pantomime. A moment later the scene was joined by a traffic policeman. His yellow rain slicker reminded Rachel fondly of the weather gear her brother Roger had worn as a patrol boy in Excelsior. But, she mused, Roger never saw the likes of this! Even downtown Minneapolis could never boast so colorful a spectacle!

The bus driver muttered an angry expletive under his breath and swerved the long vehicle so abruptly that Rachel's totebag spilled its contents onto the empty seat beside her. Several passengers called out, "Take it easy—we've made it this far" and "Let's get there in one piece."

But they were there—and in one piece. The bus had entered the dark terminal tunnel; the driver negotiated the turns at slower and slower speeds and finally braked with a screech.

"New York City!" he announced loudly over the intercom in nasal Brooklynese. "Last stop! Don't forget your belongings and keep an eye on your wallets!"

He opened the door and Rachel wrinkled her nostrils; the diesel exhaust fumes immediately filled the bus. Whew! she thought. I'm glad I don't have to sing tonight!

While passengers lined up to wait for the baggage to be unloaded, Rachel removed her single weekender bag from the rack above her head. Then she replaced the fallen items into her oversized tote and made her way to the exit.

Even the terminal building with its derelicts and winos and garbage strewn about could not dampen Rachel's spirits. Heeding the bus driver's advice, she made certain that her wallet was buried at the bottom of her totebag, and the bag itself she carried protectively against her. Her two hundred dollars in traveler's cheques were folded and tucked into her bra.

She followed the signs and only had to ask twice before she found herself on the corner of Forty-second and Eighth. The rain still poured down and it appeared as though everyone in the city of eight million inhabitants had decided to look for a taxi at the same time and at the same corner. But Rachel had learned a trick from John, another of her brothers.

She stepped off the curb, then straddled her umbrella and suitcase between both legs in order to use her free hand. She positioned two fingers as John had taught her, and whistled.

A boy next to her said, "Hey, lady, how'd you do *that?*"

A taxi pulled up almost immediately and the driver said, "That's pretty good, honey. Hop in!"

He didn't have to repeat the invitation. Rachel tossed her wet weekender bag, umbrella, and tote on the backseat and climbed in after them.

"Where to, doll?" asked the cabbie.

Rachel consulted the tiny notebook in her trenchcoat

pocket. "Allerton House" she answered. "It's at—"

"I know, doll. Every gorgeous girl arrives in New York stays there—or the Barbizon or the YWCA. You in advertising? TV?"

"Why do you ask that?"

" 'Cause Allerton's on Fifty-seventh and Lex, and that's near all the ad agencies on Madison. CBS is a few minutes crosstown, NBC is at Rockefeller Center—but walking's faster than a cab. Somehow I don't figure you for a college kid—that'd be the Barbizon—you know, secretary types and Hunter girls who don't live in the dorms. Anyway, I figured with your looks, you're in show biz. So?"

"Excuse me? asked Rachel, still filing all the information she'd just heard.

"You an actress or model? What?"

She laughed. "I sing."

"Hey, small world! I got a sister in Queens, she's a go-go dancer—does gigs in some of the clubs out near me on weekends. Rest of the week, though, she's a hairdresser. Pays better than dancing or singing, right?" Before Rachel could answer, he asked, "How old are you, anyway? Twenty?"

"I'm twenty-two," she said, "and—"

"You don't look it. My sister's only twenty, but she lied to get the club dates."

"Well," said Rachel, "I don't sing in clubs."

"You a rock singer?"

"Actually, I sing musical comedy—"

"Oh, *I* get it." The cabbie glanced at her through his rearview mirror; Rachel noticed him watching her and wondered if it might be wise to end the conversation. "You gonna be the next Barbra Streisand maybe? Or Judy Garland? Or backup on one of them TV variety shows?"

"Uh . . . not exactly." She cleared her throat. "I'm . . . well, so far I've done mostly Julie Andrews roles in summer stock . . ." Rachel suddenly felt stiff and out of place.

The taxi hit a pothole; Rachel wondered whether the driver had missed seeing it because of an aversion to her

11

current idol.

But he whistled. "Holy shit! Excuse me, honey, I don't mean to swear none. But the last time I had a legit singer in my cab was . . . let's see . . . I had to drop Jane Powell — the movie star — at CBS. Some interview — or maybe Ed Sullivan. Powell's no spring chicken, but she still looks terrific . . ."

Then he stopped his monologue. "Listen — if you're in the business, why the hell you staying all the way over on the East Side? You gotta take care of those pipes — April weather can get crazy here, y'know?"

Rachel smiled. "I'm not 'in the business' yet," she admitted. "But I am here for the New Stars Talent Search Auditions." Her heart thrummed at her own words.

"Y'mean the big contest on the radio? You gonna be in that?"

She nodded instead of speaking; she could see that he was still watching through the mirror.

"Wow! Hey, I wish you all the luck! It's a tough racket, though. You gotta be as tough as the business. That's what I keep telling my sister. You gotta be tough!"

Rachel sighed. She'd heard the advice before, although never voiced in quite this manner. She glanced at the cabbie's hack license over the glove compartment. There she saw his photograph and the name of Irving O'Connell.

"Mr. O'Connell — " she began.

"Irving. My mother hates O'Connell. My pop was Irish, but Mama's maiden name was Plotnick. She thinks Irving Plotnick suits me better. Wha d'you think?"

But Rachel didn't need to reply. They had reached Fifty-seventh Street between Lexington and Park avenues, and Irving Plotnick/O'Connell was busy scribbling on a scrap of paper.

Rachel dug out her wallet and paid the fare.

"Here, doll. My sister's number. If you need any advice, you know, inside info on the business — singing or dancing, it's still a business. Oh, yeah, she gives good haircuts, too. Give a call, no strings attached."

Rachel pocketed the number. "That's very nice of you."

"Nice, nothing. Someday, maybe I can say I knew you when. I'll listen to the auditions. By the way, doll, what's your name, in case you win?"

Rachel's hand was on the door. "Allenby," she said. "Rachel Hawthorne Allenby."

She saw Irving writing it down as she entered the hotel.

After being informed of all the house rules—no men above the lobby, no cooking or food in the rooms, no noise after ten o'clock, payment by the week or month but always in advance—Rachel took the elevator to the sixth floor and after a long walk down the winding corridor found the door that read 631. She had noted the bathroom and the showers, both at locations that seemed miles from her room.

No matter, she thought, turning the key in the lock. I'll just be here for a week or two. Once the auditions are over, I'll concentrate on finding an apartment and a job—she smiled at the thought of calling Irving's sister in Queens, something she was not planning to do—and besides, a room on the sixth floor ought to have a decent view.

She swung the door open, and for the first time since leaving her parents' large, rambling old Victorian house, she felt a flicker of anxiety. It wasn't homesickness, that she knew; she'd dreamed for years of coming to New York. But she hadn't planned on the starkness of the cell-like rectangle masquerading as a room—even if it did cost only five dollars a night plus tax.

She turned on the light switch, but with the dreariness of a dark rainy evening, the uncovered frosted bulb at the center of the ceiling did nothing to brighten the bleak surroundings. There was one window—and it faced a brick wall. The single bed, the lopsided chest of drawers, and the desk all matched; they were painted in ugly battleship gray enamel that was so thick it resembled soggy clay. The bed was covered with a hideous chintz spread that was polka-

13

dotted from cigarette holes. There was a three-legged table with a telephone on it and a small washstand in the corner. A cheap mirror hung above it.

Rachel removed her wet raincoat and opened the closet door. There were three empty wire hangers dangling on the rod; on the shelf was a mothball-smelling winter blanket—also in battleship gray.

A week or two, Rachel thought. I can put up with this for a week or two. Then she peeked in the mirror and made a silly face. "Oh God," she said aloud, "what am I doing here?"

She unzipped the plaid suitcase and carefully unfolded the burgundy chiffon evening gown that she would wear for the auditions. She was glad she had brought along its quilted satin hanger.

The gown was starkly simple, with a bateau neck and long sleeves down to her wrists. She knew that other finalists would wear glittery designer creations and parade them as if the New Stars auditions were the Miss America contest. But Rachel's preference had always run toward the dramatic rather than the showy. Her height and slim figure would carry the dress—not the other way around.

She hung the other two dresses she'd packed: the burgundy wool sweater-dress and the black silk crepe. One for daytime auditions, the other for dinners or whatever else was scheduled for the audition week festivities. Neither of the minidresses was indecently short. There were no more hangers, so she folded her jeans in half and laid them over the desk chair.

Suddenly she was tired. Not from sitting in a bus for all those hours; excitement and anticipation were instead taking their toll. Rachel cleaned her contact lenses and brushed her shoulder-length chestnut hair. It was dinnertime, but she wasn't hungry. She glanced at the phone. She'd have to let her parents know she'd arrived safely. She didn't relish the prospect; conversations with Russell and Marsha Allenby had always been strained. Her father considered long-distance calls a waste of money—as he considered this trip—and her mother would cluck on and on about vitamins and sleep and trusting no one in as "wild" a city as New York.

Nonetheless, she picked up the receiver. A card beneath the phone read: *Local calls 50 cents. All others, dial "0."* She could probably save money by phoning from the lobby. No, that meant waiting for the elevator—*and* inviting an audience to eavesdrop. She took a deep breath and dialed "0." May as well get it over with, she decided. Then I'll really be on my own.

Three minutes of the usual stilted questions and answers had exhausted the last of Rachel's waning energies. She folded down the worn bedspread. Crawling between the mended muslin sheets, she scratched her elbow. She fluffed the lead-weight pillow—and sneezed. Oh, no! she thought. I *can't* come down with a cold the very week of the auditions!

But then she saw a feather sticking through a hole in the pillow, and she laughed. She'd been allergic to feathers since kindergarten!

Relieved, she lay back and closed her eyes. Only then did she realize she hadn't turned out the light.

There was a Mayflower Doughnut Shop across the street from the hotel. The elevator operator confided that the coffee there was cheaper and better than the brew in the mezzanine dining room. "Besides, sugar," she said, "those crones get one look at you and they'll try to have *you* for lunch!"

Rachel wasn't sure that the sleepy-eyed attendant had said what she meant—or meant what she'd said. She decided not to pursue it.

The previous night's rain had left Fifty-seventh Street slick and clean, despite the building crews, who were riveting and tearing up parts of Lexington Avenue around the corner. Rachel ate a doughnut and coffee—the elevator operator had been right about the coffee; it was excellent—and then she returned to the hotel to the bank of telephone booths just off the lobby.

She called the woman at the New Stars auditions office to check in. She had arrived a day early in order to find her bearings in a city she had never visited; the other finalists weren't due in for twenty-four hours. Rachel was invited to a dress rehearsal of a new show later that week, a tea with the other national finalists and the press, a radio broadcast interview, and several parties. She was advised of the audition pianist's schedule as well as the location and availability of practice rooms for warm-up. "Welcome to New York!" gushed the auditions chairman. "We can't wait to get to know you!"

But for the moment, Rachel was on her own.

Her first stop, after a leisurely stroll through Central Park, was the theater district. She passed CBS and contemplated Irving-the-cabby, hoping that unlike his sister, *she* wouldn't have to take any jobs but those in Broadway musicals. She *would* have to sign up for jazz classes, however. The reminder came from myriad second-floor studios whose windows, covered in boldly lettered primary colors, advertised every kind of dance instruction imaginable. It's an occupational necessity, Rachel said to herself, aware of her one musical shortcoming: she moved well, was graceful enough, but she couldn't dance for beans.

She had reached the Morosco Theater, where the auditions would be held on Monday, but she paused before entering the lobby. She wanted to drink in the excitement. This elegant old building had played home to some of the greatest names in theater history, both musical and dramatic stars of generations past and present. A feeling of respect as well as intimidation washed over Rachel and then she opened the door.

But as she pulled the heavy inner door toward her, she was immediately stopped by a guard inside the foyer.

"Are you with the company?" he asked.

"I'm a finalist in the New Stars auditions," Rachel answered with far more confidence in her voice than she felt.

"Well, you'll have to come back when you've been issued a pass. Besides, this is a closed rehearsal today. No visitors."

Rachel decided to try. "That's okay, but can't I at least take a peek? I'm going to have to sing here in a week—that's frightening enough without ever having seen what the place looks like."

"Listen," said the guard, "I can sympathize. I'm studying acting, myself. But rules are rules. . . ."

He seemed close to weakening; Rachel could sense it. "I tell you what. I promise, if you'll just let me in for a minute, I'll be on my way and nobody'll ever know." She thought for a split second and added, "It'll make a big difference in the way I sing at the finals."

She had touched a fellow artist, a colleague, even, she mused, if he'd only been studying for two weeks. He glanced around and then with his hand indicated for her to follow.

They stood at the top of the aisle in the darkened theater; work lights illuminated the stage and several actors, seated on folding chairs, were running through lines.

Rachel walked down and glanced at the mezzanine and balcony. The moment almost took her breath away. "My God," she whispered, "this is twice the size of any place I've ever sung in—how will anyone ever hear me in a place so big?"

The guard leaned over. "Microphones," he whispered back with an expression clearly implying that Rachel ought to know such things.

She peered at the rows and rows of empty seats. Seats that would be filled on the night of the final auditions. Her stomach suddenly turned queasy and she only glanced at the ornate ceiling and the sparkling chandeliers before she was overcome by the urge to run from the place.

But poise was part of being a singer. In a practiced, steady voice, she said, "Thank you. I'll go so you won't get

17

into trouble." She was out on the street before the guard had even asked her name.

She decided to put anything musical on hold for the rest of the day. Once onstage, she'd somehow manage; usually her concentration and the music saw to that. It was these unexpected surprises when she *wasn't* singing that completely threw her off balance.

Rachel spent the afternoon on "safer" pursuits; she walked through the theater district, where she tried to buy three-dollar balcony seats for *Fiddler on the Roof* or *Hello, Dolly* and was told at both theaters to try again in six months. She explored Times Square, but the carnival atmosphere with its peep shows and junk shops, together with the lewd appraisals and remarks she drew from the wisecracking drunks in every doorway, sent her quickly back to the more staid but definitely less threatening area of Fifth Avenue, where she strolled past all the stores she'd only read about or seen in movies. She entered Tiffany's and browsed—but couldn't find the courage to go above the main floor with less than two hundred dollars to her name.

She almost weakened when she saw a pair of antique leather boots in I. Miller's window, but restraint surfaced in time. She did, however, buy a brown silk-velvet minidress at Bonwit Teller's Finale Shop on the third floor; she found both the clearance section and the dress itself by mistake when she went in search of the ladies' room. She smiled to herself upon exiting the store with a designer original that had only diminished her bankroll by twenty dollars plus tax. The price had been crossed out three times; the dress had once been tagged at one hundred and fifty. The bargain made Rachel feel like a bonafide New Yorker, and it was only her second day! It also helped to quell her earlier misgivings at the theater.

She dined at the Mayflower's coffee counter. The prices were reasonable enough by New York standards, Rachel thought, but a dollar and five cents for a meal consisting of a tunafish sandwich and coffee was more than she'd ever paid at the local diner back home. At the rate of two

18

dollars a day for meals and five dollars plus tax for her room, two hundred dollars—minus twenty for the dress—wouldn't last very long in New York!

Rachel didn't meet all of the New Stars finalists during the coming week. Some were at interviews while others rehearsed. Those with agents or theater connections seemed to form a private club. The two Southern belles—one a tall, buxom blonde from Texas, the other a fat, buxom belter from Alabama—giggled and blushed as though they were Siamese twins.

There were fifty finalists from across the country. The New Stars auditions were, Rachel knew, largely a publicity stunt. The competition had amassed tremendous press thus far as talent scouts searched every inch of the map—every inch with a population of more than one million, at any rate—with the enthusiasm of the armies dispatched to locate Cinderella and match her to the glass slipper.

The contest's alleged purpose was to award the male and female winners featured roles in an upcoming Havermeyer production. The name *Havermeyer* commanded the fear and awe inspired by the legendary David Merrick and the Shuberts.

The regional winners had been invited to New York for the final auditions, and each hopeful knew that the victors of next Monday's auditions were assured of instant visibility as well as immediate employment in a Broadway-bound musical.

Rachel noted at the first cocktail reception that more women than men numbered among the finalists. There were fewer than a dozen male singers or dancers, no more than there had been at the regional auditions. Ah well, she mused, so this week will turn out to be another hen party, no different from the rest. . . .

At the radio broadcast on Friday, she couldn't help but notice the most striking of the male finalists, although he had sung before she'd arrived; he was on his way out of the

19

studio and Rachel saw his face only because of a mirrored reflection. If his voice matched his looks, she thought, there would be no contest — he'd win, hands down; but he was most likely another reedy-voiced all-purpose performer, as she liked to term them: barely adequate dancers or singers but trying to masquerade as both; if they could act, local stock companies boasted "triple threats," but small towns were not ignorant to advertising.

"What're you staring at, my dear?" asked Mrs. Carleton, one of the blue-haired matrons of the auditions committee.

"Oh . . . I thought I had too much mascara on," said Rachel, looking back from the mirror as she felt her face warming.

"Well, it's not as if you *need* it, dear," said the cloche-hatted matron. "I would recommend, though, a slightly more discreet hemline. I know it's the fashion, but we wouldn't want to cause any of our male judges to have heart failure, now would we?"

Rachel heard a secretary at the desk mutter, "Small fear of that!"

Mrs. Carleton turned and asked, "What, dear?"

The desk plaque in front of the pretty brunette read Norma Kendall. "Oh, nothing," said Norma, smiling at Rachel.

When Mrs. Carleton entered the elevator, Norma said to Rachel, "It's really amazing, isn't it?"

"Isn't what?" Rachel asked.

"Just that these social butterballs like your blue fairy there spend a lifetime on the Broadway scene and never seem to get it."

"Get what?"

Norma stared directly at Rachel. "Look around this place. Do you see any *men* who could drop dead from looking at your knees or mine? Or for that matter at Raquel Welch's or Brigitte Bardot's?"

Rachel felt as though Norma were privy to a foreign language that only sounded like English, with everyday words that had a totally different meaning.

20

"Listen, I must be pretty stupid, but—"

Just then, a well-known actor passed by and Norma held up her index finger as a signal for Rachel to wait. They watched as he minced down the hall in his black Nehru suit and white silk turtleneck. He greeted friends in a higher-pitched voice than Rachel's. He also affected a pronounced lisp that had obviously been acquired; it was not a speech impediment.

"Now," whispered Norma, leaning across her desk, "do you really think *he'd* go into cardiac arrest if either of us walked past him in the nude?"

Rachel burst into laughter.

"Understand now?" asked the secretary.

"I'm certainly beginning to," answered Rachel. "I've always been a quick study—besides, Minnesota isn't *that* far away!"

"Honey, I hope you didn't come to New York to find Mr. Right. There's a lot more competition for *him*—from both sexes—than there is for any Broadway contract."

"Well, right now, the latter is what interests me, Norma."

"I figured you looked intelligent, too. I'll cross my fingers for you—and you do the same for me. What interests *me* is the *former.*"

"Well, break a leg, then," said Rachel.

"Thanks," said Norma. "The same to you."

The rest of the week sped by, with Rachel's calendar filled from morning to night. The interviews at every luncheon, tea, and reception were exhausting. The only time off from public appearances was on Sunday afternoon, the day preceding the auditions; finalists were advised to rest well for the night ahead.

"This week has only been a preliminary to the big event!" announced Mrs. Carleton to her young charges. They were assembled at Sardi's, where the finalists had been invited, en masse, for luncheon. It was Rachel's second visit to the landmark restaurant; however, on the first occasion, she had peered at a menu, panicked at the prices, and stopped in the ladies' room. Upon returning to the dining room, she had made a very hasty exit.

After the exquisite cannelloni and dessert, the already formed cliques waved and went their separate ways. The handsome blond—Rachel had overheard someone call him Jamie—had been present earlier, but he seemed to have disappeared.

Rachel walked alone toward Central Park. She didn't mind the lack of company. It was a new experience after the commotion caused by four brothers and two sisters constantly underfoot, not to mention her regularly visiting grandparents and maiden aunts.

During the frenetic activity of the week, Rachel had spent what little leisure time was granted her at the Library of the Performing Arts at Lincoln Center, next door to the Metropolitan Opera. There she had listened to her favorite shows on recordings that had often been unavailable in Excelsior or Minneapolis stores. She applied for a temporary library card and collected theatrical biographies, which she then took back to the hotel and read with the dim help of the tiny night light clamped to the headboard of her bed.

All she missed was her piano. The thought of the old yellowed keys on her grandmother's ancient upright transported her in memory back to the parlor and earlier days, when she'd had to sit atop two Minneapolis telephone directories just to reach the black-keyed sharps and flats.

Of course, there were pianos at the rehearsal studio, but there had been no time to play music simply for relaxation. An hour with one of the audition pianists was an hour in which to work and polish her song for the final, important audition.

On this particular late afternoon, Rachel entered Central Park from Fifty-ninth Street, trying not to sneeze from the horse dander as she passed the hansom carriages lined up along the street. She visited the children's zoo and the barren skating rink, and came out of the park on the Upper

22

West Side. From there, she walked back down to Columbus Circle and started east back along Central Park South. Brisk walks always helped to quell audition and performance nerves. They also heightened Rachel's appetite, especially since she had mostly picked at her cannelloni; it seemed as though each time she had placed the fork in her mouth, she had been asked a question by one of the producers or audition staff members. Finally she had given up and decided that such occasions weren't really intended for eating.

But now suddenly she was hungry. She passed the St. Moritz Hotel, where, despite the April chill, guests were eating ice cream parfaits at the outdoor Café de la Paix. Her stomach growled jealously, but she didn't dare investigate this particular restaurant's price menu.

Farther down the block she saw a Burger Heaven. The name said it all, she decided, entering the diner. There she indulged in a a gigantic cheeseburger with a double order of french fries; her furtive nibbles at Sardi's aside, she had dined on hors d'oeuvres at artists' receptions all week, eating there in order to conserve money rather than exhaust it on food; suddenly she didn't care if a dozen years went by before she saw another stuffed olive or a toast point with caviar. As the ground meat's juices oozed from the toasted English muffin and dripped onto Rachel's plate, she sighed contentedly.

When the waitress asked if she'd like dessert, Rachel hesitated only while deciding which topping to order. "Yes," she said, "I'd like a hot butterscotch sundae with whipped cream and nuts." She washed it down with a refill of coffee and smiled at herself. She'd walked miles that day—this splurge wouldn't even add an ounce to her weight.

The waitress brought the check and Rachel handed her three dollars. "May I have most of the change in dimes, please? I need them for the phone."

"Sure," said the girl, returning with eight dimes.

But Rachel was feeling both sated *and* magnanimous

tonight. She wasn't sure how soon she'd be able to be so generous again. "Never mind," she said, putting the money back on the counter. "That was delicious — keep the change."

By the time Rachel returned to the hotel, it was almost eight o'clock. She wasn't ready for bed, so she climbed the stairs to the mezzanine lounge; she'd never been there before.

The area was as drab as the rest of the residence, with split or tape-mended bottle-green leather upholstery on the chairs and forty-watt bulbs in the desk lamps at the writing tables. A few elderly ladies sat reading newspapers and whispering to each other as Rachel walked past.

She circled the floor until she found herself at one end that was deserted — deserted except for one of the oldest pianos Rachel had ever seen.

She touched several of the dusty keys, then struck an entire chord. The instrument was badly in need of a tuning. Nonetheless, Rachel seated herself on the round wooden stool and, with her right foot on the soft pedal, began to play. Her personal repertoire had always been somewhat eclectic; she warmed up with a Mozart sonata, followed by a Broadway show-tune medley, and then a Chopin étude. She was unaware of the passage of time.

When she finished her impromptu concert, there was a sudden burst of applause as several isolated groups of ladies, from various sections of the mezzanine, rose and came forward.

"That was simply lovely, my dear," said one.

"Oh, it took me back. I heard Rubinstein play those etudes when he and I were both still young," said another, touching her white hair nervously. "You really play quite beautifully."

"Thank you," said Rachel. "I didn't realize that—"

But she was interrupted by a loud, gruff voice bellowing from the lobby below. "For God's sake, can't any of you tell the time? It's ten o'clock at night—now shut that thing up!"

"But Sylvia, it's so nice to have music in the evening—it makes such a difference," insisted the white-haired lady who had heard Rubinstein years before.

"Are you deaf, too?" yelled the voice. "I said lights out!" A moment later, Rachel and her "audience" were immersed in the blackout.

The ladies' voices faded away as they made their exit in the darkness.

Rachel was growing angry. This wasn't a dormitory—it was a hotel! What right did some lackey have to turn out the mezzanine lights? What if one of those elderly women tripped and fell—and broke a hip—or worse?

Suddenly, anger turned to outrage as, feeling her way along the unfamiliar furniture, Rachel became aware of someone's hand groping her legs. She whirled about and swung at the darkness.

She struck nothing but air.

Rachel did hear, however, a soft, very stoned giggle as a voice in the blackness said, "Sorry, sweetie. Just thought I'd give it a try."

She was certain she recognized the voice; it belonged to the elevator operator—the very woman who had earlier warned *her* about some of the hotel's residents.

She waited until her eyes adjusted to the dark and then found her way to the rear elevator—the one bearing a sign that read self-service.

She didn't even notice the lumpiness of her pillow as she settled under the blankets and fell asleep. All in all, it had been quite a week.

Chapter Two

Rachel stood in the wings offstage left. She smoothed the long, flowing skirt of her gown and tried to tuck a stray wisp of hair into her upswept coiffure. She hated wearing bobby pins and combs, but the makeup man had insisted. "They expect something more formal, honey, and you can't let them down."

Her toes hurt. The burgundy silk spaghetti-strap shoes that were dyed to match her gown dug in with each step. She'd bought them at the last minute and had forgotten her father's advice about "taking her feet along." Strange thoughts, she mused, to flit through one's mind at a moment like this.

But it was precisely the moment that was causing her distress—far more than the shoes or the bobby pins and too-tight combs. Most of the other finalists had already danced or sung; her turn was coming.

Thank God the butterflies in her stomach weren't visible to the naked eye! Not that anyone would have paid attention, given the nervous chattering and pacing of everyone backstage—those who had performed as well as those who hadn't.

Rachel glanced about, trying to concentrate on keeping her breathing low. It would help her connect support with her voice once you got onstage—and might enable her to survive until then!

She noticed the tall, handsome blond again; he was leaning casually against a column with his hands in the pockets of his vested tuxedo. He was semihidden in shadow, but his head was turned toward Rachel.

She wondered if his relaxed attitude was as much pretense as her own. But there was no time left to speculate. The stage manager came up beside her and said, "Miss Allenby, you're next."

Her heart began pounding wildly, the deafening reverberation booming so loudly in Rachel's ears that she was certain everyone could hear. The carefully rehearsed illusion of poise was shattered by two little words: *you're next*.

"Break a leg," offered the tuxedoed blond as she passed.

"Thanks," she heard her voice reply mechanically as she almost tripped over a length of cable; if she didn't watch her step, she might truly fulfill the good-luck wish!

Someone beckoned and Rachel followed; she splayed her fingers, made a fist, and then released it, in an effort to keep her hands from shaking.

Stanley Havermeyer made the announcement: "Rachel Allenby will sing"—he glanced down at his index card—"from the *Cole Porter Song Book*."

Rachel fought the sudden impulse to flee as she drew another profound breath and strode, with practiced steadiness, to the center of the stage.

She found momentary comfort in the curve of the grand piano, fleeting reassurance in the accompanist's smile; she stilled her mind and centered it on positive images: yesterday's rehearsal; the microphone system; the audience, which wanted everyone to do well. The tension began to lessen. A second later, though, it returned, as Rachel realized that each of the individual members of that audience probably had a personal favorite among the finalists, and she knew *nobody* here!

All right, she told herself, if you weren't talented, you'd never have won the regionals and reached the national auditions. You've come all this way—there's no turning back, so stop this nonsense!

These conflicts between paralyzing fear and sheer determination waged their inner battle while the accompanist adjusted himself and the music. Rachel managed a weak

27

smile and wiggled her toes beneath the chiffon folds covering her sandals. Then, she summoned her muse with a prayer akin to begging and nodded in the vague direction of the pianist.

She had selected the medley of Cole Porter's songs on her teacher's advice: "With two thousand people out front, Rachel, leave melodrama to the opera singers and vocal acrobatics to the Merman-style belters. Sing what sets *you* apart."

The familiar strains began and Rachel eased into the first song of the medley. "In the still of the night," she sang, thinking of the stillness throughout the audience on this April night that could be the beginning of a whole new life if only—

If only she could focus! She gazed out at the myriad faces in the audience and grew dizzy from the blur. She was suddenly aware, as she sang myopically into the theater, that she'd forgotten her contact lenses! How could she *do* something so stupid on the most important night of her life?

But the music swept her into "Just One of Those Things," and by the time it had segued into "I've Got You Under My Skin," with Rachel's phrasing erasing any previous opinions as to the slickness of its lyrics, she had completely forgotten about the nerves of Broadway theaters, competitions, and strangers. As on countless occasions before, at lessons, in classes, and on this special night, Rachel surrendered herself to the music.

The medley continued on through a stirring "I Love Paris," followed by "Night and Day" and "Easy to Love." By the time Rachel reached the reprise, singing the words, "Do you love me as I love you?" an inner confidence had returned, soared, and echoed now through her voice, her body, and her spirit, as though she had been kissed by some mystical, intangible force. Whatever had inspired Porter to write these melodies and lyrics thirty years before had, in these final moments, transcended time and become one with Rachel. Never has she sung so movingly, not even at

28

the regional auditions that had brought her to New York and to this night.

She finished the song and a hushed silence fell over the theater. It was followed by a thunderous ovation — no paid claque *ever* clapped like this! People were on their feet shouting their unanimous approval, two thousand voices cheering as one.

Rachel bowed deeply; only her shaking knees would have betrayed her if anyone could have seen beneath the layers of burgundy chiffon.

Giddy with joy, she bowed again and slowly left the stage. She wanted to run to the anonymous safety of the wings, but her feet refused to hurry.

"Fabulous!" echoed several finalists who had sung earlier.

"I envy you," said the handsome blond who had wished her luck. "You're an artist. Most of us just sing."

Rachel was uneasy with his remark. "Thanks," she said breathlessly as she searched for her water glass.

He smiled. "You have a rare ability. You hypnotize your listener."

"I hope that doesn't mean that I put my audience to sleep," she tried to joke.

The stage manager joined them then. "Mr. Morgan, you're on."

This time Rachel told him to "break a leg," after which Stanley Havermeyer announced, "Jamie Morgan will sing from *The Student Prince.*"

Rachel only half listened. Jamie was right about one thing: most of them did "just sing." But he couldn't possibly know how long and hard she had worked to develop her "hypnotic ability" as a means of compensation for lesser vocal gifts. She laughed to herself at the irony; now it seemed that artistry would pave her way. There was no logic in the world.

Jamie finished singing and the audience broke into warm applause, although it was nothing like the ovation given Rachel after her turn. She joined in, clapping from the wings. It was a good, solid-enough lyric baritone voice, she decided, but it was his golden hair and those smoky-blue eyes that would render him irresistible. She found herself staring as he returned to the wings.

His voice interrupted her thoughts. "Well, the torture won't last much longer — only two more victims and it'll be over."

Rachel laughed and turned her attention to the girl who had just been announced. The tall, horsey-looking redhead tossed off "Glibber and Be Gay" from *Candide* with the ease of a practice exercise and created a sensation. Both the audience and backstage cast and crew broke into frenzied applause.

"God, I'm glad I didn't have to follow that!" exclaimed Rachel, her hands stinging from vigorous clapping. "*There's* your New Stars winner for 1968." She was overtaken by a sudden sadness at the realization of her own words.

"*I'd* bet money it'll be a tie between the two of you," said Jamie.

Rachel shook her head. "Her technique is sheer perfection. And what a range!" Wistfully, she added, "I wish I had something like that."

At that moment, the redhead rushed toward them. "Look out!" she cried, cupping her hands over her mouth. "I'm going to throw up!"

Rachel and Jamie stared after the flurry of pink tulle as the soprano hurried off to the restroom. All at once, the evening's tension released itself in spurts of helpless laughter. Jamie held his sides as Rachel gasped between breaths, "From out front, we all look — so — *together!*" Tears trickled down her cheeks as distant retching sounds became audible.

"Poor thing," said Jamie, his rib cage shaking, too.

"I hope she doesn't ruin her gown!" Rachel said. "She'll have to go back onstage — to accept the prize." She stopped laughing as the words sobered her. She couldn't fight off the twinge of regret.

The waiting was over. Neither Rachel nor the redheaded singer won. They weren't even among the second- or third-place winners. The first prize went to the blonde from Texas. Overfed, overdressed, and oversweet, Rachel thought, allowing her dislike to surface. Aloud she said to Jamie, "It's not so much *my* not having won—well, that's not entirely true, either. But to bypass someone who can sing that *Candide* number the way Pink Tulle can—it's just not fair!"

"Auditions are never fair," said Jamie. "Besides, it's all a crap shoot, anyway."

"If you feel that way about it, why did you bother trying out to begin with?"

"Exposure," he answered. "Agents come to these things. The radio broadcast may have reached a few people. And it's better than sitting home doing nothing, isn't it?"

Anything was preferable to sitting home, Rachel reflected. "That's why I entered the regionals in the first place. To get to New York." She was aware that not winning the finals tonight would mean that doors were still closed to her. She'd stay, anyway—winning would simply have made it easier.

"Ouch!" said Rachel as a spike heel came crashing down on her sandal-exposed toe.

"I'm terribly sorry, dear," chirped Mrs. Carleton. Tonight the lady was swathed in beige lace.

Rachel thought she looked like a mother-of-the-bride.

"I hope I didn't hurt your foot, Miss Allenby," said the matron. "I do wish I'd been one of the judges. I'd certainly have voted for you! You know, I sang in *Jubilee* 'way back in 1935 and I've adored Cole Porter's music ever since. I have recordings of all his music. But my dear, I really must tell you that *your* interpretation—and the expression in your eyes while you were singing—well, I *still* think you should have won!"

Rachel was tempted to agree aloud, but Mrs. Carleton

31

was already ambling off into a misty sea of lacy look-alikes.

Rachel grabbed Jamie's arm and whispered, "I think I'd better get out of here. I'm beginning to feel bitchy about all this phoniness and glitz."

"You can't leave now," said Jamie. "The show's just starting!" He was teasing, but it didn't help. "Look," he added, "we *have* to make an appearance at the reception. It's part of the act."

"Why can't we leave *that* performance to the winners?" asked Rachel.

"C'mon, you're an actress—even Mrs. What's-her-name can see that. What was it she said about your singing? Your interpretation—oh, and the expression in your eyes—"

"I forgot my contact lenses," Rachel explained.

"Okay . . . listen, I'll make a deal with you. Half an hour and I promise to rescue you from the vultures."

"Half an hour?" she groaned.

"Maybe less. Stick with me—I've had lots of practice."

"Practice in what?" she asked.

"Losing contests," he said with a grin. "C'mon!"

Rachel followed Jamie through the mobbed foyer as the crowd made its way to the Astor Hotel. Once inside the Grand Ballroom, they slowly elbowed a path across the polished parquet floor. Jamie craned his neck from left to right while leading Rachel by the arm. When they reached a human bottleneck, he stopped. "It's jammed," he announced. "We must be near the bar."

To Rachel the blur resembled an Impressionist painting.

A throng surrounded the first-place winner, who was holding a glass of champagne in one hand and stuffing caviar into her mouth with the other.

"I still can't believe it," said Rachel. "A typical voice student who sings like a metronome and never expresses a single emotion. Bor-ing!"

"Yeah, but they're the ones who win contests. She doesn't present a threat to anyone."

Rachel didn't understand the logic behind Jamie's remark, but she was sidetracked by one of the New Stars' staff pianists, who exclaimed to her—and to the air in general—"My Lord, I can't *believe* they'd give a prize to that *queen!*" He indicated the black baritone who had won second place. The boy was effete, almost to the point of caricature. Rachel thought he would have made a very attractive *female* fashion model.

"Oh well," continued the pianist, "someone must think *she's* in a minority!"

They were sardine-packed among hundreds of guests. Rachel tried to edge her way to a corner—away from the threat of spilled champagne on her only gown—but in the attempt, she lost sight of Jamie. Squinting to help her focus better, she edged her way across to the red-draperied windows at the opposite end of the bar. No waiters were working this side, so the spot was relatively uncrowded.

Then she saw Jamie. He was visibly trying to disengage himself from two predatory male members of the auditions committee. "There you are!" he exclaimed loudly, to the visible chagrin of his companions. "Rachel, I've been looking for you everywhere!"

Smiling politely to the two men, Jamie said, "My fiancée. You'll have to excuse us."

While Rachel turned several colors of pink, he whisked her to a clearing. "Wait here. I'm going to make good on my promise." He rushed off before she could say a word.

Rachel stood motionless as activity swirled around her. The noises and blurred images gradually blended, increasing, gaining in volume and intensity. Rachel felt like the center post of a carousel as penguin suits, sequins, diamonds, and fur floated past, each of them stopping to bombard her with questions about her career, about her future, about her plans. She experienced vertigo as she watched her distorted reflection from three adjacent, angled mirrors: were these swarms surrounding her—or was

33

she surrounding them? The silliness of her own question added to the growing strangeness of her mood.

"Rachel!" Jamie was back to the rescue. "We've got to get to the hospital right away!" he exclaimed.

"Jamie! Is everything all right?" Rachel's dizziness disappeared instantly.

"Yes! My sister's just had her baby!"

Everyone within earshot gushed congratulations and quickly prepared a wide exit berth for the couple. Jamie grabbed Rachel's wrist and they rushed first to the cloak room and then down the stairs and out onto West Forty-fourth Street. They didn't stop until they reached Times Square.

Rachel clutched her chest breathlessly and said, "Jamie, wait! I forgot to ask—is it a boy or a girl?"

Panting, he replied, "Neither. I'm an only child."

They paused at Rachel's hotel just long enough for her to change out of her evening gown and to retrieve her contact lenses. Jamie was visually devoured by one desk clerk—and ignored by everyone else. Rachel said under her breath, "They won't let you upstairs, but I guarantee you'll be safe here."

In record time, she was back in the lobby. She had removed the combs and pins from her hair and now her long chestnut waves tumbled to her shoulders. Jeans and low-heeled boots had replaced chiffon and sandals. She noted that Jamie, who was still in his tux, looked even more handsome when she could *see* him clearly.

"Let's get out of this place," he said. "It gives me the creeps."

They exited onto the street and he led her up Lexington Avenue. "I know a bar where the waiters don't wear penguin suits. Nobody there'll accuse me of trying to steal his job."

They entered the Irish pub, an old, dark, and cozy neighborhood bar with high-backed booths and sawdust

34

on the floor. They settled in—Rachel curling her legs under her on the padded leather bench—and Jamie ordered Guinness stout for both of them. "It's loaded with vitamins," he said.

"I can sure use some of those right now!" said Rachel. "I can't believe how exhausted I am! Adrenaline letdown, I guess—"

"Tell me about it!" exclaimed Jamie. He leaned his head back against the booth and clasped both hands behind his neck. "Shit, this business stinks, doesn't it?"

"I guess. . . . But the moment while you're up there singing somehow makes up for it, don't you think?" She hadn't realized she was answering a question with another question.

"Well, in your case I'd certainly agree. Y'know," he said, "I've been watching you all week, but I still can't figure you out."

"What's there to figure out?" She bristled slightly.

"Don't take offense, Rachel. I mean it as a compliment. You *had* to be as nervous as the rest of us—tonight, especially—but somehow you're able to . . . to transform that into . . ." He shrugged. "I can't even explain what I mean. But it's special."

"I *was* nervous," she admitted. "I even thought about running away—"

"That's what I'm saying. You get as crazy as everyone else—and then you go out onstage and . . . well, it's as if a kind of metamorphosis takes place. You're really . . . mesmerizing."

The admiration in his voice caused an uneasiness in Rachel. She was grateful for the arrival of their waiter and the two glass mugs of stout.

"What'll we drink to?" asked Jamie. "Your trip back home?"

She shook her head. "I'm staying. Remember Thomas Wolfe? Well, I can't go home again."

"That bad?"

"No . . . it's a nice place to visit—the usual clichés." She

35

took a long drink of the dark, cool liquid and licked the light-brown foam from her lips. "Mmmm," she said. "I know. Let's drink to beginnings. That's what tonight is—not an end. To hell with the auditions."

"To hell with the auditions!" Jamie echoed. "A great, original toast!" They clinked their mugs.

"What about you?" she asked while Jamie signaled the waiter for a refill. "Are you planning to stay in New York?"

"Yeah, but that's because I've never left. I'm a native son—part of the vanishing breed. Actually, I was born in the Bronx, but it still counts—"

"You don't sound like a New Yorker," Rachel interrupted.

"You can thank the American Academy for that. It took ages to get rid of the accent. But now"—he made a ceremonial flourish with a wave of his napkin—"now, English is my best language!"

Their waiter, arriving with two fresh stouts, remarked, "Ya talk good English for a foreigner, kid!"

The two singers doubled over with laughter.

"I don't mean to pry," said Jamie, "but do you have enough money to survive in this city?"

"No," answered Rachel. "I'll probably sleep all day tomorrow, and then the next day I'll go job-hunting and look for a place to stay. The hotel isn't cheap."

"I'll help you. I know all the inexpensive neighborhoods. I live in a dump, too, but at least it's my own—and it isn't dyke heaven!"

"You noticed." Rachel mused that in only a week, she'd come to understand a lot. "By the way, what do you do? Besides sing, I mean."

"Anything I can find," said Jamie. "I'll be touring with *West Side Story* next month. I do bits on TV soaps and extras on commercials, temp work—I hate it!—and every once in a while I land a principal in a class-A commercial. That pays for a lot of voice lessons. I lived for a year on one toilet-bowl cleanser gig." He laughed at the memory. "My mom didn't know how to explain to the neighbors—you

36

know, her *wunderkind* tap dancing inside the john! But the residuals paid me as much as ten months with *The Student Prince*, so I didn't complain!"

"Do you make rounds every day?" asked Rachel. That appealed to her only in comparison with the prospect of a nine-to-five typist's or receptionist's job.

"There are times that I make the rounds to the exclusion of everything else. Trouble is, I feel guilty afterward, like I ought to be taking classes, polishing my technique, you know. But it's a vicious circle. If I were independently wealthy, I could do both. Of course, then I'd buy my way in and wouldn't have to make rounds."

"Buy your way in? Can you really do that?" asked Rachel.

"With money you can do anything. Even get onto the roster at William Morris, I'd imagine."

"Do you have an agent?"

"Not yet. That's why I'm hoping that something materializes from the past week's charade. I'm tired of all the cattle calls where five hundred Equity singers show up to audition for one lousy role. If I spend the day at one of those, I wind up not getting cast *and* losing a day's pay at a temp job that I don't want in the first place."

Rachel sighed at the dim prospects, which seemed even dimmer in contrast with the opulence on exhibition only a few short hours before. She nibbled absentmindedly on a pretzel while Jamie continued the construction of his matchstick sculpture.

"Can't the situation be improved?" Rachel asked.

"Listen," he said, "how can anyone improve the situation, when nobody outside the business really understands the problems? Everybody tells me, 'Oh, you're in the theater. How exciting!' And if you try to tell them the truth, believe me, they don't really want to hear it. Hell, my *dad* doesn't even want to hear the truth! I could stand on my head and shout it, but until he sees me telling jokes on the *Tonight Show*, he'll still call me a bum!"

"Can't you make him understand?"

He shook his head. "I tried. It was like talking to a brick wall. You don't have to come from the boonies to be misunderstood, Rachel. You can live in the middle of it all, right down the block."

"Does it hurt?" Rachel had noticed the wistful look in Jamie's eyes.

"Not anymore. Now that *I* understand. My mom will love me whether I'm a star on Broadway or singing and dancing at St. Something-or-other's Home for the Aged — you know, bedsheets for a curtain and a pot-and-washboard orchestra. She doesn't even see the disparity — it's all the same, as long as her Jamie's onstage. She and Dad" — he paused and swallowed the rest of the stout from his mug — "oh, they love me in their way. They'd just love me a lot more if I were making money with my voice — it would justify the cash outlay for lessons all those years. Sometimes I think it's more important for Dad to get his money's worth — a return on his investment — than to see his son doing what he wants to do."

Jamie smiled, but Rachel detected sadness at the corners of his mouth. "Sure it used to hurt," he said. "But it doesn't anymore."

"You know," said Rachel, suddenly feeling very close to him, "you're as big a phony as I am. And I mean that as a compliment."

They both stared at the flickering candle in the frosted glass holder against the wall of the booth. At last, Rachel said, "There's a lot more to it than talent, isn't there?"

Jamie reached across the table and took her hands. "My voice teacher once said that ninety-five percent of all the people we audition for know *nothing* about talent. The fact that you lost tonight — and to what! — bears that out. Talent is only the first thing. First and last. It's everything else in-between that makes or breaks careers." He considered his statement for a moment. "I guess in a way, that's comforting."

"What is?"

"To know that not all the responsibility lies with a

person's talent."

"Why is that comforting?" Rachel asked. She found it the exact opposite.

"I don't know," said Jamie. "I just suppose it must be."

It was late, and now the adrenaline letdown had reached rock bottom. Rachel said to Jamie, "I can hardly keep my eyes open—it isn't your company. I've just got to get some sleep."

They walked back to the women's residence in relaxed but quiet reflection.

"I'm not going back in there," said Jamie, stopping outside the revolving door. "Talk about vibes that a place can give you!"

"It's not so bad," said Rachel. Then she reconsidered. "On second thought, it's horrible. And strange—"

"*I'll* say!" Jamie interrupted.

"No—well, that too, but I mean it's strange that until the auditions were over, I didn't really mind it. Now, suddenly, I can't wait to get out of there. Does that make any sense?"

"Sure. Tell you what. I'll phone you tomorrow night—if the switchboard accepts male callers—and we'll map out apartment strategy. Okay?"

"Okay!" she agreed.

They embraced quickly and said good night. Rachel felt as if their eyes had said much more. She felt a warm glow as she stood under the hotel canopy and watched Jamie head toward Park Avenue. Funny, she mused, we've just met, but already I feel . . . what? A closeness? She'd sensed it when he'd spoken of his family. But it went beyond that. And beyond his looks, although she knew that was part of the attraction.

We don't have to *explain* to each other, she said to herself. Jamie *understands*. With Richard, two years as lovers hadn't brought understanding. Then how was it possible for a stranger . . . ?

She smiled and amended the thought. It was Richard,

39

not Jamie, who remained a stranger. . . .

That was confirmed when Rachel checked the hotel desk for messages. There were three. One, from her parents in Excelsior, had arrived earlier in the evening, before the auditions. It read: "Good luck tonight." A second, from Richard, read: "Congratulations. When are you coming home?" She shook her head and crumpled the pink message slip.

Then she glanced down at the third piece of paper. It read: "Heard you on the radio. You were terrific. My sister thought so, too." The message was from Irving Plotnick/O'Connell.

Chapter Three

Rachel didn't sleep through the entire day, although she did awaken around noon with a grogginess that came from too much oxygen rather than too little. Her eyelids were heavy and her limbs felt weighted. When she turned her head on the pillow, a stiffness in her neck caused a cracking sound.

She sat bolt upright in bed. Sometimes shocking herself awake worked more efficiently than a languid stretch. Besides, she mused, if she stretched on this particular bed, her ankles hung over the edge of the mattress and her left elbow banged the cold, goose-bumpy wall.

No, this place would not do any longer, Rachel decided, kicking the ugly blanket aside and sliding off the bed into a standing position.

She had purchased an immersion heater at Woolworth's and before her coffee-and-doughnut breakfast across the street at the Mayflower, each morning she prepared a clandestine mug—also a Woolworth's acquisition—of instant energy. With its cereal-grain flavor, Rachel stopped short of calling it coffee. But it was hot and the caffeine helped.

She yawned to clear her head; it made her ears pop on and off. Oh great, she thought. In this state, I'm supposed to go apartment hunting!

There was a steady drizzle of rain, again, although it was too fine a mist to require an umbrella. Rachel dressed, then braided her hair, grabbed her raincoat, and went out to buy the morning paper.

She studied the apartment listings at the coffee counter. She had to find something in Manhattan so that she could walk or ride the bus to coachings and auditions. She still feared getting lost and this fear kept her above ground and out of the subways.

Rachel couldn't believe the rents. First she had looked for listings of apartments on the Upper East Side — a "good address," as she knew from magazine articles and movies. When she saw that a studio on East Seventy-second Street off Third Avenue went for the exorbitant sum of three hundred a month, she checked the listings for the West Side. But she found only a difference of fifty dollars or thereabouts.

As the hour went by, Rachel's conditions and requirements became less and less particular. Maybe something in Greenwich Village, she thought. Those one-room rentals were cheaper, but not by much. Sublets for the summer, already furnished, were out of the question.

There were apartments in the East Nineties, at the tip of Spanish Harlem, but Rachel dismissed these. As she did the area around Columbia University — too far uptown on the West Side.

She sighed deeply and ordered another coffee. If she didn't find something in the paper, she'd start knocking on doors — otherwise she'd wind up with a case of coffee nerves!

The waiter behind the counter smiled when he saw the section of the paper she was reading.

"Hey, it's none of my business," he said, "but you don't find apartments by reading the *Times* on Tuesday."

"I was getting that impression," said Rachel.

"Your best bet is buy the *Voice* on Wednesday and — you in show biz by any chance?"

She didn't ask why he assumed she was. "Yes, why?"

"Check the unions. Summer's a good time to find sublets — actors going away to stock, that kind of thing."

"Thanks!" said Rachel. "I'll do that." The idea hadn't occurred to her, and she had joined Actors Equity two years before, when a local stock company had hired her to sing in a revival of *Kiss Me, Kate*. Ever since then, all of her Julie Andrews–type roles had been with Equity companies in the Midwest.

She checked the address on her union card and walked crosstown, then down Broadway to West Forty-sixth Street. But the callboard at Actors Equity listed sublets-to-share. Rachel wanted a place of her own. Nonetheless, she did stop at the Rehearsal Club on West Fifty-third; their waiting list was *years* long. Rachel needed something now.

She was still emotionally tired from the night before, and although her physical energy had been restored by eleven hours' sleep, the sudden mobs of people emerging from the towering skyscrapers of Midtown at the stroke of five dizzied Rachel. Everyone seemed to be rushing toward her in formation, and Rachel felt as if she were the only person trying to move in the opposite direction, against the human traffic jam. By the time she reached the Grand Central area, she thought she might faint from the claustrophobic crowds.

She ducked into a Chock Full o' Nuts and ordered a glass of orange juice. The ice-cold temperature and the natural sugar helped. But what she really needed was a nap, despite having slept until five short hours ago.

She finished the juice and headed uptown; the buses were too crammed to bother with — it would take less time to walk to the hotel.

Rachel's eyes widened in amazement as she entered the lobby.

Jamie was there!

"Jamie! What are you doing here?" She hoped she didn't sound too eager or excited to see him, when in fact she was.

"I called about an hour ago and you were out. I was in the neighborhood — well, about ten blocks south at a reading for a commercial I didn't get — anyway, I thought I'd wait for you and see what you're doing for dinner."

All thoughts of a nap disappeared. "Your timing is perfect," she said. "I'm famished!"

The misty rain had caused his blond hair to fall onto his forehead in Dennis-the-Menace fashion, giving him a mischievous look. Rachel's hand went to her single braid, which was damp but intact. She hoped its little-girl effect was half as interesting to Jamie as his little-boy appearance was to her.

"Where have you been, anyway?" he asked as they exited the hotel. "I thought you were going to sleep the day away."

"I can't afford the luxury. I was apartment hunting."

"Any luck?"

She shook her head. "Everything here is so expensive!"

"Where have you been looking?"

She told him.

"Well, that explains it. Listen, I don't exactly recommend Hell's Kitchen—"

"What's that?"

"Mid-forties, west of the theater district. It's cheap, but you'd have to climb over drunks in your doorway and hookers on every corner—forget about it. But maybe you ought to try my neighborhood. It's not much to look at, but if you stay away from a couple of blocks that are drug hangouts, it's mostly immigrants—Spanish and Ukrainian and Polish families."

"I thought last night you said you live in a dump."

"I do, but it's clean—and I've got three rooms for only sixty dollars a month."

Three rooms? The ads list *studios* for three hundred—"

"Well, if you want the Ritz, sure. I mean, my place has a bathtub in the kitchen and the john is down the hall." He laughed. "But there's hot and cold running water—and the exterminator comes regularly, so I don't have many roaches."

Involuntarily Rachel shuddered at the thought of the cockroach she had killed in the hotel's bathroom down the hall.

Aloud she said, "Where is your real estate marvel of an

44

apartment?"

"The East Village. I mean *east*. Fifth Street between Avenue A and B."

"Fifth *Street?*" repeated Rachel.

"Never to be confused with Fifth Avenue," said Jamie, stopping in front of a white stucco facade on Ninth Avenue and Fifty-sixth Street. "Welcome to Angelo's. The best lasagna in town. Don't tell too many of your friends."

They entered the small, cramped restaurant. "Hey, Jamie, how'ya doin'?" called the redheaded waitress from the bar. She seemed to be the only help and was serving all the booths and tables at the same time. She busily nodded to one group in a booth. "Five more minutes—the gnocchi take longer." To a nearby table, "Red wine, right? Be right there." A wave to a couple at the back and, "The usual? Clam sauce?" The couple nodded. "Okay, comin' up."

Carrying an armload of plates, she came toward Jamie and Rachel, kissed Jamie on the cheek, and said, "Corner booth's just leaving. You can take that. You want a menu or"—this with a warm smile to Rachel—"your girlfriend having the same as you?"

Jamie said, "Rachel, meet Mary. A one-woman dynamo. Mary, I told Rachel about the lasagna—"

"Honey, he *knows*. Two lasagnas and two chianti?"

Rachel nodded to both Mary and Jamie.

"Fine. Oh—there's the table. Have a seat—I'll be over in a sec."

By the time Jamie and Rachel had edged their way through departing and newly arriving customers, Mary was wiping the blue formica surface of the table and setting down two unmatched water glasses filled with red wine. "Side order of spinaci?" she asked.

"Mary's also a mind reader," explained Jamie.

"Listen," confided Mary to Rachel, "he comes in twice a week, the best-looking guy ever, and orders the same thing every time. What's to mind-read?" Then, winking, she added, "If I wasn't old enough to be your mother, I'd give your ladyfriend a run for her money!" She laughed a hearty

45

laugh that Rachel hoped would cover her momentary embarrassment.

But Jamie was gazing at her. He wasn't staring, but Rachel felt as if he were trying to see *inside* her eyes. It unsettled her because it made her knees tremble; usually that only happened when she was about to go onstage. How was it possible, she wondered, to feel completely at ease with Jamie—and at the same time to feel nervous and uncertain?

Mary arrived with the steaming platters—they could hardly be called plates, given the size of the portions—of lasagna. All questions vanished as Rachel and Jamie dived into the tangle of melted mozzarella and chunks of ground beef and layers of homemade pasta. "My God!" said Rachel with a mouth full of food. "This is incredible!" If rents were nothing like those back home, neither were Italian restaurants!

They walked to Broadway after their double espresso coffees and a promise to see Mary in a few days.

"Have you seen *West Side Story*?" asked Jamie. They were under the marquee of the revival house where the film version was playing.

"Three times," she said. "I've dreamed of playing Maria for years, but the stock companies always cast the leads in New York."

"I could combine pleasure with homework," said Jamie, beckoning her toward the ticket window. "My rehearsals start next week."

"I'm game. I've had a crush on George Chakiris since I was sixteen."

They settled into a back row shortly after the credits rolled.

Rachel tried unsuccessfully to withhold her tears when George Chakiris/Bernardo was killed. But at the movie's end, she noticed that Jamie, too, was dabbing at his eyes. Somehow that touched her as deeply as the tragic story and Bernstein's powerful score. Richard had often accused Rachel of being too romantic. He was always so pragmatic, so logical. Rachel had once suggested that his indifference toward her career plans might have changed to enthusiasm if she had become a stockbroker instead of a singer. She recalled his reply. "Maybe. At least the stock market isn't based on air."

A twinge of resentment surfaced as Rachel wondered why their relationship hadn't ended earlier. She blushed as she answered her own question.

When the lights came up, she was still sniffling. Jamie reached over and with the back of his index finger dried a tear that had trickled down Rachel's cheek. She smiled without speaking. They remained in their seats for several minutes; again, she didn't feel the need to fill the moment with words. Apparently Jamie didn't either.

Finally they rose and, his hand around her waist as he guided her up the aisle, they left the theater and continued walking. Their hands were linked as they strolled across a dark, deserted Fifty-seventh Street toward Rachel's hotel.

When they reached the canopy, Jamie voiced Rachel's thoughts. "You're the first person I've ever done that with. All the way from Forty-sixth—and no need to fill in the gaps."

She nodded warmly. "Mary at the restaurant isn't a mind reader. You are."

"Tomorrow let's find you an apartment," Jamie said.

Rachel waited for him to add something more.

He didn't. Instead, he took her face in his cupped hands and stared into her eyes, as he had in the restaurant, as if trying to fathom something in their depths that he didn't comprehend.

Rachel closed her eyes, but it wasn't to shut Jamie out.

She felt his lips on hers, then. Just a tender, gentle kiss, but it caused every nerve in her body to tingle. She returned the kiss and looked at him. She wasn't sure whether the mistiness was in her eyes or his—or in the soft rain, which was as gentle as Jamie's kiss.

Neither of them said good night. He stood motionless while Rachel turned slowly and entered the hotel. Once inside, she looked back through the glass, but he was gone.

Rachel and Jamie spent the weekend combing newspapers and neighborhoods. They walked up and down countless streets and stopped at any building with a sign that read APARTMENT TO LET.

"I like this one," said Rachel as they examined a small studio on Seventy-first just west of Central Park.

"The owner's away for a year," said the super. "I'm not supposed to let just anyone take it."

Jamie intervened immediately. "Key money?"

"A thousand," answered the beer-bellied man, taking a swig from the brown paper-wrapped bottle.

"What's key money?" asked Rachel after Jamie had led her out of the building.

"It's hush money. And bribery. For all we know, the owner isn't even trying to sublet. Call it the super's 'cottage industry' — with someone else's cottage. You could get into a real legal hassle with that one."

"Not to mention being out the thousand dollars that I don't have," Rachel added with a sigh. Her traveler's cheques were dwindling badly; she almost regretted the dress she'd bought on sale. That represented four extra nights at the hotel.

The next apartment, on West Ninetieth, was a mess. "This place has had a bad water leak recently," Jamie pointed out.

"It's been fixed. Long time ago," insisted the super.

Jamie touched the peeling wall. "It's still wet."

"All walls feel cold in this weather," said the super.

But just then, Rachel saw a family of cockroaches parading across the linoleum floor. "Thanks anyway," she said, this time leading Jamie to the hall.

Saturday night, they bought the Sunday *Times*. They spread the classified ads over an entire table at the Crest cafeteria; while Jamie poured through the listings, Rachel watched the very odd collection of humanity assembled in

48

little groups throughout the all-night eatery. There were old ladies with all their belongings packed into plastic garbage bags and propped on nearby empty chairs; they sneered at anyone who wasn't one of the cafeteria "regulars"—including the two outsiders with their *Times*. Drunks were asleep, sprawled across the tables; several street vendors and beggars Rachel had begun to notice every time she was on the West Side found refuge here. The tall, burly white-haired man in Viking garb and helmet now sat contemplating his coffee and holding court among several unlikely subjects. Rachel had seen him in front of the Warwick Hotel and wondered where he went at night.

The man she'd seen—and heard—standing in front of Carnegie Hall was here, too. He sang operatic arias—all off-pitch and in the wrong tempo—outside the concert hall, even in the pouring rain. Rachel had walked past a few days before and guiltily dropped a quarter into his tin cup. There but for the grace of God, she'd thought. She almost laughed—sadly, though—at the memory of the woman alongside her that afternoon. When Rachel's quarter had gone *clink!* in the almost-empty cup, the woman had said, "Maybe if you throw in another one, he'll shut up!"

And yet, she mused, looking around, where else can they go? I'm down to less than fifty dollars, and *I'm* getting panicky. But then she reasoned, I'll wait tables if I have to. I'm not going to wind up in the street. And empathy turned to pity once more.

"Okay, tomorrow morning we start at the crack of dawn," said Jamie, interrupting her ruminations. He had circled a dozen or more inch-wide ads. "But we'll have to beat everyone else in New York who's smart enough to buy the Sunday *Times* on Saturday."

By Sunday evening, Rachel was convinced that every apartment hunter in the entire borough of Manhattan bought the Sunday *Times* on Saturday. She and Jamie had begun making phone calls from the hotel lobby at eight thirty-five the next morning. Most lines were busy, and by the time they had reached any prospective landlords or supers, they were told either that they were too late and the apartment had been rented—or that they could come by in the late afternoon; the earlier part of the day was already filled.

"My legs are killing me," Rachel said as they collapsed onto a park bench near Gracie Mansion. They had walked uptown and downtown and crosstown and back. The last apartment on their list was a brownstone on East Eighty-ninth, just off East End Avenue. Someone else had rented it less than an hour before.

"I knew rentals were tight," said Jamie, "but I didn't realize how bad it had become."

"I'm basically an optimist," Rachel said, "but this is really wearing me down. I guess I'm impractical, too. I thought by the end of my second week here, I'd be settled in my own apartment and going to the theater whenever I like, studying and auditioning during the day—and I haven't found a teacher, an apartment, there haven't been *any* Equity auditions—and God, I can't even get standing room to *Hello, Dolly!*"

Jamie put his arms around her. "You don't strike me as the weepy type," he said softly.

She leaned her head against his shoulder; his warmth comforted her and she felt the anxiety melting away. Together they gazed out over the East River as dusk settled.

"It's quiet here," Rachel said at last. A breeze blew stray tendrils of hair across her forehead.

Jamie's hand gently brushed them aside. "You smell nice," he murmured, his chin against the top of her head.

Rachel's heart began to hammer again. She appreciated the fact that Jamie wasn't like most of the boys—or men—she'd met back home. Even Richard had tried to rush her, although not as overtly as the rest. Jamie instead seemed to sense that rushing Rachel would have the opposite effect.

But suddenly she worried that she'd been wrong. Jamie rose from the bench and said, "Let's go to my place."

She also worried because she wasn't about to say no, and she didn't want to ruin the growing trust she felt toward

50

him.

"Jamie . . ."

"Listen," he said, "I didn't mean that the way it sounded. . . . It's just that we're both low on cash and we haven't eaten a thing since the pretzel on Fifty-seventh Street—and that was hours ago. We can take the Second Avenue bus and be downtown in no time—there's no rush hour on Sunday."

Rachel was curious to see the "dump" Jamie had described. And at least he had anticipated her reaction. He seemed to know her better than she knew herself.

Jamie hadn't told her that after the Second Avenue bus, they had to transfer at Fourteenth Street to the crosstown bus, and then, at Avenue A, to still another bus to Fifth Street. After this trip, Rachel would never confuse New York streets with New York avenues.

From the bus stop it was only half a block to number 535. All of the buildings were faced in stone that had either been painted over—mostly in a rust-colored enamel that was caked or peeling—or left gray, a gray that had turned several shades darker from grime and neglect. Most were five- and six-story walkups with two-step stoops and small inner vestibules.

Number 535 had an almost-hidden entranceway next door to a bakery whose aromatic goodies were advertised in either Ukrainian or Russian, Rachel wasn't sure which. The store was closed, but the smells hinted that someone was working, even on Sunday evening.

"I'll lead the way," said Jamie, "in case the hall light's out. Just follow me."

"Into the breach," Rachel said, stepping into a dark, musty corridor.

They climbed a steep flight of steps to the second floor. Through closed doors of other apartments Rachel could hear bits of conversation in several languages.

"It helps to be a polyglot to live here, doesn't it?" she asked.

"Yeah. But since I'm not—and neither are my neigh-

51

bors—there's lots of privacy. We gesture a lot in the halls, but we don't have to worry about secrets."

Jamie unlocked an ivory-painted door and swung it open. *"Voilà!"* he said, pulling a hanging chain that turned on the light.

Rachel was standing in the doorway, which opened into the kitchen. Jamie took her raincoat.

"You look dump-struck," he said. "I'm almost afraid to ask—what do you think?"

Rachel shrugged. "I don't know yet. Let me get used to it." The kitchen boasted a noisy, ancient refrigerator and a small stove. The table and chairs were vintage Salvation Army covered with a fresh coat of bright, orange-red enamel. A huge, old iron bathtub took up most of the wall next to the sink. Jamie explained that the claw feet had been badly chipped, so he had modeled new ones with plaster of Paris and then had "gilded" the feet and the faucet spigots with gold paint.

"There's a wooden cover for the whole thing," he said, pointing to what Rachel had mistaken for a door. He carted the cover over and laid it across the tub.

Rachel stepped into the living room. She glanced at the stained shutters on the windows; the sewing-machine table that was Jamie's desk, the Churchill green-shaded brass upon it; the cement-block record cabinets and bookshelves ("Compliments of a nearby construction site," Jamie confided.)

There was a totemic-patterened Indian rug covering the floor and velvet throw pillows in earth tones that accented those in the rug's design. Two 1940s easy chairs in unmatched tweed sat opposite the worn brown velvet sofa.

Rachel sank into it and kicked off her shoes. "Boy, do I understand the lyrics in that song from *Most Happy Fella!*"

" 'Ooh, ma feet'?" Jamie said.

"Well, my left one," she answered. "I've got a Charley horse in my instep." It shot up through her calf and she winced with pain.

"Move over," said Jamie. "Massage time."

She made room for him and soon he was easing the cramp. The intimacy of his hand kneading her foot grew more intense and Rachel cast a surreptitious glance at Jamie's face. At first she thought he was studying her instep, but then she saw that he was looking past it, to a place that Rachel couldn't see. Perhaps to somewhere in his imagination.

She breathed a deep sigh to release the building tension.

"Feel better?" Jamie asked.

Rachel thought his voice seemed huskier than earlier, but he didn't move closer.

She wondered if he had recently come out of a disastrous love affair. If Jamie *had* been in love in the not-too distant past, he might be playing it safe as a means of self-protection. Maybe that was the reason he wasn't rushing her—so as not to rush himself.

"Well, you promised me dinner," she said at last, willing her mind away from the sensations caused by his massage.

"So I did," he answered. "How's the other foot?"

"Fine," she said quickly.

Jamie busied himself in the kitchen and Rachel set the table. They drank cheap, jug burgundy, and Rachel learned to twirl the long, thin strands of spaghetti alla marinara without losing it from her fork.

"I forgot about dessert!" said Jamie suddenly, jumping up from his chair.

"Jamie, I can't eat another bite! I'm bulging—"

"It'll take five minutes. I'll run over to Ratner's and pick up something sinful. It's just a few blocks."

Her protests were useless. He grabbed his jacket and ran out the door.

Rachel saw the can of Italian espresso, but she didn't know how to use the tiny aluminum pot with its upside-down pouring spout. Instead, she refilled her wineglass and wandered through the rest of Jamie's apartment.

The other room she hadn't seen was the bedroom. It was to the left of the kitchen and quite small. The large queen-size mattress on the floor allowed room only for three suitcases stacked in the corner. A lamp hung above the mattress, and Jamie's wardrobe was supported by a metal rod that extended across one entire wall. There was no closet. The single round window was too small to offer outside light, even in the daytime.

Rachel was standing against the wall that was covered with enormous theater posters of recent Broadway hits and flops. Suddenly she heard pounding at the kitchen-entrance door.

"I forgot my keys!" Jamie called.

"What's the—" But she stopped as soon as she saw him. He was soaking wet. Only then did she notice the rain and wind beating against the kitchen window.

"You forgot your umbrella, too," said Rachel as he entered the room; he was dripping water and the forming puddle made them both laugh.

He peeled off his jacket and hung it over the sink from a clothesline stretched across the ceiling. "All isn't lost, however," he said, nodding toward the soggy pastry box with Ratner's printed in large script.

Rachel opened the wet cardboard and swooned.

"I didn't ask what you wanted, so I got a little bit of everything." Inside the box was a chunk of rich strudel, a wedge of strawberry cheesecake, and two slices of Black Forest chocolate cake.

"I was going to make coffee, but that pot . . ."

"I'll do it," said Jamie. "I'll show you how in the morning."

Her heart leapt. But Jamie calmed it.

"It's raining too hard for you to wait for a bus—three buses—to get uptown. And a taxi would cost you a fortune."

"Jamie, I—"

"It's no problem," he said quickly. "The sofa turns into a bed."

Both of them seemed hesitant as they kissed good night.

Their embrace was longer and more affectionate than in the less private setting of the hotel doorway, but again, Rachel sensed that Jamie was searching or troubled by something. She decided to let him take the lead.

Nonetheless, she did not withhold her own response to his kisses. Whatever might be on his mind, his hands reacted on their own, caressing her, touching her, and Rachel's throat grew parched as her mouth opened to his tongue. They almost fell back together onto the sofabed, but Jamie stopped them both.

"We'd better get some sleep," he said, his voice trembling. His hand caressed her cheek as he whispered, "Pleasant dreams."

Rachel hesitated, then decided not to undress. She removed only her contact lenses, after which she curled up in the middle of the bed, her body tired, her mind wide awake.

She shut her eyes and listened to the sounds of Jamie putting dishes away, then tiptoeing into his bedroom and closing the door. Gradually, the steady rhythm of the heavy rain beating against the windows lulled her into a deep and heavy sleep. She dreamed of Jamie.

Chapter Four

At the end of her third week in New York, Rachel had acquired an answering service, opened a bank account—with the initial deposit amounting to ten dollars—and found an accompanist. She had not, however, found an apartment.

Jamie was rehearsing during the day, but they spent each of his free evenings together unless Rachel was ushering. Michael Ross, Rachel's new pianist, had suggested it. "You only make four dollars a night, but if you're a substitute usher, you go from theater to theater and get to see all the shows." The meager salary paid for her meals, and she saw both *Fiddler* and *Hello, Dolly!* in the same week. She was able to walk back and forth to work, thus eliminating the necessity of using public transportation. But she was still living at the women's residence and hating it more every day.

On Tuesday afternoon during Rachel's fourth week in New York, she received a message at the switchboard. It read simply: Please call Lehman Stern. Collect. There was a number, preceded by an area code.

Lehman Stern, she thought. He was one of the best-known conductors in musical theater. They had never met. She had seen him among the guests in the Astor ballroom after the New Stars auditions, but why on earth would he be calling her? It had to be a mistake.

Nonetheless, her stomach was nervous as she dialed the

long-distance operator and placed the call.

"Capitol Theater," said the switchboard voice at the other end.

While the operator accepted the collect charges, Rachel's mind raced. The Capitol Theater in Washington, D.C.? Hadn't she sent them a photograph and résumé when they were casting for the second lead in some musical or other?

She had. The casting department had never replied. Well, they couldn't be calling about an audition now; that had been months ago.

Suddenly a familiar voice came over the line. Familiar because she had heard it before on television interviews.

"Miss Allenby?" he said.

The connection—or Rachel—seemed shaky. "Y-yes." She tried to slow her mind and speech. "Mr. Stern?"

"Thank you for calling back so soon. We're in a real bind down here and you may be able to help us."

Rachel's mind now had slowed to an almost-blank. "Uh . . . yes?"

He explained that he had heard her sing at the New Stars auditions. "It was your presence as much as your voice," he said. "And also your bio sketch in the playbill. We have a real problem just now. It's our revival of *Arrowhead*. According to the the audition profile, you're familiar with the role."

"Yes . . ." Rachel had sung in the chorus of the show in a stock production two years before. Obviously, Stern had mistakenly assumed that she had performed the second lead.

"Well," continued the conductor, "Bettina Craig, who was supposed to sing the role of Penelope, has suffered a bad fall."

"Oh, I'm sorry—"

"She'll be all right in a couple of months, but that's too late for the show, of course."

"Of course," Rachel repeated numbly. Then reason took hold. "What about her understudy?"

"That's our problem. *She's* come down with measles; we learned it just this morning. Which brings me back to the purpose of my call. Are you available—at least until we close in Washington? We're bringing the show to New York after our run here, and Arlene ought to be past the contagious stage by then."

Rachel couldn't find her voice.

"Miss Allenby?"

"Y-yes." What questions needed to be asked? Rachel wondered. "Uh . . . Mr. Stern . . . when do you open?"

"Tomorrow night. That's why I'm calling you. *Arrowhead* isn't performed very much these days, and it isn't easy to find a last-minute replacement—"

That's an understatement! thought Rachel. And most likely because the part was what she referred to as a "Nellie" role—bland, vapid, insipid. . . .

"I had an ulterior motive in calling you before looking for anyone else who's done the part," said Stern. "The way you handle Porter's lyrics would be a definite asset to the entire production."

The remark was his selling point. Rachel realized that she was being offered the kind of opportunity for which she might otherwise wait years. She had secretly felt, while singing in the chorus of *Arrowhead,* that she could have made more of the role of Penelope than the actress who had sung it.

Apparently her audition for New Stars had convinced Stern of that as well. "Can you be here in time for this evening's rehearsal?" asked Stern, assuming that she had accepted.

And, in fact, she had. He suggested the train and even had a timetable handy. "The station is only blocks from the theater," he said. "Of course you'll be reimbursed for any out-of-pocket expenses. We can work around you until you arrive. The duet in Act One isn't a complicated staging, and . . ."

Rachel was so excited by the time she went upstairs to

pack that her hands were trembling. She had left a message for Jamie at the rehearsal studio and at his answering service. According to Stern's train schedule, she had to be at Penn Station within three hours. My God! she thought as she tried to fold things neatly into her suitcase. By dinnertime tonight, I'll be in Washington rehearsing the second lead in a musical — with one of the most famous conductors in the business! Although terrified, she could hardly wait.

Just as she had tucked the last of her things into the bag, her room phone rang.

"Rachel!" cried Jamie. "Is this serious? 'Leaving for D.C. to do a show.' Is it for *real?*"

"I'm afraid to ask myself that!" she exclaimed. "I'm scared, Jamie!" She related her conversation with Lehman Stern.

"You'll be fabulous, you know it!"

"Oh, Jamie, it sounds like something out of a movie, but the truth is I don't know if I can handle it — they open *tomorrow* — I'll hardly have any rehearsal time at all!"

"That's on your side," he reasoned. "Everyone will be rooting for you. And you won't have the luxury of basking in worry." He paused. "How long will you be there?"

"He said two weeks." Then another realization hit her. "Jamie, they're paying me five hundred dollars a week — that's a *thousand dollars!*"

He whistled into the phone, then said, "I won't see you until August."

Rachel felt a twinge in her stomach. "I'll be back in two weeks—"

"I leave on Monday," he said softly.

"Oh . . ."

"Wait a second, Rachel — I have an idea. Hold on." She heard him speaking to someone at his end, but she was unable to make out his words.

Then he came back to the receiver. "Rachel, the stage manager says we're rehearsing the dance at the gym this afternoon. I'm free till five o'clock!"

Excitement surged once more. "I'm packed. Let's have a drink. Maybe it'll calm these butterflies!"

"You'll be terrific. And I'll be right over!"

Rachel touched up her makeup while humming the melody to Penelope's big third-act number.

They settled into the same booth at the same Irish pub as on the night of the New Stars auditions. Jamie handed her a list of dates and cities. "My itinerary. Write to me? The road gets lonely. And I'll be dying to know what happens with *Arrowhead*. I thought the show bombed the first time it came to Broadway."

"It did. But it's been rewritten for Gloria Doro. Fortunately, they've left Penelope's role alone. Or unfortunately, that is. She's a nebbish." The prospect of taking over such a dull part on a moment's notice suddenly made Rachel feel as vulnerable as did the thought of not seeing Jamie for six weeks.

He took her hands in his. "Don't worry," he said. "At least you've done the role before."

"No I haven't," she answered. "That's why I only listed the show *titles* in that publicity bio. Most of the stuff I've sung has been chorus or understudy. I've never even *walked* through the role of Penelope."

"Oh . . . well . . ." He suddenly seemed as unsure as Rachel. "Uh . . . listen, not to change the subject—but to change the subject—what are you doing about your hotel room while you're away?"

Rachel was relieved to transfer her thoughts to anything practical. "Keeping it, I guess. I've paid for this week already."

"That's senseless," said Jamie. "I don't know why I didn't think of it before."

"Think of what?"

"You can move your stuff to my place. Then when you

get back, you can stay at my apartment till you find your own."

"Jamie, I can't—"

"Why not? Look at the money you'll save—and that cell you live in has no cross-ventilation. August in New York can be brutal. My apartment is bearable if you open the windows—"

Rachel considered his argument. His apartment did offer breathng space, her hotel room *was* depressing—and being in Jamie's apartment might make him seem closer. "Okay," she said finally. "But I've got to catch the train in an hour."

"No problem. I'll pick up the stuff you're not taking with you and schlep it to rehearsal this evening. C'mon, we'll stop at your hotel now and you can also tell them you're leaving."

When Rachel checked out and went upstairs to collect her things, the clerk gave Jamie a knowing wink. Rachel smiled to herself. Think what you like, she mused. That's what you get when you don't allow men above the lobby!

As she and Jamie reached Penn Station, Rachel said, "Please don't come in with me. I'm lousy at good-byes." Her eyes were glistening already.

"Me, too," he said self-consciously. "Look . . . will you call me after the opening?"

"If I make it through alive!" she answered, trying to keep the mood light.

"I'll miss you, Rachel." Jamie's voice thickened then as his arms went around her.

"Take care of yourself?" she said, her own voice breaking.

He nodded and they embraced. Their kisses made it appear that two lovers were parting forever—or at the least, for a very long time.

It was Jamie who drew back and whispered, "Break a leg."

"Thanks," Rachel managed to reply. Then she picked up her weekender suitcase and totebag, turned, and hurried into the train station before her vision was completely blurred by tears.

Lehman Stern came forward to greet Rachel the moment she entered the theater auditorium. Tall, suntanned, and balding, he resembled an aging ballet dancer. His trademark black velour towel was hanging from his shoulders, and he had forgotten to leave his baton on the podium. He smiled apologetically when he realized he was carrying it in his right hand and that hand was now extended to shake Rachel's.

For some reason, this put Rachel at ease, despite the presence of a full orchestra in the pit and a stageful of actors, dancers, and singers in costume and makeup. The company had been rehearsing the second act; the Indian village from Rachel's previous *Arrowhead* encounter told her that much.

Lehman Stern led Rachel to the stage, where Gloria Doro, one of the most famous actress-singers of the American musical theater, stood waiting. She was a good four or five inches taller than Rachel, and her carrot-red hair was covered by a wig of shiny, shoulder-length ebony braids. Her broad hips were disguised by her fringed deerskin tunic, and the cleavage so often displayed offstage was covered here by a huge blanket. From out front, her strong, angular features, accentuated as they now were with inch-long false eyelashes and gooey gloss over shiny dark red lips, were dramatic, theatrically effective. From up close, Rachel observed, the woman looked like a clown.

The diva extended dragon-lady nails and said, "Welcome to our company, Miss Allenby. We appreciate your coming on such short notice."

Rachel, aware that this was, in many ways, a performance and that all eyes were upon her, smiled graciously and said, "I've admired your singing for a long time, Miss Doro." She managed to control the flutter in her throat.

Ralph Adams, the director, introduced himself. He was British and very matter-of-fact. Rachel hoped he could give her something to *do* with Penelope. "We'll stage you after supper," he said.

The male lead was Henry Ansell, a reliable if not exciting actor with a nondescript voice. Reviews always described him as "adequate" or "dependable." He worked regularly in almost any show that starred Gloria Doro. Rumors had circulated for years that the two were lovers, but Rachel had speculated that the reason was more likely Ansell's height; in fact, he had played professional basketball before a knee injury "transferred" him into the theater. He towered over the entire cast, particularly above Gloria Doro. And since her wealthy husband, Arnold Gold, produced most of the shows in which his wife starred, Ansell's career appeared as secure as a blue-chip stock.

Rachel didn't recognize anyone else assembled on the large stage, although many were camouflaged behind Indian headdresses and war paint for the production number that culminated the act.

Lehman Stern checked his watch and suggested a piano rehearsal. "The orchestra's going on dinner break, so perhaps we can go over some of Penelope's music. We had our dress run-through this morning, and I'm afraid the union won't let us do another, even for your benefit. So it's really between the two of us, Rachel." And Jamie had thought that would work in her favor! she thought as the conductor led her to a small rehearsal room backstage.

But her fears were dispelled as Lehman Stern began to play. His piano accompaniment offered all the nuances of the orchestra, and he seemed to understand and respond to Rachel's voice. He allowed her time to breathe and expand a phrase for its fullest effect. "Just remember," he said, "I'll follow you in your third-act number as long as you follow me in the ensembles. We'll help each other."

Rachel was so relieved to find a singer's conductor! She was unaware that she had sighed audibly.

"A little frightened?" he asked, smiling as he looked up from the music.

"A lot," she admitted.

"Don't worry," he assured her. "Gloria and Hank are old pros, and I'll be there all the time. Just sing the way you did at the New Stars auditions, and you won't have a thing to worry about."

She nodded. "I'll do my best," she promised.

"Good. Then I won't have a thing to worry about either," said Stern.

Rachel felt far more relaxed after a full night's sleep. The staging had required only an hour; enter here, sit, exit there. Penelope's arrival and subsequent confusion with the settlers at the fort in Act One would be served by Rachel's not having rehearsed with the chorus. "And, of course," said the director, "the other singers onstage will help you with directions if you need them. Lehman says you're very good onstage, particularly in this role."

Rachel's eyes widened. She turned to meet Stern's stare as he shook his head and whispered, "Shhh!"

He drove her back to the hotel where the principals were staying. "Mr. Stern—" she began.

"Lehman," he corrected.

"Lehman. Look, I have to ask. Earlier this evening, you signaled me not to say anything, but—"

"About Penelope, you mean?" he interrupted again. "Rachel, Ralph is one of those ultraconservative directors who never does anything new. Never takes chances. When I suggested a singer I'd seen in performance, the first thing he asked was if you'd done the role. If I'd said no, you wouldn't be here. It's one of the rules of the business. Don't tell the world your secrets. It'll only shock them and get you in trouble."

"Does he know we've never worked together before?"

He laughed. "I neglected to tell him that, too. Besides, if

64

what I heard at the auditions was any indication, we're going to work together often."

It made her nervous, but not quite as nervous as she would have been three weeks ago. She grinned as she stepped out of the car. She had been terrified only three hours ago.

The opening went wonderfully. Rachel's blond wig might have been more flattering, and there was little she could do with the stiff-collared blue gingham costume worn by Penelope, but the duet with Hank Ansell went smoothly and the applause was warm and long. Instead of retiring to her dressing room after the duet, Rachel hid in the wings to study the performance of Gloria Doro. She was impressed with the star's interpretation and voice; she was, as Lehman Stern had said, a pro.

When Doro made her exit at the end of the act, she seemed surprised to see Rachel standing just upstage of the "log cabin." Doro said, "I can't help asking. Do you always watch when others sing?"

"It depends," said Rachel. "When I can learn from them, yes."

The older woman squeezed her hand and said, "That's a lovely compliment. I'll have to talk to Arnold and see what we can do to give your career a little boost. Lehman was right; you have a beautiful voice *and* a head on your shoulders."

Rachel wondered what else Lehman Stern had said about her—and to whom.

As well as Act One had gone, it was Act Three that Rachel would replay in her mind for a long time to come.

She was alone onstage and, as promised, Lehman followed, providing a cushion of sound for the lengthy song that Rachel despised. She colored the words as much as she was able, wishing that she were singing in a foreign language—one that the audience would be unable to understand. The song had originally been written with three interminable verses, the last of which had the singer repeating the words, "Oh dear God, protect us in the wild; thus implores your Pilgrim child," over and over as the music soared. She came to the end of the second verse and silently thanked the same God for giving her a conductor who was wise enough to cut the third verse from the score.

Samuel Williams's music *was* splendid, though, and Rachel allowed that to compensate for the vapid person that Penelope was. It worked. The ovation that followed was even longer and louder than on the night of the New Stars auditions. The theater went wild with cheering and stomping. Rachel stood stock still as the applause rang on and on in her ears. She dared not move a finger, lest the public take it as the cue that it was time to settle down and continue with the show. But how long could they go on like this? she wondered. She was bathed in goosebumps as the delicious clapping showed no signs of subsiding. What was Lehman thinking now? How long could she acknowledge the ovation without stalling the show? What should she do?

She glanced peripherally toward the orchestra pit without moving her head. The violinists were tapping bows against their music stands, the highest compliment that could be paid a singer. My God! she thought as her gaze took in the conductor's podium. Lehman Stern had put down his baton and was applauding with the audience!

Rachel's head was swimming, but finally she knew it had to end. She slowly turned her head upstage as the director had instructed—everything else he'd said was, "Do it the way you've done in the past, dear"—and began to move. The audience quieted down at once and the last act continued to its conclusion.

At the final curtain, the stage manager reminded Rachel, as he had before the performance, "Okay, remember the sequence. Tableau. Then company bows together. Keep your eyes on Hank—you'll follow him for your solo call.

Gloria's on last. Third bow, entire company again. Next, you and Hank with Gloria center. Then you and Hank together. Last one is Gloria alone. Got it?"

Rachel nodded and took her place, just as the curtain opened.

Gloria patted Rachel's shoulder as they took the trio call together and said, "Well. That was quite an ovation in Act Three. I haven't seen that since Streisand's *Funny Girl.*"

Rachel diplomatically said, "And your Mame on the national tour. I saw the performance."

Gloria smiled. "Oh yes, that too."

When Rachel took her solo bow, she was given another thunderous reception as vociferous as that which had stopped the last act. This time, Rachel bowed deeply, drinking in the applause, reveling in it. She felt as though she might burst from joy.

The audience was still cheering, but suddenly from the corner of her left eye, Rachel saw Gloria Doro striding onstage from the wings. She clasped Rachel's hand tightly and as they bowed together, Doro said, "I wanted to share your triumph."

Rachel felt a combination of gratitude, admiration, and, she admitted petulantly, a touch of resentment. It had been her moment and she'd wanted to call it hers alone.

She broke the star's grip, smiled, and said, "You should have the final bow." She was wearing her contact lenses and didn't fail to notice the quizzical expression in Gloria Doro's eyes.

She left the stage as gracefully — and professionally — as she could.

The stage manager stopped her with a tap on the shoulder. "You were terrific, honey. But her hubby's paying the bills."

Rachel's dressing room was filled with people she had never seen before. Her dresser was gathering the parts of her costume; the wig man took her blond braids; someone else was checking props. Members of the cast stopped by to offer their congratulations. Autograph-seekers knocked on her door and crowded in with their programs and pens in hand. Amid the throng Rachel spotted Lehman Stern, whose bald head glistened with perspiration. Two men were with him.

"Rachel," said Stern, making his way to her, "I'd like you to meet my agent, Howard Rathborne." The handsome, gray-templed Englishman extended a hand. "This is indeed a pleasure, Miss Allenby. Lovely performance. Mesmerizing."

The word Jamie had used! Rachel thought.

"I meant that as a compliment, Miss Allenby. Few singers in my experience have had that ability."

"T-thank you," said Rachel, somewhat flustered.

"Get used to it, love," said Stern, hugging her. "I knew you'd be marvelous. I want you and Howard to get to know each other better. You need top management and *he* is *it*."

The other man with Howard Rathborne was a short, chubby man who might have passed for Humpty Dumpty had his clothes not been custom-tailored on Savile Row.

"I'm Arnold Gold," he said. "I wanted to meet you earlier, Miss Allenby, but you know the pre-performance partying a producer is *forced* into!" He said it with a victimized whine, as though partying with politicians and socialites were such a boring but necessary evil.

"Your wife's performance was wonderful," said Rachel.

"Yes, she knows how to do it," said Gold. "But you're the one who walked off with the show," he added, grinning from ear to ear. "We'll have to have a chat about your place with us in the company. After all" — he glanced at Lehman, who nodded, seemingly in anticipation — "if both of our Penelopes are unable to appear, and you can bring it off the way you did tonight . . . well, we must talk about New York. But I won't bother you right now. This is a night for celebration!" He kissed Rachel's hand and left her dressing room.

"Well," said Lehman Stern to Howard, "you and Rachel had better talk business soon—before some other top agent signs her up. This young lady's going to be a star!"

"Yes," agreed Howard Rathborne. "I do believe she is."

Every nerve in Rachel's body was alive and tingling. Arnold Gold is right, she thought. This *is* a night for celebration—how she wished Jamie were there! She couldn't wait to call him.

She was collecting her street makeup when Hank Ansell stuck his head into the room. "Rachel, you're coming to the party, aren't you? After all, you saved the show!"

Rachel reached into the closet for her coat. She'd call Jamie later from the hotel. "Yes, I'm coming," she said, beaming. "I wouldn't miss this for the world."

Chapter Five

The ringing telephone startled Rachel into consciousness. She remained still for a moment to acclimate herself to the unfamiliar hotel room. She'd neglected to draw the curtains before retiring, and now the light of the new day caused her to wince. Who could be calling at this hour? she wondered. She hadn't left a wake-up request with the switchboard. She turned to look at the blurred hands on her travel alarm clock beside the bed. Did it read nine-thirty? Not so early after all.

The phone rang again. Jamie! Maybe it was Jamie! No, she thought. She hadn't been able to reach him; he didn't know the name of her hotel.

Rachel's hand stilled the insistent jangling midway through the third ring and she murmured a dull "hello" into the receiver.

"Miss Allenby?" a sonorous male voice intoned.

"Yes . . ."

"Good morning. I'm Arnold Gold's secretary. I hope I haven't called too early."

Rachel rubbed her eyes, shook the sleep from her brain, and was suddenly awake. "No . . . not at all," she lied.

Not too early for *me,* she mused. Her own limited experience told her, however, that normal theater business—on the producer level—was not conducted before ten. This call must be important, then, she reasoned.

"I'm usually an early riser," she continued, pulling herself up to a sitting position, "although I'll admit I'm running a little late this morning."

"And after last night, no wonder!" said the secretary. "May I say we all thought you were magnificent."

"Why . . . thank you, Mr. . . . uh . . . ?"

"Pardon me. I'm Peter Nightingale. Mr. Gold asked me to call."

Rachel expected him to ask her to wait while he transferred her to the producer's line. Instead, Nightingale said, "Mr. Gold was hoping it would be convenient for you to drop by his office this morning."

She felt her heart skip a beat as she answered, "Yes," perhaps too quickly. "That would be fine. . . . What time?"

"Shall we say eleven?"

"Eleven it is."

"Good," said Nightingale. "I'll look forward to meeting you. And again . . . congratulations."

The receiver still sat in Rachel's hand after the secretary had hung up. Last night, Gold had been so enthusiastic, so effusive. This call could mean only one thing: a contract, either for permanent understudy when they moved the show to New York, or . . . or the role *itself?*

The switchboard operator's voice squawked, "Hello? Do you wish to place a call?"

"I'm sorry. No," she said, replacing the phone to its cradle.

She flopped back against the soft pillows, her hair swirling about her. Things were changing already, she thought. Even the hotel room, which was filled with Georgian pieces in polished mahogany and carpeted in rich, deep-piled rose, was a far cry from her monklike cell in New York. A successful career would mean constant travel, and although hotels wouldn't substitute for a place of her own, this *was* undoubtedly agreeable. She grinned and repeated Lehman Stern's words aloud: "Get used to it, love!" he'd said.

Gradually her grin turned into a joyous laugh.

* * *

An hour later, the doorman instructed the taxi to "take

71

Miss Allenby to the Capitol Theater." He closed the door, tipped his hat, and Rachel was on her way.

It was a clear, sunny spring day; cherry blossoms lined the streets, which shone in the late-morning light. Rachel thought she might like to become better acquainted with this beautiful town. No, she amended, *beautiful* was the wrong word. *Handsome* was more accurate; she sensed a decidedly masculine air about the city. She'd have a chance to explore it further, if the meeting with Gold fulfilled her expectations. She remembered reading of the poverty and slums, the seamy underbelly of Washington's stately facade, but none of this was apparent along the route to the theater.

The massive exteriors of the pristine white government buildings were impressive. Intimidating, perhaps, but they projected confidence, which, Rachel conceded, was probably part of their attraction as well as the architects' intent.

She smoothed the folds of her black crepe minidress and wished she had packed more than just "basics." She hadn't anticipated things moving quite so fast. She'd have to include a bit of shopping during her stay in the capital. She clutched her purse tightly. As soon as she'd met with Arnold Gold, she'd go directly to the production manager's office and see about getting an advance against her salary. Five hundred dollars a week! *That* would certainly allow for an outfit or two! Her head spun as she mentally calculated the addition of zeros—*after* the digit *one*—to her bank account.

The cab slowed for a red light and Rachel sighed, thinking back over the performance of the night before. She had sung well, and about that she was pleased. Other people—people important in the business—had thought so, too. How many singers sang well and never received proper recognition? she wondered, mindful of the redheaded soprano in pink tulle who should have won the New Stars audition and hadn't.

Whoa! she cautioned herself. You *deserve* this success, Rachel! She nodded to an inner voice that said, yes, and so had the soprano.

The cab hit a rut and the driver apologized for the bounce that had nearly sent Rachel's head into the ceiling. "We're almost there," he said.

"Good," she answered. The sudden jolt had served as a kind of slap, a reminder to concentrate on things that were happening for her—and *not* on what *wasn't* happening for others.

Her brain swam at the mental image of the luminaries who had crowded into her dressing room and later surrounded her at the party. In addition to Lehman Stern, Howard Rathborne—one of the top agents in the business, Lehman had said—had expressed interest and given her his card. Gloria Doro, despite her reputation as the ice queen, had been more than cordial, even if she *had* turned Rachel's solo curtain call into a duet. After all, the stage manager was right: Doro *was* the star—and her husband *was* the boss.

And now the boss wanted to see Rachel. That caused her to take a deep breath of the crisp spring air.

The taxi pulled up in front of the theater. Rachel paid him but couldn't add a large enough tip. "Sorry," she said, "but I didn't get paid yet."

For a moment the driver looked as if he considered it a cheap excuse. But then he softened and said, "It's okay, miss. We've all been there."

And now, she thought as she looked up at the huge white building, I'm here. Yesterday the huge brick structure with its domed roof had seemed forbidding. This morning, it beckoned with open arms. Rachel leaned forward and handed the driver an extra dollar. She'd skimp on lunch till she got that advance.

It prompted him to jump out and open her door. "Thank you, miss," he said.

"Thank you!" she answered, marveling at how quickly things could change.

* * *

The offices of the Capitol were through a door at the side of the building. Rachel took the elevator, which opened into a spacious lobby.

The receptionist complimented her on the previous night's performance, then picked up a phone. Before Rachel had time to take a seat on the leather sofa, a door opened and a tall man with straight white hair approached her. He wore gray-tinted aviator glasses and seemed in a constant state of agitation.

"Mr. Gold is tied up," said Peter Nightingale. "You can wait in my office. It's more comfortable." He turned to the girl behind the desk and said, "Barbara, would you bring us some coffee, please?"

His office was high-tech and ultra-modern, appointed in various shades of gray that matched Peter Nightingale himself. His wardrobe seemed color-coordinated with the room. When he took the seat behind his desk, Rachel wondered if he was aware that he almost disappeared.

Barbara brought the coffee, and between incoming calls, Nightingale entertained Rachel with anecdotes of other Arnold Gold productions. She listened for a time and laughed on cue, but when she stole a glance at her watch, she saw that fifteen minutes had already passed. The delay only increased the nervous anticipation of meeting with Arnold Gold, so Rachel declined the proffered refill of coffee from the silver service; additional caffeine would make the tension unbearable.

At last the phone buzzed, rather than rang. Nightingale answered it, said, "Right away," and stood. "Mr. Gold will see you now, Miss Allenby."

He held the door open. As Rachel stepped into the corridor, she heard a noise to her left. She turned to see a heavy, carved wooden door swing open. Glorio Doro swept out.

The star stopped short, smiled, and let the door slam behind her. She was dressed entirely in black cashmere, except for a blue-green silk cravat at her neck; the ensemble accented the already too-red hair.

"Hello," Rachel greeted her, returning the smile.

"Nice to see you," Doro replied, arching one perfect brow. "I had to speak with Arnold immediately about casting changes. I'm afraid it is *I* who have detained you — please don't blame my husband."

"I won't," answered Rachel as the words "casting changes" echoed in her ears.

"Besides," Doro continued, moving closer to Rachel, "I'm sure Peter has been as charming as ever."

"Oh, definitely," Rachel confirmed as Nightingale smiled nervously.

"Good. It's one of the reasons we keep him." For a moment the older woman stared into Rachel's eyes with a curious expression; Rachel wondered what she could be thinking. Then Doro said, "Well, last night was fun, wasn't it? See you tonight." As she turned to go, Doro added, "Oh, have you seen the reviews?" But Rachel wasn't permitted time to reply. "You'll enjoy them."

She sidestepped Rachel and Nightingale and walked briskly toward the elevators. Her high heels clicked along the parquet floor as Rachel knocked on Arnold Gold's door.

If the secretary's office was the quintessence of sixties modern, the producer's office was at the opposite extreme. "Imposing" came to mind, but it was hardly sufficient. The room achieved the effect of a set piece for an opera — although for what particular opera, Rachel couldn't begin to guess. Expensive, antique, ornate — obviously intended to create an impression of opulent-but-cozy; it was not unlike Nightingale's office in that it, too, lacked warmth and revealed nothing of its occupant's personality. Dracula's library, Rachel thought with a half-smile.

Peter Nightingale disappeared as the heavy door closed behind her and Rachel found herself alone with Arnold Gold.

He sat behind a massive wooden desk, also ornately carved, but he did not rise from his leather chair until Rachel had walked the entire length of the elegant Persian carpet. She did so quickly and with grace, nonetheless feeling as if she were crossing a very long stage. It did nothing to put her at ease.

"Thank you for coming, Rachel," said Gold, gesturing her to a wing-backed chair before the desk.

She took the seat, but the producer remained standing. Although a short man, he now appeared to tower over her. There was a brief exchange—his offer of coffee, her refusal—followed by unnerving silence.

The room was dark, and Rachel was thankful when Gold pulled a cord to the left of the red velvet draperies behind his desk. The sun filled the room, and after Rachel's eyes had adjusted to the light, she was stunned by the view. The office, on the top floor of the building, offered an impressive panorama of the capital.

"Magnificent, isn't it?" Gold stood with his back to Rachel as he spoke. "Originally, I had the desk against the opposite wall, but I found the view too . . . distracting."

"I can't blame you," she answered.

Gold turned then and faced her. His face was severe, his brow creased, apparently with concern. Rachel was afraid to speak, although thus far the interview had been hardly what she had envisioned.

"Mr. Gold. . . ." she began.

"Please . . . it's Arnold. After last night, you must call me Arnold."

He'd said it in a low, intimate tone—almost as if "last night" had been not a successful singing performance but a night of making love. A sudden fear rose within Rachel. Had the producer brought her to his office to make a pass?

Rachel began to squirm, trying desperately not to feel like a mouse in the lair of the cat. The waiting had been one thing; this game—whatever it was—was more difficult because she hadn't been informed of the rules.

"Arnold, then. . . . Thank you . . . but I'm . . . a little confused. Is something the matter?"

"You come to the point," he said. "That's good."

"I'm glad. But I'm afraid that I don't understand . . ."

76

"Of course not. How could you?"

Rachel wondered if she had missed a line from his script, a script she hadn't read.

Gold took his seat again and withdrew a cigarette from a silver box on his desk. "Do you mind?"

"No," she said, aware that he was stalling for time. A plume of smoke billowed about his head in the sunlight.

"My wife . . . absolutely hates it."

"Ordinarily, so do I." She paused to let him pick up the slack. When he didn't, she said, "Mr. Gold . . . Arnold, please . . ."

"I'm sorry. I have something to say, and it's . . . difficult."

"What . . . ?" Rachel tried to keep impatience from creeping into her voice.

Gold rested his elbows on the leather-trimmed blotter. "Last night, Rachel, your performance would have been stunning even if you had rehearsed all month with the company. Stepping in as you did at the last minute . . . well, in that light, it was truly overwhelming. Simply remarkable . . ."

"Why do I hear a 'but' coming at the end of that?" Rachel asked. She found herself calm and couldn't comprehend the reason. She sensed a sudden, inexplicable equality between them, although an icy shiver made itself known at the base of her spine.

"Because you're intelligent, Rachel. That's a quality sorely lacking among a great many performers." He drew a deep sigh. "Yes, my dear, there *is* a 'but.' "

Rachel realized what was coming. "You mean," she said slowly, "that last night was last night, *but* in the clear light of day you've . . . thought twice about what you said—in spite of how 'remarkable' or 'overwhelming' or 'stunning' you thought I was twelve hours ago. . . ?"

She couldn't believe her own words. She waited for Gold's answer while anger and hurt surged just below the surface of her own feigned calm. Please let me be wrong about this, she prayed. I sang well— I *know* it was at least

77

good—the audience liked me, like me a lot!—and Lehman and the rest—and Gold, himself—

"Surely it isn't 'in spite of,' Rachel," he said finally, studying the view from the window. "It's just that . . . since last night . . . well, certain factors have developed that make it impossible for me . . . to engage you . . . you know, it's *names* that sell tickets . . ."

"Glorio Doro's name is selling this show. Not anybody who plays Penelope."

He nodded, still not looking at her. "You have a very good business sense, Rachel, but . . ."

"But . . . I'm not being offered a contract . . ." She fought tears and for the first time was grateful that Gold had averted his eyes from her.

"Rachel, you've impressed a great many people. Important people. Much good can come of that."

"But no contract . . ." she said expressionlessly.

Gold picked up a stack of newspaper clippings from his desk. "Have you read these? Your reviews? They're raves— and the weeklies and magazines are still to come—"

But Rachel had risen, wanting only to be gone, afraid that her emotions would erupt before she could escape with a last vestige of dignity.

Gold continued. "Lehman Stern can be an enormous asset to you. And you must contact Howard Rathborne when you return to New York. He has a great deal of power and influence . . ."

Rachel looked at him as her hand reached the doorknob. Rage and heartbreak caused her voice to quaver as she said, "I . . . I just don't understand."

"You will," said Arnold Gold with sadness in his own voice.

She couldn't lock herself inside the confines of her hotel room, no matter how glamorous the furnishings. She had to find some small island of privacy where she could be alone with her misery.

Rachel walked aimlessly to the small, gated park. It was almost deserted. She chose an empty stone bench beside a large fountain.

The first flood of tears came and she cried openly, her sobs masked by the sound of the water surging up from the statue at the fountain's center.

"You will," Gold had said. She repeated the words over and over, their meaning still obscure. She thought back over the entire performance and the party afterward, this morning's call, the "raves" she hadn't even read. . . . Everyone had been so supportive, encouraging, enthusiastic. Everyone . . . except . . .

Gloria Doro.

In a single instant, she knew. The tears subsided as the realization crystalized and Rachel's thinking cleared.

That was it—the *but*. Now it made sense! Doro's bow with her last night, her presence in Gold's office this morning. The producer was only the pawn, helpless in the situation. Well, Rachel mused, I didn't count on making her my friend. But, she added slightly, I hadn't planned on her becoming my enemy.

It frightened her momentarily. She had done nothing to warrant such a reaction; she had not tried to compete with the star. But Rachel had unwittingly stolen the show, and that, to a woman like Glorio Doro, was akin to an act of treason.

There were two weeks of performances to endure. Twelve more days in Washington! Had she no ally—someone who could possibly understand the *cruelty*, the unfairness of what had happened?

Only Jamie. Jamie would understand.

She'd call him as soon as she was safely in her hotel room. She jumped up from the stone bench, left the park, and walked back to her hotel. She'd forgotten to ask for a salary advance, and now she was determined not to ask them for anything.

* * *

In the ensuing two weeks, nothing happened to improve the situation. Rachel's attempts to reach Jamie were constantly thwarted; messages left for him in New York—and then on the road once he'd begun his tour—were returned via messages he left for her in Washington; whenever one of them was able to call, the other one of them was out.

At the theater, Rachel remained polite while staying out of Glorio Doro's way. She fantasized having it out with the star—a genuine brawl like the staged fight among three of the "Pilgrim settler children" in Act One of *Arrowhead*—but to do so, she knew, would play into the star's hands and blacklist Rachel at the onset of her career. Only a singer of Gloria Doro's stature—and Arnold Gold's money—could afford such unprofessional behavior.

Meanwhile, as the producer had predicted, more glowing reviews appeared, adding fuel to the undeclared war. The critics decreed—in print—that Rachel had "fleshed out an otherwise insipid country girl and unearthed hidden depth in the character's simplicity, dignity in her virtue." Underscored was the unanimous consensus that "Miss Allenby managed to eclipse the most famous singing actress of our day." When *Newsweek* hit the stands, Glorio Doro began to ignore Rachel, both onstage *and* off.

Lehman Stern invited her to lunch and hinted that he was not unaware of Doro's treatment of her young colleague, but he, too, walked a fence similar to that of Arnold Gold. Gloria Doro was too powerful an adversary to cross.

Rachel put in a brief appearance at the closing night party. With part of her salary she had bought a pair of black velvet bell-bottom pants and a black silk poet's shirt. This time she knew she was upstaging Gloria Doro. As she made her farewells to the other members of the cast, she found little pleasure in either the new outfit or the party itself. The cast and crew—all but for her—were en route to New York—and to Broadway.

Worse, it seemed as though each guest felt compelled to glance surreptitiously around the room to determine the location of their redheaded leading lady before daring to openly embrace Rachel.

Hank Ansell kissed her cheek and said quietly, "It's been a pleasure, Rachel. I'm sure we'll work together again."

"Sure," she said, doubting it as much as she was certain he did.

Rachel had tried to find Lehman, but she was halfway across the crowded room and still hadn't spotted him. She did see Arnold Gold, however, with Gloria Doro's arm firmly entwined in his. While the producer's wife turned to chat with a senator from out West, Gold nodded toward Rachel. The expression on his face was pathetically help-less, but Rachel's experience had left her with little compas-sion for the man. She waved politely and moved to the checkroom.

She was collecting her trenchcoat when Lehman Stern appeared. He draped the coat gently across her shoulders and said, "I'm glad I didn't miss you."

Rachel smiled. Working with him had become her single source of enjoyment over the past two weeks.

"You are not only a wonderful performer," he said, "but you're also a lady."

Rachel's eyes misted, but she had to control herself. Too many people were watching. Perhaps Gloria Doro among them. And Rachel was more than enough actress to deny the star that particular satisfaction. Her mother had often spoken of maintaining appearances. For the first time, she was glad to have listened.

"Lehman," she said, "you've been so . . . kind. Not only for giving me this opportunity, but . . ."

"You can repay me with one favor," he said.

"*I* can? What?"

"Learn from this. Gloria's attitude costs her more than it does anyone else — in the long run."

"Does it really?" Rachel couldn't disguise the sarcasm in her voice.

"She was once a great artist. It's ebbing away, and every-one can see it. Her hide has become so tough, the soul of

81

the angel can't break through. And it is that soul which makes a great artist."

"Perhaps a tougher hide protects that angel," countered Rachel.

Stern shook his head. "You have a great career ahead of you. Don't let an experience like this embitter you. Don't let yourself turn into *her*."

"I'd quit singing first," said Rachel, amazed at her own words.

As if on cue, Gloria Doro let out a howling laugh. It was too loud, too raucous, too obviously calculated to draw the room's attention to her.

Rachel leaned over and kissed Lehman Stern on the cheek. "Thanks for everything," she said, turning as the sound of the star's "golden voice" rang in her ears.

Rachel slept a dreamless, undisturbed sleep; nonetheless, she awoke still tired in the morning. The realization that things had not changed *that* much was part of the problem. *Arrowhead* was over; she'd survived under difficult circumstances, made a few career strides, and had most of the thousand dollars she had received for her performances. But it was time to go home, to Jamie's railroad apartment in the East Village with the tub in the kitchen and the bathroom down the hall.

I can't, she said to herself. Not yet. God, I wish I could talk to Jamie!

Within moments, Rachel was out of bed, and after putting in her contact lenses, she went over the *West Side Story* itinerary. The company was at the Grand Theater in Wilmington, Delaware.

She immediately phoned the train station. The five o'clock local to New York stopped in Wilmington. She called the hotel on Jamie's list. "The cast is at rehearsal today, ma'am," said the switchboard operator. "Did you want to leave a message?"

Rachel almost said yes. But then a new idea charged her

with energy. Jamie must be missing her as much as she missed him—he'd left a half-dozen messages for her this week alone! She would surprise him! Yes! She'd see the show and drop backstage afterward!

"Ma'am, is there a message for Mr. Morgan?" the operator repeated.

"No," answered Rachel. "No message."

Rachel deposited her bag in a locker at the small station in Wilmington. It was dusk and the area around the depot was forlorn and depressing. Only one taxi, an ancient heap at that, sat waiting in hope of a fare.

The driver left Rachel at the deserted entrance to the Grand. Signs outside read WEST SIDE STORY. LIVE. ONE WEEK ONLY.

Suddenly Rachel was aware of a nameless, unsettling pall. It's exhaustion, she reasoned. That and tension and the emotions of the past two weeks. Jamie would make it all right. He would take her in his arms and love her—love her as he almost had that night in his apartment. Surely her need for understanding and tenderness would break through whatever shyness or past hurt had thus far held him back. The wall had begun to crumble. . . .

The first snapping fingers were heard, then seen, as the members of the warring Sharks and Jets appeared, one by one, on the small stage of the Grand Theater. The tough, angry boys began to tell the story in movement, their casual strides growing seamlessly into dance.

Rachel knew that Jamie/Tony's entrance didn't occur until after the ballet overture. It was difficult to control her anticipation; the element of surprise excited her as much as Bernstein's music. This was heightened by the powerful beauty of the choreography, the aggression of the dancers, the strength of their lean, muscular bodies. The Bernardo, dark and swarthy with an animal sensuality that defined

83

his role from the outset, was every bit as riveting as George Chakiris had been in the movie.

And then there was Jamie. He stood at the center of the stage, his golden hair and smoky blue eyes flashing in the light as he sang of Tony's premonition. "Somethin's comin'," his clear voice rang out, full of the optimism and hope in the song.

Rachel beamed with pride at the sight and sound of him; her knees went weak as various sensations washed over her and made the previous fourteen days seem only memories of a distant past.

"Could be," he sang. "Who knows?"

Rachel tried to find patience; she could barely wait until the show was over. The intermission was the worst of it, seeming to cause an unnecessary delay in their meeting.

But at last, the final words of the lovers, Tony and Maria, were spoken. *"Te adoro, Anton."* The performance was over and the curtain closed. When it reopened, the audience was on its feet. Rachel wanted to rush from the auditorium to Jamie, but she had to stay and witness his curtain call. She, too, stood, applauding joyously, tears in her eyes and her heart filled to bursting.

The curtain fell for the last time and the houselights came up. Rachel joined the throng in the crowded aisle and made her way from the theater. She tingled with excitement, a feeling that was all around her, in the air an exhilaration Rachel herself had experienced every night at the end of her number in Act Three. Gloria Doro hadn't robbed her of that!

She found herself pushing around and through the crush of people to avoid the halting, swaying rhythm of the crowd.

And then she was at the head of the aisle. She walked swiftly to an usher and asked, "Where's the stage entrance?"

He nodded toward the main exit. Rachel followed his directions and took a left turn, then ran down a dim alley that shone red from the bare bulb over a battered door that stood open.

"Mr. Morgan's dressing room, please!" Rachel cried to the old man who sat in a straight-backed chair inside the entrance.

"One flight up, third door on the left," he said. But she was already on the stairs. She cursed the high heels that slowed her pace up the steep steel steps, and she gripped the handrail firmly as sweat-soaked dancers excused themselves and rushed past.

The first and second doors were open, the rooms filled with well-wishers and cast members.

There, straight ahead of Rachel, was the third door on the left. It bore a small plastic sign that read **Mr. Morgan**.

Rachel's heart swelled and her throat suddenly went dry. There were tears in her eyes and she felt the blood surging through her veins as she turned the knob and threw open the door. "Jamie!" she cried.

He stood with his arms still coiled in a fierce embrace around the body of the dark-haired dancer who had played Bernardo. The boy's lips parted from Jamie's and both broke away from each other as Rachel stood in the doorway unable to move or to speak.

The dark-haired boy averted his eyes, while Jamie's face went from bright scarlet to stark white.

At last, Jamie, in a choked voice, said, "Rachel . . . this is Paul."

Chapter Six

The bar was mobbed. Rachel was grateful for that. She was filled with too many conflicting emotions to permit any one in particular to surface. The conversation was stilted, light, and impersonal. It was an agonizing performance.

Paul was as friendly as could be expected under the circumstances. Rachel caught him stealing occasional glances in her direction, but there were half a dozen "Sharks" at their crowded table. No opportunity for explanation; no time for discomfort to thoroughly subside. The discussion centered around that evening's show, what had worked and what hadn't. Rachel purposely lost herself, pretending to hang on to every syllable, all the while aware that Jamie detected her retreat.

Paul excused himself early. Shortly afterward, Jamie said to Rachel, "I'll walk you back to the hotel." They said good night to the rest of the cast and left the bar.

At last they were alone. They walked in silence along the deserted tree-lined street. It was quite unlike the comfortable quiet they had shared after a very different evening of *West Side Story* in New York.

"I should have told you I was coming," Rachel said at last.

"I guess," said Jamie. "But it wouldn't have made any difference unless I had lied to you, and I . . . I don't want to do that." Turning his face to her, he said, "Rachel, I . . . I didn't mean for you to find out like this. I . . . I don't know how to explain before. . . ."

"All you had to do was . . . say it," she answered in a choked voice.

"Say what? Just out of the blue? Just 'Rachel, I'm gay'?"

She nodded with a deep sigh, and they continued to walk with these new, staccato silences.

Finally, Jamie said, "Are you very angry with me?"

"Angry?" Rachel reflected for a moment. "No . . . yes . . . I didn't know, Jamie." She swallowed. "Maybe I am a bit because . . ." But she didn't know why; she only knew it was so.

"Because you're . . . attracted to me? Because you . . . think I was leading you on?" he asked with self-conscious hesitation.

"Because I feel like a fool," she blurted out. "And that's probably my ego talking." She hadn't intended to speak the latter remark aloud.

"Rachel, I wanted to tell you . . . I guess I thought, or hoped, that somehow you just knew—that we understood each other well enough. . . ."

"Apparently we didn't," she said with a slight edge to her voice. "I'm sorry, Jamie. I'm feeling . . . strange. . . ."

"About Paul and me—or about you and me?" This time he was looking away from her.

"About everything," she answered. "You, me, the past two weeks. I guess I'm not as strong as I thought. I've always kidded myself into thinking I could handle anything." Tears threatened, but she didn't have the energy required to stop them. "Maybe I did know, or wonder, subconsciously. But I wanted to be wrong." She stopped walking, drew a deep breath, and admitted, "I wanted you to love me."

He turned his face to hers and touched her cheek with his hand. "I do love you. I don't expect you to understand. *I* don't, myself. You're the first woman I've ever felt this way about, and . . . it's confusing me. That's why I couldn't tell you before."

He was right. She didn't understand. "Jamie, look, I won't deny that I wish you'd been honest with me—"

"Rachel," he said slowly, "it's taken a long time to become honest with *myself.* This wasn't a little self-discovery I made over breakfast one morning. . . ." He had absent-mindedly taken her hand in his and was fondling it gently, stroking her fingertips.

"I don't feel close to that many people, Rachel. And I do love you . . ." His voice faltered again.

"I love you, Jamie," she said.

"For now," he said. "But that'll change."

"Never," she insisted.

"Sooner than you think," he answered softly.

They had reached the hotel. Jamie collected their keys and walked her to her door. "I don't want anything to ruin our . . . closeness, Rachel. Promise me that much."

She could only nod; her voice refused to comply. She wanted to reassure him, to embrace him, but an invisible, intangible barrier restrained her.

Jamie tilted her head upward, and she closed her eyes so he wouldn't see the heartbreak there. She felt his lips upon hers, but it was a good-night kiss, nothing more. She managed a weak smile, all the while aware that Jamie's admission had set a burden upon her, a knowledge that there existed a part of him locked away in a place Rachel was unable to reach, to fathom, or to share.

Rachel returned to New York on the early train the next morning. She ached from an emotional numbness, an incapability to continue the masquerade. She felt an intense dislike for Paul, and for nothing he had done.

She splurged and took a taxi to Jamie's apartment, where the super had been given an extra set of keys to hold for her arrival. The weather had turned hot and humid, and even with all the windows open, the air was stifling; in addition, Rachel felt Jamie's presence throughout the place. She tossed her suitcase onto the mattress on the floor in his room and went out again. She bought a newspaper, picked a movie, and spent the rest of the afternoon sitting alone at Loew's Sheridan on Twelfth Street and Seventh Avenue, where she stayed through two showings of *Fanny* and cried until more tears refused to flow.

On Monday morning, she rose early, treated herself to an almond paste–filled Danish at Ratner's for breakfast, and shortly after ten o'clock, returned to the apartment. There she rummaged through her things until she found the business card that read: Howard Rathborne Artists, Limited, New York and London.

"Rathborne Limited," said the woman at the other end of the line. "May I help you?"

Rachel thought the voice sounded familiar, but she couldn't identify it. "My name is Rachel Allenby. I'd like to make an appointment with Mr. Rathborne," she said. "He gave me his card in Washington and suggested that I call."

"Please hold, I'll check."

Rachel tapped her fingernails against the rim of the bathtub while she waited. Jamie's "office" was the kitchen table.

A moment later, the voice returned. "Mr. Rathborne is with a client, but he said that he can see you at two o'clock tomorrow afternoon, if that's convenient."

"That'll be fine," said Rachel. Two o'clock. Only twenty-eight hours to kill until then.

At one fifty-five the following afternoon, Rachel entered the Getty Building on Madison Avenue. She was wearing a simple ecru-colored cotton minidress; only when she saw her reflection in the lobby mirror did she realize that in a certain light the color made her appear nude. She wondered if Howard Rathborne would turn out to be gay, in which case it wouldn't matter. He certainly hadn't appeared to be gay when she'd met him in Washington. Neither, she reminded herself, had Jamie. She forced the knot in her stomach to untie as she pressed the elevator button and waited for the car to take her to the top floor of the building.

The chrome doors opened directly onto the reception area of Howard Rathborne Artists, Limited. Apparently, no other firm shared the top floor. The lobby, in elegantly appointed gray and ivory and accented in gold leaf, boasted a breathtaking view of Central Park on one side. The remaining three walls displayed oversized photographs of some of the leading actors and singers handled by the agency.

Rachel gave her name to the receptionist and seated herself on a gray-and-ivory striped loveseat. She was leafing through the current issue of *Variety* when she heard her name and looked up.

"Well, I don't believe it!" said Norma Kendall. *"That's* why I thought I knew the name!"

Rachel immediately recognized the receptionist from the radio station and the New Stars audition-week interview. "No wonder your voice sounded so familiar on the phone! But what are you doing here?"

"The station was driving me nuts. Too much work for too little pay. Mr. Rathborne had an opening, and as they say, the rest is history. I've been here since May."

Norma's presence helped Rachel to relax. By the time Howard Rathborne buzzed the intercom, any trepidation had completely dissipated.

"Follow me," said Norma. "He's really terrific. English and terribly handsome, even if he *is* pushing forty. She winked and, in a decent Oxford accent, added, " 'Veddy charming, I say.' "

"I met him in Washington," said Rachel. She proceeded to fill Norma in on as much about *Arrowhead* as was possible before they reached the ivory door on the side of the corridor facing west.

"Well, break a leg—on *both* counts," said Norma. "I don't think *I'm* his type, but you just may be. . . ." She gave Rachel a thumbs-up and headed back down the corridor.

Rachel knocked and turned the knob at the same time.

Howard Rathborne was immediately on his feet. "I'm sorry," he said. "I got tied up with a call from London. Please come in. It's so good to see you again."

He extended a hand in welcome and Rachel's nerves resurfaced. She was led to a gray silk loveseat that matched those in the lobby except for their missing ivory stripes.

"I wish I could have remained in Washington longer than just for your opening," said Howard Rathborne, "but business demanded my presence here. I did read your reviews, though; apparently the press concurred with my first impression."

"They were . . . very generous," Rachel replied, uncomfortably warm.

"No, the reviews were on target, for a change. That's always a pleasant surprise. So often the critics write as though they really know and—" He stopped and stared at Rachel. "Is something the matter?" he asked.

"No," Rachel answered, suddenly aware that she'd been daydreaming. "I was just thinking back over the performances. They seem so far in the past, and yet the last show was only a week ago."

Howard Rathborne leaned over to the carved walnut coffee table in front of them and reached for the silver cigarette case. "Will it bother you if I smoke?"

"Not unless I'm singing," she answered.

"Good. I'm trying to stop. I'm down to four or five a day. They still calm me when I'm . . . unclear on how to handle something."

"Unclear? What about?"

He laughed, which made her smile. "You have a lovely smile, Rachel," he said. "May I call you by your first name?"

She nodded. "Mr. Rathborne—"

"Please. If we're going to work together, you must call me Howard."

He hadn't said it in the predatory or intimate manmer of Arnold Gold. But he *had* said they were going to work together!

91

"Howard, then," she corrected. "I don't mean to sound theatrically naïve, but I don't understand your use of the word *'unclear.'* "

He shook his head. "Rachel, you're not naïve. Your honesty is refreshing, and in this business, that's unusual — a definite plus. I am unclear — or was — about how to broach the subject of your ordeal with Gloria Doro. I see now that I can be direct with you, and that *is,* as they say, a real load off my mind."

Rachel crossed her legs, then uncrossed them. "Then I . . . I guess you've heard about Gloria — Miss Doro — and me."

Howard took a cigarette from the silver box, lit it from the matching silver lighter alongside the container, and said, "Everyone has heard. As well as the way in which you dealt with the situation. And, of course, Lehman Stern rang me about it from Washington. Unfortunately there was nothing he could do to alleviate the, er, problem. Gloria Doro is a very powerful woman in the business."

"I gathered," said Rachel, thinking back to the "morning after" interview in Arnold Gold's office.

"Well, from all reports," Howard said, "she's cutting her own nose. She insisted on reviving *Arrowhead* — against the best advice — because Samuel Williams will write *anything* she pays him to write. She couldn't carry the show in D.C., and I'm afraid the critics here won't be so kind." He paused to look at Rachel, then continued. "Don't be too disappointed about the outcome. The show's in trouble. They've fired the director, and the new Penelope . . . well, Gloria's found a girl who won't steal the last act from her, that's for certain."

Rachel lowered her eyes. "I didn't *steal* it," she said.

"Well, you took one of the most ridiculous roles in recent musical history and magically turned it into flesh-and-blood. No thanks to Ralph Adams, I might add."

Now Rachel was laughing. "I *hated* the role. And he gave me no direction at all. But the music *was* lovely."

"You are, too," said Howard. "But I've said that already."

Rachel thought his face had warmed slightly. Norma was right; he *was* "veddy" charming.

Howard rose and crossed to his desk. He shuffled through some papers and said, "I also said we're going to work together. I didn't mean to be presumptuous. I think you're headed for an important career, Rachel. That requires guidance as well or more than talent. The talent you already possess in abundance. I'd like to represent you, beginning now, if you're interested."

If I'm interested! she thought. The biggest independent agent in the business was offering to manage her—of course she was interested! She wanted to pinch herself to make sure they weren't discussing someone else—someone who wasn't there.

"I'll need photographs—eight-by-ten glossies," Howard said.

"I've brought some with me," answered Rachel, reaching into her totebag that doubled as a portfolio. She handed an album to Howard and studied his eyes while he studied the photos.

"Excellent," he said, leafing through the clear plastic folio pages. "Especially with your hair flowing as in this one." He looked up, then, adding, "And the way you're wearing it now. It's very . . . attractive."

"Thank you," she said, a fluttery nervousness returning.

Just then, Norma knocked at the door and entered. "Mr. Champion is due in five minutes. You asked me to remind you."

Howard glanced at his gold Rolex. "Thank you, Norma." He rose. "Rachel, if you'll leave a dozen or so copies of"—he thumbed quickly through the photographs once more—"this. Yes, this is the one we'll use, definitely. Give them to Norma along with copies of your résumé. And then reorder another batch, all of that same picture." He nodded again, to himself. "Yes. Wonderful. We'll get things moving right away."

"Thank you, Mr. Rathb—Howard. I'll order copies this

afternoon. Thank you so much!"

"It's *my* pleasure," said Howard Rathborne as they shook hands. Then they said good-bye and Rachel, in tandem with Norma, left his office.

They parted at the front desk. "Honey, you're on your way. Howard doesn't waste a minute."

"That's exciting, but it's scary," Rachel admitted.

"What is? Having these things move fast?" Norma feigned a shocked expression. "Are you crazy? One of these days we'll have to talk, over lunch. Things moving fast *always* beat things moving slow, honey!"

"Yes," said Rachel, "I suppose you're right."

But everything else appeared to be moving like molasses. The staff at Max's Photo Service, where actors went for reproductions of their eight-by-ten glossies, was up to its ears in orders, and Rachel was told that one hundred copies would take a week. The résumé service said five days. Rachel's personal life, what there was of it, she mused, seemed more sluggish than the sticky, humid weather, which made everyone move in slow motion. She felt like a rose in a time-lapse film—a wilted rose, she amended as she tried to keep the various cottons in her spartan wardrobe from clinging too closely to her skin.

Auditions came to a standstill in summer, too. Rachel stopped buying *Variety,* whose casting notices had shrunken from two full pages to less than three columns, most of them in places so remote that they made Excelsior, Minnesota, grand by comparison.

She read *Backstage,* however. On first glance there appeared to be dozens of shows casting. But when she reached the bottom of each notice, the words *no pay* or *showcase* or *nonunion* caused her to cross them out with her red pen. She seldom circled more than two auditions in any one week. And every time she stopped by the union, out-of-work actors, sitting on the old, worn sofas, commiserated with the equally ⸝worn excuse, "Well, it's summer. . . ."

She also signed up with a temp agency for secretarial work; her typing speed was an asset, and the novelty of substitute ushering had worn off by the time Rachel had seen those shows she'd wanted to; now she preferred to augment her bank account.

However, after three weeks of the nine-to-five routine in which the heaviest workload—and the blame for anything left undone by anyone—went to the newest "temp," she was growing restless. She had willed Jamie from her mind, despite his postcards and letters, which arrived with regularity. At least, she mused, Paul doesn't sign them, too! But she realized that she hadn't found an apartment—hadn't actively *looked* for one—since her return, and she'd have to come to terms on the matter of Jamie—and her feelings about him—before the tour of *West Side Story* was over. She wondered whether Paul would be moving in with him—another reason to resolve certain matters, first in her mind and then in her life.

But it was so hot! Thinking required energy, and at the end of the week and thirty-five hours of nonstop typing and broken fingernails, that energy was spent; in its place was a craving for . . . for what? A reward? No wonder Sophie, the office manager, weighed two hundred pounds. She'd worked at the same company for almost twenty years. Twenty years of food rewards could make anyone fat! Or Agnes, the receptionist who spent every penny on her wardrobe. The clothes were stunning, but wasted; there was only one man in the entire leather goods importing firm, and he was at least sixty-five. Norma was right, after all. Things moving fast *were* preferable to things moving slowly.

And so, on a Sunday when the thermometer topped ninety-two degrees with humidity to match, Rachel found herself walking uptown along Fifth Avenue instead of apartment hunting with *The New York Times*. She strolled east to Madison on one block, then the next street brought her west, back to Fifth. She passed expensive boutiques and fashionable restaurants, all closed for their wealthy clientele's summer exodus to the Hamptons or Fire Island or Martha's Vineyard or the Cape. The metal gates across shop windows served only to intensify Rachel's increasing feelings of isolation. Everywhere along the avenue she saw people in pairs.

When she reached Fifty-third Street, she hesitated, contemplating a visit to the Museum of Modern Art. But she soon dismissed that idea at the sight of three tour buses unloading; all the passengers made a beeline for MOMA's revolving doors. Rachel wasn't in a mood to be jostled.

Turning back, she took the west side of Fifth Avenue and meandered farther uptown toward Fifty-seventh Street. Those new fall boots in Andrew Geller's window would lift her spirits, she decided; a visual reward that was neither costly nor fattening.

She was unaware of passersby until she heard her name.

"Rachel! For goodness' sake, it *is* you!"

She turned at the sound of the familiar British accent and at the sight of Howard Rathborne reflected in the shoe store's window.

"Well, this is marvelous luck!" he said. "I dislike working on Sunday, but it's the only time the damn phones stop ringing. And now you'll provide the perfect excuse for my procrastination!"

"*I* will?" She looked at him blankly. He was dressed casually in white duck pants and a navy V-necked shirt. His slightly windblown silver-gray hair shone in the sunlight and framed his deepened tan. His smile momentarily made Rachel forget her loneliness.

"You will," Howard said, taking her arm. "We'll have a cooling drink at the Café de la Paix and spend some time people-watching—"

Just then, two good-looking young men passed by with their arms locked together. Rachel's mind darted back to Jamie's dressing room. "Howard, I don't know. . . . I may not be the best of company this afternoon."

"Why don't you let me be the judge of that?" he asked as

he steered her west on Fifty-seventh Street. "If you like, we can talk business." But he was teasing, Rachel could tell. She appreciated his attempt to lighten her mood. And she still hadn't had the time or money to indulge in one of those ice cream parfaits.

"Why not?" she said rhetorically, allowing Howard to lead the way.

She opted, however, for a gin and tonic. They were seated at a table that caught the occasional breeze; it was late enough in the afternoon so the sun now faced the north side of Central Park South; it baked the hot dog vendors, and melted ice cream cones dripped along after children who tried to gobble them up before they turned completely to liquid. No horse carriages were in sight; Howard explained that the heat wave had driven them from the streets.

"It's true, you know, about mad dogs and Englishmen—and their clients, it seems. What *were* you doing on Fifth Avenue all by yourself on a day like this?"

"Oh," she said, "just thinking. Sometimes I do that to excess."

"But according to your résumé—if I'm not mistaken—you live *down*town."

"You're right," she said, smiling. "It's *way* downtown. And if you knew what it looks like, you'd understand why I came *up*town." Her comment produced a small laugh.

The waiter brought them a second round, and Rachel's head buzzed from the gin. But it cooled her at the same time that it warmed her, and she liked the relaxing glow. She hadn't realized how tense her body had been lately.

"I haven't been able to send you on any auditions since we met in my office," said Howard, "but this time of year in New York is deadly."

"I know," said Rachel. "I've been reading the trade papers."

"Oh, well," said Howard, "most of the casting notices you see in print are for jobs that are gone—cast—already. The showcases aside, that is."

Her eyebrows rose. "They're already *cast?*" Her voice had risen as well.

"The unions require interviews and auditions for every member who wants to go up for a part. But the leads are cast before the calls are even listed. That's why you need me — or an agent like me," he quickly added, watching her as he sipped his drink. "I'm sorry, Rachel, you bring out some sort of protective instinct in me and the words seem to come out that way. They aren't intended to be possessive. Please don't be offended."

"I'm not, Howard," she answered. "But I can protect myself."

"You're right," he agreed. "Anyone who can handle Gloria Doro is pretty self-sufficient. How *did* you manage that, anyway?"

"Gloria Doro?"

"No, no. How did you learn to take care of yourself?" He grinned and Rachel noticed tiny creases at the corners of his mouth and eyes. It made them twinkle and appear to be smiling.

"Is something funny?" she asked.

He took her hand in his. "I'm trying to find a way to draw you out, to tell me about yourself. And I'm not succeeding. Guess I'm out of practice."

"I don't understand."

"I'm not in the habit of sitting at an outdoor café on a hot Sunday afternoon while prying into the personal affairs of a new artist on my roster."

"*Are* you prying?" asked Rachel.

He laughed again. "I'd like to, but somehow I think you're smart enough to see through it."

"Thanks. But my 'personal affairs' would bore you. I'd rather hear about yours." She turned beet-red and quickly said, "I mean, I'd rather hear some of the theater stories you've heard or witnessed — " She was embarrassed by her faux pas. She was also aware that her hand was still enclosed in Howard's strong, tanned palm and that she had made no attempt to remove it.

"You can read those anecdotes in books," said Howard. He was studying Rachel's eyes. "You're fascinating," he said. "And your eyes have the appearance of . . . well, of intensifying whatever they see."

"That's because I can't see without my contact lenses." This time she laughed heartily and he joined in. The gin and sun were doing their part in lowering Rachel's defenses.

"You're also not an egotist," said Howard. "And in this business, *that* is rare, indeed." His other hand closed over the one in which Rachel's hand still rested.

"Have you always been an agent?" asked Rachel, trying to change the subject.

"No. I began my career as a solicitor in London. Hated every minute of it, but in those days, one did what one's family had always done. Then my wife"—Rachel's hand involuntarily flinched—"or rather ex-wife, who used to be a singer, was offered better opportunities in the States. I couldn't practice here, and Cecily needed someone to handle her contracts, so what started as a sideline gradually took over. I seem to have the knack, as they say, and when other artists began asking me to handle their contracts, well . . . one thing just led to another." He laughed softly at a private joke. "In a way, I owe it all to Cecily."

"May *I* pry?" asked Rachel.

"Certainly."

"Why is she the ex–Mrs. Rathborne?"

"Oh, when the agency became a full-time job—and an overtime job as well—Cecily claimed that I had left her and married my business. So *she* left. Ran off with a very intense-looking Italian director who had some 'new concepts' or other."

"And?"

Howard shrugged. "I've neither seen nor heard from Cecily since our divorce."

Rachel twirled the remaining ice cubes in her glass with the straw she was using as a swizzle stick. "Was it true what Cecily said? About your being married to your business?"

"Not in the beginning. I suppose when we started drifting apart, it was then that I found myself staying late at the office. She accused me of having a mistress hidden away somewhere. We had a few hideous rows."

"Did you?" asked Rachel. "Have another woman, I mean?"

Howard shook his head. "My business was my mistress. It gave me more pleasure than my marriage, I'm sorry to say. For example, Cecily and I could never have had a conversation such as this. We hardly ever talked to each other. When she left, it only added her physical absence to what was already missing."

"What happened to her career?"

Howard finished the last of his drink. "Well, that's the odd part. She dared me to retaliate for her walking out—"

"Retaliate? Really?" Rachel asked incredulously. "And did you?"

"I didn't have to—even if I'd been so inclined. Three years later, Cecily's Italian dropped her and it was over. Her career, her affair, finished. She tried to come back, but three years' time is too long to be out of the public eye." He motioned for the waiter and reached for his wallet. "Cecily was always talking about people doing in other people. But she did herself in professionally. All by herself."

"You don't say that with much satisfaction in your voice," Rachel noted aloud.

"It didn't give me any," Howard said.

They walked through Central Park, which was cooling from the late afternoon shadows. They paused beside the statue of Alice in Wonderland. "You know, Rachel," Howard said, "show business is like that young lady's world," indicating the bronze replica of Lewis Carroll's heroine. "It's exciting and unpredictable, filled with mazes and choices—which road to take, which potion to drink. It's not so different from life. In the final analysis, most of it *is* probably just a pack of cards. But," he added, turning to her, "I wouldn't trade it for anything."

Rachel smiled. He had voiced her sentiments exactly.

They exited the park at Seventy-second Street and turned up Fifth Avenue.

"By the way," said Howard, "earlier you gave me the feeling that you've been troubled about something. If there's any way in which I can help—"

"Thanks," she interrupted, "but it's a personal matter." She experienced a sudden visceral reaction as the thought of Jamie crossed her mind.

"I expect it involves a young man then, if you're reluctant to discuss it."

Rachel didn't reply. When they were several blocks beyond the Metropolitan Museum, Howard said, "I live just there, across the street. Would you care to come up? I have a far smaller collection of Impressionists than the Met's, but some of the oils are worth seeing, I promise."

Rachel hesitated. But the gin had added a slightly devil-may-care recklessness to her mood, and she heard herself answer, "Sure. I'd love to see your paintings."

She was hardly prepared for a Monet, but there it was, a small seascape in an antique frame, hanging directly opposite the fireplace in the living room of the sumptuous penthouse. Howard led her past the vast expanse of windows and French doors overlooking the park. They entered an adjacent room, furnished in antique white pieces and white rugs on which lay smaller jewel-toned Persian carpets.

Howard crossed to an imposing inlaid mahogany cabinet and opened the brass-grilled doors to reveal a hidden bar. He prepared two gin and tonics, then handed one of the glasses to Rachel.

"Care for the deluxe tour?" he asked, joining her.

"Your etchings?" she asked, only half joking.

His look told her that he understood her question. But he didn't answer it. Instead, he led her down a parquet-tiled hallway. "This is my den. I work out the details of my clients' careers in here. My office-away-from-the-office." He switched on one of the antique brass lamps to exhibit a room Rachel had envisioned only when reading English whodunits — the library in which all the suspects were assembled for the wrap-up and solving of the crime.

Bookshelves lined two walls; the third displayed a marble fireplace. A leather-topped desk with matching leather sofa and two high-backed chairs completed the furnishings, all of which rested upon another splendid Persian carpet.

Howard took her hand. "Come and tell me if you like the music room. It's just down the hall."

"Oh, Howard!" Rachel exclaimed as she caught first glimpse of the sleek ebony finish of the concert grand piano. Her eyes, fastened to the instrument, failed at first to notice the exquisite Sisley snow scene or the small Cezanne beside it. She had gone since April — not counting the decrepit hotel upright — without the physical pleasure of playing the piano. The temptation was too great. "May I?" she asked, seating herself on the bench without awaiting Howard's reply.

It was a simple melody, haunting and delicate. Howard joined her on the piano bench. "That's exquisite. What is it?"

She shrugged her shoulders. "I don't know," she said, continuing to play. "It's whatever comes into my head." She went on, improvising variations in a minor key.

"But where did the *idea* come from?" Howard asked.

"I don't know. It's just something I'm able to do." Her fingers moved effortlessly over several octaves as she was drawn deeper and deeper into the music.

"You *are* fascinating, Rachel," he said. "Fascinating, talented, and . . . puzzling."

She didn't stop playing to reply. This was a dream, and she wasn't ready to awaken. She was aware of the lightness in her head, of Howard's closeness, of the musky scent of his cologne, of his breathing beside her.

It was Howard who spoke. "Frankly, Rachel, I'm not sure as to the next step. . . ."

She took her hands from the keyboard. "What do you mean?"

He brushed a wisp of hair from her temple. "I guess I'm trying to decide whether to put you in a taxi and send you home, or"—he hesitated, seeming to search Rachel's face for a sign of encouragement or rebuff—"or whether I should pour us another drink and run the risk of making a fool of myself if you stay."

"I . . . I don't think you'd be . . . making a fool of yourself, Howard," she said slowly, surprising herself. Only then did she look directly into his eyes. The gin had warmed her, relaxed her, and her cheeks were flushed. But she wasn't drunk, and this wasn't the gin speaking.

"I don't want anything to interfere with our professional relationship," she said. The words struck her as stiff and priggish the moment they were uttered, but Howard didn't seem to mind.

"One has nothing to do with the other, Rachel." His voice was lower.

They rose and went back to the bar, where Howard refreshed their drinks.

"Lots of gin, please," she said.

Howard did as she asked and handed her the glass.

Rachel walked to the French doors, opened them, and stepped out onto the terrace. It was still quite warm outside, but the humidity had dropped and now, at dusk, high above the street, the breeze was exhilarating. She was unaware that Howard had joined her until she felt his breath on the back of her neck and his tanned hands on her bare shoulders.

"You're going to have a bit of a sunburn tomorrow," he said tenderly. "With such delicate skin, you ought not to wear a halter." He ran his palms lightly back and forth, causing a pleasant chill wherever his fingers lingered. Rachel closed her eyes, and Howard bent to kiss her left shoulder. His arms went around her waist as he drew her to him. He cupped her breasts, which were still covered by the light cotton fabric. His hands felt so warm, and Rachel wanted so to be held, to be needed and loved.

Suddenly the word *retaliation* flashed through her like a

103

lightning bolt.

She shrank away. "I'm sorry, Howard, this isn't fair. *I'm* the one behaving like a fool." She walked to the bar-cabinet and set her glass on a coaster. "It wouldn't be fair—to either of us. It would be for all the wrong reasons."

She turned toward the door.

"I'll ring for the lift," said Howard, accompanying her to the elevator. "Let me know if you come up with the right reasons." He lowered his head and kissed her lightly on the mouth.

The brass doors opened and Rachel stepped inside the cubicle. "I'm sorry, Howard. I guess I have some sorting out to do."

"Don't apologize," he said, unoffended. "Some things take longer than others. We'll talk tomorrow. Meanwhile, see to that sunburn."

And the doors closed between them.

Chapter Seven

Several messages awaited Rachel upon her return to East Fifth Street; they included two from Jamie. The first, read to Rachel in the indifferent monotone of the answering service operator, said, "Jamie called, he is not at a number where he can be reached, and he will call back." The second, left four hours later, was more urgent. "Have tried you all day. Will phone tonight. Must talk. Jamie."

The telephone rang as Rachel was pouring a glass of iced coffee from a pitcher in the asthmatic refrigerator.

Nervously, she picked up the receiver. But it wasn't Jamie; it was Howard.

"I know I said we'll talk tomorrow," he began, "but I came up with an idea and I need to be certain you'll be at home in the morning."

"The morning?" said Rachel. "Yes . . . I'll be home, I guess." She was surprised to hear from him so soon after her awkward departure from his apartment.

"Good. Then I won't keep you," said Howard. "I'll . . . let you see to that sunburn." There was no malice or sarcasm in his voice, for which Rachel was relieved. On her way downtown, she had reflected on her behavior with him, and it had worried her; Howard was a powerful agent, and Rachel had accepted, then rejected, his invitation. She didn't want him to consider her a tease; she'd never been one, and wasn't about to become one now.

She heard herself say, "I'm glad you called, Howard. I . . . appreciate your understanding . . . earlier."

"Not at all, Rachel. We'll talk tomorrow then. Have a

good night's sleep."

She suspected that was the single thing she wouldn't have.

Jamie telephoned around midnight. Rachel had stretched out, wide awake, on the unopened sofabed.

"I had to wait till the performance was over," he explained. "Are you all right?"

"I'm fine," she replied. But her breathing went shallow at the sound of his voice.

"I was worried about you . . . about not hearing from you . . ."

"I've been busy," she said. "And I—" She stopped before inventing a lie regarding the loss of his itinerary list; it was on the kitchen table beside her address book. "I haven't known what to say, Jamie." That was the truth.

"Well, that makes two of us," he said. Rachel thought he sounded tired.

"H-how are you?" she asked. She refused to include Paul in the question.

"I'm okay. But you're sure you are, too?"

His concern suddenly irritated her. "I'm *fine*. You don't have to ask!" Then she realized the harshness of her tone. "I'm sorry, Jamie," she said more gently. "It's terribly hot and I just need to get some rest."

"Look, the tour ends in a week, and—"

"I'll be out of here by then," she said quickly, wondering where she would go.

"No—*that's* why I wanted to reach you. I . . ." His voice faltered and Rachel heard him sigh into the receiver. "Rachel, I've been thinking. In a way, it's easier that you . . . that you know about Paul and me . . ."

She knew he expected a reply, but she had none to offer, so he continued.

"Why don't you stay? We can share expenses. I . . . I like the idea of . . . of your closeness . . ."

She paused, her mind filling with questions. She gave voice to the first one. "What about Paul?"

106

"He has his own apartment. And . . . and I prefer it that way."

She wondered why, but decided that a long-distance call was not the appropriate moment to ask.

"Rachel?" said Jamie when she didn't speak.

"I'm here. Listen—can we play it by ear? You know, we'll see how it works out once you get back?"

"Sure." Another pause and then Jamie said, "I miss you."

Her eyes misted. "I know. Me too."

The operator cut in. "Three minutes are up. Please signal when through."

"Rachel. I'm out of change. I've got to run."

"Take care of yourself," she said.

"I will. See you in a week." And the line went dead.

Rachel closed her eyes sometime after 2 A.M. She had gazed myopically at the luminous dial of her Baby Ben alarm clock until its soft ticking lulled her into a deep, exhausted sleep.

She was awakened by the loud door buzzer at ten twenty-five in the morning. Lazily she rose and tried to smooth the halter and skirt she'd worn all night. Rachel felt as crumpled as the outfit; she'd slept in a curled-up fetal position on the sofa.

She opened the door and went to the top of the stairs. "Who is it?" she called down; the apartment didn't have its own intercom system.

"Allenby?" barked the gruff voice from the dark vestibule hallway.

"Yes." She covered her mouth as a wide yawn escaped.

"Jack Kahn delivery."

"Delivery of what?"

"Your piano," came the annoyed reply, as if Rachel had to know without his answer.

"A piano? There's a mistake—I didn't order a piano!"

107

"Hey, lady! This is Five thirty-five East Fifth, right?"

"Yes, but—"

"Second floor, rear, right?"

"Well, yes—"

"Then this is your piano. We'd like to bring it up, so ya mind clearing anything in the way? This hallway ain't exactly cooling us off!"

Within minutes, the delivery man and his partner were maneuvering a quilt-covered spinet up the creaking stairs. As they reached the second floor, Rachel caught sight of patches of ebony peeking through holes in the quilting. They only hinted at the glories to be unveiled.

Rachel stood motionless in the doorway to Jamie's kitchen. This was impossible, she thought; she hadn't ordered a piano!

But suddenly she knew who had.

The shorter, chubbier man stopped to wipe sweat from his face and neck. He peered past Rachel and grinned when his eyes fell on the bathtub. "Well," he said, "at least you didn't order a concert grand!"

His tall, wiry assistant at the rear snorted. "C'mon, Al, let's get this show on the road, huh?"

The first man nodded. "Well, lady, where ya want it? Not that there's much choice, huh?" He laughed at his own joke. Then, obviously realizing that the living room was the only possible place for the instrument, he grunted and silently hefted his end. He was careful to cover the corner that otherwise might have scraped along the edge of the bathtub. The task took five minutes more as the two men positioned the piano along the one available wall, opposite the sofabed.

"Presto!" announced the taller man, removing the protective quilt with one swift tug. Rachel gasped when she saw the polished black wood, as rich an ebony finish as that on the grand piano in Howard's music room. She tipped the delivery men and offered both of them beer. Only after they had left did she begin searching her mind for the way to tell Howard Rathborne of the joy he had brought into her day.

She splashed cold water on her face, inserted her lenses, and made a pot of coffee — she had finally mastered the art of preparing espresso in Jamie's tiny upside-down napolitano pot. Then she dialed Howard Rathborne's office number.

He wasn't in yet. Norma was. Rachel told her about the piano. "Norma . . . I'm thrilled — but I can't accept it, and I don't know how to tell him."

"What do you mean, sweetie? You need a piano, don't you?"

"Yes, but I don't want to give Howard the wrong idea . . ." Her face flushed at a mental image of the previous afternoon on Howard's terrace. She didn't share the thought with Norma.

"Rachel, honey, you have no control over Howard and his ideas. Or his gestures. Look, I've been around the block, and I've learned that if a guy wants to give you a present, you're only slapping him in the face if you turn it down."

"But Norma — a *piano?*"

"Well, I think a diamond would be more intimate, but you haven't known each other *that* long, have you?" She laughed, but when Rachel didn't join in, Norma added, "Rachel, if Howard Rathborne thinks enough of you to send you a piano, the least you can do is respect his judgment and acknowledge it."

"What do you mean? How?"

"The old-fashioned way. By thanking him."

That was what concerned Rachel. "Norma . . ."

"He'll be in around noon today. Why don't you just call and tell him what you told me? It doesn't have to be complicated."

"You make things seem so easy to handle, Norma."

The secretary laughed again. "Rachel, I'm serious. One of these days you and I really *must* have lunch."

"It's a deal," said Rachel, feeling somewhat less uneasy but not wholly comfortable. "I'll call back in an hour."

"Good. You were right that day at the radio station."

"About what?" asked Rachel.

"About your being a quick study. You *do* learn fast."

Rachel seated herself at the matching bench that had arrived with the piano. She ran her fingers over the gleaming keys, and as so often in the past, melodies began to appear. She became totally absorbed in the music; the real world faded away and, with it, the real world's problems. Whether this was comfort or escape, Rachel couldn't be sure. But music provided the tranquility she needed and desired, just as it always had.

When she rose from the bench to telephone Howard again, three hours, not one, had passed. It was almost two o'clock.

His voice came on the line immediately. "Well, Rachel . . . good afternoon!"

"Howard! I've been rehearsing some kind of speech—the proper way to—"

"Nonsense. Just tell me in a word: Do you like it?"

"Like it! I love it! I've been playing since the delivery men left—"

"Ah," he said with a smile in his voice, "so *that's* why you didn't call earlier."

"I *did* call. You can ask Norma—"

"She told me. You mustn't take me so literally. How's the sound? Shall I arrange to send over a piano tuner?"

"Howard, it's perfect—and you've done . . . far too much already."

"I'd like that to be only the beginning," he said.

"As it is, I . . . still feel very odd about accepting such a gift, Howard. Especially—"

"Rachel," he interrupted, seeming to sense her discomfort, "call it a business expense. You need a piano so you

110

can practice for auditions without being dependent upon an accompanist. I'm just looking out for my client. Does that make it any better?"

She paused. "I don't know."

"I promise to take it as a tax deduction. Meanwhile, you can promise me something."

She waited for him to continue.

"Just remember what I said yesterday. That one thing has nothing to do with the other. All right?"

This time she sighed heavily and made no attempt to hide it.

"Rachel?"

"Yes, Howard . . . I promise." She would remember—she only hoped that Howard would, too.

Rachel's mind was very much on the word *retaliation* during the following week; *Arrowhead* opened, was panned unanimously by the city's daily papers, and closed on its third night without awaiting further condemnation from the weeklies. As with Howard's conversation regarding his ex-wife's career demise, Rachel, too, experienced no feeling of triumph.

Nor did she sense the expected anxiety when Jamie called from Penn Station upon his return. Rachel had given the matter considerable thought, and while not relishing a threesome with Paul, she had concluded that being with Jamie on these new and very different terms was still preferable to not being with him at all. If that became intolerable, she would make the necessary changes and come to another decision; for now, the status quo was better than no status. Retaliation would have done Rachel more emotional harm than Jamie; either way, he still had Paul.

She examined her sentiments toward Paul and tried to separate the shock of her discovery in Jamie's dressing room from any actual dislike for the handsome dancer. She

111

was aware that for the present, she would have to monitor her own responses, record her reactions, as if she were a spectator watching herself on film. It was for her sake as much as for Jamie's, even if Paul might benefit from her accommodation. But Rachel's motivation, she knew, was for purely selfish reasons. *She* hadn't completely accepted the reality of the situation.

The adjustment, she learned, would be tested almost immediately. Half an hour after his call, Jamie was there, standing in the doorway to the kitchen. He and Rachel embraced as though nothing had occurred in Wilmington. They hugged until both were short of breath.

"You look wonderful!" he exclaimed. Her mild sunburn of the previous Sunday afternoon had faded and was now a rosy tan.

"So do you," said Rachel, observing the deep bronze of his skin and the golden sun-bleached streaks in his blond hair.

"I hope you're hungry." She had stopped at Ratner's and now an assortment from the delicatessen-bakery lay on the opened red-and-white-checkered tablecloth Rachel had bought on Fourteenth Street that afternoon.

"I made coffee, too," she said.

"I brought wine." Jamie unearthed a bottle of Valpolicella from his bag. "The place looks great—" Suddenly he saw the piano. His eyebrows rose. "Where on earth—"

Rachel warmed slightly. "It's a long story. I've found an agent, and, well, he knew I needed a piano and couldn't afford one—"

"An *agent* gave you a *piano?* Are you *crazy?*"

"Well . . . it's more a case of *his* being crazy, I guess," she said self-consciously.

"Who in God's name is he? The president of MCA?"

"An independent office. Howard Rathborne—"

Jamie interrupted her with a whistle. "Holy shit! How did all *that* come about?"

Over wine and strudel, then cherry cheesecake and espresso, Rachel told him of her introduction to Howard after the Washington opening of *Arrowhead* and her subsequent interview in New York. She omitted only the part that she had also neglected to tell Norma.

"Well," said Jamie finally, "it sounds like you've really lucked out. I mean, Howard Rathborne himself! I've been sending him pictures and résumés for two years—not even a Xerox 'thanks-but-no-thanks.' Guess you're more his type than I am." He seemed to realize then that his joke had stirred unpleasant subjects. He reached for the wine bottle and added, "Paul wants us to come to dinner tomorrow evening . . . if you're willing."

"How do you feel about that?" she asked.

Jamie took her hand. "I'd like for both of you to know each other better. I really would."

All the previous week's rationalization and intellectual analysis hadn't prepared Rachel for the sudden little visceral tugs and the quick catches in her voice, but she decided that facing them head-on would be better for all concerned than hiding and evading such issues.

"Sure. I'd like that too, Jamie."

"Good," he said. "I'll call and tell him." He rose and took his suitcase into the bedroom. As he dialed, he called to Rachel, "Listen. That piano is gorgeous. Just make sure the guy doesn't chase you around his office."

"Howard's not that type of man," Rachel said.

"What type *is* he? Short and fat with a Hollywood-style cigar?"

She laughed. "Tall, distinguished, silver hair. Deep tan." The sudden memory of Howard's strong arms around her caused Rachel to blush, and her voice trailed off.

Fortunately, by that time Paul had answered his phone.

Jamie's jazz class wouldn't end until seven the next evening. Rachel was temping until five. For convenience, they agreed to meet at Paul's apartment, which was between Seventy-eighth and Seventy-ninth streets on Second Avenue. If Jamie hadn't told Rachel beforehand that it was a narrow doorway between the hardware store and the barber shop, she would have missed it altogether.

Now, as she rang the bell beside *P. Jacobi*, she prayed that Jamie had arrived ahead of her. She also hoped that Paul had invited other friends or members of the *West Side Story* tour.

She had thought Jamie's building in the East Village was grim; Paul's entranceway was far worse. It was narrow, dark, and smelling of an unlikely combination of urine and cockroach spray. The mustard-yellow walls revealed large chunks of peeling paint and plaster; from within various apartments on the ground floor, one could detect sounds of bronchial spasms alternating with booming bursts of profanity and static-ridden music.

"C'mon up," welcomed Paul from six flights above. "I'm the penthouse. Start climbing!"

Rachel was panting by the time she reached the top. "Do you . . . do this . . . every day?" she asked between gasps.

"Several times," he said. "It's great exercise for the cardiovascular system. Unless you're schlepping groceries."

She inhaled deeply and wrinkled her nose. "Whew! What *is* that—rarified air?"

Paul laughed. "Sour milk. I forgot to dump the garbage." He beckoned her inside and hastily shut the door against the awful stench.

Rachel's eyes perused the small living room and settled immediately on the card table in the corner. There were places arranged for three. So be it, she thought, resigned to make the best of the evening.

"Jamie's on his way," Paul said. "He called about fifteen minutes ago."

"Oh . . ."

Paul indicated the threadbare easy chair. "Have a seat. I'll get us something to drink." That was when Rachel remembered to give him the white wine she'd brought.

"I'll chill it," said Paul, making space in the knee-high refrigerator. The apartment was so small that Rachel could see every detail of the so-called kitchen from her sight lines in the corner chair.

"Something to drink in the meantime?" asked Paul. "I have beer and . . . Pepsi . . . unless you'd like something stronger. I have bourbon—"

"I hate bourbon," she said. "Beer's fine. As long as it's cold." Rachel kicked off her sandals and curled her legs under her on the tufted cushion. "Your place isn't wired for air-conditioning either, is it?"

"This building isn't wired for *anything*—you'll see when I turn on the oven. The lighting is pure theater. Or bordello . . ."

They were both making an effort at small talk and Rachel sensed that each of them knew it. They laughed too readily at every appropriate comment.

But the small talk stopped abruptly when the doorbell rang. Paul jumped up and hurried to the door. He suddenly seemed as self-conscious as Rachel. She wasn't sure if that helped to put her more at ease or made her less so.

"Sorry I'm late," said Jamie, entering the room. He wasn't at all out of breath.

"Well," said Rachel, rising to greet him, *"your* cardiovascular system must be in great shape!"

"It only takes a day or two—" But Jamie cut the sentence short as the meaning behind his answer made both Rachel and Paul look away.

Rachel shook her head in self-reprimand. If the three of them were going to endure a hot, humid evening together, it was senseless to add to the discomfort. "You never did get me that beer," she reminded Paul.

"That sounds good to me, too," said Jamie, flopping down on the pillows scattered about the floor. Rachel sank back into the same chair as before, while Paul took three cans of beer from the refrigerator.

Rachel observed Paul, who appeared in the peripheral

115

vision of her right eye as he puttered about the kitchen. He was almost as good-looking as Jamie, although the two were at opposite extremes: Paul's jet-black hair fell in soft waves; dark eyes and a deep tan made him seem Spanish or mulatto. He was only an inch or two shorter than Jamie, whose boyishly handsome looks suggested a casual indifference; instead, Paul's strong, muscular body had clearly been cultivated, either at a gym or in strenuous dance classes. He, too, was striking, but Rachel would never have found herself sexually attracted to him; something hinted at his predilection, although if asked, she could not have explained. It didn't matter. She wasn't in love with Paul.

As the evening progressed, Rachel was relieved to find that all three of them, with the wine's assistance, were relaxing and gradually loosening the reins on their earlier, guarded behavior. She sensed that her awareness was shared by both men.

Paul's homemade manicotti was excellent, although, as Rachel commented, the heat generated by the oven was enough to asphyxiate them all.

"That would require gas," said Paul. "This little stove is electric."

"In *this* building?" Jamie and Rachel exclaimed.

"Well, you *did* notice the lighting effects, didn't you?"

They nodded. The lights had dimmed until Paul turned off the oven.

"How long have you been living here?" Rachel asked.

"Too long," answered Paul. "But it's cheap and—"

He was interrupted by the sounds of very loud shouting from the apartment on the other side of the wall.

"Don't you *dare* say that to me!" screamed a woman in a high-pitched yell.

A man's voice yelled back, but his words were unintelligible.

The woman cried, "You got one helluva nerve, George!"

Again, his undecipherable reply.

A glass object crashed against the wall. Rachel turned from Jamie to Paul. "Sure sounds like Greek to me," she said.

Paul, in the attempt to keep from laughing, began to choke on an unswallowed piece of manicotti. Jamie quickly jumped up from his chair and pounded Paul on the back. The mouthful of pasta became dislodged and finally traveled down the proper pipe.

"*What* did I say?" Rachel asked when he was beyond the danger of choking.

"Oh, Rachel!" The laughter threatened once more and several giggle spasms escaped before Paul could explain. "Rachel — *George* — *is* — *Greek!*" He doubled over in a convulsive fit, this time joined by Rachel and Jamie. The neighbors next door continued their relentless exchange, the woman in broken English, the man in his native tongue.

At last, a thunderous crash was heard. The woman screamed — in very clear English — "Go to hell, George!" The door to the neighbor's apartment slammed so violently that the wineglasses on Paul's table shook from the impact.

Rachel excused herself. "The laughter and the wine," she explained. "Where's the john?" She shuddered at the thought that Paul might share the facility with the madman next door.

But he didn't. "See that closet door, Rachel? Behind the pots and pans on the pegboard?"

What from the living room had appeared to be a pantry was instead the smallest private bathroom Rachel had ever seen. When she positioned herself on the seat, her knees touched the wall in front of her. The wall dividing Paul's bathroom from George's apartment on the other side was so thin that every sound was intensified. She heard the Greek muttering under his breath as he stepped on or stumbled over broken pieces of china and glass.

George's voice boomed louder once more. Just as Rachel pulled the ancient chain, flushed, and rose from the commode, a fist punched its way through the plasterboard partition. Rachel screamed as she lowered her skirt. Cries of pain roared from the other side of the wall.

Jamie and Paul were instantly on the scene—just as the scratched, bleeding, though not severely wounded, hand was withdrawn from the gaping hole in the wall. Fierce, bloodshot eyes replaced the fist; they stared through the protrusion as the bulbous red nose snorted like a bull about to storm the matador.

His audience didn't dare laugh or make a sound, for fear that the entire wall might be next; it provided a skimpy barrier to a Greek bound for vengeance.

George was the first to back away. As he did so, he began to laugh—a grumbly, corrugated, croaking laugh, but without a trace of anger.

Rachel, Jamie, and Paul stared at one another in shock. They still stood at the entrance to the cubbyhole closet. George's door slammed as it had shortly before, and a moment later, there came a pummeling against the door to Paul's apartment. A roaring voice yelled, "Open up! Open up for George!"

The three stood frozen in the kitchen. The pounding came again. "Open up the door! George say open *now!*"

Rachel was the first to move. "We may as well," she said, going to the door. "If we don't, he may put a hole through that, too."

She swung open the door. Standing menacingly on the threshold was a very large man. He was bald, with a white handlebar mustache, and wore a dirty sleeveless undershirt. It barely covered an enormous belly, which protruded over shiny brown baggy pants. He was expending great effort to maintain his balance and was not succeeding too well.

He cleared his throat, housed within the thick, leathery neck, and bellowed, "Today is birthday! George today make seventy years!" Then his mouth forced a petulant shape and he added, "George hurt his hand." He entered the room, apparently unaware that no invitation had been

118

extended, and drew a bottle from behind his back.

"That bitch gone! Now we celebrate! Now we drink!"

Paul quickly grabbed four small glasses from a shelf and joined the others.

"Sit!" ordered George.

And they sat. George took the place of honor—on the floor—and Paul, Jamie, and Rachel arranged themselves in a semicircle around him.

"Ouzo!" cried George, pouring generously into each glass. "Good for the blood! Good for the soul! Without ouzo, George's hand hurt!" He lowered his voice and confided to himself, "With ouzo, *nothing* hurt! We all drink! We drink to George!"

The others obeyed and clinked their glasses.

Rachel's nose wrinkled at the licorice aroma. It was one of her least favorite tastes or smells. That, together with the heat, plus the beer and the wine already consumed, convinced Rachel that it might be wise to forgo this phase of George's celebration. She managed a weak smile. George was watching her.

He scooped the glass from her hand, lifted it to his lips, and in one gulp drained its contents. Then he refilled it to overflowing, returned it to Rachel, and announced, "Is easy! Now *you* drink!"

Rachel wasn't about to argue. Shuddering, she drank.

The impromptu birthday festivities continued. George dominated the proceedings, most of which occurred in Greek, since no one else was given an opportunity to speak. His captive audience laughed on cue—whenever George laughed—and nodded—whenever George nodded. And they drank whenever George poured. The celebration came to an end well after midnight but sometime before dawn, when George's guests, however willing, one by one passed out.

Rachel lay curled in her wrinkled skirt and shirt among

119

the cushions on the floor. Her head pounded with a louder sound than that created by the gridlocked trucks and cars on the street six flights below. An ambulance siren blared in the immovable traffic; five minutes passed before Second Avenue opened and allowed the vehicle to pass. At last, the wailing cry died away.

Rachel's eyelids were in agony; she had slept in her contact lenses. The intense discomfort caused tears to form, and she blinked repeatedly until they had helped to lubricate her eyes and clear her vision; then she glanced about the room. Jamie's head was buried under a pillow; his long, slim body was rolled into an embryonic coil. Paul was absent, but the aroma of freshly brewed coffee made Rachel turn her head toward the stove. There, pouring the steaming liquid into giant mugs, was their host. Rachel massaged her temples, but the hangover refused to budge.

"G'morning," said Paul, stepping over Jamie and the empty overturned ouzo bottle to hand Rachel one of the mugs.

She stretched her arms and forced herself into a sitting position to accept the coffee. Paul nudged Jamie several times with the toe of his bare foot; then, after receiving no response, he settled on a free cushion next to Rachel.

"How are you feeling?" he asked.

"I'm beyond feeling," she answered. "My head may never be the same. I didn't know ouzo had such a 'morning after' effect."

"Maybe not by itself," he said. "But we drank all that wine and beer before . . ."

She began to recall the earlier part of the evening and nodded. "I hope you made a few gallons of this stuff."

"Not to worry." They both leaned their heads back against the wall. "I'm sorry about your headache," he said at last, "but I'm glad you came with Jamie last night."

"You are? Why?"

He concentrated on his coffee mug instead of looking at her. "Well . . . I had a different impression of you . . . the first time. . . ."

She inhaled deeply. "I didn't know about . . . Jamie hadn't told me."

"He explained later. But he didn't tell me you were in love with him." Now his eyes met hers. "Or that you still are."

"What makes you think that?" She was certain her voice betrayed her.

"I was studying you last night."

"Really?" She felt a sudden sting.

"Don't get defensive — you were studying me, too. I saw it."

She couldn't deny it; Paul was right on the mark.

"Rachel, I'd like us to . . . to get along. I know Jamie would like it, too. And you and I — well, we're in the same boat."

"Not exactly the same boat, Paul," she said.

He didn't seem to take offense. "We're both in love with Jamie. That's what I mean."

"We're talking about different kinds of love," she said. This time it was Rachel who didn't look directly at Paul.

"Not so different. You'd like to be his lover, wouldn't you?"

The sudden color in her face answered for her.

"Rachel, I'm not . . . competing with you."

"Of course not. You've already won — if there ever was a contest." Why, she wondered, did every word she uttered imply that she felt left out of some conspiracy? That she hadn't been invited to the party?

"Paul, you've got to understand . . . or I've got to, somehow." But she didn't have an explanation that she could have shared with him.

"Look . . . I've been jealous of you, if that makes us even," he said. "All I hear, from morning to night, is 'Rachel this' and 'Rachel that.' Jamie does love you. It's just that —"

"That he likes men instead of women," she finished for him.

121

He took a long drink of coffee. "Rachel, there are as many ways of being close as there are ways of avoiding closeness. Jamie is still finding that out. He's a lot more . . . well, complicated, I guess, than someone like me."

"What does that mean?"

He smiled and moved his cushion closer to her. "In the first place, I knew I was gay by the time I was twelve. Boys that age experiment, you know, but I discovered that I liked it. And forget the psychological bullshit about domineering mothers and wimpy fathers. My dad is a peach, so's my mom, and they're still on a honeymoon after thirty years of marriage. I just dig guys." He cast a glance toward Jamie, who still exhibited no signs of life.

"Jamie, on the other hand, has fought it. Homosexuality goes against everything his parents taught him, his friends, lifestyle, et cetera. Finally, just a couple of years ago, he woke up and realized that he couldn't fight his own body. Okay, so he came out — still feeling lousy and uncertain about it. Then, just about the time he'd accepted it — and himself — you came along and stirred up emotional and sexual feelings he's never had before — for a woman. It's been tearing him apart, too, believe me."

"Then *why* does he want me to stay at his apartment? That doesn't make sense —"

"Because he *loves* you."

"But —"

"Rachel, I'm not a shrink. I'm just . . . just trying to be a friend." He placed his coffee mug on the floor and reached for her hand.

She released a deep, pent-up sigh but allowed Paul to squeeze her fingers and returned the pressure.

"Rachel, be patient with Jamie. He needs you. He's very confused. Y' see, he and I — well, before we met, I guarantee he led a very different life from mine."

"What do you mean?"

"Just that Jamie's not the type to cruise the bars or hang around Third Avenue. And he'd feel like a freak at Cherry

Grove on Fire Island. He'd go straight if he could . . ."

"And he can't?"

Paul shrugged. "I don't know. I've met guys who switched—who even got married and had kids. But I've always felt they did it for appearances. For example, I think you're damned attractive—but you're a woman; you just don't turn me on."

For some reason, it made Rachel laugh. Possibly because she felt the same about Paul; gorgeous, but . . . nothing there.

Jamie stirred then. A long, sighing groan emanated from the pillow-covered head. Paul rose from his cushion. "I'll reheat the coffee and get us all aspirins. I think we're going to need them."

Whether it was the caffeine or her conversation with Paul, Rachel found that her own hangover and headache were completely gone. She was cold sober.

Chapter Eight

October 1968

Summer faded into fall. After her conversation with Paul, Rachel had accepted him and was making every attempt to accept his relationship with Jamie. She kept the physical aspect from her mind, not because it would have repulsed her, but because, on some deep, subliminal level of her brain, she hoped that Paul might be wrong, that Jamie was the exception and could change . . . and that if it occurred, it would not be simply "for appearances."

The light breeze cooled to a brisk chill and sent a tingle of exhilaration through her. Rachel was nearing Cooper Union and the Astor Place subway entrance. The sight brought relief to her toes, since she'd walked to the destination wearing the new black kidskin boots purchased—in half a size smaller than usual—at Geller's pre-autumn sale; the three-inch-high heels were not exactly designed for walking tours, but she needed the height for auditions.

Now, after breaking in the boots for a month, they were almost comfortable, and she had enjoyed her stroll. Her spirits had lifted considerably since closing the apartment door.

Instead of the usual heightened excitement that accompanied an imminent audition, she had been uncertain— even depressed—at the prospect. Strange reaction, she mused, since it was her first audition in more than three weeks.

During that time, Jamie had been very busy with two callbacks for an Off-Broadway show, followed by a booking for a local bank commercial. Then came the news that he'd landed the show. He had started rehearsals two weeks ago. Paul, too, had had a full schedule since getting a job in a textile industrial show now being staged at the Waldorf. While Rachel was happy for both Jamie and Paul, their successes brought a twinge of envy in the comparative light of her own recent inactivity.

No matter how pleasurable, there were only so many evening hours she could spend at the piano while Jamie was at rehearsal. Howard Rathborne had invited Rachel to dinner several times, but she had declined, except once, when she knew there would be others present. Even that occasion had presented its problems.

Rachel hadn't told Howard that she shared an apartment with a roommate, let alone a male roommate; she hadn't envisioned Howard ever going near her neighborhood. However, on the evening that she and several of his clients, including Lehman Stern, had dined together at Charles V, Howard had insisted upon accompanying her home.

Fearing a repeat performance of the afternoon on his terrace, Rachel began to panic as the taxi neared Fifth Street. When the car stopped in front of number 535, Rachel jumped out and said, "Howard, thank you for a lovely dinner. Good night."

He was out of the taxi in an instant. "I don't like the thought of your going up alone." He preceded her into the dark hallway. "At least I can see you to your door."

She tried again once her key was in the lock. "Howard, it's late. And I have to get up very early for my temp job."

His hand was on the doorknob. "I'm not asking for a nightcap. I just want to make sure you're safely ensconced."

As the door opened, Rachel shrank back, half expecting Jamie to be reading or watching television or—worse yet—to be with Paul, since she'd told them she'd be late. But her fear turned to wonder as she stepped into the kitchen.

Howard stood directly behind her.

Jamie wasn't at Paul's; she knew, because the lights were on, and Jamie always turned them off when he went out. And he had to be home, because although it might have escaped Howard's eye, Jamie's suede jacket was on the door hook. It was too cold to be outside without it. His other outerwear was too light or too heavy for the weather.

The bathroom? she asked silently. Was Jamie suddenly going to burst in on them? She tried to put her thoughts together, but nothing made sense; the apartment seemed somehow . . . changed.

Howard said, "Well, I must say it's cozy. And you keep it neatly arranged. Very organized."

Then she realized what seemed so different. Nothing lay about. Usually, Jamie's sweaters or shoes wound up in the living room, or his dance leotards and tights were tossed wherever they happened to land until he got around to washing them. Tonight, instead, the apartment looked as if . . . as if, thought Rachel with a smile forming, only *one* person occupied the place!

"Care to give me the grand tour?" asked Howard.

Before Rachel could protest, Howard opened the door to the bedroom. Rachel gasped — Jamie *had* to be lying there, asleep — but Howard said only, "Well, it's small, but livable, I suppose."

Where *was* Jamie? Rachel wondered.

Howard reclosed the door and walked into the living room. "The piano looks fine, here," he said.

"And I love it. I play it till all hours." She'd formed the sentence purposely. "Speaking of hours, Howard, please don't think I'm being rude, but . . ."

"I'll go," he said. "I just wanted to have a better picture in my mind."

She didn't ask why; it might have opened other doors. They kissed good night, but the kiss was on middle ground, somewhere between passion and friendship. Howard wasn't pushing her.

When he was gone, she leaned back against the kitchen

wall and heaved a sigh. She heard muffled laughter coming through the closed door to the bedroom.

"Jamie?" she whispered as she turned the knob.

"Boo!" he cried, parting the dozens of hangers and stepping out from behind the clothes rod. Only then did Rachel discover his hiding place: he had jammed together the longest coats and pants; towels, dance paraphernalia, everything usually left scattered throughout the apartment had been thrown across the top of the rod to create an impenetrable clothes fortress.

"I just wish you'd given me a little more time!" he teased. "I was sitting here, minding my own business, when I heard voices and the key in the lock. Then I remembered you had a business dinner with the great Howard Rathborne and knew it couldn't be anyone else."

"Jamie, you're amazing!"

"You're right!" he said. "Would you care for a spot of tea?"

Since that night, she hadn't accepted dinner invitations from Howard, for fear of unintentionally leading him on. Too, she wanted to be with Jamie as often as he was free. He seemed to understand and respond to this, because he seldom stayed over at Paul's more than twice a week. But soon his show would open and she'd be alone every night. Meanwhile, despite whatever understanding she and Paul had reached about their respective relationships with Jamie, its very nature still gnawed at her, simply because Paul and Jamie were lovers, and she and Jamie were not.

Her upcoming audition had not come through Howard Rathborne Artists, Limited. During the heat wave in August, in what Rachel had termed the "summer of her discontent," she had "blanketed" the city's casting offices with a mass mailing of pictures and résumés. Her follow-up phone calls had netted only two interviews, neither of them leading anywhere.

So Rachel's dwindling funds, despite the money from

two weeks with Washington's *Arrowhead,* had demanded her acceptance of whatever mundane employment the temp agency continued to dole out. During the work week, she lived for her coffee-break call to the answering service. Perhaps there would be a message, an audition, an interview. . . . The days and weeks had moved on, the weather had grown cooler and the days shorter, and . . . nothing.

Then, one day there *had* been a message. One of the two casting directors who had interviewed her months before had called with an audition: a national tour revival of *Camelot*. The show and the role of Arthur were being reworked as a vehicle for an aging film star whose career was fading. Rachel had heard about the forthcoming production, which was largely viewed as a "last-ditch effort" to salvage a career on the skids.

So it wasn't Broadway. So the production would lack a certain amount of prestige. But appearing in it would still be a good — and sorely needed — credit on Rachel's résumé. She had understudied the role of Guinevere in stock — another Julie Andrews impersonation — but most of all, it was a *job* that offered to pay her to do what she loved most — and at five times the money she made in the temporary typing pool.

Nonetheless, she was surprised at her lack of enthusiasm. The audition was for the role of Morgan Le Fay, who never appeared onstage; she was heard as a disembodied voice from the wings as she entreated King Arthur to temptation. The contract also offered understudy to the leading lady, who, like the Broadway Penelope in the ill-fated *Arrowhead,* had been cast with an adequate but unexciting singer who would present no threat to the male star.

Rachel had been requested to bring something from the show. Since she would have to be convincing as both Morgan Le Fay *and* Queen Guinevere, Paul had suggested two songs — Morgan's seductive, evocative "Follow Me" and Guinevere's lively, mischievous "Simple Joys of Maidenhood"; the former would display her voice; the latter would show that she could act.

Rachel would have preferred to sing something from another show — any show. All the singers auditioning would choose either or both of these two songs. After the first dozen renditions, the director and conductor would either be lulled asleep or bored to death. Rachel's audition was scheduled for two o'clock; unless she could embue the songs with a fresh, original approach, she'd be forgotten the moment she left the stage.

She hadn't told Howard about the audition, and it made her feel disloyal to accept a call from someone else. She had tried to reason that Howard's office hadn't arranged an audition in several weeks, and he could have submitted her for this job, even if it was less prestigious than those generally handled by his office. That he hadn't sent her — and someone else had — combined to create a conflict of feelings — those of guilt *and* mild resentment, with a dollop of insecurity. *Why* hadn't he submitted her name? Surely Howard's influence and her success in Washington with *Arrowhead* were enough to impress the producers, make them know she wasn't without talent. The show itself had flopped, but she hadn't been part of its failure; she'd been its major asset. It seemed that no one cared, that *Arrowhead* had never happened and was now relegated to merely one line on the sparse résumé of a neophyte.

Why hadn't Howard submitted her? Didn't he have faith in her ability? But he'd sent her the piano — could he simply have overlooked her for the role? Not thought of her at all? That hurt even more, which was why, finally, she had decided not to tell him about the audition. She would do it on her own.

These thoughts had preyed on her mind all along the walk to the subway. She ran over the two songs and concentrated now on the intentions of the lyrics.

A gust of wind brushed her cheek. Suddenly, in that instant, the words took on the meaning she had sought to find and convey: a return to youth, to joy, to beginnings—an escape from the coming frost of a dying year.

Had she only been here six months? Had April been so very long ago? The lyrics, the melody's simple beauty, evoked a sweet nostalgia—the very nostalgia with which Morgan Le Fay was trying to entice the king.

But looking to yesterday, however seductive, Rachel reflected, was hardly the portal to tomorrow. One stepped into the future from the present, not from the past.

She'd turned the corner of Second Avenue onto St. Mark's Place, when a rush of autumn wind swept the chiffon scarf about her neck. As she walked, there was a new spring to her stride; she was leaving April behind for the burnished elegance of October—and its meaning.

No longer did she perceive the fall as symbol of a dying year, but rather as an arrogant, bracing reminder that life, thank God, must change.

Rachel crossed to the subway entrance, but when her hand touched the steel banister, she paused. A woman and child were walking past the street where panhandlers stationed themselves, as usual, outside the Cooper Union school building. The woman carried a huge, cumbersome pumpkin in one arm; her other hand was held by the little girl at her side. The child clutched a shopping bag filled to overflowing with Halloween candies. Then the pumpkin began to slip from the mother's grasp. The little girl grabbed the bottom just in time. The two laughed at the near mishap as they continued on their way amid a flurry of colored leaves that decorated the sidewalk pavement.

Rachel smiled at the scene. It would be pleasant to walk crosstown, perhaps stroll through Washington Square Park, on such a day as this. She glanced at her watch. One-thirty. There wasn't time.

Still, it *was* autumn in New York, and *she* was on her way to an audition.

If only she could tell Howard!

He'd be so proud of her! Of course that would only happen if she landed the job. They'd told her the callbacks would be soon—but how soon, no one had said. One step at a time, Rachel reminded herself as she joined the throng that spilled from the train onto the platform.

They *had* to call her back! Guinevere's song had gone very well—she had relaxed enough to have fun with the words, and the wit and devilment of the lyrics had more than carried her through. Paul had been right, she grudgingly admitted; she *had* been asked for a second song. Fortunately, too, since it was with "Follow Me" that she had achieved real success. At the end, she had held the last note and allowed it to fade away slowly, as though she, too, were drifting off and away, beckoning, tempting them to follow.

She and the pianist had remained alone on the bare stage, lit by a bank of lights whose glare had prevented Rachel from seeing the faces of the casting people out front. She had squinted, trying to determine how many "judges" were seated in the house, but all she had seen were shadows. After a seeming eternity of silence, a man's voice had called from about halfway back, "Miss Allenby. I've rarely heard that number sung with such genuine understanding. Thank you *very* much."

She had come to know that at an audition, "Thank you very much" was synonymous with "You may go." But the compliment preceding the dismissal had more than compensated; it had sounded sincere.

Sure enough, when she returned to the apartment and checked the answering service, there was a message from the agent, Jerry Mason. She had a callback audition for the following week—this time to read a scene from the script!

She hung up the phone and gave an uncharacteristic whoop. I'm in the running! she almost shouted aloud. She was bursting with excitement, aching to tell someone . . . Jamie! She had to tell Jamie!

His show was still in rehearsal. He'd be home around six-thirty. And Paul had a performance that night. She'd have

131

Jamie to herself. Alone.

It reminded her that one evening before Jamie's show opened, the two of them would have to put in an appearance at the Waldorf to see Paul's industrial. Not that it would be an ordeal; industrials were always as polished as Broadway hits, and Paul was a good singer and an even better dancer. No, it was something else. Although she had grown to like him and understood in her mind that he was not to blame for Jamie's "preference," in her heart she still coveted the time the two spent alone together, without him.

Never mind! she chided herself. I have him tonight. I'll cook a wonderful dinner—and *not* spaghetti; they'd been living on spaghetti. That was for lean days. But Jamie was working, and maybe soon, she might be, too! No spaghetti tonight!

As soon as Jamie arrived home, however, and learned of Rachel's news, he dashed to the telephone and left word for Paul at the Waldorf. The receiver was in his hand before Rachel could say no. But she knew he hadn't meant to hurt her; he was simply ecstatic for her and probably assumed she'd want to share the happiness with Paul. His enthusiasm was infectious; Rachel almost smiled at the guileless innocence of his action. And they'd have *some* time together while Paul was doing his show.

They talked and drank while she prepared dinner. It felt like old times, despite the briefness of their history together. Jamie had a strange and wonderful knack for recalling simple joys. Rachel smiled at the words from Guinevere's song as she basted the chicken with her spicy marinade.

When Paul arrived, he instinctively moved to kiss Jamie. Rachel noticed that Jamie stepped back to put physical distance between them. He seemed embarrassed, or perhaps self-conscious, with her present. Rachel saw, or thought she saw, a quick flash of resentment pass across Paul's face. But then he planted a kiss on her cheek and produced a small, wilted bouquet of carnations from behind his back.

"I bought them before the show, 'cause I wasn't sure there'd be anyplace open this late," he said by way of apology.

Jamie lit the stove to warm the leftover chicken for Paul. Rachel was arranging the flowers in a vase. "Rachel—we need dessert!" Jamie said suddenly. She grinned and together they yelled, "Ratner's!" They both laughed, then; Paul looked from one to the other, and Rachel knew he'd been unintentionally excluded from the joke. But Jamie had his coat on already and was moving toward the door.

Once he was gone, an awkward silence filled the kitchen. Rachel handed Paul a plate of the heated food and, to create conversation, began recounting the day's events.

"Listen," said Paul, pouring more wine for them both, "I don't mean to be a downer, but—"

"I know," she interrupted. "It's only a callback and doesn't mean I've got the job. But it's *something*, you know?"

He nodded. "You'd be touring for six months?"

The hope in his voice was unmistakable. Rachel had tried fighting the perception that his presence was intrusive; suddenly she realized that Paul must be viewing *her* as an interloper. With Rachel out of town, there would no longer be a triangle, even a triangle-of-sorts.

Their eyes met for an instant as understanding passed between them. Then Rachel answered, "Yes. I'd be gone for six months . . . Happy?"

Paul placed his wineglass on the table. "That last remark was unnecessary."

She sat and faced him. "I know. I'm . . . sorry. Still, it would be . . . convenient. For you, I mean. Right?"

She hadn't said it as a dare, but as an ackowledgment of the given situation. Finally he nodded again and said quietly, "Right."

She had forced him into the admission, and his answer had stung. But at least it had cleared the air. They understood each other.

Rachel had read and loved T. H. White's *The Once and Future King* while still in school. The book that had inspired *Camelot* had remained vivid in her mind; nonetheless, she borrowed a copy of the play from the library.

She had a temp office assignment that week, so she studied the script en route to work and on her lunch hour. Unlike most musical heroines, Guinevere was interesting: complex and flawed. The role offered an actress the opportunity to express dramatic ability as well as comedic flair. And, thank God, she didn't have to dance.

Her boss at Acme Container Corporation wasn't pleased to hear that Rachel wouldn't be in on Wednesday. She had considered working half the day and going to the callback directly from work, since she needed the money badly. But the callback was too important; she mustn't arrive tired. Mr. Kaplan complained, but Rachel reminded him that she was paid only for the hours she worked. Besides, she found it impossible to feel guilty over not invoicing the cardboard boxes manufactured by the firm.

On the evening before the audition the radiators were ice-cold in Jamie's apartment. Landlords had been forced to supply heat as early as October this year, but no law could control temperamental boilers. Jamie was spending the night at Paul's, but Rachel was forced to spend it shivering beneath the blankets. A good night's sleep was essential for tomorrow; audition butterflies were starting to surface, and the freezing cold did nothing to help.

But on Wednesday morning, she awoke to the slow, faint hiss of steam rising from the pipes. Rachel tentatively lifted one arm from under the blanket and tested the air. Yes, it was warmer. Thank God for small favors, she thought. I can take a hot bath.

The callbacks were at the Broadhurst Theater, where the

initial auditions had been held. The familiar environment served to ease some of the tension.

There had been twenty other girls waiting in the drafty passageway near the stage door. Now they were down to six, including Rachel, and were allowed to wait in a vacant dressing room in the theater's basement.

The other five girls looked Rachel's age or older, except for one girl who seemed barely out of her teens. Rachel was clearly the tallest, especially in her high-heeled boots, which she had worn because Zane Whitney, the star who would play Arthur, was six foot four.

As Rachel took a seat beside a pretty blonde, the stage manager called a name and escorted one of the girls upstairs.

"What a cute guy," the blonde said.

"You're right," Rachel agreed. "Which one of us is next?"

Quietly, the blonde whispered, "Micro-mini in the corner."

She smiled and glanced across the room at the brunette in the shortest skirt she had ever seen. Another half inch, mused Rachel, and she might be arrested for indecent exposure.

"Do you know her?"

"Sort of. From other auditions. I hate to admit it, but she *can* sing."

"But today's a reading, isn't it?"

"I hope so. I didn't warm up. Are you new? I've never seen you before."

"You haven't. My name's Rachel Allenby."

The blonde offered a manicured hand. "Beth Burns. Nervous?"

"Yes."

"Me too. The hardest thing for me is trying to appear as if I don't need this job."

"I know just what you mean."

135

By the time "Micro-mini" had finished singing, Rachel thought perhaps she'd found a friend in Beth Burns.

"They're taking a five-minute break, Miss Burns," said the stage manager. "I'll be back for you then."

Beth thanked him and opened the script she'd brought along.

"I'll leave you alone so you can look it over again," Rachel offered.

"It's all right. I know it by heart already."

Rachel grinned. "So do I."

"But I *do* have to hit the powder room first," she whispered, rising from the chair. "It was nice talking with you. I don't like many other women."

"Neither do I," said Rachel. "Good luck."

Beth looked at her for a moment. "You really *mean* that, don't you?"

"Well, 'break a leg' gets a little tired, doesn't it?"

"Here," said Beth, withdrawing a card from her purse. "This is my number. Give me a call. We can have coffee sometime."

"I will."

"And good luck to you, too. I hope one of us gets this gig."

Rachel was surprised that Zane Whitney was present. She was more surprised by the overwhelming whiskey stench as he said a groggy hello.

As before, the stage was bare and the lights too bright. With the stage manager, Rachel read a love scene between Guinevere and Lancelot. It was easy enough, and the stage manager was a decent actor, which helped. But Zane Whitney read opposite her for the scene at the play's end. Fortunately, she had worked repeatedly on the most difficult and highly emotional moment in the role. Although short, it comprised admission of shame and guilt. An actor such as Richard Burton would have "given" her something, but Zane Whitney was obviously too drunk or bored—or both—to bother. He recited the lines without inflection, offering nothing. Frustration surpassed nerves, and Rachel used the former to finish the scene with the tears required by the script.

"Miss Allenby," called a voice from the darkness of the house, "one question. Why do *you* think Guinevere joins a convent?"

Rachel thought for a moment. "Penance, for what she thinks she's done."

"Thinks?" exclaimed the director. "She's ruined a man and her marriage!"

"And a country, too," Rachel added. "And she's caused a war and killed a dream . . . but after all, Lancelot isn't entirely blameless, is he?"

She could hear muffled conversation out front. Zane Whitney was smiling at her. The stage manager winked.

"Very well put, Miss Allenby. I was right. You *do* understand the character—and the play. Thank you *very* much."

Chapter Nine

Rachel's return to Acme Container on Thursday was hardly triumphant. No one asked about her audition, and she worked through her lunch hour to compensate for the double load of billing that had accumulated on her desk. She telephoned the answering service four times a day. No word.

She wished she had asked how soon a decision would be made; that would have told her how soon to stop hoping.

By six o'clock on Friday night there was still no message. An entire weekend open to wonder. She was certain she would hear; she had read well, even if producers seldom knew what they wanted. Maybe they'd call on Monday.

But Monday brought no news. At two-thirty that afternoon, she reluctantly phoned Jerry Mason. She didn't want to be a pest; nonetheless, not knowing was getting to her.

The call only made matters worse.

"What *is* it, Rachel? My receptionist is out sick and I'm handling all the phones alone."

"I was wondering if you'd heard anything about the understudy job."

"What? What job?"

"*Camelot*. Zane Whitney . . ."

"Oh, that. If I remember, I'll call and find out what they thought. G'bye."

Either he never remembered or found out nothing, since Tuesday and Wednesday brought no further word. She was afraid to bother him again.

Wednesday. A week. Could it take *that* long?

Friday, Rachel took a sandwich to the office and ate there, while leafing through that morning's *Times,* which someone had left on a nearby desk. She noticed a press release in the theater section. Final casting for the Zane Whitney *Camelot* had been completed. The names were listed alphabetically.

Beth Burns's was the first.

Rachel felt tears welling in her eyes and quickly closed the paper. Hurriedly, she escaped to the privacy of the ladies' room. Suddenly she hated Acme Container Corporation more than anything she had ever despised; she was stuck here, indefinitely, with no imminent hope of anything better.

At least it had gone to Beth Burns. If she couldn't have the job, she was glad for Beth. Maybe over the weekend, when — if — it stopped hurting, she'd even call to say congratulations.

In the meantime, she had to talk to someone. To Howard. Or Jamie.

No. To Howard.

She splashed cold water on her face and then returned to her desk and dialed the number.

"Hi!" said Norma cheerfully.

"Hi, yourself," she answered, attempting the same brassy edge that was Norma's style. But it wasn't Rachel's, and her voice cracked. "Oh, Norma," was all she could manage.

"What's the matter? Are you upset?"

"I was . . ."

"Anything I can do? I'm great in a crisis."

"It's not a crisis . . . really," Rachel said. "I'm sorry to sound mysterious. It's just hard to talk about. Is Howard there?"

"Sure. Listen, you need anything, call me at home. Let's go to a movie. My treat."

"You're on," said Rachel as Norma put her on hold.

Suddenly, panic seized her. Howard would be sure to ask how she'd gotten the audition in the first place! What could she say?

139

"Hello, stranger, happy Halloween," said Howard.

Rachel sighed. "Could I make an appointment to see you?"

"Anytime. You don't have to ask."

"Good. I . . . I have a confession to make."

She left the office early on the excuse of a headache and went downtown. She would try to calm herself before changing clothes and meeting Howard uptown for dinner.

Jamie was home. As soon as he saw her face, he asked, "What's up?"

She felt as if she had answered that same question a hundred times already. She lacked the energy for one hundred and one. Listleissly she dropped the theater section on his lap. Then she flopped onto the bed.

She was resting her eyes when she heard, "I'm sorry, Rachel."

"So am I," she said.

She decided on the brown velvet minidress; she hadn't had an occasion to wear it before; maybe it would give her a lift. She rolled her hair into a French twist, then applied extra blusher to her cheeks and iridescent shadow to her eyelids. Her spirits rose as she began looking forward to an evening with Howard Rathborne in an elegant restaurant. But then she remembered the purpose of the evening: to admit that she had broken a trust by not telling Howard about the audition. It didn't matter that she wasn't signed to an exclusive management contract; Howard was her agent. She regretted ever having accepted Mason's audition call in the first place. Even if she had gotten the job, she'd still owe Howard an explanation. In retrospect, Rachel realized that she could have refused Mason and then asked Howard to submit her.

But she hadn't thought of it before. If nothing else, at least she was a little wiser.

She fastened the tiny pearls to her earlobes and reached for her trenchcoat. It was time to face the music. . . .

Despite the expense, she had opted for a taxi; she wasn't in the emotional state required for public transportation tonight.

One of her earrings began to pinch, and she removed it to massage the lobe. Maybe pierced ears were the thing to do. The pearl lay in her gloved hand and she smiled. The earrings had been a birthday present from her parents last year.

She'd have to call them soon; she never did with regularity. Letters were easier; they filled in the pauses left by the phone.

Howard was waiting for her in front of Voisin. He rushed forward and paid the driver before Rachel could voice her protest. His face seemed to brighten as he took her hand, and the dark blue of his eyes, the cleft in his chin, seemed deeper, more pronounced in the harsh glow of the overhead heat lamps under the restaurant's canopy. His hair was tousled from the wind; obviously he'd been waiting for more than a few minutes. As they walked to the coatcheck, Howard placed his arm around her; it felt strong and good.

"I was concerned. You're not usually late."

"I know. We got stuck in traffic."

"Well, no matter. You're here. We have a table in the corner, where we can talk."

Rachel was aware as they crossed the crowded dining room that many eyes were following them. Of course, Howard was probably known here. Every few tables, she heard a soft voice ask another, ". . . but who is *she?*"

Howard had selected a bottle of Meursault to accompany their poached salmon. Over dinner, he talked quietly about the season, his office, other clients. Rachel's original impulse had been to blurt out the truth and have it over with. But seated in the booth beside him now, she found it easier, more comforting, to listen. Howard had a way of elevating even polite gossip to the level of a Robert Benchley or Dorothy Parker anecdote. Every word seemed to have a point, a reason, but was laced with wit and humor.

When he finished his entrée, he crossed the handles of his knife and fork on the edge of the empty plate. Rachel asked him why.

"It's a carryover. On the continent, it signals the waiter that he may clear it away. Perhaps quaint, but useful. Efficient."

"There," said Rachel, following suit and crossing her own knife and fork. "It can be my coat of arms."

Howard laughed. "Certainly more realistic than mine!"

"Howard," she said, "you actually *have* a coat of arms?"

He nodded. "Someone in the Rathborne family was distantly related to a second-rate peerage—from which my grandfather gained undue pleasure. My father, fortunately, took it with a grain of salt. Our only real claim to royalty was probably illegitimate—and that was two hundred years ago."

"Well," she said, leaning her head back against the booth, "I must call you Sir Howard. And I'll write home that English royalty has shown an American commoner a wonderful evening."

"It's hardly rare," he answered, looking into her eyes. "The monarchy was once abandoned for an American commoner." He took her hands in his and Rachel felt pulses beating within their entwined fingers; she wasn't sure whose was beating faster.

"Excuse me, Mr. Rathborne," said their waiter, breaking the mood. "You have a telephone call."

The waiter had cleared their "coats of arms." When Howard returned, he slid into the booth and settled closer to Rachel.

"That was Norma," he explained.

"Was it anything important?"

"She'd forgotten to remind me that I'm meeting Abe

Burrows in the office at noon tomorrow. She tactfully said she didn't want to bother me later." He took Rachel's hand again and stroked her long, slim fingers. "I hope Abe is enjoying his evening as much as I'm enjoying mine. Shall I order cognac?"

Rachel nodded. "I'd love some. Although I haven't had this much to drink since . . ."

"Since when?"

"Nothing. It's . . . I'm just a little fuzzy from the wine." She was grateful when he didn't pursue her hesitation.

"Cognac. I won't let you drive."

"Plying me with liquor for licentious intent?" She was surprised the words hadn't slurred.

"Byron couldn't have said it better," he said in a good imitation of Noël Coward. Then he leaned in more closely. Rachel could feel his lips against her ear. "I have a really good brandy at home . . ."

Rubinstein was playing Rachmaninoff from across the room. The fireplace offered the only light in the room, other than a candle burning in a crystal holder on the marble-top coffee table.

Howard's arm rested on the back of the sofa, his fingers playing with a wisp of hair at the nape of Rachel's neck. She leaned forward and reached for the brandy snifter. The color of its contents was deepened and its blazing center glimmered in a burst of firelight prism, reflected by the candle's glow. Rachel inhaled the heady aroma, sipped, and sighed.

"What's that for?" he asked when she didn't lean back again.

"I have something to tell you."

"The famous confession?" There was amusement in his voice.

"Yes," she replied. "And you may not find it humourous." Her head remained bowed as she studied her brandy and searched for the way to begin.

143

"Well?" he asked without impatience.

"I've broken our agreement." There. She'd said it. It was out.

Slowly, deliberately, she told him the entire story, from Jerry Mason's call to the announcement in the *Times*. There seemed so much to tell, to make clear, so that Howard would understand why.

". . . and then," she concluded, "I saw Beth Burns at the head of the cast list . . . and I called you."

Rachel had not looked at him during her monologue, afraid of the hurt, anger, or disappointment she might see in his face. But now she had finished her story, and she turned her head to him.

Howard had removed his jacket, vest, and tie; the white of his shirt stood out against the pearl gray silk of the sofa. His face was immobile, impossible to read.

Finally, he said, "I know of Beth Burns. She's talented. Not ready for a major career yet—as you are—but she will be."

It wasn't what Rachel had expected him to say.

"Howard . . . don't you care that I . . . I lied to you?"

He rose from the sofa, took his snifter and hers, and crossed to the bar. "Of course I care. But you've told me, haven't you? Your ambition doesn't ultimately interfere with your honesty." He refilled the two glasses but didn't return to the sofa. "And honesty is what I want of you . . . even if it hurts."

Now he seated himself again, close to her side, and handed her the brandy. "Am I the first person you've told?"

"About Beth Burns . . . yes."

He seemed to ponder that for a moment. "It's not your fault," he said then. "I should never have let three weeks pass without an explanation. I allowed my personal feelings . . . to color my business instincts."

"What do you mean?"

He gazed deeply into her eyes. "I thought it best to . . . give you time . . . not to hound you. There hasn't been a day that I've not thought of you, but . . . I feared making a

144

nuisance of myself."

"But Howard —" she began, resting a hand on his wrist.

"Wait," she interrupted. "You see, if you were merely a client — just any client — I'd have rung you at least once a week to reassure you that I was working in your behalf — despite the absence of any auditions. But I didn't. What else could you think but that I'd been careless, had overlooked you?"

"You . . . you *do* understand, don't you?" She was almost incredulous.

"Yes, I do. And you're right. I *could* have arranged an audition for *Camelot.*"

"But then why . . . ?"

"There's something *you* don't understand. You never had a chance of landing that job. I'm frankly amazed — and proud of you — for getting as far as the callbacks."

"Howard . . . ?"

He rose to flip the Rachmaninoff. The first strains of the Second Piano Concerto drifted from the stereo as Howard said, "Arnold Gold is producing the *Camelot* tour."

"What?" The newspaper had mentioned a different name, an acronym.

AGCAMP—*Arnold Gold Camelot Productions!* Suddenly it all made sense, as though a blurred scene in a film had been forced into focus. "You mean . . . Gloria . . . ?"

"Of course. You said you couldn't see the faces out front because the stage lights were too bright. Arnold was certainly there — for your callback, if not before. Gloria may have been there, too. Arnold likes you. But you'll never work for him as long as Gloria Doro had anything to say about it. And she always will."

"My God, Howard, I feel like an ignorant, ungrateful fool."

"No reason to. Other than *Camelot,* there's been nothing to submit you for. It's been desperately slow. But activity is picking up, and we're going to find the right role to showcase your talent. This will stop hurting, and —"

"But Howard," she said, surprised, "that's just it — it

145

doesn't hurt—not anymore!" She put her glass down beside his on the table. "It's all right, now—now that I understand."

The dying embers were flickering in his dark blue eyes. He took a step forward and rested his hands on her shoulders, drawing her close to him.

At his touch, Rachel's brain began to fog, and she felt the familiar sensation of her knees weakening. Familiar, yes, but to whose touch? Jamie's? No, this was Howard, so different. Nonetheless, the *feeling* was familiar. Was that possible? A thousand images and questions echoed inside a cavern of jeweled and glittering lights, lights that grew darker as the flames smoldered and at last were gone. The room was suddenly colder, yet warmer. Howard seemed farther, but nearer.

Then she was aware of his lips brushing against her shoulder in a shower of quick, tender kisses as he moved up to the delicate spot under her neck. His breath was so warm, so good. Rachel let her head fall back and gave herself to the sweet sensation. She felt Howard's hand at the back of her head, felt the pins come out and her hair falling free. It cascaded through his fingers as they pulled gently, caressing the waves. Then his lips were on her mouth and she opened it to his tongue as their bodies molded closer together. She felt a chill as he moved the zipper of her dress slowly, agonizingly slowly, deliciously down her back. His hands slid the sensuous velvet the rest of the way over her hips until it fell to the floor. He was pressed hard against her now, and as she became aware of his desire, she became aware of her own. It surged through her as his caresses became more urgent, as her need became as powerful as his. And Howard seemed to know, from her arms locked around him as she tried to both pull away and still to draw him closer, that she was at long last saying yes. Yes with her mind, yes with her body.

He had unhooked her bra and his mouth moved to her breasts. Rachel heard herself, from far away, moaning with delight. She took his face in her hands, her fingers tracing the cleft chin, the sensuous lips, the strong eyebrows. The tips of his fingers made light, feathery strokes across her breasts and teased her hardened nipples before his hands moved down across her flat stomach, to the elastic of her pantyhose, and pulled them down. Their eyes locked as she lifted each foot and he removed the nylon that had separated them.

The dizziness was no longer from the brandy. Rachel's head was swimming. As the fire in the grate went out, a very different fire ignited inside Rachel and threatened to drown her with sensation. Rubinstein's fingers played magic on the keyboard while Howard's hands sought another magic. And then he found her special place; Rachel's legs buckled but he was there, catching her, holding her in his arms and lowering her to the plushness of the soft carpet.

Her hand grabbed at his hair and pulled his head down to meet hers. As their lips explored each other's faces, she fumbled with the buttons of his shirt, his belt, his pants, until he was as naked as she.

"Let me look at you," he whispered, kneeling before her. Their eyes searched each other's body; his chest was firm and muscular, his stomach taut and lean. His legs . . .

His fingers were moving inside her and driving her wild. She reached out and stroked his erect penis, its head as moist as she was now.

He kissed her gently, then with increasing strength, and her legs opened to him, wrapped themselves around him, clung to him desperately as he thrust himself inside her again and again. His words seemed to reach her from far, far away, while their bodies came closer and closer to being one.

She screamed with joy and heard him cry, "Oh my Rachel! I love you!"

She lay watching him as he slept beside her in the enormous bed. How beautiful he was! Richard had never made love to her like this; perhaps it was Howard's maturity and experience, in contrast with Richard's youthful haste. No, she reflected as Howard's chest rose and fell in peaceful rhythm. Howard Rathborne had given her as much pleasure as he had taken for himself. Richard had been a selfish lover, and Rachel doubted that any amount of time would change that.

Howard had carried her to bed and they had made love again. Now, despite the languid aftermath of passion, she was fully awake.

The draperies were drawn and the room was pitch-dark, except for the luminous dials of the alarm clock on Howard's night table beside the bed. The hands pointed to two-fifteen. Was it so late? Or so early?

Suddenly, Rachel bolted upright. Jamie! she remembered. She had promised not to be late. How could she stay the night?

For the first time, she guiltily wished she had never met him. If there were only Howard, here beside her, so many questions might remain unasked.

Silently she dressed and left the apartment.

Rachel didn't notice the quizzical expression on the doorman's face as the elevator deposited her in the spacious lobby. All she did when he asked, "Taxi, ma'am?" was nod her head and say, "Yes, thank you."

There was no traffic in the middle of the night; Rachel was amazed at the speed with which the car reached East Fifth Street—ten minutes' ride all the way from Upper Fifth Avenue; the trip by bus would have taken an hour at midday. The cabby's expression was as curious as that of Howard's doorman, but Rachel's mind was occupied with thoughts of Jamie.

She wearily climbed the stairs to the second floor; her body still ached from Howard's lovemaking, but it was a relaxed, pleasant ache; she felt warm all over, despite the dampness of the night air. She wondered how she would tell Jamie—*if* she could indeed tell him. Could she *not* tell him? That seemed dishonest; at the same time, he knew her

148

well; too well for her to lie and for the lie to go undetected.

But her quandry was unfounded. Jamie wasn't home. He hadn't planned to stay at Paul's that night, but obviously he'd changed his mind.

The air outside was cold and the winds had begun to bluster, beating against the kitchen window as Rachel removed her coat. She shuddered, wrapping her arms around herself against the chill. The radiator wasn't producing its customary hiss. Rachel walked to the element beneath the window, touched it, and drew back at the icy touch. The apartment air was frigid cold because there wasn't any heat. Damn! she thought. No heat again!

She slipped back into her coat and went downstairs to ring the super's bell.

"Hey!" came the wheezy voice from within as a ribbon of light came on under the door. "Ya know what time it is? Whaddya want?"

"Some heat in the apartment!" Rachel called out.

"Boiler's broken again. Ain't no heat tonight."

"But it's freezing!" Rachel protested.

"So turn on the stove! I can't do nothin' about it tonight!"

Rachel saw the sliver of light along the door threshold disappear. Any further communication before morning would be one-sided.

She returned to the apartment. The stove was out of the question; its unreliable pilot light had caused her enough concern when she was wide awake and cooking; she wasn't about to trust it while she slept.

This is ridiculous! she decided. The only reason she'd left Howard's bed was so Jamie wouldn't worry. She hesitated a moment longer, then grabbed her totebag and headed back to the street in search of a taxi.

Chapter Ten

The same doorman was still on duty. He tipped his hat and didn't ask her name. His nod said as much as "Go right up, ma'am."

Howard's reaction held more surprise than the doorman's. He was wearing a silk paisley robe and Rachel noticed a brandy snifter on the marble-topped coffee table.

"I'm glad you had a change of heart," he said, taking her coat but not asking for an explanation.

Rachel peered about the room. "Are you alone?"

He shook his head and laughed. "Rachel, my dearest, did you actually expect to find someone *else* here? After . . ." He paused, then said, "What brought you back? Or" — he looked into her eyes — "why did you leave in the first place? I thought — "

"The boiler's broken at my apartment. There's no heat in the building."

"I see." Howard reached for his brandy. "That's not very flattering — to be preferred over a freezing flat."

Rachel couldn't tell whether he was angry or joking. He probably had a right to be furious.

"May I pour you one?" he asked. "It'll warm you up."

"Thank you." She tried to avert her eyes. "I would have called, but I don't have your home number."

He handed her a glass of swirling amber liquid. "I'm in the telephone directory. Under *R*." With his free hand he led her to the sofa. His long, slim fingers lightly brushed aside a stubborn wisp of chestnut hair. His hands were warm and strong, and the memory of their touch brought color to Rachel's entire body. She felt good here, but was still a bit shocked by her own earlier behavior.

"I don't want to frighten you off, Rachel," said Howard, "but I also want you to know how I feel." He turned her face toward him. "As I've said before, it has nothing to do with your career, if that's what caused you to leave."

"It wasn't that," she said slowly.

"Well, I just wanted to state my case." He reached for the brandy decanter and refilled their glasses. "Forgive my asking, but is your boiler really broken — or are you still . . . sorting things out?"

She nodded, sighing deeply. "The apartment was freezing."

His index finger was tracing the rim of the brandy snifter. "Well," he said, "selfishly then, I'm glad. I missed you when I awakened and found you gone."

Rachel experienced an odd moment of guilt as she leaned into Howard's arms. She felt needed and wanted — all that she had hoped to have with Jamie. But she wasn't using Howard, that much she knew. When they had made love, she hadn't wished for it to be Jamie; in fact, Jamie hadn't crossed her mind until later. It had been Howard. Only Howard.

And that, Rachel realized, was why she was feeling guilty.

Still, when their glasses were empty and Howard beckoned her, she followed him back to bed.

Rachel's sexual appetite had only served to heighten the rest of her senses; she was ravenously hungry, and the delicious smells emanating from the kitchen drew her from under the covers.

Howard had left a second silk robe at the foot of the bed. She slipped her arms through it and joined him.

"Well, good morning," he said, leaning down to kiss her forehead. "Have a seat."

Rachel settled on a bright green stool at the long butcher-

151

block counter. She observed the menu: hot cinnamon biscuits, crisp, lean bacon, steaming hot coffee, and an omelet-in-progress.

"Do you treat all your guests so well?" Rachel asked, inhaling the wonderful aromas.

"I couldn't say," Howard answered. "You're my first . . . overnight . . . guest in quite a long time." He'd said it lightly, but then added, "Rachel, whatever you choose to think is up to you. But I do wish you'd believe that I don't go about trying to seduce every talented young woman who crosses my path. It just happens I've fancied you from the moment we met."

"Fancied?" The word stuck her with a pejorative thud.

"It's the language barrier. You Yanks use other terms."

"Like what? *Lusted?*" But it made her laugh.

Now he laughed, too. "That as well. I didn't want to scare you"—a sudden seriousness entered his voice—"or I might have used the word *loved.*" Before she could react, he tossed an egg in the air. "Quick—catch it!"

Rachel's arms darted out and the egg landed gently, without breaking, in her cupped hands. "How did you know I wouldn't let it drop?"

Howard placed a perfect omelet in front of her. "I saw you land on your feet in Washington. You're impulsive, you're spontaneous, too. And your reflexes aren't half bad."

"You seem to know me pretty well," she said.

"Not half as well as I'd like," he replied. "Come on, start your breakfast. Omelets have to be eaten hot."

She didn't argue; he was an excellent cook.

Rachel knew that somehow she would have to tell Jamie about Howard. If she had hesitated the night before, spending an entire morning at Howard's convinced her that there was no alternative. It was only a matter of how.

Howard and she walked together to Sixtieth Street; he was en route to the office; she was on her way downtown.

152

"Rachel," he said at the corner, "I don't want to pressure you in any way, but I do hope you'll . . . well, don't just ring my bell when your boiler's broken, hm?"

"Howard—" But she didn't know what to say. In the cold sunlight, certain realities had to be faced.

"I've said I can wait. Last night doesn't change that. A man who's falling in love tends to abandon his pride."

She looked up into his clear, deep blue eyes. She wished she might tell him what he wanted to hear, that she was falling in love with him too. She almost spoke, then stopped herself. It wouldn't be fair to either of them just now. Or to Jamie.

Jamie was at the apartment when she arrived this time. The boiler apparently had been repaired; the radiator was puffing away as Rachel entered the kitchen, and already the dry smell of steam heat filled the room and pinched her nostrils.

"Where were you last night?" he asked the moment she'd closed the door.

"I got home late. It was freezing. Were you at Paul's?"

"For part of the night. When I got home, though, you weren't here. Where'd you go so late?"

"What is this," she asked, "twenty questions?" She removed her coat and walked into the living room.

"Paul and I had a fight. We're . . . not going to see each other for a while."

Suddenly Rachel's stomach churned, although she didn't know what a fight between Jamie and Paul had to do with Howard and her. This wasn't the moment to tell him. That was all she knew. Instead, she said, "I'm sorry. What was it about?"

"Commitment. I hadn't thought he was the type to get serious."

"Oh."

"So where were you? You still haven't told me."

Rachel sat down on the piano bench and silently traced

several of the black keys. "I . . . had an appointment with Howard."

"He keeps late office hours, doesn't he?"

"We . . . had dinner together." She was growing increasingly warm.

"It must have been a very late dinner. Into breakfast?"

At Jamie's mention of breakfast, Rachel's mind conjured an image of the omelet Howard had prepared — after they had made love for the second time.

"What happened, did the great Howard Rathborne try to seduce his protégée — and succeed?"

"Jamie, I —"

"Maybe you'd better not tell me." But Rachel's face had gone from pink to crimson.

"Shit," said Jamie. "You already have."

She hadn't planned for him to find out in this manner, and she certainly hadn't expected him to guess.

"Jamie —"

"Never mind," he snapped. "That just makes us even." His voice had taken a sarcastic edge. "I *am* curious about one thing, though, if it isn't getting too personal . . ."

"What?" She desperately wanted to avoid an argument.

"Well . . . do you really think that screwing Howard Rathborne will advance your career?"

Before Rachel could collect her thoughts, her hand involuntarily swung out and slapped him hard across the face. "Don't," she said hoarsely, grabbing her coat, *"don't* turn into a *bitch!"* She whirled around and stormed out, slamming the door so hard that it almost came off its hinges.

This time she didn't head uptown for Howard's. Instead, her body fueled with heat from her exchange with Jamie, she walked up First Avenue all the way to Fifty-seventh Street, then west, past Second and Third avenues until she reached Lexington. She shuddered at the prospect, then entered the revolving door of Allerton House and checked in for the night. She needed time alone. Time to think; time away from both Jamie and Howard and audition pressure and expected behavior; time to figure out, as she sat on the

154

lumpy mattress and stared out the window at the brick building across the way, what in God's name she was doing here.

Rachel returned Howard's telephone messages without telling him where she was calling from. She invented an excuse—that of auditing a class at Actors' Studio—as the reason for not seeing him that night. But when he said, "Tomorrow night, then?" she was unable to say no; she found herself torn between wanting him and trying to stay away. But for whose sake, hers or Jamie's, she wasn't sure. Observing her feelings had the advantage of nonjudgmental awareness, but at the same time brought with it the disadvantage of perhaps too much detachment.

Jamie didn't leave a message at the answering service until late that night. All it said was: *Jamie. Urgent.*

Rachel opted for the privacy of the phone in her room, despite the service charge. Whatever she and Jamie might say to each other was not anything she cared to share with the ladies who loitered beside the bank of open pay phones off the lobby. Let them listen on someone else's dime, she thought impatiently while the switchboard rang Jamie's number at home.

He answered on the first ring. "Rachel?"

"I'm returning your call," she said.

"Look, I . . . I feel really lousy about what I said earlier."

"You should," she replied, still feeling the sting.

"Look, I . . . I'm sorry. It was . . . well, it was the fight with Paul and then . . ." He heaved a sigh into the receiver. "I'm really sorry about the whole thing."

"So am I, Jamie. But . . . it hurt." She thought for a moment. "I guess it was intended to, wasn't it?"

He paused. "Rachel, I . . . I didn't mean to . . . I was . . . I . . . listen, can we get together for coffee? So we can talk face-to-face?"

"I don't know, Jamie. Maybe it's better this way. I can stop by to pick up my things, and—"

"Rachel, please?" He sounded close to tears.

She thought and then said, "All right. But I'm still not sure it's a good idea."

They agreed to meet at the Waldorf—not the luxury hotel on Park Avenue, but the all-night cafeteria opposite Bloomingdale's. It had been another of their haunts during Rachel's first month in the city.

His eyes looked as tired as hers, Rachel reflected as Jamie entered the dingy restaurant. His clothes were disheveled, although compared with the Waldorf's seedy clientele, he was dapper in his suede jacket and faded jeans.

Rachel was seated at a rear table. Jamie waved nervously, stopped to buy a coffee, and joined her. He busied himself arranging the jacket over the back of his chair, stirring cream in his coffee, and taking a spoon from the next table before facing Rachel directly.

She, meanwhile, had been studying him. She had asked herself time and again *why*—why she felt this way about him. And each time, the question had drawn a blank.

"You . . . you didn't say . . . where you were calling from," he began.

"It wasn't from Howard's," Rachel responded. "If that's what you wanted to know."

"I'm sorry. Rachel, I swear—"

"Jamie, I've been doing a lot of thinking." She took a sip of the tepid coffee to stall for time. "I can understand some of the reasons you reacted the way you did."

"Look, I know I had no right, considering—"

"I won't argue that point," she said. "But . . . but it's important that *you* understand something, too, if we're going to save our, well, our friendship, at any rate."

"What's to understand?" he asked. "You and Howard are lovers." But this time he didn't say it maliciously. Instead, he spoke flatly, in a voice completely devoid of emotion.

She focused her eyes on his. "Yes. Howard and I are lovers." Her heart raced as she voiced the fact. "And I hope it won't come between us"—she drew a breath, which caught—"any more than your . . . relationship with Paul has come between us." She was pained for Jamie and didn't want to bring Paul into the conversation after he and Jamie had argued, but it was unavoidable if she and Jamie were going to narrow the chasm between them.

"Are you . . . are you in love with Howard?" asked Jamie slowly.

"I . . . I can't answer that. It's too soon." She reached across the table and rested her hand on Jamie's. "It's different from the feeling I have for you," she said, not clearly comprehending her own meaning, "but . . . I'm not *using* Howard, whatever you think."

"Look," said Jamie, "I realized the moment I'd said it that you'd never, well, I mean . . . it's just that I saw you sitting at the piano—the piano *he* gave you—and I suddenly saw red." He squeezed her hand so tightly, it made her knuckles turn white.

"Rachel, I love you. And I'm having trouble handling this. I . . . I wasn't really lashing out at *you*. Please understand."

She withdrew her hand from his. "Jamie . . . let's both try to forget it." She wasn't certain it was possible, but she refused to give up hope. "You probably ought to know that I'm . . . seeing Howard tomorrow night. And . . . I may not come home till morning."

He nodded without answering.

"I just wanted you to be aware of the situation. I don't know where any of this is headed, but I'm not going to lie about it. Not to you or to Howard."

"No, I . . . I don't want you to."

A moment's awkward silence ensued.

"Have you spoken to Paul since last night?" Rachel finally asked in an attempt to change the subject.

"Not yet," he replied listlessly.

"Well, maybe you ought to call him. Some things take longer than others." She suddenly realized she was using Howard's words.

"Maybe you're right. I just don't like being pressured or

157

rushed into things," he said. "Y'know what I mean?"

Now it was Rachel who nodded. "I know exactly what you mean."

Rachel began spending more evenings—and nights—at Howard's. She hadn't told him of her altercation with Jamie; however, she gradually realized that if he should decide to ask, she would tell him. Everything.

Meanwhile, Jamie was either adjusting to, or accepting, the situation, just as Rachel had forced herself to do toward his relationship with Paul. In deference to Jamie and his feelings, Rachel made a point of returning to Fifth Street at least three nights a week. On these occasions, Jamie never questioned her, although whether it was for Rachel's benefit or his own, she didn't know.

Rachel finally met Norma for lunch; Howard's secretary had made a passing remark after Rachel and Howard entered the office together one morning. She tactfully waited until Howard had gone to his office to take a London call.

"Congrats, sweetie!" she whispered.

"For what?" Rachel looked up in surprise.

"*You* know for what. Don't try to hide it; it's written all over your face. His, too. I think it's terrific!"

After that, it was merely a matter of choosing the restaurant. Norma didn't pry; she only wanted the external details—where they dined, what shows they saw. It relieved Rachel's mind to be able to gossip with a friend and not feel compelled to weigh or analyze every word.

One evening in late November, Howard said, "I'll be in Boston over Thanksgiving. Lehman's conducting a new show. Care to come along?"

"Howard, I can't," said Rachel. "I'm doing a perfume promotion at Saks. I'm working Wednesday and Friday. And—"

He interrupted. "Then how about a Dickensian Christmas?"

"What's that?"

"An invitation to London," he said. "I thought we might spend the holidays in England. Show you off to the family."

The casual tone of his "invitation" took her breath away. "Howard! London? *Really?*"

He was seated on the floor in front of the fireplace; she was curled up on the leather sofa. Now he reached up and pulled her down beside him. Her hair was tangled from the fall, but he brushed it off her face and kissed her. "Yes, my love. London. Really."

He seemed almost as surprised as Rachel did when she smiled radiantly and said, "Yes! I'd love to!"

"Good. We'll see about getting you a passport right away—unless you already have one?"

She laughed aloud as her arms went around him. "Howard, until I came to New York, the longest trip I'd ever taken was to Minneapolis!" She considered that for a moment. "Actually, in many ways, London's much closer."

Rachel spent Thanksgiving week, except for the holiday itself, spritzing shoppers with Givenchy III; she had treated herself to a bottle with her store discount, although, she mused, the air was so permeated by the perfume spray that her wardrobe would reek of the stuff until Easter.

She shared Thanksgiving dinner with Jamie and Paul at Paul's apartment. George the Greek was absent—working at the Paradise Restaurant downtown all day, Paul explained—so a hearty red wine—no ouzo—accompanied their meal.

And then came December and packing for London. Jamie and Paul were seated at the kitchen table while Rachel crammed the last of her clothes into the Mark Cross fortnighter suitcase Howard had given her as a pre-trip present.

"I thought you said you like to travel light," teased Paul.

"Well, I don't know what people wear to the theater in

London, or to dinner, or to museums—"

"*I* thought you said you're going to meet his family," said Jamie. "That sounds like country and tweed, to me."

"I've got that, too," she said. "I'm a very organized packer."

"Good," said Paul. "Because you'll need to make room for this." He reached under the table for a package and then handed her a large gift-wrapped box from Henri Bendel's.

"My God! Did you make *that* much on the industrial?" Rachel had been inside the posh store only once—to look.

"It's from both of us," said Jamie. "Your Christmas gift."

Paul grinned as Rachel tore off the silver wrapping. "You might say it's from my industrial show *and* Mr. Morgan's Off-Broadway stint—we *all* know how much Equity minimum pays, so you can guess who got the short end of the deal!"

They laughed as Rachel opened the box. "Ohhh!" she exclaimed, parting the tissue to reveal yards and yards of black silk-velvet. It was an ankle-length evening cape, completely lined in red silk. Delicate silk-braided frogs decorated the front closure.

"It's gorgeous!" Rachel cried, immediately sliding her arms through the slits—also edged in silk braid—and modeling it for them. "Oh, I love you both!" She hugged Paul and then turned to Jamie. Only when they embraced did she feel self-conscious about the words. From his face, Rachel could tell that Jamie did too.

But the door buzzer averted further awkwardness.

"That must be Howard." Rachel opened the door and called down, "I'll be right there!" Then she carefully folded the cape inside the suitcase and closed it.

Paul and Jamie accompanied her downstairs, Paul carrying the fortnighter and Rachel and Jamie following behind.

A group of neighborhood children had surrounded the sleek gunmetal-gray limousine in front of which Howard was standing. Grown-ups from the block seemed as curious, but they only pointed or exclaimed in languages Rachel didn't understand. Nervously, she introduced Howard to Jamie and Paul. Then, to all three, she said, "I hate farewells. Merry Christmas!" She quickly hugged Jamie and Paul one last time and hurriedly ducked into the safety of the car. Howard climbed in after her and the chauffeur closed the door.

Rachel felt both a heaviness and lightness, as though a battle were raging within her and she could do nothing about its outcome. She sensed that she was at a turning point — they all were — from which none would emerge unchanged.

She waved to Jamie and Paul, who were surrounded by a dozen small children at the curb. Except for his height, Jamie in that moment looked no older than the little boy standing beside him. My God, she thought, are we ever more than children — simply grown taller?

The limousine headed up First Avenue, where new audiences stared and pointed. Rachel felt as though her emotions, as well as the car, were on public display.

Howard hadn't spoken since he'd slid into the backseat. Rachel removed her gloves and placed them in her lap. All the while she gazed absently out the window as they turned onto the FDR Drive and toward the bridge that would lead them to the airport.

Finally, Howard said, "The two young men." It was neither a question nor a statement.

"Friends," she answered automatically.

"The blond — Jamie — looks familiar. Is he a singer?"

She nodded. "I . . . met him at the New Stars auditions. He's done some TV commercials. You've probably seen one of them."

"Is he working now?"

"Here and there. Auditioning, looking for an agent, the usual." She was curious at the emotion welling as she spoke about him.

"It's a damn tough business," said Howard. "But if he has staying power, he'll be all right."

"I suppose . . ."

After another silence, Howard ventured slowly, "Has Jamie anything to do with that sorting-out of yours?" He'd asked it casually, but Rachel felt a visceral impact nonetheless.

"I . . . yes . . . no . . ."

Howard took her hands in his, causing her to turn and face him. "Rachel, I've said before that it's none of my business, and it isn't. But he—well, that other young man with him—" He looked with hesitation into her eyes. "I mean, they *are* lovers, aren't they?"

She closed her eyes at the word, then reopened them and said, "Yes. They're lovers."

"I see." Howard nodded, more to himself than to her. "And Jamie is the one you're . . . in love with." His voice betrayed a flicker of disappointment.

"Not anymore. . . . Please, Howard, I don't want you to think that I—"

His index finger covered her lips. "Shh. You needn't explain. I just, well, selfishly, I like to know what I'm up against, that's all."

Tears filled Rachel's eyes, but they weren't only for Jamie. "Howard, please give me some time?"

"It's one of my ulterior motives in taking you to London," he said. "Not to get you away from him—but to have you more to myself. That will become more difficult when career demands start monopolizing your time. But for now—for the next two weeks, at least—I don't have to share you."

She leaned her head against his shoulder. "You're too good for me, Howard."

"Not true," he said. "I only hope I'm good enough."

Chapter Eleven

December 1968

Rachel had expected to suffer from jet lag, but she was so thrilled when the plane landed at Heathrow that her energy soared instead of lagged. Perhaps, she mused, first-class passengers weren't afflicted by the malady; or perhaps jet lag was a mental condition. Rachel's elation was a happy surprise, coupled with a strange sensation: on her very first visit to the city—while still at the airport—she felt as though she were coming home.

For seven o'clock in the morning, the customs line was lengthy. However, at last the entry forms had been processed and Howard and Rachel were settled into the backseat of a huge black London taxi. It had rained, and the sound of the tires as they went round and round on the slick pavement produced a lulling effect as the car made its way into the heart of the city.

"What would you like to do first?" asked Howard as their driver hefted their luggage from the boot of the taxi.

"Oh, freshen up a bit, then find a place for breakfast." She looked up at Howard and added, "I don't suppose anyone in England makes omelets the way you do."

"We'll see what we can drum up," said Howard as they entered the revolving doors of the Savoy Hotel.

Rachel noticed the clerk's eyebrows as he collected their passports. But no remark was made; Howard was a regular guest at the Savoy and apparently commanded respect. Still, Rachel was aware as they crossed the dark, elegantly appointed and columned lobby to the "lift" that she now had an inkling of what a kept woman must feel like. She didn't share the observation with Howard.

The windows of their suite overlooked the Thames. The richly carpeted floor invited Rachel to kick off her boots and wiggle her toes as she explored the rooms, twice or three times the size of Jamie's apartment.

Howard rang room service. Within half an hour, Rachel discovered the meaning of an English breakfast. She was aware that Howard sat watching her; his eyes displayed amusement as she devoured kippered herrings, marmalade-covered scones, bacon, sausages, kidneys, and a mountain of scrambled eggs.

"Haven't you neglected something?" he asked.

"Have I?" She glanced at the empty plates on the table.

"Your tea," said Howard.

"I'm not a tea drinker," she said.

"Well, we'll have to see about that."

There was also a pot of coffee. Rachel and Howard drank their respective brews and then, fully sated, stood together at the windows and gazed out over the river. "I think you'll like London," said Howard.

"I do already," she said, leaning back into his arms.

Even after high tea at the Savoy, during which time Rachel sampled myriad varieties of the leaf and ate her first cucumber sandwiches, even after duck with currant sauce in the wood-paneled luxury of Rules', followed the next night by dinner at Simpson's on the Strand, the meal that would remain most vivid in her memory was, nonetheless, the room service feast each morning. She and Howard slept late, usually after an evening of theater, followed by brandy and their private view of the Thames, after which they invariably made love. Rachel's earlier qualms about meeting Howard's family began to dissipate as she grew more and more comfortable with him.

During the day, they visited the British Museum, the

Tate, and the Victoria and Albert. They lunched lightly at quaint pubs — Rachel became addicted to Cornish pasties and shepherd's pie — and later fed crumbs to ducks and geese as she and Howard strolled through Kensington Gardens.

They were scheduled to spend Christmas weekend at Hertfordshire, with Howard's cousins, Jennie and William. They spent much of Friday at Harrods buying presents. After a late lunch of roast beef and Yorkshire pudding at Ye Olde Cheshire Cheese and a visit with several of Howard's newspaper friends on Fleet Street, they stopped back at their suite to change clothes. Two of Howard's clients were appearing in *Robert and Elizabeth* at the Savoy Theater across the street from the hotel.

Rachel was wearing a new evening dress that she'd bought that afternoon; it was black wool crepe with a boat neckline; the back, however, swooped provocatively down to her waist. With black-tinted pantyhose and black silk sandals to complete the picture, Rachel mused that she looked perfect for the role of Mata Hari.

While she rummaged through her costume jewelry for a faux pearl or ruby brooch to add as a colorful accent, Howard said, "I'll be right back. I'd almost forgotten something." Rachel hoped he wasn't going for cigarettes; he'd cut down even more lately and she secretly hoped he was in the process of stopping altogether.

He was back in ten minutes. "Close your eyes," he said playfully. Rachel thought his voice sounded as excited as a schoolboy's. It took her back to Excelsior and her brothers' anticipation as they'd handed her their homemade presents on Christmas morning: a name plaque made in wood shop at school; a handpainted leather bookmark; a papier-mâché pencil holder.

Obediently she closed her eyes.

She felt Howard's arms as he raised them over the back of her neck. He struggled for a moment with what was obviously a clasp, and then Rachel felt the coldness of metal against flesh.

Howard spun her around, stepped back, and said, "You may look now."

He had turned her so she was facing the mirror. When she opened her eyes, she let out a gasp of delight. "Oh, Howard!"

His mouth formed a large grin. "I take it that 'Oh, Howard!' means you like it?"

"It's *beautiful!*" she exclaimed. The necklace was a bold, hammered yellow-gold collar that came to a pronounced *V.* At the center of the *V* was a perfect cabochon ruby, in a cusp setting surrounded by a circle of tiny diamonds. It was a uniquely modern design, while at the same time bearing a classic, regal stamp that made Rachel feel like an Egyptian princess.

"I thought it might add the right touch to your dress," said Howard, unpinning the ten-dollar imitation ruby brooch she had pinned to the black crepe while he was downstairs. "I want you to wear only the very best."

"Howard, I—"

"Shh," he said. "Happy Christmas."

Suddenly she wondered if the cashmere scarf she'd bought him—with her own money saved from perfume modeling at Saks and her hated temp assignments—would be enough.

Apparently, he'd read her mind. "A man can't wear jewels, so the next best thing is to buy them for the woman he adores."

His taste and hers were alike; Rachel had seen the necklace in one of the mahogany and glass cases in the lobby. Of all the pieces in the jeweler's display, it was her favorite.

The Savoy Theater wasn't filled to capacity; possibly because *Robert and Elizabeth* had been running for quite some time, but more probably because it was the last night of Christmas shopping before the holiday. Heads turned as Howard and Rachel entered the theater, but she assumed it was because they were a striking couple; nobody knew her, and the audience didn't seem to be a theater crowd; Howard had mentioned that he only saw one or two familiar faces.

He seemed as unprepared, then, as Rachel, when he heard his name called at intermission. They had gone outside, despite the frigid air, to escape the blanket of cigarette smoke filling the lobby. Rachel had added a warm red cashmere scarf over her new dress and under the black velvet cape, but still her teeth chattered. A further chill was added when "Howard!" issued from a silken voice and one of the most stunning women Rachel had ever seen approached them.

Howard visibly stiffened, but recovered immediately and said, "Cecily. This *is* a coincidence."

Cecily! thought Rachel. Howard's ex-wife! She'd seen the face before—on covers of magazines such as *Theatre Arts,* in books such as *Theatre World.* Cecily *Wilton* was the ex–Mrs. Rathborne!

Rachel's knees weakened as the inevitable occurred; the two women were surreptitiously sizing up one another; Rachel didn't relish the experience; Howard's former wife was the ultimate in sophistication and glamour. She wore a full-length chinchilla coat and matching hat, and enormous diamonds sparkled from each ear. Suddenly the black velvet cape on which Jamie and Paul had spent a small fortune became plain by comparison. Rachel couldn't help wondering if Howard had given Cecily the earrings.

It was little consolation that Cecily was trying too hard to impress both her ex-husband *and* whatever she took Rachel to be. That thought quickened Rachel's pulse and for some reason triggered a protective instinct—she was ready to take Howard's side if Cecily dared to be nasty.

Rachel hadn't paid attention to the conversation, since Cecily, after the obligatory introductions had been made, proceeded to ignore her. Rachel's mind went to Gloria Doro and Arnold Gold. But she hadn't become Gold's lover, and Gloria Doro wasn't her lover's ex-wife. For appearances' sake—and Howard's—she decided to be utterly and completely charming.

"I saw you in the film version of *An Everyday Dilemma*," said Rachel. "I enjoyed your performance very much."

"That's sweet of you," replied Cecily. "And what do you do?"

Rachel couldn't tell whether the question had contained any innuendo or if she was misinterpreting from her own discomfort.

"Rachel's in the business," said Howard. "A fine singer and actress."

The ex–Mrs. Rathborne flashed an insincere smile at Rachel. "I'm sure of that. Howard has always had an eye for talent. What brings you to London? A new show?"

Howard answered for both of them. "We're spending the holidays with William and Jennie," he said.

"Oh, the country cousins. Do give them my love." Then Cecily turned to Rachel. "It's very rustic. I was only there once."

Bells signaled the beginning of the second act. Rachel was grateful that it wasn't a three-act show.

As they settled into their seats, Rachel whispered to Howard, "Why did Cecily only visit your family once? Is 'rustic' that primitive?"

"Not at all," he said. "They never invited her back."

Rachel spent the rest of the evening wondering just what she might expect of Christmas in the country.

William and Jennie Sterling lived up to their last name. Rachel took an instant liking to the couple from the moment they came out to greet their guests.

Howard had rented a Mercedes for the weekend; the rest of the time, since they were staying in the heart of London, it was more convenient to travel by taxi. Rachel was secretly pleased; there was something old-fashioned and romantic about the clunky, oversized English taxis—a nostalgic throwback to 1950s movies on television. She half expected

Laurence Olivier or John Gielgud to step from a Rolls — or Wendy Hiller or Maggie Smith, dressed in tweeds, to ride by on a bicycle. The "hired" Mercedes, despite its elegance, failed to impress her at all.

Jennie Sterling was a woman in her late fifties; she was the very definition of the phrase "pleasingly plump" without being fat. She wore no trace of makeup and employed no artifice whatever; her hair was wiry and gray and she didn't seem to care.

William, Rachel learned, was the head of a nearby hospital. He looked to be in his early sixties; Howard's height but thinner; the heavy cable-knit cardigan hung from his shoulders, and his tanned face — in a climate not known for its sun — was creased and craggy. His dark blue eyes were similar to Howard's; they were the intelligent, interested eyes of a good physician, but lacked the powerful intensity of his cousin's.

Jennie bent to pick up Rachel's suitcase, but Rachel insisted. "I can manage. It's very light."

"Well, now. I see Howard has brought us an unspoiled guest."

William heard her and laughed. "He's learning."

Rachel wondered, but didn't ask, if the last lady guest had been Cecily.

Jennie led the way to the comfortable living room. It was nothing like Howard's apartment on Fifth Avenue. Nor was it a country cottage. Solid, traditional pieces were placed for balance, but clearly the Sterlings had furnished their home for function; all the chairs and sofas faced the fireplace, for warmth; the rolltop desk was near a window, for light; it was an attractive, unpretentious, middle-class home, something that Cecily *would* have termed rustic.

Howard and William stayed behind outside, while Jennie led Rachel down the center hallway.

Rachel hesitated for a moment when they reached the guest room and Jennie said, "Just toss your things on the bed. There's time to unpack later." Rachel didn't know whether she and Howard were expected to stay in separate

169

rooms.

But Jennie added, "I hope you won't feel obligated to keep yourselves at arms' length for our benefit. We only have the one guest room — and besides, we know he's quite taken with you."

"He's spoken about me?" She wondered when he'd had the time. They'd been together since their arrival in London, except for the ten minutes when he'd gone to buy her Christmas present.

"He doesn't have to. It's not often he arrives with a guest. Just his bringing you for the holiday tells us a lot. I'm glad. He's too fine a man to spend the rest of his life alone. And I have a good eye for people. I can tell you're good for Howard."

Rachel didn't answer. For some reason, Jennie's comments made her think of Jamie.

The foursome trimmed the tree after Jennie's sumptuous meal of beefsteak and kidney pie. Once the last ornaments were hung, they settled around the fireplace, where the logs crackled in the hearth and a Bach harpsichord concerto played in the background. Finally, after midnight, the two couples said good night and went to their respective rooms.

"I have another present for you," said Howard after they had closed the door. "But I think it's a bit too personal to put under the tree."

Rachel had been undressing and now she looked up. "Too personal?"

He reached into his suitcase and brought out a box from Harrods. "Well, the cousins aren't narrow-minded, but . . ." He handed her the package.

Inside was an ecru satin nightie trimmed in lace. Indeed, it wasn't something to open in front of Jennie and William.

"It reminded me of that minidress you wore to my office the day you came for your interview," said Howard.

She smiled, remembering back to the hot summer afternoon. She'd all but forgotten the dress.

"Will you wear it for me tonight?" asked Howard.

Rachel nodded and slid out of her remaining clothes. She was constantly discovering new sides to herself and to Howard. The first few times they had made love, she had been self-conscious about undressing in front of him, and now, aware that he enjoyed watching while she did so only heightened her desire for him.

And he'd remembered the ecru dress! "You're a romantic," she said aloud as she reached for the nightie.

"What gives you that impression?" he asked, grinning from the edge of the bed.

"You are. It's one of the things I love—" She caught herself and stopped.

Howard rose and took her in his arms. "Someday, my dearest Rachel, I hope you'll be able to finish that sentence." He brushed her hair aside and began to kiss the nape of her neck. "But for now, I won't be greedy."

A light snow fell during the night. They slept under two quilts and awoke to unusual quiet. After joining William and Jennie to exchange presents around the tree, Rachel and Howard partook of Jennie's legendary Christmas breakfast—it put even the Savoy to shame—and then went for a walk in the nearby woods.

On Boxing Day, December 26, they hiked in the bracing cold for almost an hour—the snow wasn't deep, and the wind was calm—and paused for a pint of stout at a neighborhood pub. It had a cozy, characteristic charm—Rachel mused that the word *rustic* didn't have to be pejorative—with its low, beamed ceilings and leather booths. Dark wood was everywhere, and the original windowpanes, bordered in lead, shone like diamonds as a hazy sun filtered through the amber glass. Pewter ale tankards stood lined up along one end of the bar. Patrons standing there helped themselves; this was obviously their second home.

A pot-bellied bartender with black, center-parted hair and a matching handlebar mustache called out, "Why if it isn't Mr. 'oward! Visitin' for the 'olidays, are ye?"

Howard nodded. "Happy Christmas, Mike," he said.

"And to yourself and the lady. Two Guinness, will it be?"

Rachel's heart gave a sudden start at Mike's mention of the drink she had shared with Jamie at the Irish bar in New York. It seemed centuries ago and worlds apart.

Mike set down a glass tankard for Rachel, pewter for Howard. An elaborate letter *R* was etched into the design.

"Mr. 'oward's one o' the regulars, even if 'e don't come round the way he used to," explained Mike.

Howard smiled. "You're welcome to mine. Mike wouldn't even need to change the monogram."

They clinked pewter against glass and drank. Then they walked back in the afternoon chill, took time out for a snowball fight, and pink-cheeked and exhausted from their walk, reached the house in time for tea.

All in all, reminiscences aside, it had been a perfect Christmas holiday.

Chapter Twelve

Rachel mailed postcards to her parents in Minnesota; she wondered what they would be thinking—she hadn't mentioned Howard, and they were intelligent enough to realize that her meager savings could not afford a trip to Europe. But she would call them when she and Howard returned to New York and answers would present themselves. She was gradually learning that they usually did, once the questions were identified and the answers were sought.

She and Howard spent an extended weekend in Hertfordshire; Jennie and William insisted, and business in Howard's London branch of the agency was even slower during the holidays than in the New York office. So it was that Rachel became acquainted with the picturesque countryside, neighbors, and friends. She was greeted by Mike at the pub as one of the "regulars." On the day before their departure, she and Howard stopped in for a pint. Mike toasted the coming year with them. "Bring 'er back soon, Mr. 'oward, and we'll put another pewter on special order."

Howard, looking into Rachel's eyes, said, "I'll do my best, Mike."

Once they had returned to the Savoy, Rachel found that she had several hours each afternoon in which to explore the city; Howard's schedule, despite the holiday slack, and required personal attention and his presence at the office.

Rachel didn't mind. She loved walking. She did take her kidskin boots to a cobbler's shop, and while she waited, he lowered the three-inch heels to a more comfortable two-inch walking height. Rachel marveled at his expert craftsmanship. The man, an Italian in his seventies, barely spoke English, yet he communicated the pride he took in his work. From there, Rachel strolled through the mod boutiques on Carnaby Street, purchased a plum-colored, plum-flavored lipstick at Mary Quant, and stopped to buy souvenirs for Paul and Jamie: old-fashioned biscuit tins, shaped and painted to resemble London's red double-decker buses and filled with Scottish shortbread.

She toured the area of Tottenham Court Road as her personal homage to Eliza Doolittle, another favorite of her stock-role repertoire, but was disappointed to find the street filled entirely with stereo and hi-fi stores. Piccadilly Circus reminded her of a more cosmopolitan Times Square, and some of the street crossings, despite bobbies waving in frantic semaphore, appeared more hazardous than the drag strip on the outskirts of her hometown.

Rachel and Howard had agreed to meet back at the hotel for tea. She set down her packages on the chair opposite her own at one of the four tables inside the gazebo. Within ten minutes, Howard joined her. Each afternoon he had introduced her to a different kind of tea, and her former prejudice against the leaf as only a remedy for the common cold gradually waned, although she still preferred a strong dose of espresso in the late afternoon when her energy needed a lift.

When they rose from the table, Howard looked at Rachel quizzically. He glanced down at her boots, but the cobbler's expertise kept Rachel's secret. The boots didn't appear to have changed. "You've shrunk!" teased Howard.

"No," answered Rachel. "Tea tends to stunt one's growth. It must be the tannic acid."

He shook his head as they stepped out of the gazebo. "You can take the Yank out of the colonies," he said.

She laughed. Tea notwithstanding, her first trip to England had transformed her into an Anglophile.

* * *

They stopped in for the second act of *Robert and Elizabeth* even though they had already seen it. There was talk of bringing the show to New York, and Howard remarked to Rachel, "You'd be perfect for the female lead."

Rachel hadn't thought about performing for more than a week! "Howard! Do you mean it?"

"Well, it suits you. If you're interested, I'll mention your name."

Interested! she thought. She could send a million résumés on her own and never even get an interview! "Of course I'm interested!" she answered.

"Good. I'll make a few calls."

Is that all there was to it at Howard's level? she wondered. Is it really about connections, about knowing the right people? Doesn't talent enter into it at all?

Rachel dismissed these thoughts as she spotted a chinchilla coat from across the lobby. She prayed that Cecily wasn't viewing *Robert and Elizabeth* for a second time as well. But when the coat's owner turned, Rachel saw that it was worn not by Cecily but by a man who was almost as feminine as the ex–Mrs. Rathborne, although far less attractive. She breathed a sigh of relief as she and Howard entered the theater and the usher led them to their seats.

Howard didn't mention Jamie until they were settled into the first-class section aboard the New York–bound jet. Rachel was sipping a Bloody Mary when, out of the blue— or so she thought—Howard asked, "When we land, shall we stop by to pick up your belongings, or will that cause problems with your . . . friend?"

"I don't understand. Why should that cause problems?" But she sensed that it would.

"Well," said Howard, "you *have* been sharing that flat with him, haven't you?"

Her eyes widened. But she'd made a pact with herself. She wouldn't lie to Howard or Jamie. "How did you know?"

He smiled gently. "That night I brought you home. I admit it was an excellent attempt."

"Did you *see* him behind the clothes rod?" she asked, incredulous because he'd never mentioned it.

"No — you mean he was *there?*" But instead of anger, Howard laughed. "In that case, it was a marvelous act!" More seriously he said, "And he does care for you. I appreciate that. But no, I didn't see him. I noticed a pair of tap shoes on the radiator." He looked into Rachel's bewildered eyes. "You've often told me that you don't dance."

She was embarrassed for two reasons: for having tried to fool him — *and* for his having found out. "You never said a word about it. Why?"

He traced the outline of her lips with his finger. "I knew it was important to you because you didn't tell me. But I realized it had to be brought up before we landed in New York."

"Howard," she said, sipping more of her drink, "about that. I . . . I don't know if it's . . . well, if it's right for me to . . ."

"What? To move your things to my flat? Why not?"

"Well, it's just . . ."

"Are you concerned for Jamie? What he'll say or think? Or is it his feelings you're worried about?"

"I . . . I'm not sure."

"Rachel, darling, you can't crawl inside his head and change him, no matter how you'd like to. I'm a patient man, but I'd hate to see Jamie come between us."

"So would I, Howard," she said. Odd, she thought as the vodka and the engines' roar lulled her into a limbo of suspended emotion, those were almost her identical words to Jamie.

Rachel had decided to telephone Jamie from Howard's apartment. On the way from the airport, they had reached a silent agreement that Rachel would stay uptown while not removing all of her things from Fifth Street; that would have suggested permanence, and Howard seemed to understand Rachel's need to remain free of ties—at least visible ties—as well as any action that might imply restraint.

But Jamie wasn't home when Rachel called. She dialed the answering service, left a message that she'd try again in the morning, and hung up.

She pulled off her boots and walked to the terrace windows while Howard checked through his accumulated mail in the den. The lights in windows across the park glittered in the indigo night; Manhattan's skyline appeared as it had upon the plane's approach to JFK: a giant Christmas ornament, the private greeting to each of its observers. "I love this city!" she exclaimed to the air.

Howard had entered the living room. "I thought you'd become an Anglophile," he said, joining her at the window.

"Can't I be both?" she asked, leaning against him.

He didn't reply, which drew Rachel's attention to the ambiguity of so much of her life these days.

"I've hung your clothes in my closet," Howard said, drawing her closer to him. "It reminded me about New Year's Eve."

"What about it?"

"Business parties. Usually boring. But I've got to put in an appearance at two or three. Will you join me?"

"At a business party? Would I fit in?"

He snuggled his cheek against hers. "You fit in anywhere. And your presence will make it all the more bearable. How about it?"

She accepted. She hadn't made end-of-year party plans.

"Good. We'll go to Bergdorf's tomorrow and buy you something smashing to wear."

She withdrew from his embrace. "Howard, this may sound very prim, but I . . . I don't really approve of your buying my clothes. I feel strange as it is about the black dress and the luggage—not to mention the necklace—"

"Christmas presents," he insisted.

"Well, Christmas is over. I'll buy my own dress for New Year's Eve."

"Birthday?"

"Not till spring. The answer is no. Thanks, anyway." It was one thing to garner a certain glance from the desk clerk at the Savoy; it was another where her own feelings were concerned.

The next day, Rachel was still unable to reach Jamie. The answering service said that he hadn't picked up her message.

"Is there a number where you can call him?" she asked.

"He didn't leave one," came the reply.

She left another message, then looked up Paul's number in the telephone directory. He wasn't home either, and she didn't know which answering service he used. There was nothing else she could do.

She headed for Saks, where she took advantage of Cheryl's offer; the regular salesclerk in the perfume section had promised the use of her employee discount card at any time that Rachel needed it.

Half an hour later, she emerged from the Fifth Avenue store carrying a single package: a claret silk minidress completely covered with matching bugle beads. It had been an extravagance, but Rachel justified the expense—a week's temping salary—by rationalizing that she could wear the burgundy sandals she had bought for the New Stars auditions and only worn the one time. They would be as uncomfortable as before, but she could endure them for the length of a few parties.

She hailed a taxi; even the detour downtown to Jamie's to pick up the shoes—he still wasn't home—and a taxi back to Howard's would cost less than a new pair of shoes. And spending ninety dollars on the beaded dress had been a heady experience; Rachel knew that if Howard had paid for the dress, she wouldn't be half as thrilled with it.

His appreciation, when she entered the den an hour before the first party, made the expense worth every penny. She had parted her hair low on one side; the result was a very mysterious look, with one eye hidden by a silken wave every time she tilted her head. The spaghetti-strap neckline didn't permit a bra, and she was aware that she'd have to be careful when bending over.

Howard noticed immediately and told her she had dropped an earring. He roared with laughter when she fell for the bait.

"We won't stay out late," he promised. "You look too delicious to share with the night." His hands caressed her through the shimmering, undulating beads. "Mmm. Why don't you stop wearing a bra all the time? After all, women have been burning them for quite some time."

She nodded. She liked the feeling, made all the more pleasurable by Howard's fingers.

"Now," he said, "women just have to get rid of that other horrid invention."

Her eyebrows rose.

"Pantyhose," he explained. "The ancient Romans had the right idea. Just tunics and togas. Nothing underneath to get in the way."

Rachel's knees weakened suddenly. Hours ago her mind had been occupied with Jamie. Now, she couldn't wait to return from the night of partying to be held and loved by Howard. She was increasingly bewildered by herself.

The first party was a standing-room-only affair. The two hosts, a set designer from the Metropolitan Opera and his male lover, a famous stage director from the same company, had choreographed the cocktail-and-canapes gathering fully mindful that guests would have a drink or two and continue on to other celebrations.

Rachel recognized many of the faces among the throng, although she hadn't been previously introduced to any of them. As she and Howard edged their way to the terrace between exchanges of "Hello, Zero" or "Nice to see you, Rock," a flashy blonde in gold sequins leaned against a white piano and warbled unintelligible lyrics to several songs. When Rachel recognized one of them as "Night and Day," she shuddered; Cole Porter was fortunate not to be alive for this rendition.

The apartment itself was a lavish penthouse on Central Park West in the Upper Seventies. Like Howard's on the East Side, it boasted a spectacular view of Central Park.

"It's practically straight across," Rachel remarked.

"Yes," agreed Howard. "With binoculars, they have a perfect sighting of the master bedroom."

Rachel's cheeks turned as deep burgundy as her dress.

"I love that about you," said Howard. "You look so smart, sophisticated. But underneath—"

"You *like* when I blush?" she asked. She'd always hated it.

He nodded. "It's one of the first things I noticed about you. In your dressing room. A woman who can blush—especially in this business—is rare. Shows that she's genuine."

"Or that she embarrasses easily," Rachel said, trying to focus on which of the rooftops across the park was that of Howard's building.

"Funny," she mused aloud.

"Did I miss something?" he asked.

"I was thinking about your apartment. Aside from the den, it's so . . . well, cold. And you're not."

"I thought you rather liked it."

"It's gorgeous. It belongs in *Architectural Digest*. But it doesn't look like a place where someone *lives*. I don't mean it as an insult—but it isn't *you*—"

"Well, I'm not insulted, because Cecily decorated the

180

flat — or had it done, that is. I take credit — or blame — only for the den. And the Impressionist paintings."

"The music room?"

"Cecily. So her taste wasn't all bad, was it?"

Rachel smiled. "She married you. And the apartment is a designer's dream. She just didn't seem to know you very well."

"That, you might say, is the story in the nutshell. Would you like to redecorate?" he asked suddenly.

This time she turned beet-red and nothing she could do would stop it.

The second party, on Riverside Drive, was similar to the first. Rachel wondered how anyone could talk "business deals" with all the music and noise. Nonetheless, as she and Howard stepped out into the cold air, he took her arm and said, "I'm sorry, but apparently *Robert and Elizabeth* isn't coming to New York, after all."

"Don't be sorry," she said.

"I am, only because you were perfect for the role. But there'll be better shows and better parts. Once the holidays are over, things will start moving again. Be patient, darling."

Rachel thought from the expression in his eyes that he was reminding himself of the same advice.

The third and final party was at the enormous apartment of Myron Klein. Nobody really knew what he did for a living, but he seemed to have a finger in every Broadway pie. At one time he had been a night club crooner, but when rock and roll came in, he had faded from public view. Several years later he had resurfaced after having married and divorced a paper towel heiress and now appeared on the arm of a beautiful showgirl or Hollywood starlet at every film or theater premiere. His name was constantly in the columns, his picture always in the news. Rachel had wondered if his little black book of phone numbers came in a three-volume set.

And then she met him and realized that he was gay.

He was handsome in a Hollywood "honey-sweetie-baby" kind of way. His gold brocade dinner jacket would have played second fiddle only to Liberace—and the latter had not been invited. He wore makeup, which created a Caribbean tan on both his face and the pink collar of his ruffled shirt.

When Howard introduced Rachel, she was immediately renamed by Myron as "Doll-face." She hated the expression as much as she had loathed cheek-pinching aunts as a child.

But she played her part and was as gracious as on the night she had met the ex–Mrs. Rathborne. So far, she mused, she was doing far more acting offstage than on. She was grateful when a passing waiter stopped long enough for her to take a glass of champagne.

An hour and several glasses later, Howard, who stood out in his custom-tailored black tux and white silk shirt among at least two hundred men in black tuxedos and white silk shirts, returned from a tête-à-tête with Gloria Swanson and whispered, "How would you like to get out of here?"

He had to repeat it twice at louder volume before Rachel could hear him above the din. "Let's go!" he finally shouted into her ear.

As they made their way to the bedroom, where the coats had been thrown across two king-size beds, the flashing strobes suddenly spotlighted two familiar faces.

"Rachel!" said the handsome dark-haired dancer. It was Paul!

And standing beside him with an arm possessively around the dancer's slim waist was a very well-known face: Lehman Stern!

Her thoughts darted immediately to Jamie. Why wasn't *he* with Paul tonight? Why weren't they at a party—any party—together?

Lehman Stern greeted Rachel warmly. "It's lovely to see you! Howard has told you that we're going to work together, hasn't he?"

She was still speechless from seeing him with Paul.

"I . . ."

"How was London?" asked Paul, obviously sensing her confusion.

"Wonderful. I . . . I tried to phone you when we got back."

"I haven't been home much the past week," he replied. The forced cheerfulness had suddenly faded from his face and voice. Rachel wondered if she alone had noticed.

"Yes," she continued. "I stopped at the apartment to pick up some things. I . . . I didn't know where to reach you. Or . . . Jamie." There. She'd said it, despite Howard's and Paul's presence. She'd had to say it.

Paul nodded. "I think he's . . . spending some time with his family."

"Really?" That seemed strange; he didn't get along with his parents; why would he be celebrating the holidays with them? "How long will he be there?" She tried to sound nonchalant and still glean information.

"I don't know," said Paul with a trace of sadness. "I haven't seen him since Christmas."

Lehman cleared his throat and said, "Paul's been visiting me for the holidays. I told him not to leave word with anyone—I always disconnect my phone until January second."

Rachel heard herself say, "That's a good idea." But she was miles away.

Howard seemed eager to leave. "Lehman, since your phone is off the hook, will you ring me on Monday? We have to talk about Rachel."

"Sure thing, Howard."

Paul said, "And Rachel, call me. I don't know where to reach you. And I'd love to hear all about London."

She knew they wouldn't spend more than thirty seconds

183

on the subject. "I will. We can meet for lunch." She wondered if Howard had read every word between the lines, if he knew she wasn't ready to announce publicly that she could be reached at his apartment.

And then Lehman Stern and Paul were swallowed up by the revolving strobe light and the hundreds of dancing guests.

Rachel and Howard made their way down the hall. Howard retrieved his coat from the rack outside the bedroom. Rachel had laid her cape across one of the beds, since the cape would have fallen too easily from a hanger.

A battle was raging inside. Myron Klein, standing just inside the door, was trying to referee a screaming match between a square-faced, truck-bodied woman and a fashion model whose face Rachel had seen on the cover of *Vogue* more than a few times. The model was dressed from head to foot in gold lamé; the "truck" was wearing a man's gray gabardine suit.

"I paid ten grand for that mink, Myron!" screamed the lesbian in trousers. "And that bitch is trying to steal it!"

"Liar!" screamed the gorgeous blonde in gold. "This is *my* coat!"

"I'll kill you!" cried the first woman. "That was my Christmas present to Olivia!"

Myron's pleading voice was almost comical. "Ladies, please, *please*—"

"Shut up!" The gray lady again: "We're talking ten thousand bucks, you jerk!"

Miss Vogue pulled herself up to a full height of just under six feet and screamed back, "I know mink, Beverly! That rat you gave Olivia was worth twelve hundred— *retail!*"

While Myron backed up against the wall to dodge a flying vase, Rachel spied her velvet cape on the floor. "Excuse me," she said, grabbing it and ducking at the same time. "I'm sure neither of you is interested in *this* . . ."

Howard pulled Rachel through the doorway. "Happy

New Year, Myron," he said.

The door slammed as another round began.

"Howard," said Rachel fuzzily as they entered his apartment, "I want you to know something. It's *very* important." She had drunk four glasses of champagne and her speech was slurred.

"And what's that?" he asked, tenderly kissing her temple.

"I'm here—with you, I mean—because I *want* to be."

"I know that, darling—"

"I mean, it's *not* to advance my career—nothing like Lehman Stern and Paul—"

"Rachel, you don't have to tell me that. I *know* it. I've known it from the start."

"Good!" she said. "Then I don't care what anybody thinks!"

"Why? Did someone make a remark?"

"Jamie. Before London. And he *knows* it isn't true!"

"Well," said Howard, removing her sandals, "don't be too hard on him. We tend to get upset if our saints fall from their pedestals."

"*I'm* not a saint!" She giggled a champagne laugh.

"That's precisely what he can't forgive. And he's a little jealous, too."

"Of what, Howard?" His voice sounded far away and dreamy to Rachel.

"Of you. Of me. Perhaps of us. You can't control that."

"That's *so* sad. . . . Don't you think it's sad?"

"Well," he said gently, "*I've* never been in love with Jamie, so I'm not as affected by it as you are." In a softer voice, he added, "My dearest Rachel, we have no control over others, not even of those we love."

She yawned. "Ooh, I'm *so* tired!" She yawned again and flopped to the sofa.

"Come, darling. It's late." He began to undress her; she

185

was already dozing. He lifted her into his arms and carried her to the bedroom. "I love you, Rachel," he said. But she was in that sleepy state where words sometimes only seem to be what they are.

Chapter Thirteen

While Howard met with Lehman Stern the following Monday, Rachel telephoned Paul and made a date to meet him for lunch. They agreed on the Evening Star, a midtown coffee shop across the street from Angelo's on Ninth Avenue; the choice eliminated most likelihood of bumping into Jamie at the Italian restaurant or Howard and Lehman Stern at any of the neighborhood's fashionable French bistros. Rachel needed to talk to Paul in private.

Paul obviously felt the same; he was already seated in the booth farthest back from the door. Another few feet would have landed them in the kitchen.

They ordered hamburgers and waited until the waiter had left them alone. Then Paul began. "You looked ravishing at the party."

"You looked pretty good, too. I . . . I admit I was surprised to see you with Lehman Stern, though."

"Life goes on, as they say."

"I guess it does."

"Rachel, what you saw isn't what you think you saw."

"Care to translate?" she asked.

"Your conductor friend has . . . well, his tastes are a little . . . bizarre, even for me."

"Now I'm sure I don't understand."

"It's a new vocabulary for me, too. And I thought I'd tried everything." He didn't elaborate, and then their waiter returned with two cups of coffee. When they were alone again, Paul changed the subject. "You seem happy with Howard Rathborne. Are you?"

Rachel sighed. "It isn't just a holiday fling, if that's what you mean. I'm not sophisticated enough for that."

"Is that supposed to imply that I am?"

"Well, you were with Lehman Stern the other night. And you were with Jamie when Howard and I left for London."

"Well, let's say I just don't have Howard Rathborne's patience." Paul was stirring his coffee without realizing how much milk he was adding to it until it spilled over into the saucer. Rachel quickly grabbed several paper napkins and made a cushion to mop up the excess under his cup.

"Sorry," he said. "It's just a case of Jamie not knowing his own mind. One minute he thinks he cares, and then — well, it's not so different from you and Howard Rathborne. I understand what he must be going through — we're in the same boat."

"How do you figure that?"

"He's in love with you; I'm in love with Jamie. You and Jamie are both sitting on the fence." He smiled gently. "That's not intended to sound like an indictment; it's just the way things are."

She couldn't deny a word. "Is Jamie really in the Bronx with his family? Or was that just party talk?"

"I don't know. He said he'd probably visit them. Then he mentioned something about getting away for a while. He's got some money saved from the bank commercial. And he hates January in New York."

"But the season's just starting up again — now's the time to be here."

"Well," said Paul as their burgers arrived, "it depends on what you're looking for."

"And he still doesn't know, does he?" she asked rhetorically.

"Who does?" Paul answered. "You're better off than he is, at least."

"Why? Because of Howard, you mean?"

"No. You're only confused about Jamie and your feelings toward him. But you have a pretty fair idea as to who Rachel is. Jamie's confused about himself. He's still seeking answers outside—in you, in me—but there's part of him that's afraid of what he might find if he digs deep enough."

"Like what?"

"Like maybe he's empty inside and can't love anyone. You know the old cliché—you have to love yourself first, before anyone else can love you. It has nothing to do with gender or persuasion."

She reflected on his statement. "I can't believe that he's incapable of love. Otherwise we couldn't love him, could we, Paul?"

"I don't know, Rachel. Lots of people make that same mistake."

A sudden image of Cecily Wilton crossed Rachel's mind. The better she was coming to know Howard, the more she was convinced that the breakup of his marriage had not been his fault. Paul was right, after all. She only hoped he was wrong about Jamie.

Was the world changing, or was she? Both, she reasoned, aware of new perceptions in her everyday life. She had begun to examine and question so-called logic and reason. At times it brought frustration, but she refused adamantly to return to an old way of thinking, even when the latter might have proven more comfortable.

Every night the illuminated marquees of *Hello, Dolly!, Fiddler on the Roof,* and *Man of La Mancha* advertised their seeming obliviousness to the changes on the streets and in the crowds who filled the theaters. The trio of shows had become a symbol of sorts to Rachel—a defiant holdout of "the old guard"—they were evidence of an almost bygone era. That these entertainments still played to sellout houses offered a peculiar comfort, and Rachel endowed them with personalities of their own.

However, by the early part of 1969, these stubborn mainstays had begun to acquire a label of quaintness. The Love Generation had been christened; the sexual revolution was born. Mary Quant and Sergeant Pepper had already changed the look and the sound of the world. The first large influx of surviving draftees returned from Vietnam no longer the boys who had left, their hometowns no longer the insulated hamlets of post–World War II naïveté. There were many who said that "nothing is quite as sure as change." Howard had likened events to the Chinese curse, "May you live in interesting times."

Rachel had just finished her daily routine of vocalizing. Michael Ross had taped the warmup session for her, and when she switched off the cassette recorder, she could hear soft music coming from the den.

"It's only five o'clock!" she called. "You're home early!"

"Josh canceled our meeting at Twenty-One," said Howard.

"Everything all right?" she asked, running her purse comb through her hair, then hurrying down the hall to join him.

"He's not feeling well . . . again. Come here. I have something for you to see!"

When she appeared on the threshold to the den, he was seated behind his desk and had already changed into a crewneck sweater and slacks. He looked up and grinned. "You're in good voice."

"Yes . . . thank you—if I may say so myself."

"You may. Cocktail?" he asked, rising.

"I'd love one—but let me. You stay where you are."

Rachel looked forward to this time of day. She had recently acquired the skill of mixing a good martini and enjoyed the hour when they sat with their drinks and talked about their day.

She kissed him on the cheek, then placed the glass with the pearl onion in it in front of him and kept the olive one for herself.

On Howard's desk was a script, bound in red leatherette, the title obscured by his hand.

"Is that what you wanted me to see?" she asked.

"Yes. Read it. If you like the book, I have a tape of the music as well as the written score in my briefcase. I'm curious to know what you think of it."

Rachel knew that Howard and Norma had been scouting scripts in an effort to find a "property" for her. She also knew it hadn't been easy. So new to the city and to the profession, Rachel knew it was unrealistic to expect a leading role so soon—even with Howard's influence. He had been hunting for a good vehicle that would introduce her in a supporting role. Only once before had he brought home a script he'd thought worthwhile. That had been a month ago, and in the meantime, the show had lost its backing.

Seating herself on the edge of the desk, Rachel sipped her drink and turned to the cast page. It read: "In order of appearance: Little John, Friar Tuck . . ."

"Robin Hood?" she said skeptically.

"The working title is *Knights in Nottingham*—but that's subject to change."

"Okay," she said with a sigh. Her eyes traveled down the page until she reached Maid Marian.

"She's the only woman in the cast?"

Howard nodded.

"Then it's the *lead?*"

"Not quite. Read it."

"*You* like it, don't you?"

"Whether I do or not doesn't matter unless *you* like it. And the role."

"All right. I'll read it tomorrow."

"Do we have plans for this evening?" he asked.

"No . . . why?"

"Well, I thought I could build a fire after dinner and you might leaf through it tonight."

Rachel leaned across the desk and kissed him. "You *do* like it . . . a lot. . . ."

By nine o'clock that evening, she was curled up on the sofa in front of the fireplace and had read halfway through the script. Without looking up, she asked. "Darling, where's your briefcase?"

Howard didn't answer. When Rachel brought her eyes up from the page, he was smiling at her from his chair. "Curious?" he asked.

"Well," she said, "the lyrics are wonderful. . . . I'd like to hear the music."

By eleven o'clock, she had scanned the entire score while listening to the tape. The composer was accompanying himself at the piano. Even with his scratchy voice hardly singing the lyrics, there were tears in Rachel's eyes when she reached the last page.

"Oh, Howard . . ." she said softly.

"It's lovely, isn't it?"

"It's . . . it's . . ." She was at a loss for words.

"A bit reminiscent of *Camelot*, God knows, and Marian's not the lead, but she does have that one scene and the one song."

"And Howard—*what* a scene! What a song!"

"Then you like it," he said.

"I *love* it!" She wiped a salty tear from her cheek.

"It's yours."

Had she heard him correctly? *"Mine?"*

"There'll be an audition next week—for the producer. Just a formality. The director saw you in *Arrowhead,* and . . . there's an added bonus."

"What's that?"

"Lehman Stern is musical director. He'll be conducting."

"Oh!" she exclaimed, crossing the room to him. She removed the book he'd been reading from its face-down position on his chest and he pulled her down onto his lap. A log crackled in the fireplace and the flames dimmed to an intimate glow.

"Howard, I . . ." she began.

But he silenced her with a kiss. "I know," he whispered.

As Howard had promised, the audition was just a formality. Rachel began rehearsal for *Knights in Nottingham* during the second week in February.

She had tried to contact Jamie about her good news. After three attempts, she gave up and found that she was almost relieved at *not* having reached him. Reflecting on her conversation with Paul, she wondered if Jamie would have been happy for her—or whether he'd have been resentful. If he was still without work, the latter was probably the case.

She made the obligatory call to her parents. As expected, her father was unimpressed. Rachel knew her mother was excited—considering that Marsha Allenby had no real idea of the job's importance. Rachel explained about the two-month rehearsal period. "Then we preview in Los Angeles for four weeks and open in New York in June."

"That's wonderful, dear," said her mother. "But it seems ages since we've seen you. It's too bad you won't be previewing in Minneapolis."

"Mom," Rachel suggested on a sudden impulse, "why don't you and Dad fly here at the beginning of July? I can show you around New York — and you can see your daughter on Broadway!"

"Where would we stay, dear?"

"Well, with . . ." She caught herself. They couldn't stay at Howard's. Or at Jamie's. "I . . . I can put you up at a hotel."

"You're not living at your old address anymore, are you?" said her mother.

Rachel had checked the mailbox at Fifth Street once a week since moving in with Howard. Her parents hadn't written in a month. "No . . . I . . ."

"I've called your old number *twice,* dear," said Marsha.

That was a surprise. Russell Allenby was strict about the expense incurred by long-distance calls. "That's what the mail is for," he'd always said. If her mother had called twice, it could only mean that she suspected something. And Rachel was *not* about to be maneuvered into the admission that she was living with a man. She'd never hear the end of it.

"Is anything wrong?" she asked her mother.

"Wrong? Why no. Does something have to be wrong before I call my daughter?"

"Well, no, Mom, it's just that . . . you *never* phone, and . . ."

"Are you implying that I don't care? Rachel, how can you say that?"

It never failed to amaze Rachel the way her mother could take good news and turn it sour — while manipulating the topic of conversation away from her daughter and back to herself.

"Mom . . . will you come to New York? Yes or no?"

But her mother held few surprises. "Oh, dear, it's so hot in July, and so far away, and I've never flown. Your father, of course—"

"Take a train," Rachel suggested.

"Well, that's a three-day trip, and you know how your father hates to travel. . . ."

On it went. What should have been the joy at delivering good news had instead diminished into a depressing impatience. In the past, such exchanges had affected Rachel for as long as a week.

But, she noticed later, this time the feeling of rejection had dissipated in a matter of hours. The conversation was always the same, and it was losing its punch. Either she was growing weary, she reflected, or she was growing up.

Rachel found it odd that, aside from Paul, the only other person she was eager to tell was Beth Burns. She felt that somehow Beth would be happy for her. But *Camelot* was still on tour and Rachel didn't have the company's itinerary.

When she told Paul over lunch, he hugged her tightly. "That's fabulous! You'll be a beautiful Marian. I hear the score is great."

"It is. And Lehman's going to conduct."

"Oh."

"I'm sorry, Paul. I didn't mean to bring up—"

"No, no. He's good. Well, I mean . . . he can conduct."

The first day of rehearsal was on Tuesday.

Howard dropped her off at the studio on Broadway at Fifty-third Street. "Say hello to Lehman for me," he called as she closed the taxi door. The car sped down Broadway, and Rachel crossed the street to Bickford's for a coffee-to-go. Then she ran against a red light in the cloudy winter wind and entered the Broadway Arts Building.

Studio B was large and—thankfully—warm. Rachel saw

immediately that the takeout coffee had been unnecessary. A huge metal urn, surrounded by bagels and Danish pastries, stood on a table just inside the door. Groups of people, most of them strangers to her, were gathered in conversational clusters. A dark man in Levis offered his hand. "I'm Chuck, your stage manager. You must be Rachel, right?"

She nodded while removing her coat. "I'm not late, am I?"

"Not at all. But Lehman will be. We'll start without him, though. Have some coffee. You've got a script?"

"Yes, thanks," Rachel replied. She took a bagel with cream cheese and said good morning to Drew Colton, the show's Robin Hood and her leading man. She'd ushered for *Kelly's Folly,* the musical for which he'd won the previous year's Tony Award.

At the center of the room, four long tables had been arranged in a square. A miniature scale replica of the set stood like a dollhouse at the center of the smallest table. In the corner was an upright piano covered with sheet music. Coats and umbrellas had been hung over the backs of some of the folding chairs.

Rachel glanced at the other tables and saw an empty space with an envelope bearing her name. She sat down and withdrew the cuts and revisions, the new pages to be replaced in the script.

By ten-fifteen, the rest of the company had assembled, after apologizing for their tardiness. A sleet-rain was falling, affecting all transportation. At ten-twenty, the rehearsal began.

When everyone had taken a seat around the table, Chuck introduced Bennett Jerome, the director, who offered a few words of welcome. Then, starting on Jerome's right and moving clockwise, the members of the cast introduced themselves and their respective roles. Lehman Stern had still not arrived.

The hours preceding the lunch break were used for filling out union insurance forms, after which Barry Milton explained the details of the set design. There were only two other women present besides Rachel: Anita Oates, the choreographer, and Fiona Ridgley, who had brought along her costume sketches. She was a two-time Tony winner and an Oscar nominee, and her designs reflected her talent.

She was midway through a display of the first-act sketches when Lehman Stern made his entrance. He tiptoed in, obviously trying not to intrude, but Rachel could see from the designer's eyes and the slight rise in her voice that she hadn't appreciated the interruption.

As Fiona continued to discuss the first act, Rachel nodded a greeting to Lehman, who had taken the chair opposite hers. He seemed agitated at being so late, but what concerned Rachel was the black-and-blue mark over his left cheek. Had he been in an accident?

But Fiona was saying, "And Rachel . . . this is your gown. Since you open the second act, I wanted it to be spectacular."

She held up the sketch. The word *spectacular* applied. The swatches of cloth stapled to the bottom right side of the board showed that the heavenly blue in the colored drawing would be of softest velvet; the brown trim at the low-cut squared neckline would be of sable. And Rachel's wrists would be studded with glittering jewels.

"My assistant will be here around two, and we'll start taking measurements then."

"Now," Bennett Jerome said at last, "Chuck will pass around our first week's schedule. Please let him know of any conflicts—commercials, auditions, filming, et cetera. We've got studio A down the hall for musical rehearsals, which will begin tomorrow. Lehman will give you his breakdown of songs. When you're not in room A with him you'll be in here with Anita and me for dancing and staging."

Anita Oates hadn't spoken yet, and Rachel was curious about her. During the late 1950s and early 1960s, Oates had been one of the best dancers on Broadway. Now nearing her fifties, she had moved gracefully, over the past seven or eight years, into a new career as a much-sought-after choreographer.

"Gentlemen . . . and lady"—she smiled at Rachel—"the dances will be very physical. I expect everyone to be warmed up and ready when we begin each morning. Next week a fencing and fight director will be here to help us integrate the duels and stunts into the movement and music."

As the choreographer continued speaking, Rachel found herself growing more and more excited. She was surrounded by the best talent the business could offer. And she was part of it.

I'm here! she thought. *I'm in a Broadway show!*

She had hoped to have lunch with Lehman, but as the room cleared for the hour's break he was deep in conversation with Bennett Jerome. He looked up briefly and waved at her not to wait for him.

In the afternoon, they had the first read-through. Alex Sussman, the composer and lyricist, took his position at the piano and began to play the overture, which carried the melodic line to Rachel's solo song, "A Light Through the Trees." As the last soft note was sounded, Chuck spoke: "Act One. Sherwood Forest. Offstage, we hear someone whistling the tune to 'While Richard's Away.' The whistler appears. It's Little John. Another whistler is heard, in harmony. Then another and another, until the stage is filled with Robin's men, whistling the song *a capella* as they start

198

the campfire. Music comes in quietly under the melody and builds until, as the first flame of the fire is seen, Robin Hood swings in through the trees — on a rope from upstage center."

The story was completely original. Robin and his legendary band of lovable thieves were the only familiar aspects to the production. Still, Rachel was enraptured and sat listening, immersing herself and almost forgetting that she *wasn't* a member of the audience.

After a ten-minute break, they returned to read Act Two and Rachel's scene. Earlier, the script had established Prince John's promise of Marian's hand in marriage — unless she confided Robin's whereabouts. Misunderstood by court gossips — and at the same time remaining silent to protect her bandit rogue — Marian's soliloquy and the following love scene with Robin contained undoubtedly the most inspired writing in the show. By the time the dashing outlaw had stolen into Marian's palace bedchamber, the audience would be with them completely — and vicariously.

It was a wonderful scene: Robin, swearing to abandon all hopes and dreams for England in order to have Marian set free; Marian, pleading and then convincing Robin that their duty to King Richard was more important than mere personal happiness.

Instinct guided Rachel from the moment she and Drew began to read. Without playing into the sentimentality, she found the chord of nobility that was the backbone of Marian's character.

Rachel had already learned the song and now she asked to try it herself, rather than having Alex Sussman speak it. The composer and director seemed pleased at her eagerness. Lehman Stern smiled as he had during the piano rehearsal in Washington.

The dialogue moved smoothly into the lyrics of Rachel's solo, which ascended to a final, glorious high note as she sang:

> I'm not really alone in the night,
> Though the world thinks it knows what it sees.
> What appears to the rest as a flickering fire,
> I know as my light through the trees.

There was a brief silence; then, from the piano bench, Alex Sussman began to applaud. It served as a cue, and the rest of the company joined in.

Only the leading man, Drew Colton, sat still, with his hands folded before him on the table. Their eyes met, and the smile faded from Rachel's face as she recognized his jealous challenge.

That can't be, she thought. It's ridiculous. It's my song, after all. He's the star—with two solos of his own. Besides, he's a *man*. Drew Colton *couldn't* sing this song!

Could he?

Howard and Rachel's only late night out was now Sunday, since Monday was her one day off. Although she cared deeply about the show and most of the people involved in the production, she also coveted her time away from it. She needed a day to clear her mind and to be with Howard, who was working half days on Saturday to compensate for his absence from the office on Monday.

They had one free weekend, however, and agreed to join Anita Oates at her home in Connecticut. By Saturday night, Rachel and Howard realized their mistake. Rather than a relaxing country weekend to escape the tensions of a show nearing readiness, nerves only increased. Anita talked incessantly of *Knights*—she went so far as to run over the steps of Rachel's choreography. Although Howard made no vocal objections, it was clear that he was bored.

Rachel had looked forward to the visit, to hearing first-hand Anita's stories of her early days in theater with legendary productions and stars who had been household names. Several of her ex-husbands had been famous dancers, and Rachel knew there had to be a repertoire of anecdotes.

Nonetheless, Anita talked on and on for three full days about the sets, costumes, dancers, and everything else concerned with *Knights in Nottingham*. Rachel couldn't wait for Monday evening, when she would finally escape *into* the city with Howard.

"Some people can't help it," said Howard as they pulled out of Anita's driveway. "It's their demon."

"I suppose. It's taxing, though!"

He nodded in agreement. "They say the Lunts didn't stop rehearsing even after a play opened. They went over their lines in *bed*."

"God!" exclaimed Rachel. "Where does devotion leave off and obsession take over?"

"Well," said Howard, "I do have two other clients who perceive no difference. And, too, love *is* a kind of obsession, don't you think?"

Rachel considered his remark without replying.

In a different tone, then, Howard said, "A friend of mine calls it show business of the brain."

That made her laugh. It summed up all her thoughts on what she felt was more akin to disease than to occupation. Odd, she mused, there had been a time when she had entered a theater the way some people would enter a church. When had that changed?

Rachel's total onstage time in *Knights of Nottingham* took barely twenty minutes. Once her part was staged, she was given the luxury of several free hours each day while the men rehearsed. She used the time to work on her voice and also signed up for an acting class and a grueling hour of dance—after which she rewarded herself by going shopping.

She still wasn't completely relaxed about spending money—even though she was earning her own—but she had opened a savings account, to which she added more than half her salary each week, and she did need clothes both for rehearsals and for the eventual month in California. She continued to search the clearance-sale racks, but if she couldn't find exactly what she wanted, she didn't avoid the retail section.

Lehman was shocked when she told him of the opening night gown—in a blue silk that matched her Marian costume almost perfectly—she'd bought, full price, at Lillie Rubin.

"Darling," he said, "Mother inherited millions—and *she* told me *never* to buy anything retail!"

Rachel didn't tell him of the "high" it had given her; he wouldn't have understood, having come from so much money. This was the first time in her life she'd been able to afford silk that wasn't reduced or secondhand. And she liked the feeling. She remembered the year before. Spaghetti with Jamie. Pooling their loose change to buy *one* of them a subway token—whoever had the audition. Somehow these nostalgic fancies always returned Rachel to the harsh reality that, no matter how her life had improved, she had received no word from Jamie.

March continued February's onslaught of snow and rain. By early April, the weather began to clear. Running *Knights* from beginning to end—twice, when there was time—became the daily schedule. This was followed by an hour of notes from Bennett Jerome and Lehman Stern.

Rachel hadn't mentioned Drew Colton to Howard. Although her fears of the star's jealousy had faded, there remained something—an intangible warning—that sounded within her and caused her to withhold her trust from him. He exuded the charm, the magnetism, that all stars possessed. And Drew Colton *was* a star in every sense of the word. At first, Rachel hadn't understood her fascination with him; she could sense that he was attracted to her, but from his notorious reputation she knew he was attracted to *all* of his leading ladies and had usually taken them to bed by the end of a show's run. Rachel wasn't interested in a casual affair, so she had assumed that her own physical attraction to him was a subconscious carryover from their onstage romance.

But one day it dawned on her, during their love scene. Drew Colton was more rugged and taller, and not quite as blond. But he very strongly resembled Jamie. That could be dangerous.

Chapter Fourteen

April 1969

Friendships had formed within the company. Rachel's and Drew's behavior toward each other had been both polite and professional, despite discomfort whenever she glanced up and found him undressing her with his eyes. If he smiled, she blushed and looked away. So far, he had remained tentative and unaggressive during their love scenes. Rachel hoped it would stay that way.

Everyone in and out of show business knew of Drew Colton's reputation with women. It was not only well deserved but much publicized by a battery of press agents working long hours for that purpose. Just the month before, the demise of his affair with a famous older beauty had made headlines. Since then, other women, mostly actresses, had made attractive appendages.

In addition, Rachel learned that Drew was one of Howard's former clients. For two years he had appeared on a popular soap opera. However, his lack of discipline had presented a constant problem.

"Eventually," Howard told her, "I had to drop him."

"Are you sorry?" asked Rachel.

"Sorry?"

"I mean because he's a star now."

"Rachel," answered Howard, "Drew Colton was a star the day I met him. The fact that he can sing and act is only a plus. No, I'm not sorry. Fortunately for him, alcohol isn't one of his weaknesses — otherwise he might end up another

Zane Whitney." In the columns that morning were reports of Whitney's having missed three performances on the *Camelot* tour.

So it was with some reluctance—even fear—that Rachel accepted Drew Colton's invitation to lunch, even if he had said he wanted to discuss the show.

The sun was shining and despite the chill in the air, the streets seemed more crowded than they had been so far that winter.

"Where to?" he asked, taking her arm.

"Let's go to the Stage Deli," Rachel suggested for several reasons of her own. She had never eaten at the famous delicatessen, which was only two blocks away. Moreover, she knew it was always mobbed with people. There was "safety" in numbers.

"We can't," said Drew. "I didn't make reservations. Besides, we'll have no privacy."

Where he expected to find privacy at lunch hour in Midtown Manhattan was beyond Rachel, but she shrugged and said, "Okay, your move."

Taking it as a cue, his hand left her elbow and went around her shoulder. "I know just the place."

Ten minutes later they were being shown to a back booth in a little French bistro on Fifty-eighth Street. Though the place was hardly empty, there were a few vacant tables. A flurry of whispered exclamations followed the couple as Drew was instantly recognized.

They ordered immediately, and over her white wine, Rachel asked, "What's it like?"

"What?" he replied, sipping his beer.

"Fame."

Drew smiled. "You'll find out soon enough."

"Thanks for the vote of confidence, but—"

"Excuse me!" came a loud, adenoidal female voice.

They turned to see a portly matron in green paisley. The dress was too short and too tight, and its owner almost fell

205

onto their table. She held a napkin in her hand.

"Drew," she cooed, bringing her voice down by several octaves, "my daughter just thinks you're—oh, what does she say?—groovy! That's it! And she'd *kill* me if I didn't—"

Drew took the napkin from her. "Do you have a pen?"

"Oh! No, I—"

"Here," said Rachel, proffering her own. As Drew scrawled his name, the woman said, "Could you make that 'To Bellissima Ann'?"

"Bellissima Ann?" He and Rachel asked together.

"That's her *name,*" said the woman indignantly.

"Okay." Drew smiled and added the inscription.

Bellissima Ann's mother grabbed the napkin and stuffed it into her purse. Then she announced vehemently, "You know, Giacomo Pazaratti isn't any better!"

"No," he agreed quietly, color rising in his cheeks. "That's why I changed it. Maybe Bellissima will have the sense to do the same. *Ciao!*"

"Bellissima *Ann!*"

"Good-*bye,* lady!"

The woman turned and stormed off, while Drew sipped his beer and exhaled deeply. "*That's* what it's like," he said to Rachel.

"But you want it."

"Yes I do."

"And you're *really* Giacomo Pazaratti?" She couldn't hide the surprise in her voice.

He nodded. "And who are you—really?"

"The same. Rachel Allenby."

"Funny, somehow I believe you. Well, it sure beats the paisley lady's daughter."

"I suppose we *were* rude to her."

"Oh, Rachel, come on. *Bellissima Ann?*"

They both dissolved into laughter; tears filled Drew's eyes as he tried to stifle his guffaws. Through her own giggles, Rachel watched the corners of his dark eyes wrinkle as a lock of hair fell across his brow.

Eventually the laughter subsided and their food arrived. Drew raised his beer mug and clinked it against the edge of Rachel's wineglass. Taking her hand, he said, "Let's toast. To . . . to you . . . Bellissima . . ."

"Thanks . . . Giacomo."

The laughter started all over again.

For the run-throughs, Fiona and Bennett had suggested that Rachel begin accustoming herself to moving in a long, flowing dress and the tiny-heeled slippers designed for her. An old wraparound challis skirt was found for her to slip over her own rehearsal wardrobe of Levis and sweater. Shoes with an appropriate heel were provided, and while they were a size too tight, Rachel managed to squeeze her feet inside and then took her place for the start of Act Two.

The last scene of Act One was being rehearsed. She noticed that for the past two days, Drew had wisely chosen not to sing full-out, thereby saving his voice. He had the lion's share of music in the show, and Rachel knew that two run-throughs in one day at full voice could exhaust anyone's energy. She was grateful that Maid Marian was a small enough role to permit singing her song twice a day without greatly taxing her vocal instrument. Each of her rehearsals was done at performance level, which enabled her to sing the role "into her throat."

"Curtain!" Chuck yelled. "And we'll go right into Act Two, please! Set up for Act Two!"

Tape had been measured and placed on the floor of the large rehearsal room to mark the perimeter of the stage and the actual playing area. Within its boundaries, folding chairs, boxes, and tables were either removed or rearranged by the assistant stage manager and production assistant to simulate what and where the real set pieces would be. A small "flight of stairs" with only six steps on it represented the grand staircase from which Maid Marian would descend into the palace garden for her clandestine meeting with Robin Hood.

"Places!" shouted Chuck when all was ready. "Places for Act Two!"

Rachel climbed the six steps and faced stage left, where Sherwood Forest and the light from Robin's campfire would be. The music began, Chuck called "Lights up!" and after a count of ten, Rachel turned, lifted her long, heavy rehearsal skirt, and began pretending to descend the staircase. She was to stop midway on a musical cue, then Robin would enter below, and the action would be played not unlike that of the balcony scene from *Romeo and Juliet*. However, since there were only six steps in the rehearsal staircase, timing would have to wait until technical run-throughs began the following week, with the full sets and costumes, at the theater in Los Angeles. Rachel could hardly wait.

She and Drew—Marian and Robin—greeted each other, and she sang the first few bars of the song. Then, during an interlude in the music, she ran down the "staircase" and into his opened arms. A long embrace had been staged. But this time the kiss was different.

Instead of holding Rachel at a distance with his hands on her shoulders, Drew pulled her into him and folded his arms around her.

Rachel's hand was against his chest, and she could feel his heart pounding in her palm. Very slowly, he brought his slightly parted lips down softly upon hers as the music swelled. She felt a thrill dart through her, yet instinctively she felt herself fighting the sensation. She drew back, breaking the kiss and gasping for air.

Bennett, Lehman, and the rest of the cast were whooping and clapping at the moment's intensity. Rachel moved to make her rehearsed cross downstage left and begin the chorus of the song, but Drew kept her hand in his. Their palms were moist, their fingers entwined together as she sang.

The music came to an end, and the scene's dialogue continued until her exit up the staircase.

Bennett cried out, "Now *that's* a love scene! Wonderful! Leave it all in!"

Rachel looked down at Drew. He wore a wide smile across his face, and his eyes were boring into her.

Oh no! she thought.

She said nothing about it to Howard. Though trying to remain friendly with Drew, she accepted no further luncheon engagements with him. Certainly not because she wouldn't have enjoyed it; she might have enjoyed it too much. Robin and Marian had shared that kiss. It couldn't be—*mustn't* be—Drew Colton and Rachel.

Her birthday fell on a Friday. At the end of the rehearsal day, Chuck brought out a cake with ten candles on it, and champagne was uncorked as the entire cast sang "Happy Birthday" to her. Rachel was touched by the gesture. "But Chuck," she said, wiping away a tear, "how did you know?"

"When I collected the insurance forms, I jotted down everyone's birth dates—assuming that all of you told the truth!" The room resounded with laughter. "Hopefully," he added, "we'll all be together for a *long* time—long enough to celebrate everyone's birthday at least once!"

Drew came forward with a plastic glass of bubbling champagne and offered it to Rachel. "I was going to buy you something beautiful and expensive, but I figured you probably wouldn't accept it."

"You were right," she said, sipping. "But thank you, Drew."

"Well, I did get you . . . this . . . for your dressing room."

From behind his back he produced a mirrored, five-pointed star. At its center, in tiny, black-stenciled letters, was the name "Bellissima Ann Pazaratti."

"You *do* make me laugh!" she said.

"That, dear lady, is my fatal charm."

Rachel picked up the day's mail when she returned to the apartment. Howard wasn't home yet, which tonight pleased her. She hated to see him working late, but on this occasion it would give her the extra time needed to bathe and do her hair. They were going out to celebrate her birthday. He hadn't said where, but only "Dress to the nines."

She threw her coat over a chair and poured herself a glass of white wine before calling the answering service for messages. Then, wineglass in hand, she settled down on the sofa to sort the mail. Credit card bills, an invitation to a benefit performance, and . . . a letter addressed to Rachel and postmarked in the Bronx.

Trembling, Rachel opened the envelope. The plain white notebook paper was covered with a familiar, but shaky, hand. She read:

Dearest Rachel,

Since it's your birthday, I thought I'd write the apology I've owed you for some time. I've written to Paul as well. I'm trying to make amends to all the people I've hurt, especially you.

I've been staying with my folks for a while. I needed to get away, time to think, time to become whoever I really am. Hibernation doesn't seem to help, so maybe now that it's spring, I can come out of hiding. In the past, I've always felt a kind of rebirth in the spring. Last April we met. I still can't believe it's been only a year. So much has happened . . . for us both. We're such very different people now. Or are we, really?

Whoever these two new people are, maybe they can still love each other, accept each other, on each other's terms. Until then, I'll continue on my journey and borrow a lyric from a favorite song: "I'll remember April, and I'll smile."

Happy Birthday with love, Jamie.

Rachel sat motionless for a moment, her emotions warring. First came relief that Jamie was safe somewhere and that he cared, loved her. Then, a great sob from a place deep within her, accompanied by an aching loneliness. She missed him so much! He was right; they *were* different now, and though she could not regret the changes, she was sad for the way in which the changes had come about. She wept for what seemed to be their dying youth, an end to their mutual innocence. She cried for Jamie, and for Paul, and for herself, still unable to close the chapter of her unresolved feelings for Jamie, in spite of everything.

And she cried for Howard, who waited.

"You look—you are—magnificent," said Howard, as their waiter poured champagne.

"Thank you," Rachel answered, grateful that the puffiness around her eyes had subsided. She had forced herself to concentrate on her appearance for Howard's and her sake as well. The scoop neck of her teal blue silk dress accentuated the alabaster luster of her shoulders, and her hair fell in graceful waves around her shoulders. The only jewels she wore that evening were long earrings—rhinestones, to be sure, but they caught the glimmer of the single candle at the center of the table, and even diamonds could have offered little more.

She turned her head toward the window and looked out at the shimmering city, the glow of the streets some fifty stories below.

"What are you thinking?" Howard asked.

What could she say? The temptations presented by Drew Colton were bad enough; that they were a constant reminder of Jamie was worse. Even if she hadn't been physically unfaithful to Howard, in soul and mind, her fidelity was being tested. By Drew's behavior, by Jamie's letter.

At last she answered, "I'm thinking about the future, I guess." She reached across the table and took his hand.

"Not unusual. We all get a bit reflective on birthdays. And . . . so . . . ?"

"So?"

"What *of* the future?"

She shrugged. "No matter how hard we wonder about it, it's . . . just not ours to know." She sighed and shook her head, the chestnut waves forming a frame around her face. Then she grinned. "There, now wasn't *that* profound?"

"Rachel, what's the matter? You're not . . ." He stopped, seeming to rephrase his thoughts, and said instead, "There's something else on your mind."

She laughed ruefully. "You know, I never dreamed anyone would come to know me as well as you do, Howard."

"I feel as if I've hardly scratched the surface," he said.

"Oh, Howard, that's not true. You have."

"No." He shook his head. "If I had, you wouldn't be avoiding an answer to my question."

"What's on my mind, you mean?"

"Or *who* is. But I don't like assuming. I'd prefer to hear it from you."

"All right . . ." She took another sip of champagne. "I've heard from Jamie."

He was looking directly into her eyes. "You felt you had to keep that from me?"

She wasn't pleased, but she admitted it. "Yes. I . . . I did."

Howard continued to study her for a moment, then

212

brought his eyes down to gaze at the candle flame. "Oh, Rachel," he murmured, "it's sometimes so difficult . . . wondering when you'll comprehend."

"But I do," she insisted. "I understand."

"You don't. You say I know you so well, but if *you* knew *me*, even half as much, you'd know that keeping things sealed away inside isn't . . . necessary. I . . . I want you to open your heart to me, not close me out."

"But Howard — how can I be so cruel as to unburden myself to you about—"

"About someone you love? Rachel, I'm also your friend, not just your lover. It can never be complete without that."

From his pocket Howard withdrew a small black velvet box. "This is for you," he said. "If you'll excuse me, I'll be right back."

He rose from his seat and left the table.

"Howard—" she called softly after him.

But he didn't turn back.

"Are you coming to bed?" Rachel asked tentatively from the doorway of the den.

Howard sat in his silk robe before the cold, unlit fireplace.

"I'd like to sit here for a while."

"All right," she answered. Then, "Howard . . . don't be angry with me."

"I'm not, Rachel." He paused, and without looking up, said, "I love you." Almost abruptly, he added, "Unconditionally."

She felt she should go to him, but something stopped her. "I'm trying not to hurt you, Howard."

"Darling," he said, turning now to face her, "you listen . . . but you just don't hear me."

"Please, Howard . . . come to bed."

"In a few minutes. You go on."

213

Rachel walked slowly to the bedroom. On the dresser was the velvet box Howard had given her in the restaurant. She opened the lid and gazed once more at the tiny diamond pin fashioned into an arrow. *You are my Marian*, was written in his neat hand on the small card that had accompanied the gift. *Happy birthday, darling.*

He still hadn't come to bed by the time Rachel drifted into a fitful, restless sleep.

The company was ready to move to Los Angeles, and the following week was spent in preparation for the trip.

Final New York fittings were scheduled at the costume shop to ensure against future problems out West. Rehearsals were choreographed around physical demands incurred by a production leaving for "the road," even if it was to be a fully equipped theater in one of the nation's largest cities. It was not—yet—a *New York* show, and anywhere away from the Great White Way, no matter its size, was nonetheless deemed the road.

At the last rehearsal before the move, Rachel noticed that Drew, for the second time that day, had engaged Lehman in private conversation. Occasionally the star's eyes darted over toward Rachel, but the moment she looked up, he averted his gaze.

Lehman had seemed annoyed. When she asked about it later, Drew answered, "Just a little difference of musical opinion. We'll work it out in L.A." But he appeared as irritated as the conductor. Rachel decided not to pursue it further.

She wondered if the same would apply with Howard. He'd promised to fly out on weekends, but two days in seven would make "working it out" somewhat difficult.

They had made up—and made love—twice since her birthday the week before. If matters were still tenuous, at least their physical bond was more than intact.

He drove her to the airport and kissed her tenderly as the skycap loaded her luggage onto a cart.

"I'll say good-bye to you here," he said.

"You're not coming to the gate?" she asked, disappointed.

"I think not. Most of the cast will be there—and Lehman. We'd have even less privacy than now."

"I'll miss you, Howard."

"I'll be there on Saturday night." He kissed her again and got back into the cab. As it pulled away, he mouthed the words, "I love you."

Rachel had telephoned Jamie repeatedly before departing for the airport, but apparently he hadn't returned to his apartment from his parents' in the Bronx. She decided to try once more before boarding her flight.

The phone rang six times, more than enough time to reach the phone from anywhere in the apartment. Rachel was just hanging up when she heard his voice sleepily say, "Hello?"

"Jamie! I was afraid I was going to miss you altogether!"

"Where are you?" he asked.

"At JFK. I've tried for days—"

"Why . . . is something wrong?"

"No. I . . . I wanted—I'd hoped—to see you before I left."

"But you're at the airport," he said numbly.

"Yes. Listen . . . did I wake you?"

He yawned into the receiver. "I was lying down."

"Are you all right?" Rachel thought he sounded sedated. "Did you take something?"

"What's that supposed to mean? You think I'm on drugs?"

"No, of course not—"

"Look, Rachel, I hope the show is a big success. I just

don't feel like talking now."

"Jamie, I'm leaving for L.A. in ten minutes—I won't see you for a month—"

"Have a nice trip," he mumbled.

"Thanks," she said dryly. "It's nice to know you care."

"It isn't you," he said. "It's just . . ." His voice trailed off.

"Oh, Jamie." Rachel felt suddenly like a parent abandoning a lost child. "I wish I could help."

"Yeah," he replied. "I wish you could, too."

There seemed little else to say. Rachel hung up with a numbness of her own. Of all the varying forms and degrees of loneliness, she reflected, self-pity, made of passive choice, had to be by far the most damaging. But what could anyone do for Jamie unless he was ready to do something for himself?

She had seen Paul, so she knew part of Jamie's reason for depression. The tables had turned professionally, and where six short months ago Jamie had been the one with work and money coming in, now it was Rachel. "It isn't that he's jealous," explained Paul. "It's just that his inactivity gives him too much time to brood. He isn't going on auditions or making rounds. He sleeps all day so he can avoid facing reality."

"I thought he was looking for an agent."

"The last two who were interested came on to him. I think he's as disgusted with the whole business right now as he is with himself."

"I could ask Howard about—"

"I wouldn't," he interrupted. "That would only rub it in."

She sighed deeply. "Look, while I'm away, will you . . . keep an eye on him . . . for me?"

"For both of us," Paul answered sadly.

* * *

The drive from the airport into Los Angeles proper told Rachel little of what the City of Angels was like. That it sprawled *out* rather than *up* was all she could glean. Dusk had bathed the town in pink light, but it was a smoky, dusty pink, shrouded in smog.

Once arrived at the hotel, Rachel unpacked and then joined Lehman and Chuck for dinner in the restaurant downstairs. Drew was immediately whisked off to a television studio for a talk show taping to plug the tale of Sherwood Forest.

Rachel's call for the next morning was scheduled for nine-thirty, where she found Lehman, Bennett, and Drew in the lobby. The producers, in an uncharacteristic gesture, had "gone Hollywood"; a stretch limousine and driver were waiting to take them to the theater.

A new, heightened excitement was apparent in them all; this was the first day they would move *onstage*. In a week, preview performances would begin.

"Dear boy," said Lehman as the limo pulled away from the hotel's main entrance, "how did your taping go last night?"

"You mean you didn't tune in?" Drew returned.

"To be perfectly frank, no. Air travel exhausts me. I went to bed . . . alone, unfortunately"—here he laughed to the air—"I even missed the monologue."

Drew looked from Rachel to Bennett. They both shook their heads.

"You mean *none* of you watched me on TV last night?" He seemed stunned. At first, Rachel thought he was feigning his indignation, it was so melodramatic. But he slumped into the velvet seat, folded his arms, and stared out the tinted window without speaking another word for the remainder of the drive.

The ride continued in silence until the car turned off the freeway. Bennett leaned forward and said, "Driver, take us

217

to the lobby entrance instead of the stage door, please."

The driver nodded and Bennett explained, "I came by last night to have a look. The set is up and it's wonderful. I want you all to see it from the back of the house."

As always, a strange feeling crept over Rachel as she entered the theater. Perhaps the churchlike awe had not left her completely, she thought. Two thousand unoccupied seats inside the cavernous space produced an eerie effect. Somehow, its size, its emptiness, served as a reminder that Rachel and her peers were the ones responsible for bringing it all to life. As in the past, she was both humbled and exhilarated by it.

The proscenium curtain had been raised. The lights hadn't been set up on the grid, and the lamps that were mounted remained dark. Only a worklight with its bare bulb stood at the center of the stage.

What had been until this moment a twelve-inch cardboard model of the designer's vision now stood life-sized and majestic.

Even her more seasoned colleagues were obviously impressed.

Before them *was* Sherwood Forest.

"Oh, Bennett!" said Rachel in a hushed voice. "Wonderful is an understatement!"

Chapter Fifteen

Any thoughts of seeing the sights of Los Angeles were quickly forgotten once "hell week" got under way. When Rachel was not onstage rehearsing, last-minute nips and tucks were being taken to ensure her costume's perfect fit. It was even more stunning than in the original sketches, but she had not rehearsed with a six-foot train trailing behind her. Her new satin slippers, which had replaced the too-tight pair in New York, were a size too large. For the first time she was working with the two-foot-high pointed hat that matched her blue velvet gown. The "dunce cap" was promptly knocked from her head by the rose trellis surrounding her entrance "door." With her first cue only seconds away, a light had to be reset. Or the electric carriage conveying the palace unit jammed. Constant delays postponed her entrance, often for five minutes, sometimes for an hour.

Rachel's "free" time, whatever was left after the arduous hours spent in rehearsal, was filled with newspaper interviews arranged by the company's publicity man. However, since she was on call for ten of every twelve hours each day, those interviews took place in her dressing room or out in the last row of audience seats at the back of the house.

Each night she returned to the hotel exhausted. Run-throughs with full orchestra had begun, and although she was at ease under Lehman's able conducting, it still seemed that her song was being taken too fast—certainly faster than they had rehearsed it with piano in New York.

On the third day, Drew appeared onstage in costume for

the first time. Predictably, he was dressed in various shades of green, with matching tights and brown suede ankle boots. The "picture" had been designed to accentuate his ample masculine endowments, and he definitely fulfilled the physical requirements of a matinee idol.

He and Rachel hadn't seen much of each other, except for their onstage scene together. During a long rehearsal involving all of Robin's men—but not Robin himself—Rachel suddenly found him approaching her aisle seat halfway back in the house.

"Hi," he said cheerfully.

"Hi," she returned.

"Listen, can I ask you a favor?"

"Sure."

"I'm a little shaky on the new dialogue for our scene. Would you mind running lines with me?"

"I'd be glad to. I can use the practice myself."

"Great. But let's work in the lobby, okay? I'd like to go over the blocking while we're at it."

"Fine," she said, although she couldn't understand the necessity of walking through the stage moves and crosses; they hadn't changed.

On the way up the aisle, Drew said quietly, "I guess I'm a little nervous. . . . I'm the 'title role' now, you know."

"Oh? They've changed your name to Nottingham?" she joked.

He laughed. "No . . . I just found out. They've changed the name of the show. They think *Robin Hood* will sell better."

"They're probably right," she said.

They decided to use the foot of the mezzanine staircase to run the scene. Rachel walked to the top and began miming the lyrics to the first part of her song, then ran down the stairs and into his arms.

Since the afternoon weeks ago when the love scene had taken on such intensity, Rachel had come to expect Drew's reaction. It hadn't changed since then. The effect upon her was no longer quite as unnerving, since it was no longer new; still, she had retained a slight giddiness at the touch of his arms and lips.

But it had never been like this. Perhaps it was because no one was watching, no one could hear. The dim glow of the lobby was more intimate than the glare of overhead fluorescents in a rehearsal room or the flood of lights on the stage.

Drew pulled her against his body with uncommon force and immediately crushed his lips on hers in a hungry embrace. His mouth opened, his tongue searching, and she was filled with his breath. Rachel felt a familiar dizziness as his pelvis pressed into her. Involuntarily, her mouth opened to his kiss. Her legs weakened and she stumbled, but recovered and threw her arms around his neck. As his arms tightened around her, she gave in to the sensations swirling through her. Warm waves traveled upward to the spot at which his now-full erection kneaded her.

With little remaining strength, Rachel pushed him away and turned toward the wall.

He was coaxing her back to him.

"No, Drew—stop it!" she whispered breathlessly. "Please. No more!"

He was standing behind her. "You like it," he said hoarsely. "And I like it. Why not?"

"Drew . . . please!"

"I repeat . . . why not?" He spun her around and looked into her eyes. From the stage inside the theater the men's chorus was singing about "following Robin into the fray." It struck Rachel as ridiculous, under the contrasting circumstances, and she was helpless to resist a smile.

"Because," she answered at last, "I'm living with your former agent, and you know it."

"He's not here, is he?"

"He will be. This weekend. And that's beside the point. No."

Drew smiled too and, backing up several paces, pulled his tunic toward his knees. "It's a good thing I've got this to cover what my tights won't hide."

Rachel laughed. "Listen . . . do you still want to run lines?"

"Over dinner tonight?"

"Drew . . ."

"Please?"

"No."

"I swear, no hanky-panky. Just dinner. Talk. About the show. Music. Your song."

"My song?"

"If you don't mind. I've got some ideas that would help make the scene stronger. It's the best song in the show. It deserves all we can give it."

"Like what?"

"Have dinner with me?"

She hesitated, then said, "Oh, all right."

There was a two-hour break for dinner, after which the company was called again; evening rehearsals began at seven.

Rachel had agreed to meet Drew in the hotel restaurant at five forty-five. Half an hour before that, she entered her room and, as she had every night since her arrival, called Howard in New York.

Speaking with him this evening had only heightened her anxiety. She tried to find excuses to keep him on the phone, even after they had exchanged mutual news. Rachel sensed that he was tired, and he had a long day ahead, starting with a five o'clock drive the next morning to Long Island, where a client was making in a movie. They discussed the producers' decision to rename the show *Robin Hood,* Rachel told him about her interviews, and there was nothing more to say.

"I miss you," she said.

"I'll see you on Saturday," he replied.

She had expected him to add that he missed her, too.

Rachel washed her face and applied a touch of makeup. She was buttoning a fresh blouse when there was a knock at the door. Glancing at her wristwatch, she saw that it was five thirty-five. Annoyed, she reached for the knob and said, "Drew, I told you—"

But it was Lehman Stern. His thin face wore a worried expression.

"May I come in? I'll not keep you." He took a seat on the sofa and crossed his long legs. "You're having dinner with Drew, I understand?"

She nodded. "But how did you—?"

"He told me. In fact, he bragged about it."

"Lehman, it's only dinner." She thought for a moment and then added, "There isn't *time* for anything *else!*"

"Darling, the 'anything else' is neither my business nor my concern. Just look out."

She was suddenly confused. "For whom? Drew?"

The conductor smiled as his face colored. "Of *course* Drew. Did you think I came here in a jealous rage?"

"Forgive me," she said, smiling. "I didn't know what else you could mean. I *am* aware of his reputation, Lehman. And I'm a big girl."

"Your potentially broken heart isn't what I'm talking about either. You don't know everything about Drew's reputation."

"Meaning?"

"I may be wrong," he said, shrugging. "Still, Bennett feels as I do. Drew has said things . . . to both of us . . . that have us on guard. You'd do well to follow suit."

"What has he said? What 'things'?"

"Suggestions. Regarding you."

She paused. "And my song."

"Then he *has* mentioned it to you?"

"In passing. We're talking it out tonight."

Lehman sighed and lit a cigarette. "Excuse me, darling, but I *must* smoke. Perhaps I'm being an old-maid gossip about all this . . . but believe me . . . Drew is up to no good."

In the elevator on her way to the lobby, Rachel reflected over her conversation with Lehman. He had finished his cigarette and left, without supplying more specific information.

She considered telephoning Howard again, but he had to be up so early the next day, and the three-hour time difference meant that although it was only nine o'clock in New York, causing him needless worry might keep him from a good night's sleep.

She entered the restaurant, where Drew was seated, waiting for her. "Right on time," he said, rising from his chair.

"Good. I was afraid that I'd be late."

The waiter arrived and was advised that they were in a hurry. White wine and beer appeared almost instantly.

When Drew took her left hand, Rachel felt her pulse quicken again. She smiled and covered the sensation.

"You look beautiful," he said.

"Thanks . . . flatterer . . . I needed that. I'm exhausted."

"I said you're beautiful." His hand squeezed hers. With her free hand she sipped her wine.

"What did you want to talk about?" she asked.

"First the show. Then us. Later. Tonight."

Rachel removed her hand from his with some difficulty. "First things first."

"Okay." Drew took a deep breath, a swig of beer, and another breath. "Think of Marian's bedroom light in the palace."

It wasn't what she had expected. "All right . . ."

"Now," he continued in a low, intimate voice, "think of

224

Robin, alone and missing Marian. In the forest. Seeing that light, knowing she's there."

Slowly, Rachel felt a sinking in her stomach. No, she thought. Don't jump to conclusions. Hear him out. Still, she said, "You mean . . . in the same way that *Marian* sees *Robin's* campfire light in the forest *from* the palace—the way it is *now?*"

"Well . . . yes . . . sort of," he answered, his rhythm faltering slightly. "But the dramatic power, the impact on the audience—from *his* point of view—would be really heightened. You see what I mean?"

Rachel sat back in her chair as dinner arrived. When the waiter was out of earshot, she said, "I think I'm just beginning to, Drew. Go on."

"That's all, really. I think my slant on it helps the show and underscores both of our characters."

"Excuse me," she said, leaning in closely and placing her chin on her hand, "but then the song would be sung in the Sherwood Forest set?"

"Yes," he answered innocently.

"How does that strengthen *my* character?"

"By keeping the audience guessing what you're like," he said easily.

"Drew . . . you mean . . . I don't appear onstage?"

"Of course you do. Robin's wish is fulfilled at the end of the song as you run through the trees to him."

Am I really hearing this? she wondered. She felt a cold tingle at the base of her spine as her shoulder muscles and neck began tensing.

"And the palace set?" she asked. "My scene? My *only* scene?"

"Well . . . let's try to keep our egos out of the way. We're trying to make the show better."

Rachel removed the napkin from her lap and threw it on the table. "Let me make sure I understand you. The show gets better by *your* singing 'My Light Through the Trees'?"

225

He nodded. "Don't you agree?"

"No, Drew," she said flatly, trying to contain her fury. "I can't."

"You don't understand. But you will. Tonight."

"Oh, I understand plenty right *now!*" She leaned across the table and whispered, "All this . . . this coming on to me . . . this so-called seduction attempt. It was all to get my song."

"How can you think so little of me? Of yourself?" In his best leading-man voice, he murmured, "I *want* you, Rachel."

"Oh, please! You *want* my *song.* You were just hoping to get laid in the bargain!"

"That's not —"

"Go to hell," she said, and without having touched her dinner, she left the restaurant.

She felt like a fool, but it all made sense. Horrible sense. Rachel then remembered the expression on Drew's face when she had sung the song at the first rehearsal in New York. It had been on his mind from the start.

Lehman had been right. For the second time, his advice had helped her. Before her entrance at the top of Act Two that evening, she thanked him.

"I'm sorry to have been *so* correct," he replied.

Now in place at the head of the high staircase, Marian turned to Robin as he called her from below. The music began and she started down the steps, her six-foot train trailing behind her. She stopped on the musical cue, began her dialogue, then ran down the rest of the stairs and into Robin's waiting arms.

Drew held her closely, fiercely, and once again started the exploration of her mouth with his tongue.

She bit it. Very hard.

As Drew cried out and ran from the stage, Rachel peered

out into the orchestra pit. Only Lehman and Bennett understood what had happened. They were both laughing.

"Take ten, everyone!" called Bennett.

Rachel headed for her dressing room and a candy bar, since she hadn't eaten her dinner. As she passed Drew's door, she heard a whimpering moan from within. She grinned at the knowledge that only Marian's onstage relationship with Robin was real.

But for Rachel, the man professionally named Drew Colton had, from that moment, ceased to exist.

Chapter Sixteen

It seemed forever before Howard arrived. In actuality, it was only days, and he was in Los Angeles in time for the first complete dress rehearsal of *Robin Hood*. He and Rachel hadn't found a moment to steal more than a quick kiss in her dressing room. Then they had hurried into the auditorium to watch Act One from out front. Rachel wasn't required backstage until the break before Act Two.

Butterflies were beginning to form in her stomach. Knowing Howard was seated beside her in the darkness helped to calm the nerves that had increased as the opening grew nearer. Sunday would be the tenth day of twelve. Monday she'd really need the rest. Whether they would be called to rehearse Tuesday morning depended on how smoothly the show ran tonight and tomorrow. Tuesday night was the first performance for paying customers. Preview week: the time for setting the pace, holding for applause, for laughs. Hopefully, by next week's end, the show would be in shape for its official opening, when ticket prices soared to top dollar and critics came to pass judgment. On the production. On Rachel.

Drew Colton and Howard were politely civil to each other, but no more than that. Rachel wondered what exactly Drew's "discipline problem" as Howard's client had been. Howard wasn't given to rash statements. Nor was he the type of agent to suddenly drop a client from his roster. Could it have had anything to do with Cecily? she wondered. Too, she had thought about his attempts—both to sabotage her song and to seduce her. The latter ploy was

228

easier to comprehend. But how could he feel any competition with her? Never mind that he was the star—the title role, as he'd said—but he was a *man*. How on earth could an actor playing Robin Hood be jealous of an actress playing Marian? Gloria Doro's behavior—in the light of Drew Colton's—was more understandable. Well, she mused, not quite *understandable*. . . .

The lights dimmed and the "dress" began. Rachel put her arm through Howard's and tried to relax.

By any definition, it was a disaster. From the opening curtain, things seemed to go awry. Robin Hood made his entrance swinging through the trees upstage center; Friar Tuck was two feet off his mark and was knocked flat by Drew Colton's flying feet. The felled actor wasn't hurt, but his burlap habit was badly ripped. In the audience, behind the eight-foot wooden board laid across the top of seats in front of them, the heads of production were all bent over their yellow legal pads and hastily scratching notes. Squinting under the single small table lamp at the center, Bennett and Larry Dule, the technical director, puffed on cigarettes and guzzled coffee while they wrote.

So far, choreography and lights had escaped mishap, but the moment two dancers bumped into each other and a bank of lamps began flickering on and off for no apparent reason, Anita and Walt Channing, the lighting director, grabbed their pencils and began scribbling. Then the actor playing the sheriff of Nottingham forgot to sing a line in his scene with Prince John; the latter was almost a full minute late for an entrance and finally appeared half-dressed and only half-buttoned. Fiona leaned over to Chuck. "I told Carol to change all of his buttons to oversized snaps. Ask her what happened."

Chuck spoke into the mouthpiece of his headphones, which put him in speaking contact with both the lighting booth and the backstage area. He called the name of the assistant stage manager and said, "Put Carol on headphones, please."

Then he listened, after which he turned to Fiona and answered, "Carol says Drew wanted his shirt washed and pressed for tonight, so she didn't have time to do the snaps."

"Tell her to tell Drew that laundry night is tomorrow and Wednesday," Fiona announced at top volume. "No exceptions! And get those snaps sewn in!"

"I think she heard you," said Chuck.

In Act Two, Rachel's six-foot train caught on a nail in the stair unit, thus making further movement impossible. But without missing a beat of music or a line of dialogue, she walked back up the steps, disengaged the fabric, and continued with the scene.

She approached Robin in character, so while Marian hungered for his kiss, Rachel remained wary. She knew Howard was watching, although she was sure he hadn't heard of the tongue-biting incident. *She* certainly hadn't told him. Her fear was that Drew might retaliate.

As he took her in his arms, she fought the revulsion rising inside her. I am Marian, she told herself. He is Robin.

The kiss was executed as it had been staged. No tongues. Rachel finished her song and climbed the steps as the lights dimmed to a slow fade. She was relieved, glad it was over, as she reached her mark at the top of the staircase. The only illumination onstage was a "baby pin-spot" encasing her face.

The remainder of Act Two proceeded without serious incident, although hardly without mistakes. It was quite late when Bennett, Fiona, Lehman, and Anita finished giving their notes to the cast and crew.

"Bad dress, good opening," Chuck said dejectedly to Rachel as she and Howard were leaving the theater.

"There's still another dress tomorrow night, Chuck," Howard offered with encouragement. "It'll come together. Don't worry. It always does."

* * *

Rachel and Howard had barely closed the hotel room door before they began undressing each other. They made love with voracious appetites, inspired by the week's separation and performance energy. Rachel was silently grateful that all thoughts of temptation were gone; she gave herself to their lovemaking with a wish to satisfy Howard totally; it was genuine, not born of any need to assuage guilt or remorse.

In the middle of the night, they awoke and laughed in the dark over the mishaps incurred during the dress rehearsal. She was able to laugh because she was growing confident of her work in the show.

The company had not been dismissed until almost 1 A.M., so, in accordance with Equity rules, they could not be called to rehearse before noon. During the afternoon, all of the trouble spots were run and rerun, polished and perfected, in the hope that by that evening's dress rehearsal all hitches would be eliminated.

When Howard and Rachel returned from the dinner break, the poster bearing the new title had been set inside the glass showcase out front. DREW COLTON IS ROBIN HOOD! it boasted in glowing green letters.

"That's driving the budget up, I daresay," Howard commented.

"Expensive?" asked Rachel as they passed through the lobby.

"Indeed. Title change in newspaper advertising, reprinting of programs. Still, it's a wise move." He put his arm around her waist. "You know, in case I haven't said so already, you're wonderful."

When they entered the theater, the wooden production table was gone, and Rachel felt the tingling sensation in her stomach once more. Tonight's final dress run-through wouldn't stop—couldn't stop—for any mishaps. Tonight was a performance. The single missing ingredient was the audience. She gripped Howard's hand.

"What is it?" he asked.

"I won't be able to sit with you out front tonight. I have to stay backstage for the whole show."

"I can stay with you in your dressing room, then go out front for Act Two."

"No," she said, smiling. "Later on, yes, please. But I want you to see the show tonight from beginning to end."

They kissed, and she ran down the aisle to the backstage entrance.

Beyond a complaint about too much backstage noise, the dress rehearsal went off, in Chuck's words, "without a hitch." When Howard left for New York on Tuesday morning, Rachel faced the coming week of previews with renewed strength and confidence.

She called him after the first preview.

"Hello, darling," he said. "You're back early, aren't you?"

"Early?" She laughed. "It's three in the morning in New York—I was certain I'd wake you!"

"I've been waiting for you to ring, but I thought you'd be much later. Why aren't you out celebrating?"

"We're all exhausted. Some of us dropped by Bennett's room for a drink, but we're saving the partying for you and the official opening night."

"You sound good. It went well?"

"Oh, Howard . . . the audience yelled *brava* when I made my exit!"

The cheers continued at every performance, including the matinees.

By week's end, word of mouth had spread the news around town: *Robin Hood* was a smash—and the actress-singer playing Marian was a real "find."

Howard flew back to Los Angeles on Saturday and stayed in Rachel's dressing room through Act One on that night and Sunday. Opening night, the following Tuesday,

...d before they knew it.

The change in the atmosphere backstage was palpable. Thirty minutes till curtain; the time seemed insufficient, even if Rachel's entrance wasn't for another hour and a half.

She checked her name on the company callboard, then took Howard's arm. "Look," she said, pointing to a large notice pinned to the cork board. It was the announcement of the party after the show—a lifetime from now.

Howard joined her in the dressing room, but tonight she again insisted that he stay out front from the start. "I want you to eavesdrop," said Rachel. "I want to know what they *really* think."

He smiled and drew her to him.

When she closed the door to her dressing room, Rachel surveyed the five enormous bouquets of flowers crammed onto the table. One was from Howard, another from her parents, one each from Lehman and Bennett. And one from Paul.

She tucked the telegrams from Beth Burns and Norma into the framing around her mirror and moved the flowers away from the heat generated by the border of bare bulbs. The third telegram was from Jamie. It read: "I'll be there with you." Rachel drew a deep breath and put the message in her purse.

She had finished applying her Pan Cake and was beginning to do her eyes when the "squawk box" came alive with sound. Chuck's voice said, "Five minutes, ladies and gentlemen. Five minutes, please."

The sounds of the unseen audience could be heard through the speaker; two thousand people taking their seats, talking, laughing, coughing, turning the pages of their programs, the activities blending to create a constant rush of white noise.

Rachel's costume hung on the rack behind her, but she

233

would wait until intermission before stepping into it. palms and underarms tingled with excitement and perspiration, and she wanted Fiona's spectacular creation to remain as fresh as possible for her entrance.

She carefully lined her eyelids and added shadow. She had glued on the thick eyelashes before coming to the theater to ensure a steadier hand. Now she leaned back in the chair and smiled at her reflection. Tonight could be a dream come true — or an embarrassment. She envied the actors who went on at the top of the show. Sitting it out until Act Two was sheer agony. But nerves must not hinder you, she reminded the image in the mirror. You must channel them into energy! She began to concentrate, first with deep breathing, then with stilling her mind and all the little demon voices that tried to plague her during the long wait.

"Here we go, kiddies!" Chuck announced quietly. "Places! Places, ladies and gentlemen, for Act One of *Robin Hood* — and knock 'em dead!"

For two full minutes there was nothing but the static white noise again. Then, a drum roll began. Slowly, softly, building in speed and volume until it peaked and the orchestra joined in. The overture had begun.

The show unfolded, its story and music so familiar to her now. Over the squawk box it seemed like a radio play. The audience laughed and gasped. To Rachel's delight, they even hissed the villains, Prince John and the sheriff of Nottingham. Things were going well.

Intermission came. Carol knocked at the door to help Rachel into her costume. Chuck gave the five-minute call just as the high, pointed hat was balanced and fastened to Rachel's hair. "Break a leg," said Carol.

Rachel powdered down her makeup once more and left the safety of her dressing room with minutes to spare.

She stopped at the edge of the proscenium near the stage manager's desk. Giving in to temptation, she peeked through the tiny eyehole in the curtain and peered out into the house.

Immediately, she knew it was a mistake.

At the back of the theater, she could see the lobby lights blinking on and off, signaling the audience to take their seats for Act Two. Down the aisle the patrons came, tuxedoed, gowned, jeweled. But this was not just a well-dressed crowd.

This was an opening-night audience that included some of the most famous and beautiful faces in the world. The heavyset man in row two Rachel recognized as Orson Welles. Three rows behind him, Richard Burton whispered to a stunning Elizabeth Taylor, while Natalie Wood laughed at something said by Robert Wagner. Everywhere Rachel looked, the glittering stars were clustered in what appeared to be a meeting of the most exclusive of clubs, the elite of Hollywood royalty.

She searched among them for Howard, but she had forgotten to check the row and seat number on his comp ticket. A glimpse of him now would soothe her rising nerves. But he was impossible to find.

Rachel's hands began to shake and she turned quickly away from the curtain.

"Places," Chuck said, squeezing her hand as he spoke into his headset.

Rachel took three profound breaths and climbed the back steps of the staircase unit. Passing through the archway, she took her position to the left of the flowered trellis.

The stairs leading down to the stage suddenly seemed steeper, narrower than before. The bodice of her velvet gown felt too tight; how would she breathe for those long phrases in the song? And her heart was racing at breakneck speed.

The music began and the stage lights came up. The curtain that separated reality from fantasy slowly rose to reveal Maid Marian in her palace garden. It was up to Rachel to give her life.

* * *

Twenty minutes later, Rachel retraced her measured steps and turned, singing the last phrase of her song with a fullness of voice and feeling. The final, ethereal note drifted up and out into the house on a cushion of the orchestra's voluptuous sound. Rachel was lost in the lyric, in the moment. With tears in her eyes, she raised a hand in farewell to Robin, and the lights faded.

The theater erupted into pandemonium. A wall of noise and energy, which she could *feel* as well as hear, forced her back half a step. The audience was cheering wildly, their voices and hands raised in overwhelming agreement. Approval.

Love.

The ovation came once more, twice as vociferously, during her curtain call at the end of the show. The audience was now on its feet. The crème de la crème of Hollywood itself was yelling, stomping, some were even whistling. From the side boxes, people were tossing flowers and calling, "*Brava*, Marian!" As she bowed repeatedly, Rachel suddenly realized that the clapping was coming from *behind* her as well as out front. She turned to find the entire cast applauding her. Her heart swelled and her throat closed. She nodded in acknowledgment and then bowed again, this time to the balconies.

As she lowered her head, she spotted Howard, at last, in the middle of the fourth row. He, too, was on his feet and applauding. Their eyes met and he mouthed the words, "*Brava!* I love you!"

Rachel took her final and deepest bow directly to him.

Now the remaining well-wishers had exited her dressing room, and there was quiet. She seated herself at the makeup table and gazed at Howard's reflection in the mirror. He put his hands on her shoulders and massaged gently. Rachel leaned back, enjoying the sensation, and felt

236

his lips as they kissed the base of her neck.

"Tired?" he asked.

"I should be, shouldn't I?" She looked up at him and smiled. "But you know . . . I'm *not* tired. I'm thrilled and excited and . . . oh, Howard, I'm so happy!"

"No more than you deserve to be . . . and it's only the beginning. You were magnificent, my love."

"Thank you . . ."

"But there's something else you should be feeling, in addition to happiness."

"What's that?" she asked.

"Pride. I don't consider it a deadly sin."

She laughed. "I don't either. And . . . I guess I *am* proud, too. I think I sang well."

"And *acted* well." He grinned broadly. "I love being right."

"About what?"

"You. You're marvelous. And you're going to be a great star." They kissed again. "Now," he said, changing the mood, "you'd better dress. I'll wait at the stage entrance." He moved toward the door, but before turning the knob, he added, "I left a box beside the flowers. Open it and wear what's inside to the party."

Rachel had scrubbed her face and reapplied her own makeup. She slipped into the flowing blue silk gown and piled her damp waves high on her head. Then she put on the earrings that she had found inside the small Cartier box that Howard had brought all the way from New York. She had gasped upon first sight of the long, thin row of rubies and diamonds, so long that they almost touched her shoulders. They accentuated her swanlike ivory neck, while the dazzling jewels trapped prisms of light and sent shooting sparks of color to her aristocratic jawline.

Wrapping the three yards of teal blue ostrich feathers around her as a stole, she reached for her matching teal

237

blue beaded clutch purse. Then she surveyed the image in the mirror and beamed. She looked terrific and she knew it.

More applause greeted Rachel as she and Howard entered the ballroom of the hotel. The sextet of musicians engaged for the opening night festivities broke into Marian's song, while the bejeweled guests stood clapping as she strode to the table.

The caterer had planned the seating arrangements with discretion; Drew Colton had been placed at the table *next* to Rachel's, not at the same one. But Lehman sat across from her and took her hand. "At the risk of plagiarizing . . . a star is born."

Before she could answer, Chuck popped a champagne cork. "We were saving this for your arrival!"

He poured, and they toasted her. It was only the first of the night. Champagne began to flow at every table.

Five television sets had been mounted high above in order to be visible from anywhere in the ballroom. At eleven o'clock, the music stopped and the small screens came to life. The late-evening news was on. Couples returned from the dance floor to their tables, and voices hushed as the broadcast reviews began.

"*Robin Hood* opened tonight in Los Angeles before its journey to a New York run—and run it *will*," the first critic said. "A big, colorful, bouncy show with great songs and a swashbuckling title performance from Drew Colton. But the surprise of the evening comes in Act Two, with the appearance of newcomer Rachel Allenby. Her Maid Marian is a skillful, beautifully wrought performance that strikes a perfect balance between innocence and passion. Her voice has been touched by the Muse. It's a shimmering sound, enhanced by glorious phrasing. If audience reaction is any gauge, this critic isn't going out on a limb in saying that here is a talent destined for stardom."

War whoops resounded from the assembled crowd as the

next critic on the next station echoed the first. Within the hour, Wednesday's morning papers were delivered. Harold Beckman, the producer, rose to a microphone to read the reviews aloud. "More of the same!" he cried.

The critics seemed to be vying to outdo each other in a search to extoll the virtues of Rachel's performance. She sat quietly, tears welling at her eyes, as she listened to rave after rave. "Brilliant!" "Luminous!" "Radiant!" were but a few of the adjectives used.

Howard's arm was around Rachel as she glanced at the vast ballroom and the sea of faces smiling at her. She thought back to the moment just before Act Two, when she had peered at this same crowd from the peephole in the curtain. Only a few hours ago, she had felt like a Christian about to be fed to the lions. But she had not been torn asunder. She had been triumphant. A victor. I was right, she reflected. This *is* a kind of exclusive club. A royalty of sorts.

A chill swept through her, then, at the sudden realization: They were telling *Rachel* that she was one of them— that *she* belonged!

Chapter Seventeen

June 1969

Rachel's dressing room in New York was filled with flowers. She had received countless telegrams, phone calls, cards, and letters. The local papers in Excelsior had run feature stories as former classmates formed a line to "share the secrets"—Rachel laughed aloud at this; she had *never* confided a single secret to any classmate because she hadn't felt she was one of them.

"This is crazy!" she exclaimed as she leafed through all the clippings her mother had sent.

"That's nothing," said Howard. "If the show's as big a hit here as it was in L.A., it'll just be the beginning."

"I hope you're right," she answered. "Now, if I can just stop my knees from shaking . . ."

He kissed her lightly so he wouldn't disturb her makeup and said, "I'll go and greet the press. You'll be theirs at the party. Break a leg, my love."

The entire cast was assembled at Sardi's in typical Broadway tradition. There was abundant food and drink, but most of the guests were too anxious for the reviews to partake of the former. Champagne flowed, and an atmosphere of celebration was everywhere; even before the papers made it official, everyone knew that *Robin Hood* had scored a hit.

Jamie hadn't come backstage, although Rachel had

240

glimpsed him among the throng and confusion. Now she spotted him off to one side, a cigarette hanging from his mouth. Since when, Rachel wondered, had he begun to smoke?

She made her way to him. "There you are! Did you ever see such a mob?"

"I recall a night at the Astor Hotel," he said. "But on that particular occasion, you and I were both eager to get away from all the racket and the phoniness."

"God," she said. "It wasn't so long ago, was it?"

"A year and a half. As they say, so near and yet so far."

"Did you enjoy the show?" she asked, wondering if Jamie's subtext was his invention or her imagination.

"Sure," he answered. "You were terrific. Thanks for the ticket." But he had spoken with almost no inflection.

"I'm glad you came tonight, Jamie."

He stubbed the cigarette—which he had hardly smoked at all—into the ashtray on the table beside them.

When he said nothing, Rachel asked, "How have you been? I . . . I thought about you while we were in L.A. I'm sorry you weren't there."

"I'd have thought you were too busy with your show to think about anyone."

"Jamie," she said cautiously, "I'd . . . be happy for you . . . if this were your opening night."

"Well, it *isn't* mine, is it?" A waiter passed, and Jamie accepted a glass of champagne. From his speech it obviously wasn't his first of the night.

"Jamie." Rachel spoke his name as she reached out to squeeze his hand. She sensed that he had recoiled slightly from her touch. "You've . . . you've changed," she said.

"We've all changed," he said flatly, draining his glass.

Now Howard appeared at Rachel's side. "Hello, Jamie," he said, extending his hand in greeting.

"Well," said Jamie. "Congratulations." He looked from Howard to Rachel. "To both of you." Then he put down his empty glass and disappeared into the crowd.

241

Rumors predicted that Rachel would win the New York Drama Critics and the Drama Desk awards for Best Supporting Actress. The Tonys would have to wait until next year; *Robin Hood* had opened three weeks after the awards. She was featured in *Time* and *Newsweek,* both of which amazed her. "I thought only famous people got in those magazines!" she exclaimed to Howard.

"And people on their way to becoming famous. Enjoy it."

Norma was collecting so much mail that she had to hire a temp assistant just to handle Rachel's correspondence. There was an unfamiliar face at Howard's office on Monday of the following week. A *temp* wearing designer clothes? Rachel wondered. What agency had Norma called?

But the woman wasn't a "temp." Her name was Mina MacDonald, and she was a publicist. Rachel liked her firm handshake and her innate self-confidence.

"But," she whispered to Howard when they were alone, "do I really need someone to publicize me? Aren't the reviews — and those blurbs in the magazines — enough?"

"Blurbs, as you put it, darling, don't lead anywhere beyond New York."

"But this is Broadway — where else can it lead?"

Howard was holding an unlit cigarette; he had finally stopped smoking altogether in Los Angeles, but every once in a while he still liked to hold a cigarette as others might hold a pen or pencil. "Rachel. You know there's talk about a film version of the show."

"Oh, yes, but you've always said it's only talk until it's in writing."

"That's my point. Mina is going to make certain that your name is very much alive when that film talk firms up into writing. Otherwise, when studio bosses return from their summer vacations, you'll be old news — someone who's appearing in a hit Broadway show that's been running since June. By September, there'll be new shows opening. New news. See?"

She saw, but still felt uneasy about *paying* to have her name in the papers. And she believed only half of what she read.

But she believed all of what she read when she saw the next morning's paper. Howard was a devotee of the *Times*—both the New York paper and its London namesake, although he never read them thoroughly until the weekend, unless a client was opening midweek in a show. Rachel, instead, made a habit of leafing through the *Daily Mirror,* usually over her late-morning coffee.

And it was on the front page of the *Mirror* that the full-page photograph of Jamie appeared. He and two other young men had been captured—by the camera and by two policemen—as they tried to kick themselves free of the lawmen's grasp. Above the picture was the banner, in two-inch-high letters: HOMO BAR RAID—RIOT AND ARRESTS. In smaller letters: *Full story on page 5*.

Rachel tried to blink away a sudden nausea. She'd made a mistake—that couldn't be Jamie! But her brain hammered away until she finally accepted what she had seen.

Jamie was front-page news.

Frantically, Rachel tore through the paper until she came to page 5 and the "full story." The police had raided a homosexual bar called the Stonewall on Christopher Street in Greenwich Village. She knew the place—she'd walked past there dozens of times on her way to Sheridan Square!

Howard had gone to the office at ten. By the time Rachel had calmed her shaking hands sufficiently to dial the phone, he had just left.

"He's having lunch with Alan Jay Lerner," said Norma. "I can try to reach him if it's important."

Rachel was trying not to hyperventilate.

"Honey, is everything all right?" asked the secretary.

Gasping between breaths, Rachel told Norma about the headline. "What can I do?" And then tears choked off her voice.

"Sweetie, did you call the police? The precinct station?"

Rachel hadn't thought of that.

"Let me do it for you and I'll call you back," offered Norma. "You go take a Valium and try to relax."

There were no tranquilizers in Howard's medicine cabinet, so Rachel poured herself three fingers of Chivas Regal. She shuddered as the liquid hit her empty stomach. But its numbing effect allowed her to think.

The phone rang within minutes. "They've released your friend," said Norma. "On recognizance."

"On what? Is that like bail?"

"It means they're trusting him to show up when they tell him to. He left a number in the Bronx, but that's all I could get out of them."

"The Bronx," repeated Rachel. "His . . . his parents." But she knew that Jamie wouldn't go to his parents. Not after something like this. "Norma . . . thanks. Let me try to call him. I'll talk to you later. Okay?"

"Will you be all right, Rachel?"

"Yes . . . I—I'll be all right." But she wasn't sure Jamie would be. She looked up Morgan in the Manhattan-Bronx directory. There were five columns of Morgans listed. She had no address or first initial to narrow it down. She dialed the apartment on Fifth Street on the chance he might have gone home. There was no answer. She telephoned Paul.

"I've been trying to find him, too," he told her. "God knows where he's gone. He's probably trying to crawl into the woodwork."

"That's what I'm afraid of, Paul. You . . . you don't think he'd do something . . . stupid . . . do you?"

"Rachel, don't start thinking all kinds of weird stuff. He's mixed up, but he's not suicidal. And he wasn't the only one arrested."

"What was he doing there in the first place? You said he never cruises the gay bars."

"He never *used* to," said Paul softly. "People change."

Was that what Jamie had meant at the cast party? she wondered, dreading the answer. Aloud she said, "Call me if you hear anything, will you?"

"I promise. But I doubt that he'll get in touch with me."

Rachel doubted that Jamie would contact her either. Not knowing sent her back to the Scotch decanter. By the time Howard arrived at the apartment, Rachel had cried herself—and drunk herself—asleep.

At the theater, there was little talk of anything else. Howard, Rachel, Paul, and everyone they spoke to had assumed that the sensational aspects of what was being called the Stonewall Riots would subside within a day or two; even additional raids the following night didn't quell the general optimism among the members of the cast, mainly, Rachel speculated, because half of the dancers in the company had frequented the Stonewall themselves and had emerged unscathed. In addition, Paul had tried to reassure her by explaining that the Stonewall was "tame."

"What do you mean?" she had asked.

"Well, some bars—not my kind, mind you—are into all sorts of scenes. The Stonewall is just a bar. A gay bar, sure, even a drag bar"—he paused, but when Rachel didn't ask for a definition, he went on—"but it's nothing kinky, like the leather bars or wrinkle rooms or the chubby chasers—"

"Paul, I'm beginning not to understand a word," Rachel interrupted now.

"Okay. Wrinkle rooms are for aging gays. Or for guys who get turned on to old men. Chubby chaser bars are for fatties. Chicken bars—"

"What bars?"

"Chicken. For gays who like young boys. And there's also your 'piss elegant' bar, which is out of my income

245

bracket, and then, of course, there's heavy leather."

"Heavy leather?" said Rachel.

"For guys who like what's known as rough trade." Then, seemingly aware of Rachel's discomfort, he added, "Listen, I could write a book about it, but it's mostly based on what I've read or heard. None of my information is based on actual experience."

Nonetheless, Rachel was amazed. She'd had no inkling of the homosexual subculture. She wondered if the rest of the "straight" world could possibly be as ignorant as she felt in this moment.

"Paul," she said, "why did the police pick the Stonewall, if it's just another gay bar?"

"Who knows? Maybe the mob owns the kinkier places. But that's why it has to blow over in a few days."

Rachel's next question was voiced more softly and slowly than those preceding. "Paul . . . has Jamie ever . . . been to these other kinds of bars?"

"I doubt it, Rachel. He used to feel funny about meeting me at Julius's."

"Julius's! But *I've* been there with actors from my scene study class—that's an *ordinary* bar."

She heard him laugh into the phone. "Rachel, honey, it's an 'ordinary' bar during the afternoon. Have you ever been there in the evening?"

She was forced to admit she hadn't.

"Things aren't always what they seem to be," he reminded her. "But the Stonewall, aside from guys who like to dress up in satin and eyelashes, isn't anything out of what you call the ordinary. That's why it can't do much harm to anyone. Maybe it'll bruise Jamie's ego. It might be good for him—get him off the fence we've talked about. He'll be okay. Everybody will. Not that much will change."

But Rachel sensed change everywhere, only some of which involved Jamie and the Stonewall. She wasn't surprised when the incident was enlarged out of all proportion by the media as well as by any factions who might benefit from the publicity—those who were gay and those who weren't.

Rachel, Paul, and Howard had all expected Jamie to surface, once the publicity died down. But one week stretched into another without a trace. Several chorus boys in the company had worked with him on the road in *The Student Prince*. When word reached Rachel, she enlisted their help. Eventually everyone she knew was trying to find Jamie.

As were the police. Rha-ji, the Indian biology major who came in twice a week to clean Howard's apartment, was recruited to take telephone calls—precisely because his English was excellent and his Oxford-inspired accent was just off-putting enough to intimidate all but those callers with whom Rachel or Howard wanted to speak. Once the police learned, probably after gaining access to Jamie's apartment, that Rachel had shared it with him, Rha-ji became a godsend, shielding her from the supermarket scandal sheets who threatened to write their own version if they weren't granted personal interviews.

"Yes, fine," said Rha-ji. "Go right ahead and print it. Then we shall take immediate legal action." Most of the time, it was enough to frighten them off.

Although Rachel feared that it bordered on the melodramatic, she hired a private investigator. He turned up only two pieces of new information: one, that Jamie had moved out of his apartment. Either that, or someone had broken in; according to the super, only the large pieces of furniture—including Rachel's piano—remained. Everything else was gone.

The detective had located Jamie's parents' address in the Bronx. However, the telephone number had been changed and the new number was unlisted. No one was at home, and the neighbors refused to answer any questions.

The only other information of note was that Jamie had spent two years in the U.S. Army. He had been stationed in Belgium and was discharged—honorably—in June 1967.

247

That explained to Rachel why he hadn't served in Vietnam. It also told her something more: Jamie had a valid passport. He might be anywhere.

His disappearance was exacting its toll on Rachel; tiny, all-but-imperceptible lines around her eyes and mouth betrayed a constant concern. Professional discipline did not permit Jamie to interfere with her nightly onstage life, but he seldom left her thoughts during offstage hours. She marveled at Howard's patience, at his ability to soothe her distraught nerves. When words failed, he made love to her; he seemed to know intuitively whether she needed quiet, coaxing tenderness or unabated passion. And never once did he remark on Jamie's invisible presence, made only more vivid because of his absence.

Chapter Eighteen

The summer of 1969 provided constant distraction, in direct contrast with the preceding year when Rachel had had too little activity to occupy her time and too much time to occupy her mind.

She was performing in *Robin Hood* every evening but Monday, when Broadway theaters were dark, with matinees on Wednesday and Saturday. The show was sold out at every performance, and her single number never failed to captivate her audience.

Her days were filled as well, partly from Howard's attentiveness, partly from the scores of scripts they were both constantly reading. The talk of a film version of *Robin Hood* had diminished into just that: talk. Howard had explained that movie musicals were falling from vogue, and to produce another remake of the tale of Sherwood Forest — without the music — seemed pointless, since the original that had starred Errol Flynn and Olivia de Havilland was a classic.

As a result, while efforts to locate Jamie had not been abandoned, Rachel recognized that, as Paul had said on the previous New Year's Eve, life went on. And she had to find the right role to advance her career. Howard was right. The fall season would begin and Maid Marian, no matter how touching her portrayal, would be last season's news, garnering no more attention than yesterday's newspaper.

Now that she knew that shows were set by the time they were listed as "casting" in the weekly trades, she concentrated on those scripts suggested to her by Howard. He had asked her to trust his judgment, and she would not repeat her *Camelot* mistake again. "My career is in your hands, Howard," she warned him gently.

"And I shall guide it as though it were my very own. It is, in a way, you know." She pored through at least half a dozen scripts a week. Those with good stories unfortunately lacked decent musical scores. When the singing roles were well written, the books were pedantic, heavy-handed, and labored. And on the rare occasion that both book and music were uniformly excellent, the leading woman's role called either for a belter, which Rachel was not, or for a legitimately trained singer who could dance. Rachel could follow the choreography required to "dance" Eliza Doolittle or Guinevere, but a Gwen Verdon or Cyd Charisse? Never!

This was why she was excited with Howard's news one Monday evening in late August. On her free night each week, they usually stayed in; on the other six evenings they met Midtown for a light dinner before the show; even after a full day at the office, Howard accompanied Rachel to the theater and never missed a performance.

He entered the apartment and found her in the den. "Put down whatever you're reading!" he said, bending over the sofa to kiss her. "I think we have a role for you."

Rachel returned the kiss, and then her arms went around him. Howard was holding a script behind his back. She drew it from his hands and glanced at the title in the middle of the black leatherette cover. *"The Red Shoes?"* she asked quizzically. "It's one of my favorite movies, but Howard—she's a *dancer!*"

"Ah, but this isn't the movie. The role isn't going to be played by Moira Shearer, this time." He smiled as though he were keeping something secret.

"What is it, Howard? You're not telling me everything, are you?"

"Well, not exactly everything," he admitted. "But let's ring down for Chinese food, first, shall we?"

She knew he was teasing her. "You know I can't think of food until I hear all the details—"

"Hmm . . ."

"Howard!"

"All right, I give in." He seated himself beside her before she pulled him down onto the sofa. "I had a business chat with Lehman Stern the other day. As a result, he has decided to move into directing—"

"Details, please."

"I'm getting to them. By the way, would you care for a gin and tonic? I'm so thirsty—you've no idea how bloody hot it is outside—"

"Howard!"

"Well, then. I've explained that before *Robin Hood* becomes a dead issue, he's got to move on. And conducting musical comedy simply leads to more of the same—it isn't like opera or the symphonic world where the baton wields power. So Lehman has decided to take my advice, and he is going to *direct*. He's thought about it for some time on his own—which he hadn't told me until we spoke about it—and he's always dreamed of transporting *The Red Shoes* to the stage. It's tailor-made for a musical. And the role of Victoria Paige is tailor-made for—"

"A *dancer,*" Rachel interrupted.

"Not necessarily, darling. Remember the ballet in *Oklahoma!?*"

She knew what he was getting at: The ballet sequence in the Rogers and Hammerstein musical had been danced by a "dream" Laurie and Curley, both onstage and in the film version.

"I think *The Red Shoes* is a wonderful idea for a show, Howard, but Victoria Paige is the *lead*—"

"You may not believe this, but you were Lehman's choice before I had an opportunity to mention your name."

"You're right. I don't believe you."

"Rachel, feel free to ask him. But I'm telling you the truth."

She didn't have to ask; she knew he wouldn't lie to her. "But do you—and Lehman—think I'm ready to carry an entire show?" She wasn't totally convinced of it herself.

"In a word, yes. Of course, the producers will want to hear you sing and go over some of the script, but . . ."

She was only vaguely aware of the rest of what he was saying. She was already envisioning the confrontation between the beautiful ballerina and the megalomaniacal impresario, Lermontov. Would they be able to find a singing actor with the stage magnetism of Anton Walbrook? The sobering thought that followed brought her back to the present: Would *she* be able to portray a ballerina to whom dancing meant everything—when, without the patience of a brilliant choreographer, she could barely manage an arabesque without losing her balance?

Rachel had formed several friendships over the past months. She continued to meet Paul every other week for lunch—still at the Evening Star on Ninth Avenue—that was when she allowed Jamie to monopolize their time; she met Norma regularly, too, primarily because she didn't know or take to many young women of her age; other actresses seemed too competitive, too egotistic.

The one actress who didn't, despite a strong ambition, was the singer to whom she had lost the understudy role in *Camelot*. Beth had returned—the entire company had returned—prematurely from the tour because Zane Whitney had suffered a heart attack.

"We didn't get any severance pay," Beth explained as she poured out her disappointment to Rachel over coffee at Schrafft's. "They consider a heart attack as *force majeur*. You know, an 'act of God.' That clause even

Equity can't fight."

*Rachel was genuinely sorry for Beth. She hadn't told her new friend the Arnold Gold–*Gloria Doro story. It might have hurt Beth to know that she had gotten the role for reasons other than talent. Besides, Rachel had no guarantee that she would have been cast, anyway. And, as were so many matters these days, it was in the past. Why even bring it up at all?

". . . so after we closed in Chicago," Beth was saying, "I spent an extra few days there with this producer I met—unfortunately, he's married, but he does run a solid little regional stock company, so you never know . . ."

"Is he planning to divorce his wife?" asked Rachel.

"Oh, honey, don't be naïve. Of course not. But he likes me, and as I said, he *is* a producer. A fling can't hurt, and it may help if I need work. You know how it is—you've got your agent, I've got my producer. Right?"

Rachel didn't answer. Few people aside from Norma—and perhaps Howard himself—would believe a denial. She supposed that Paul and even Jamie, wherever he was, had their doubts.

Aloud she asked, "Well, what's next, then? Are you staying in town for a while?"

"Got to. This is where the action is. Unless you look like Jean Shrimpton. Then you go West to Tinseltown." Beth nibbled at her English muffin. "I did make a decision, though, while I was on the road."

"What kind of decision?"

Beth leaned closer. "Well, just this. There were girls in the show—the chorus—who started out without any solo lines and all of a sudden, bingo! A small part here, a little solo, there."

"But you don't sing in the chorus."

"That's not my point. Remember that cute stage manager?"

Rachel nodded.

"Straight. And since he was in a minority, he had the

pick of the crop. And you could tell at each rehearsal who had and who hadn't—according to which girls got solo lines. Follow me?"

"It's one of my favorite songs. But I'm not sure you're getting at what I think you're getting at."

"Okay, then. Bottom line is this: I've been in New York for five years. Hundreds of auditions. Maybe I land one job in every fifty. Time was when I felt really good that I got that one job on talent—you know, didn't sleep for it, play the kickback game for it, whatever. But I'm practically thirty"—Beth nodded to Rachel's raised eyebrows—"yes, thirty, honey, even if it doesn't show yet. And lately, the bit about 'to thine own self be true' doesn't have the same ring it used to. About the first of every month, when the rent comes due. You know—you've been there."

Rachel had been there—at least the latter part.

"So I'm trying a new attitude. At AA—my brother's a charter member—they tell you 'change your attitude, change your life.' Well, I'm changing mine. Whatever I have to do to make it, I'm ready—and to hell with my conscience. Conscience doesn't pay the bills. And I'm not getting any younger. If I don't make it soon, I'm never going to make it."

Rachel wasn't aware that she hadn't spoken for almost ten minutes, but apparently Beth had noticed. "You're quiet. Does that mean you disagree with my new philosophy, or—what's that old Italian saying—*chi tace consente?*"

Rachel shrugged. "I'm just not saying anything because I don't have much to say, one way or the other. It's not up to me, Beth."

"That sounds a little like 'it's your life, Beth.' My mother said that to me. My pop said only tramps go into theater in the first place. So now I can tell him I'm guilty as charged." She tried to laugh, but Rachel detected a false note.

"Look," said Beth, "being good hasn't done me a damn thing. So I won't be good, I'll just be careful." She signaled the waiter for their check. "Listen, Rachel, I'm only telling you because one, you're a friend, and two . . . well, you understand. We're sisters under the proverbial skin."

Although she liked Beth, Rachel had returned from their conversation somewhat depressed. Howard had left the script for *The Red Shoes* lying on the leather sofa in the den. She kicked off her sandals, turned the air-conditioning several degrees cooler, and curled up to read before it was time to dress and meet Howard for dinner, followed by another performance of *Robin Hood*.

She admonished herself for having grown slightly bored with the role of Maid Marian. She was lucky to be in a show at all, given Beth's reminder of the law of averages. That the show was a smash hit and her role a supporting lead, not to mention a standout in the otherwise all-male cast, was a stroke of luck. Whatever part talent played in the fortunes of careers in the theater, Rachel was aware that plums such as hers did not come along every day of the week. She didn't need Beth Burns to tell her. She also didn't need to hear that it was Howard's connections—and her relationship with him—taking her out of the cattle-call auditions and placing her in the limelight. Howard's contacts hadn't brought her the rave reviews or the offers and fan mail that crowded Norma's desk. Her mind settled for a moment on Mina MacDonald and the "visibility" she was creating for Rachel. Nonetheless, Mina had arrived *after* the fact. Talent must have *something* to do with it!

Howard had seen to it that Rachel hadn't signed a run-of-the-play contract for *Robin Hood*. As the fall season

opened, she saw the wisdom in his counsel. Perfor-
mances were still sold out, but now the talk was of the
new shows opening. It was true: theater parties and
women's clubs flocked to the hits of last season, but the
"beautiful people" wanted only the latest and the newest.
Sondheim was in; Rodgers and Hammerstein were out.

Lehman Stern was leaving the show to embark upon
his Red Shoes project; Rachel hadn't mentioned her
conversation with Howard because Lehman had been so
busy; she saw him only at the theater, and then they were
constantly surrounded by other members of the cast. In
addition, a sixth sense advised her to leave the matter in
Howard's hands; to thank Lehman would sound prema-
ture and presumptuous at the same time; to wait until he
broached the subject seemed far more professional.

Lehman's replacement in the pit was a young black
conductor named Phillip Greene. Rachel wondered
whether the modestly talented substitute was one of
Lehman's current or former lovers; he bore more than a
slight resemblance to Paul.

But she dismissed the thought. Not from its possibility,
but because the matter of Paul meant the matter of
Jamie, and Rachel refused to let it govern her life—
except for the back booth at the Evening Star. Their
waiter no longer asked how they wanted their biweekly
burgers; they had become "regulars"—one medium rare
with cheese, the other dripping with blood. A side order
of fries, two coffees, and talk of Jamie. The menu never
varied.

"I may be doing a new show," said Paul on one of
their lunch dates.

"In New York? Or out of town?" He seldom went for
very long without work; chorus "gypsies" often went
from show to show on the recommendation of choreog-
raphers with whom they had rapport.

"If it materializes, it'll play Boston and New Haven
and then come into the city. But I don't see how it can

work—can you imagine The Red Shoes as a musical?"

Rachel didn't mention that she was being considered for the lead. Instead, she said, "These days, everything's fair game. I've heard about plans to do it."

"Well, if you ask me, a Broadway audience won't sit still for ballet unless the music is by a Bernstein. Even if Lehman Stern is going to try his hand at directing."

Now Rachel looked right at him. "Is that why you're doing the show?"

Paul shook his head. "No. He doesn't 'owe' me. Or, put in another way, he and I are a fling of the past. If he had to give a job to every one of his former lovers, Rachel, *The Red Shoes* would require a cast of thousands!"

They both laughed. For a change it was an easy laugh, something that didn't often occur between them, because most times when they were together, they talked of Jamie. They had spoken of him today, too, but had moved on to other subjects, those over which they exercised a modicum of control. Rachel, however, was starting to see how little control anyone on the performing side of theater actually possessed. Moreover, she was beginning to wonder if talent had anything to do with it.

She would come to wonder even more over the following weeks.

After Rachel had read through the script, she confided in Paul about her role and elicited his promise to coach her on any difficult dance movements she might be called upon to execute. She also accompanied Beth Burns to ballet class.

"It's just to brush up and see what I remember," Rachel told Beth. Howard had suggested she keep the subject of Victoria Paige under wraps until Lehman himself broached it. Beth hadn't questioned the idea; singers and actors frequently took a few classes to keep *in shape between shows.*

"*I don't know about you,*" said Beth as they changed into their leotards in the small dressing room, "*but these intermediate classes are a real workout. Sometimes I think I ought to go back to the beginner level. But that's laziness; I need to stretch myself.*"

Rachel smiled as she straightened her tights. "*Beginners' class would be stretching it for me. I don't know how I'll get through the next hour!*"

She survived, although she was painfully aware—both physically and through the unavoidable reflection in the wall-length mirror—that most of the dancers in the class, including Beth, belonged at the advanced level. As sweat poured down the back of her neck, Rachel observed her friend's extensions and marveled at Beth's agility. Beth wasn't just a singer who could move; she could really *dance.*

Nonetheless, as Beth confided later over ice cream at Howard Johnson's, neither her singing nor dancing had paid off that week. "I went to five auditions, got callbacks for all of them, and lost out to Miss America types with that scrubbed-but-come-hither look in their eyes. I tell you, Rachel, I'm getting fed up. I mean, *I'm* willing, but so far, even with my change of tactics, nobody's coming on to me! What do I have to do? Kill someone?"

Beth laughed, but Rachel detected a growing bitterness in her friend. She speculated that perhaps less talented performers, if they possessed only driving ambition, were lucky; they could rationalize losing a job without looking for logic—a logic that both Rachel and Beth seemed more and more to recognize as nonexistent. Rachel further suspected that the awareness was due not to superior intelligence, but to the very fact of their talent. Funny, she mused, talent was supposed to be a blessing, not a curse.

Rachel and Howard met Lehman Stern for dinner on

the following Monday evening. They discussed The Red Shoes, and as Howard had told Rachel, Lehman *had* immediately thought of her for the lead.

She didn't admit to prior knowledge as Lehman outlined his ideas. "A friend of mine, Oliver Woodward, wrote the script and the lyrics. Dunston Shaw composed the score, which I think you'll really like. The vocal range is perfect for you, and we all agree that the emphasis should be on the story, rather than on the ballet. After all"—he laughed here—"we wouldn't want the audience to be looking for Moira Shearer and Robert Helpman, would we?"

Rachel was glad he had laughed; it allowed her to vent her own relief. "I'd be thrilled to take a look at it, Lehman," she said. "Just let me know when."

"Good. I thought we might get together with Dunston and Ollie—an informal gathering at my place—and run through some of the show. Then we can invite the producers up and present them with a sampling. What do you say?"

Rachel said, "That sounds fine—as long as the producer isn't Arnold Gold."

Now all three of them laughed. Lehman said, "Hardly. Some members of the Stern family are investing, and a few of their more adventurous friends—"

"Your family?" asked Rachel, surprised. "Are you from the department-store Sterns?"

"Uh, no . . ." he answered. "Actually, I'm the only renegade. The rest of the menage is into Wall Street." He glanced modestly at his wineglass. "In fact, my grandfather owns . . . a few . . . of those glass towers downtown."

"Well," said Rachel, "for heaven's sake, don't *apologize* for it!"

He didn't.

Rachel was in high spirits by the time she and Howard returned to the apartment. If Lehman Stern's family *would be investing in The Red Shoes* and their "renegade" would direct the show, singing a few numbers at an informal gathering was nothing more than a formality; she had the role sewn up.

She had telephoned her parents in Minnesota but had sworn them to secrecy. "No 'exclusive interviews' in the local papers until I've signed the contract. Promise me!"

They gave her their word.

That Sunday afternoon, Dunston Shaw, Oliver Woodward, Lehman, Howard, and Rachel assembled at Lehman's enormous apartment on Park Avenue and Eightieth Street. Three hours passed as they went through the entire score of *The Red Shoes*. Rachel sang all of Victoria Paige's music, which, as Lehman had promised, was written in her range and allowed her to color the lyrics with her voice. She read several scenes, enlisting Howard to read opposite her; they had already done this at home in anticipation of Sunday, but it remained their knowledge alone.

"Howard," said Oliver when they had finished, "did you ever consider going on the stage? You'd make a wonderful Lermontov!"

He laughed. "Perish the thought. One star in the family is enough!" He had said it spontaneously, but Rachel's nerves went on alert.

Those nerves were nothing like her reaction to Howard's news two weeks later. He seemed preoccupied during dinner, but when Rachel asked him if anything was wrong, he said they'd talk after that night's performance.

All through her song and soliloquy, despite her commitment to the role, Rachel couldn't help wondering if Howard had received news—terrible news—of Jamie. By

*the end of the show, her anxiety had increased; Howard
had not kept her company in the dressing room between
acts as he customarily did. Obviously he didn't want to
discuss whatever it was until they were at home.*

She waited until they had closed the door and turned
on the foyer lights. Then, before she removed her coat,
she said, "Howard, I can't stand waiting any longer—
what *is* it?"

He answered slowly, "I don't quite know how to tell
you."

"Jamie! It's about Jamie, isn't it?" She was growing
frantic now.

But he shook his head. "No. It isn't about Jamie."

"Well, then—*what?*" Impatience crept into her voice.

"It's . . . it's about *The Red Shoes* . . ."

"What about it? Has it been postponed?"

He didn't reply.

"It's been canceled?"

"It's going into rehearsal next month." Howard wasn't
looking directly at her.

"Then *what's* the matter?" She was trying not to burst.

This time he lifted his eyes, but their depths held a
puzzling, lost expression. "They've signed . . . someone
else."

"Someone else for wh—" But she stopped as realization struck her. "You mean . . . the role of Victoria
Paige?"

He nodded helplessly.

"But . . . *who?*"

He drew a profound breath. "A friend of yours, I'm
afraid. They've signed . . . Beth Burns."

Chapter Nineteen

Rachel was stunned; the conductor who had given her a chance in *Arrowhead,* who had cast her as Maid Marian and had continued his enthusiastic support—until now; the friend who had trusted and confided in Rachel—but not completely. She felt a double betrayal, and the delicate balance between anger and shock left her numb.

It wasn't exactly as it appeared. "If it's any comfort," said Howard as he poured each of them a brandy, "Lehman truly wanted you for the role. But there have been changes in the script and Victoria Paige will have to do her own dancing after all. He insisted that the matter was beyond his control."

"If he's directing, the casting decisions are up to him," she said. "And if his family is backing the show, he has more than a little input regarding the production—dancing, singing, everything. It sounds more like a cheap excuse for a change of heart. Especially since *he* was the one who originally suggested me to you."

Howard seated himself in the leather chair opposite her. "He mentioned that pressure was being brought to bear. Believe me, he didn't seem very happy about the situation."

Rachel only half heard him. "I just don't understand." What kind of pressure did he mean? Beth couldn't have gone to bed with Lehman Stern, because Lehman Stern didn't sleep with women.

"No," agreed Howard after she had voiced this aloud. "But he said something about the Wall Street Sterns. Your friend may have . . . well, she may have *used* someone in Lehman's family. They're putting quite a lot of cash into *The Red Shoes*. If Beth Burns is as desperate as you've said, she had her pick. The Sterns are all married and extremely well connected. Lehman is the only 'black sheep.' With their social position—"

"Of course," Rachel cut in bitterly. "Julius Caesar *said* position is everything in life." She sighed ruefully. "And I never gave Beth a hint that I was up for the lead." Still, she couldn't envision Beth's "strategy" as working in the long run. Somewhere along the way, she'd have to answer for her actions—if not to anyone else, at least to herself.

"Is everything finalized already?" she asked, wondering if there was any point in pursuing it further.

"Lehman left today for the family compound in Connecticut. He said he hadn't the courage to tell you to your face."

"So he left his agent to do the dirty work," she said. "And *he* told *me* not to become another Gloria Doro! Doesn't *anyone* ever make it in this business without conniving and cheating and stabbing people in the back?"

Howard placed his glass on the bar and came to her. "I'd like to answer that by saying 'all the time,' Rachel. But I've been in the business too long. One learns to accept it and look the other way. It's a means of survival."

Of the entire episode, that upset her the most.

When Beth Burns telephoned with her news about the show, the subject of *how* she had landed the starring role

263

in *The Red Shoes* never came up; Rachel couldn't broach the matter without expressing disappointment in her friend, and she felt it was unfair to judge. If Rachel had confided that *she* had been offered the part and *then* Beth had used whatever influence or "hold" she had on Lehman Stern's family to steal the role from Rachel, that would have been another matter. But, Rachel reasoned, since Beth hadn't known beforehand, why compound the situation after the fact?

Besides, Howard had said that Victoria Paige would now do most of her own dancing. That would have presented obstacles from the start. At least Beth wouldn't need a "dream" Vicki to compensate for any balletic inadequacy. She might not be another Moira Shearer—and certainly wasn't a Margot Fonteyn—but she *had* danced her way through stock productions of *Brigadoon* and *Pajama Game,* and wearing a black wig in photographs that made both Beth and Rachel laugh, she had also played Anita—not Maria—in the national company of *West Side Story*. If the revised script of *The Red Shoes* called for a dancing-singing Victoria Paige, Beth, whatever she had done to get the part, deserved it more than Rachel. Maybe there *was* a touch of logic involved, after all.

At least she chose to hope as much.

By the time Rachel met Paul for lunch the following week, the news that he would be in the show's chorus made little impact upon her. She had decided to be happy for Paul—and for Beth, too—although wishing for Lehman Stern's success was forcing the issue and would have made her feel like a hypocritical Pollyanna.

She did tell him all that had happened, however.

"So you'll stay with the gang in Sherwood Forest for a while longer?" he asked.

264

She nodded. "Howard is looking over scripts with a bit more urgency now," she answered. "I think he's feeling responsible because there wasn't anything he could do about *Shoes*."

"He must love you very much," said Paul.

She didn't answer. Instead, she asked, "You said on the phone you'd heard from Jamie?"

He pulled a postcard from his pocket and handed it to her.

"Paris!" she exclaimed. "Why on earth—?"

"I guess because he speaks French—those two army years in Belgium. Anyway, read what it says."

She glanced down at the familiar handwriting. "Just so you'll know I haven't left the planet." His signature was scribbled at the bottom.

"That's *all*?" she said. "Over four months and one single sentence? How generous of him!" And why was she growing angry? she wondered. But she knew. Because he hadn't sent that one single line to *her*.

And Paul knew her well. "Rachel, he can't write to you. It's as though you read into his soul. That's enough to frighten anyone off."

"You're just trying to placate me."

"Not at all. I've always known that one day he and I could be friends, even if we can never be lovers again. Most of my male friends are former lovers. But with you . . ."

"With me, what?" Her voice still betrayed an edge.

"He can't be friends with you unless he makes peace with himself. It's as if you and Jamie are flip sides of the same coin. What's the Zen thing about balance . . . ?"

"Yin and yang. Sure. Jamie and me." And she laughed, even if she found it less than amusing.

However, on her way back to Howard's apartment, Paul's words replayed in her mind.

* * *

265

A suitable script arrived at last, although it came as a complete surprise to Rachel. It was neither a musical nor a show at all. It was a film script. The closest Rachel had been to a movie camera had been doing extra work on the film version of *Hello, Dolly!* during her first summer in Manhattan. She had risen at dawn to be herded off, together with several hundred other "background players," to Garrison, New York, where an exact replica of the film set in Hollywood had been constructed. That job, as well as one day on *Sweet Charity*—a day that was canceled because of Robert Kennedy's assassination—comprised her motion picture "experience."

Nonetheless, Howard felt it was the right move to make at this time. "The big, extravagant musicals are on their way out, Rachel," he explained. "Just look at the new vogue—shows like *Hair* are what the public wants. With the rest, box office attendance is down—even with theater parties at the matinees—yours, as well as the other shows around town. I even have strong doubts about *The Red Shoes* . . ." He paused only for a moment, then quickly routed the conversation in a different direction.

"Anyway, with production costs and ticket prices going through the ceiling, and more so-called 'message' shows in protest of Vietnam, my business instincts are pointing to another path."

Rachel couldn't argue; Howard's instincts had protected him when less wise but greedier agents had been forced to close their doors or relegate their clients to the growing unemployment lines.

"I'm glad you have faith in my acting ability," she said, glancing down at the script.

"I've told you before, it's the way you *interpret* the songs you sing that impress me with your voice. Pure sound just for sound's sake—like so many opera singers who put me to sleep—is just what a writer friend of mine calls 'luck of the genetic draw.' Perfectly formed vocal cords are an accident of birth. Acting ability requires far more."

She narrowed her eyes. "Then why have I studied voice all these years?"

He returned her look with one of his own. "Because you hadn't been offered an acting role such as this, I'd gather. Why don't I fix us a drink and we'll have a read-through?"

Rachel didn't know which appealed to her more—the part, that of a sensitive, intelligent woman journalist who risks her life and that of the man she loves in order to write her story *and* see justice prevail, *or* the exciting, romantic locations listed: Paris, Tel Aviv, and much closer to her experience, London, where the interiors would be shot at Pinewood Studios. It only occurred to her later that Jamie's postcard had been mailed from Paris.

After reading the script with Howard, Rachel was convinced that he was right; although she wouldn't sing a note, the role could expand her career possibilities and obtain for her the higher visibility that Mina MacDonald had been forced to invent, as of late. Too, with *The Red Shoes* going into rehearsal and her own show going on twofers, it was time for a change of scenery.

By the end of October, Rachel had read for the director and met with the producers. Only the contract was yet to be signed; she had been packed for a week.

She and Howard would spend a few days in London on preproduction work before departure for Israel. The technical aspect could be handled more easily at Pinewood, since even with the most sophisticated equipment flown to Tel Aviv, location was, nonetheless, location.

Rachel was pleased that they would have time to visit with William and Jennie. She had spent every night but Mondays onstage since late spring; now she looked forward to free evenings of relaxing dinners and leisurely discourse.

However, when they arrived at the Savoy, Howard learned that William was at a medical conference in Dublin, and Jennie was leaving to visit friends in Edinburgh, Scotland. "The best I can do," she said, "is offer you the keys to the house."

It sounded too delicious to refuse. Rachel wasn't surprised when Howard reached under the straw mat on the front step to retrieve the latchkey. She had missed that kind of trust, but New Yorkers, no matter their origins, didn't dare extend such an "invitation."

When they stopped in at the local pub, Mike greeted Rachel as he had Howard on the previous Christmas. "If I'd a-known you was coming, miss, I'd a-ordered you yer pewter." However, by the second day Mike had located a splendid tankard in the dull silver-gray metal. Only the monogram was missing. "What's the initial, miss? I'll 'ave it engraved before the week is out."

Rachel felt a warm glow of belonging. "An *A*, Mike," she said, smiling. "For Allenby."

"An *A* 'tis, then," he said.

When he had left their booth, Howard turned to Rachel and took her hand in his. "This is a bit public for what I have in mind," he said, "but I thought it might be wise to mention it now, before"—he glanced up at the bar—"before Mike has the wrong monogram engraved."

Rachel looked up into his eyes. "Howard—"

"In case I'm not making myself clear," he interrupted, "that's a proposal. I want to marry you."

268

She lowered her eyes as her heart began to race. What, she wondered, was holding her back? "Howard . . . I . . . can't we wait . . . just a little longer? Till I'm back from Israel? I have so much to think about."

"It isn't complicated. My proposal requires only a 'yes.'" With his index finger, he tilted her head up so her eyes were forced to meet his. "I can't wait forever," he said. "I'm too much in love with you."

What was the matter with her? she asked herself. It was a question she had silently repeated, over and over. But an answer still eluded her grasp.

"Some things take more time than others," she said aloud, replying both to Howard and herself. "You've said that in the past."

"So I have," he agreed. "And I may have been mistaken."

Howard didn't bring up the subject for the rest of their stay in Hertfordshire, nor in the subsequent week at the Savoy when they returned to London. Rachel sensed only the slightest emotional withdrawal—or perhaps it was her imagination. In reality, she reflected, he may have been responding the way he felt she wished him to. At one time it would have relieved her. Now she wondered if she had any clear idea of what she did in fact want—from Howard as well as from herself.

Rachel's wardrobe fittings for *The Sixth Day* went speedily; most of the time she would wear khaki safari-style shirts with matching skirts or slacks. She was pleased, but realized this was due to her own prejudice and inexperience; she'd seen too many Marlene Dietrich "desert" sagas on late-night television.

Therefore, when she was informed that she would wear minimal makeup and let her hair blow free in the hot desert breeze, she began to think that Tom Jarrod understood the script. His depiction of Israel's six-day war of 1967 would not be just another excuse to show off biblical epic locales while cashing in on the controversy encountered whenever a film was made in any of the world's "trouble spots."

Howard had planned to accompany Rachel to Tel Aviv. However, on the night before their scheduled departure, plans changed.

"There's a problem with one of my clients. Malcolm Campbell is threatening to tear up his contract at the National. I'll have to stay here until it's settled—it may take a week or two."

Rachel wondered if he had invented the excuse. "Is it absolutely necessary that you stay?" she asked.

She thought his eyes looked tired as he answered, "If I let him handle it alone, we could easily wind up in court. He has a wretched temper—it's only matched by his abominable business acumen."

"Oh . . . I thought . . ."

"What?" he asked. "That I didn't want to be with you?" He crossed the room to her and took her face in his hands. "Rachel, my darling, if I didn't want to be with you, I wouldn't fabricate a reason. And if I felt that we needed time away from each other, I'd tell you so."

"I know. It's just . . ."

"It's just that you don't believe me completely. Look, I don't deny that this will give you a chance to . . . well, to breathe a bit. But I didn't create a delay for such a purpose. I didn't create it at all."

"I'm sorry," she answered. "How soon do you think it'll all be settled?"

"Hopefully within the next week. Malcolm will come to his senses and realize that ultimatums have destroyed careers far more important than his. If he can understand that before it's too late, he may survive his own ego."

"Does it always come down to survival?" Rachel wondered half aloud.

The phone had rung, and Howard either hadn't heard or else he didn't know the answer to her question.

It was a pleasant, uneventful flight, despite an unscheduled stopover and an hour's delay in Athens. Rachel arrived at Lod Airport in Tel Aviv on a very hot and humid November morning. A swarthy, stocky man in his late thirties stepped forward the moment she entered the terminal building.

"Miss Allenby?" he asked in thickly accented English.

He introduced himself as David Bar-El of the second unit production office. "I will get you through passport control. Do please wait here." He hurried off to a uniformed guard and both began conversing rapidly in Hebrew.

Rachel observed the airport's interior. Soldiers stood at every checkpoint; each man carried a machine gun and carefully scrutinized the arriving passengers and those people who had come to collect them. Departing travelers were directed into small booths for customs inspection. One elderly grandmother repeated over and over, "I can't open all the packages—they are gifts for the children!" Ignored by the customs official who tore off the wrappings, she wailed, "This isn't fair! I have nothing to hide!" She was advised to cooperate lest the plane leave without her.

"It is for your own protection," said an El-Al official as David Bar-El returned to Rachel.

"I am sorry for the delay," he apologized, "but we must comply with regulations. A thorough check must at all times be made. Surely you understand."

271

Rachel did; it made her feel safer, although she sympathized with the distraught grandmother. David Bar-El saw her looking at the opened souvenirs and said, "I have seen harmless toys that contained bomb devices, Miss Allenby. One cannot be too careful."

She nodded and followed him out of the terminal.

Even with dark lenses in her sunglasses, the glare was blinding, the heat scorching. David's car, an ancient, rusting relic dating back to Rachel's childhood, stood baking in the pre-noonday sun. As she climbed into the front passenger seat, her arm brushed against the red-hot leatherette upholstery, and she flinched.

"I am again sorry," said David, "but air-conditioning would cost a fortune. Our inflation is murderous as it is." He settled uncomfortably behind the wheel and retrieved a wrinkled towel from the backseat. He offered it to Rachel, who mopped her forehead and the back of her neck before returning it to him.

"Miss Allenby, we wish to make your stay as pleasant as possible. Anything I can do—for example, should you wish to change dollars into Israeli pounds, let me know. I can arrange a good exchange on the black market."

She was surprised by his open referral to the "exchange."

"You must understand," he explained, "that our black market is available to all. It is simply that a foreigner who does not speak Hebrew—unless of course you do—would not receive the highest rate. Do you speak the language?"

"No, I'm afraid I don't. And I appreciate your offer." She reached into her totebag first for Kleenex, with which she again wiped perspiration from her neck, and then for her makeup case. She spilled a dozen bobby pins into her lap as the car made its way along the dusty, sandswept desert road.

By the time they had reached the outskirts of Tel Aviv

proper, Rachel's long, damp waves had been lifted off her neck and pinned into a haphazard French twist. Even her sunglasses seemed to take on added weight in the sweltering heat, which, judging from the rusted, overturned trucks along the highway, broiled everything in sight.

"From one of our previous wars," David explained. "They are not Israeli trucks."

Rachel nodded as she gazed at the golden-beige sand everywhere. "It really *is* the desert, isn't it?" she asked.

"Tel Aviv itself is built on the desert," answered David as square buildings of two and three stories on cement-piling stilts began to dot the horizon. They reminded Rachel of her beloved Russian fairytale witch, Baba Yaga, whose house stood atop chicken legs. "Everything here sits upon the sand."

Nonetheless, trees and shrubbery gradually became visible, first sparsely and then in greater profusion as larger clusters of buildings came into view.

David proceeded to point out various government landmarks and monuments. "And we have occasions for cultural enrichment, too," he said as they passed the Mann Auditorium. "Home of the Israel Philharmonic," he said proudly. "The hotel, by the way, where all the foreigners will stay, is the Dan. It is situated on the beach, just past the opera house."

"You have opera in Israel?" Rachel asked, surprised.

"Yes. They used to be at the Mann, but they were thrown out. The woman who runs it fights with everyone. Now they perform at the Knesset—that was our first Parliament. You shall see. We shall drive by it."

"Oh, that's not necessary." What Rachel wanted most in the world—far more than a guided tour—was an air-conditioned hotel room and a bath.

"Excuse me for asking, but you have come here from London, still you do not speak with a British accent. Yet your name is British."

"It is?"

He nodded. "Lord Allenby was part of the British mandate when Israel was still Palestine; he played an important role in our history and helped many Jews. Look, see for yourself." He pointed to the street sign.

"Allenby Road!" said Rachel, surprised.

"What is your nationality?" asked David.

"I'm American."

"No, I mean where your people come from. Your family. You know, we have Israelis who are Russians, Israelis who are Romanians, the Yemenites, then there are the Sabras, who were born here. They are like your native Americans, I think."

"Our native Americans are Indians," said Rachel. "I was born in America, and so were my parents and grandparents, but—"

"Then you *are* like a Sabra."

Rachel was confused, and David only made it worse. "Of course, you will also meet many Yekehs—excuse me, that is what we call the Germans—"

"I don't understand all the classifications. Isn't everybody Jewish?"

His mouth formed a broad grin. "Miss Allenby, it is easy to see that you are new to our state—New York, in your America, is not the so-called melting pot. It is Israel. I have not even mentioned the Christians living here. *Israel* is the . . . the mixed pickle!" He laughed now, pleased with his simile.

Rachel was still studying the street sign. Allenby Road was leading the car to water; the Mediterranean sparkled in the distance with blue diamonds as bathers splashed, sprinkled like Seurat's dots of color across a canvas that was the sea.

"Allenby," David was saying. "Well, what's in a name, as they say. But you will be asked about it often while

274

you are here. Israelis are very direct. If they wish to know a thing, they ask."

"Excuse me," said Rachel, "but you keep referring to Israelis as 'they.' Aren't you Israeli?"

"Now, of course. It was a great day for me when I came here from my town of Riga—it is now part of Russia, but it used to be Lithuania. Most people you will meet here came from elsewhere. Only the Sabras were born here. They feel that Israel belongs to them alone, yet they envy those who leave, because most Sabras have no place else to go. This is also why so many Yekehs are bitter. They came here during the Second World War to escape Hitler and found themselves trapped in another kind of—" He threw his hands in the air without finishing the thought. "Those who cannot leave both love and hate Israel, you see. They band together only in times of war."

"But why?"

"Because," he said solemnly, "Jews in other countries offer their money. Israel offers her sons."

Rachel's introduction to the Holy Land was already unlike anything she had imagined or expected to encounter. She filed it in her memory; David Bar-El might not know it, but he was enriching the character she would portray in *The Sixth Day.*

Just then, the car swerved to avoid an oncoming bicycle. David nodded in the direction of a crumbling architectural disaster. The building's facade was salt-streaked and reached toward the skies with ugly, oddly pointed turrets. Rachel wondered if it had been a victim of one of Israel's recent wars.

"That's the opera house," David said. "We're almost at the hotel." He turned right then, onto Herbert Samuel Drive along the beachfront. Rachel could see the marquee of the elegant Dan Hotel.

"I shall deposit you at the front entrance, which is

around on Hayarkon Street. By the way, the staff speaks English—everyone here does, for the most part—but if you need anything at all, do not hesitate to ring the office. I will give you the number. You are free until Sunday, which is when everyone will arrive for work. Some personnel will be here tomorrow afternoon, but they, too, are ahead of schedule. We begin on Sunday. In the meantime, I suggest that you do not tire yourself; the climate can be debilitating. A *chamsin* is expected soon and it will not be very pleasant."

"What's a *cham-sin?*" asked Rachel as she tried to unglue the back of her blouse from the wet, sticky upholstery.

"It is an Arabic word for fifty. Half a hundred. A wind which sweeps in from the Arabian Peninsula. It occurs fifty times each year and comes quite suddenly. One feels as if there is no air, as though one might suffocate. It is best to remain inside where it is air-conditioned. It passes. Just be advised that it is not a matter of willpower or mind over matter. It is *very* real—and most uncomfortable. But one survives." Winding up his monologue as he parked the car in front of a modern white tower, he added, "And do enjoy your stay."

Wisps of damp hair dangled from Rachel's neck, her skirt and blouse were wrinkled as if she had wrung them out without ironing, and she was certain her mascara had run halfway down her face by the time she was checked into her room. But the hotel was as modern as any she'd seen stateside, and the room—air-conditioned and downright cold—was large, modern, *and* equipped with television, telephone, and a small refrigerator. Someone had thoughtfully provided a welcome basket of fresh pears and avocados, and a bottle of Carmel wine.

She ran water in the bathtub and undressed while a

black-and-white segment of *Star Trek* played in the background. The only disconcerting factor about Israel thus far, despite David Bar-El's less than optimistic portrait, was that the television image was all but obliterated by subtitles; while William Shatner and Leonard Nimoy exchanged orders in English dialogue, Israeli television provided simultaneous translation, in white lettering, for its polyglot viewers and bordering neighbors. Rachel recognized French, Hebrew, and Arabic trailing across two-thirds of the screen. The moving white letters made her dizzy after the heat and humidity outside; she finished drawing her bath and turned off the set.

She tried to place a call to Howard's office in London to let him know she had arrived safely, but she was told by the hotel switchboard operator — in perfect English — that all circuits to England were engaged and to please wait until later.

A note beside the telephone reminded guests that on Saturday, the Sabbath, everything shut down. Restaurants were open in the nearby Arab village of Jaffa, but not even coffee was available via room service from sundown Friday until sunset on the following evening.

Well, this is only Thursday, Rachel mused. I can still eat tonight! She stepped into the welcoming water, to which she had added a healthy dose of Givenchy III. As she did so, she wondered if Israelis ever compared their state to a Venus flytrap.

Rachel flopped onto the inviting queen-sized bed. Her windows overlooked the blue-green sea in which bathers were immersed as far as the eye could fathom. Rachel stretched her relaxed limbs and sighed aloud. The tub had been delightful. Maybe she'd even try the hotel pool. But the natives — David's "mixed pickle" — were welcome to the beach; she wasn't about to suffer the effects of a *chamsin!*

At dusk, further refreshed after an afternoon's nap, Rachel decided to explore the terrain. From the small terrace she could see the ancient city of Jaffa, but she didn't feel that ambitious. She slipped into a chocolate-colored cotton chambray minidress and decided to test the neighborhood.

She headed along the now deserted Hayarkon Street, past decayed dwellings and gutted buildings. When she reached the intersection and the street bearing her family name, she took a right and strolled the block past the hideous structure that she'd seen earlier. Even in the evening's shadows, it brought to mind a sleazy beach house. Nonetheless, high above the movie marquee—which advertised only in Hebrew lettering—was a rusted sign with huge letters. They spelled, in English, ISRAEL OPERA.

Rachel noticed that the lobby was filled with patrons. However, they were not dressed as opera- or theatergoers would be in less remote parts of the world. They wore briefest beachwear—women were in backless halters and shorts; men sported T-shirts, Bermuda shorts, and sandals. And most of them were eating.

The food reminded Rachel that she had skipped lunch, except for an avocado after her bath. She stopped into the café adjacent to the opera house and ordered a coffee. It was served to her in a glass. The proprietor spoke first in Hebrew, then in French, and when he realized that Rachel was proficient in neither, he smiled and said, "English?"

When she nodded, he beckoned her to a table outside where it was somewhat cooler than in the café, which was not air-conditioned. A moment later, he set down a pastry filled with almonds and dripping with honey.

Several women in theatrical makeup exited the stage door; they were fully costumed in heavy woolen skirts

and shawls. They wore black or gray wigs and babush-
kas. Their physical appearance made the air seem twice
as hot as it was. They chatted noisily among themselves
until a tray of coffee glasses arrived; they paid and
reentered the theater. Other women, wearing as much
makeup as those who had just exited but in far scantier
"costumes," eyed Rachel suspiciously. A fat, greasy man
with several chins and matted, dyed black hair approached her and began to speak in what was obviously
Hebrew. His leering grin revealed yellow, cigar-stained
teeth. Rachel understood nothing he said, but instinct
translated his business proposition. She felt her cheeks
reddening as the café owner stepped forward. "You are
an actress, perhaps? A singer?"

Rachel nodded. "Both. How did you know?"

He said, "Never mind. One moment." He turned to
the obese intruder and sharply intoned a reprimand. The
man shrugged and shrank away. The owner seated himself beside Rachel and said, "My name is Henri. That
one mistakenly took you for one of the working girls
instead of an *artiste*."

"*Merci*, Henri," she said. "I didn't know it was *that*
easy a mistake to make!"

"Well," he explained, "the opera *is* in the heart of
the—how you say it?—the red-light zone? Do not be
offended. At times, the zone's 'girls' are mistaken for
singers!"

Rachel laughed with Henri as she sipped her espresso
and reflected on the irony; she had already decided that
Israel was a state of such ironies.

After thanking Henri—the pastry was 'on the house,'
he'd said—Rachel walked again to the corner at the foot
of Allenby Road. Latecomers were filing into the theater.

"Excuse me," she said to a young woman entering the
lobby. "Do you speak English?"

"Of course!" came the reply.

"Well, can you tell me what opera is playing tonight?"

"It is *Fiddler on the Roof*. And it is not an opera, it is a musical from Broadway, in America. It is written by—"

"Yes, thank you," interrupted Rachel. "I'm familiar with the show." She could be as direct as any Israeli. "And is it being performed in English?"

"Of course! It is *written* in English!" She gave Rachel a quick once-over and marched haughtily into the theater.

The lobby was pleasantly air-conditioned, and the air outside, although cooler now that the sun had set, was still quite humid, even after a damp London autumn. Well, Rachel mused, at least it'll be live and in color—with no subtitles. That certainly was a plus compared with Israeli television!

The theater was devoid of ornament or physical enhancement. The orchestra pit was built beneath the stage, and instead of wood to assist the acoustics, this auditorium had walls of pale blue stucco and floors of asphalt tile. Even politicians, Rachel mused, had possessed the wisdom to move the parliamentary arena to a more suitable "theater."

She examined the program handed her by an usher. The top half was printed in Hebrew. The lower portion in English, she assumed, was a translation of the Hebrew. As the orchestra warmed up and a tuba sputtered loudly in the pit, Rachel wondered if television might have been a wiser choice.

The conductor entered, turned to face the audience, bowed quickly, as if to dispense with that part of the performance immediately, and took the podium. A sudden transformation occurred: the short, paunchy, stoop-shouldered old man with the thick, hornrimmed glasses lifted his baton, and, as if wielding a magic wand, he came alive.

First were the familiar strains of the title music. When

the string section joined the harmony, Rachel found herself smiling. This conductor, whoever he was, conveyed a keen sense of phrasing. As the villagers made their entrances onstage, their multinational backgrounds not only revived David Bar-El's conversation in Rachel's mind but also added a special flavor to the singing. Instead of finding the mixture of Hebrew, Polish, Russian, Yiddish, Spanish, Australian, and God-knew-what-other accents disconcerting, they heightened the charm and poignancy of the show.

The Tevye was perhaps several decades too young for the role, but he was amusing, and the audience loved him. The rest—Golde, Yente, and the daughters and their beaus—were excellent. Rachel found herself almost humming the strains of "Sunrise, Sunset" with the people seated on all sides. She reminded herself in time that despite local custom, she *was* a member of the profession; one did not hum with the singers onstage!

She settled back into her uncomfortable seat and enjoyed the scene between Tzeitel and her beloved tailor, Motel, then the sad scene when Hodel sang good-bye to her father and went off to marry Perchik in Siberia.

And now came the scene between Chava and her Russian gentile, Fyedka. His earlier lines had been covered by the loud talking and eating going on in the audience—Rachel wondered how anyone could concentrate with such commotion and distraction. Her contact lenses were irritating her eyes, and even with wetting solution, she had blinked through his entire first scene.

But she wasn't blinking now. The audience had settled down, perhaps because their candy wrappers were finally empty and discarded. The couple in front of Rachel had changed their seats, and at last she had a clear, unobstructed view of the stage—and a clear, unobstructed view of Fyedka.

Suddenly, before her brain had time to compute the

information, Rachel found herself gasping for breath.

The tall, slender, handsome blond didn't have to speak his lines to tell Rachel that his English was American. She had only to look at his face.

The Fyedka was Jamie.

Chapter Twenty

Rachel sat, immobilized, unable to form logical thought, incapable of movement.

When the curtain fell, she fled to the street to commandeer her senses. A mere *chamsin* could never rival this!

She gazed at the Mediterranean, now an ominous, inky black. To the left, silhouetted against a moonlit sky, the city of Jaffa painted a surrealistic landscape. Nothing seemed real.

Should she run away—as Jamie had—and share her discovery with no one? *Could* she convince herself that she had *not* seen him? She knew the answers. She had traveled halfway around the world, and some invisible guiding force had brought her to him. There was no turning back.

She found the stage door and heard a voice—her own—ask for Fyedka. "Upstairs, left," came the reply.

His dressing room was empty, but the cossack shirt he'd worn was flung over the back of a chair. Rachel leaned against a metal wardrobe armoire for support. Her hand still clutched the program. She glanced down at the lower portion—the English half. It read: "Fyedka: Boris Bar-Lev."

Her earlier dizziness returned as she heard footsteps on the stairs. He turned in the doorway and froze.

"Hello, Jamie," she said.

His mouth opened, but no sound issued from his throat. Silently, they stepped forward and, without words to aid either of them, held out their arms to each other. She raised her hand to his left cheek, as if seeking tactile reassurance of his presence. He kissed the hand that touched his cheek. Then they embraced with a ferocity that no onlooker could have fathomed. Neither had spoken but for Rachel's two words of greeting. Now they both endeavored to speak at once.

"I thought I'd never see you again," she said. "What are you doing here?"

"Me! What about *you?*" he asked.

"A film." She couldn't take her eyes from him. "You never wrote—"

"I couldn't," he said. "Not . . . not then . . ." He reached for his sweater. "Can we get out of here and go where we can talk?" he asked.

"I'd like that," she answered.

His eyes smiled with a light she remembered from the very first night they had met. "Me too," was all he said.

Their conversation, as they walked, was punctuated by silences—or perhaps it was the other way around; Rachel couldn't tell. A rocky expanse between the edge of Tel Aviv and the approach to Jaffa, probably serving sunbathers by day, provided, on this occasion, a private place shared only with the moon. They spoke of travels, of Rachel's burgeoning career, of Jamie's self-exile.

"After the Stonewall incident last summer, I had to get away, to hide from the world. I went to Europe with some money I'd saved—I wrote Paul so he wouldn't worry—and I backpacked through France with some people I met. Finally, two of us wound up here. He returned to the States, but I decided to stay."

He continued, explaining how in a state where he had

sought to lose himself, he had instead found himself. "I worked on a kibbutz when we arrived. The sheer physical labor didn't allow time for self-pity. Then I began taking care of sick children. They taught me so much! They couldn't do anything about their own suffering, but I learned from them that I could do something about mine. I studied Hebrew, picked up some Yiddish, and last month I realized there was no point in hiding anymore. So I sang for the opera, and the crazy woman hired me. I sing the leads in the musicals and operettas—you should hear *The Student Prince* in Hebrew! They only do Broadway shows in English, so you were lucky tonight." He paused to touch her hand. "No. *I* was lucky tonight."

She squeezed his fingers gently. "We both were," she said.

"It's funny, Rachel, but in a way, the Stonewall mess forced me to face the truth. At first I fought it, rejected it, God how I hated myself! And yet, now that I've finally accepted my homosexuality, I find that nobody else cares or judges me. It's brought me a certain peace that I've never felt anywhere else. Strange that I should find it in a country so often at war, but . . . I don't look for logic any longer."

"I've given that up, too," she said.

He accompanied her to the Dan Hotel shortly before dawn. They had walked along the beach, hand in hand, as the moon faded and the day began to break. Not once did they encounter another living soul, no witness to their unrehearsed reunion.

"I have a brush-up at ten o'clock," he said. "I'll be through around two-thirty. Then we'll have till Sunday."

"Where shall we meet?" she asked, barely able to keep her eyes from closing.

285

"In your hotel's lounge, downstairs. Beside the lily pond at three." He bent and kissed her eyelids, but she was too exhausted to notice. When she reached her room, she even forgot that she hadn't made a second attempt to telephone Howard.

Rachel slept past noon. When she awoke, the bathers on the beach far below were collecting their blankets and belongings and heading home, she surmised, to begin the Sabbath.

She put through a call to London; this time the hotel switchboard informed her that although the circuits were clear, Howard's line was engaged. The operator promised to keep trying.

Half an hour had passed before the telephone rang. Rachel had showered and helped herself to an apple and instant Nescafé. Her immersion heater needed a power adapter, so the coffee was prepared with hot water from the tap.

She wondered if Malcolm Campbell's contract was "out of danger" so that the actor could stay in London on his own and Howard could fly to Tel Aviv.

She still hadn't fully absorbed the shock of finding Jamie. It was probably one of the reasons why she told Howard about it—to convince herself of the fact—although she didn't share all of Jamie's disclosures; in some way, these belonged solely to Rachel and Jamie. To repeat them, even to Howard, she perceived as a form of betrayal.

Howard's voice reflected no feelings other than concerned interest. "Jamie's been all right, then, these past months?"

"Yes. That's what he says, at any rate."

"I'm glad to hear it. And . . . how are you adapting to Israel? Have you had a chance to see any of its history?"

Was Howard purposely avoiding further talk of Jamie? Would he feel the need to do so if he knew that Rachel and Jamie would never be lovers?

He said then, "I miss you, darling. I'll be there as soon as I can."

She couldn't deny missing him, too, although she speculated that part of missing him was due to Jamie's acceptance of himself; while happy for him, his new-found peace had unsettled her, and she didn't understand why. She knew only that it had nothing to do with sex.

They spent the Sabbath strolling up Ben Yehuda Street, past the countless jewelry shops and fur stores, each semihidden by amber plastic sheets covering the metal gates across their windows. The parks were deserted, too, as were the tables outside fashionable cafés on Dizengoff Street.

In the late afternoon, they walked all the way to Jaffa and ate *shishlik* kebabs with turkey disguised as lamb. The café was in the oldest section of the village, which had been so thoroughly renovated that it resembled a movie set rather than a living, breathing colony restored to the simplicity of biblical days. The stone pavements, the steps, the artisans' galleries were too pristine and too perfectly fashioned to conjure any sense of history. Rachel found it both disconcerting and anachronistic; from the rooftop terrace of the café, she could see the modern buildings that lined the shoreline of Tel Aviv. Neither setting fit the other.

On Sunday morning, David Bar-El called for Rachel at the hotel. The air was as hot as on the day of her arrival, but this time she wore a comfortable cotton safari outfit—beige slacks, matching shirt, and a large straw hat as protection from the sun. Except for the single, thick braid into which she had arranged her hair, the wardrobe reminded her of desert ensembles worn by famous actresses before her: Deborah Kerr, Ava Gardner, and—who was the third—Jean Simmons?

In one of the hotel's souvenir boutiques, she had purchased a Japanese fan. It wasn't appropriate to either the big-game-hunter trappings or to the scene, but it was very necessary to the climate.

Rachel was wearing only a minimum of makeup. Her totebag was packed with cooling astringents and cologne; she hoped that any location quarters would include an air-conditioned trailer instead of a tent; camping out was as alien—and distasteful—to her as ballet classes. No matter that her appearance offered an image of a practical woman who was accustomed to "roughing it."

But they weren't headed to a remote desert location. "Today we are shooting just outside the walls of Jerusalem," said David as the car passed more rusted trucks along the road. They were similar to those Rachel had noticed on Thursday and she didn't ask about them this time.

"It will not be a long day," he said. "It is the scene in which you try to learn from a soldier what has happened to Ben-Aron."

"Will he be on location?" Rachel hadn't inquired beforehand which members of the cast were required for exteriors, since a note accompanying her script had said that revisions would not be ready until the first day of photography.

"No, we will use his stand-in, since it is your scene. Of course, the embassy scenes will be shot in London. The situation here is too delicate to expect the government to open the doors to its official buildings. Cameras could contain . . . anything."

"Of course." Rachel wondered if David's overriding paranoia was founded in reality from past experience, or whether working in films had expanded his imagination.

"How many films have you worked on here?" she asked.

David's eyes lowered for a moment. Then he said, "I had hoped you wouldn't notice, but apparently you have. This is my first film. I am looking forward to working with you because I know how advanced film techniques are in Europe. I"—this he said almost sheepishly—"I thought I might pick up some pointers from watching you work."

Rachel burst into nervous laughter.

"Have I offended you?" asked David. "What have I said?"

She shook her head and reached out to take his hand. "David, this is *my* first film."

"It *is?*"

"You mean it doesn't show?" She stopped laughing. "Miss Allenby—"

"Rachel. Please."

"Thank you. Rachel. No—it does not show at all!"

A broad smile spread across her face. "Well, then, I must be a better actress than I thought."

The quizzical expression in his eyes told her that he hadn't quite understood her meaning. She was grateful for that. It wasn't something she had meant to share aloud.

Aside from one genuine "acting" scene, most of her location work was merely to provide authenticity of atmosphere. Her leading man was Guy Hanover, a British actor, who would start filming only after the troupe returned to London. He would balance his role of the devoted, adoring, older man in her life with his nightly Henry IV at the Old Vic.

Howard had told Rachel it was more than Guy's busy schedule that allowed him to stay in London while she had to travel to Israel. "You're prettier than he is, darling. The audience needs a bit of relief from the heat and sand—and the dramatic tension—at about this point in the film. Showing you against the ruins will add to the story, not detract from it."

Rachel hadn't been thrilled at the reason. The role required far more than a pretty face. But she saw the point. Guy Hanover was good-looking, but in the rough-hewn, craggy way of a Jack Hawkins or a Peter Finch. And as they approached the walled city of Jerusalem, both phrases came to mind as descriptions of the location: rough-hewn and craggy.

Several trucks were set up already, but no luxury "star trailer" seemed to be anywhere. "Well," mused Rachel as she stepped from the car, "it isn't just like in the movies."

"Excuse me?" said David.

Rachel shook her head. "Never mind. It wasn't important."

Tom Jarrod, the director, came forward. Rachel recognized him from photographs in film anthologies. He, too, wore safari clothes—including the kind of hat Rachel remembered as worn by Stewart Granger and Gregory Peck in desert "location" films. She tried to recall whether Humphrey Bogart had worn one in *The African Queen,* but memory failed her. Oh well, Tom Jarrod had seen the same movies she had, and *he* was a veteran of scores of films.

"Hmm," he said by way of greeting. "I see our leading lady doesn't need a wardrobe fitting. That getup's perfect—except for your hair."

Rachel extended her hand and introductions were exchanged. "This isn't exactly a place for glamour, is it?"

He gallantly replied, "But you've brought it, just the same."

They both smiled as he led her to an open tent. "We'll stay at the King David at the end of the shoot tonight, since we have two days here." Apparently he saw the relief on Rachel's face, because he added, "You didn't think we'd let you sleep out here!"

"I frankly didn't know what to think."

"Well, never fear. We'll work while the sun is high, and we'll wrap around four. Tomorrow I want to start at sun-up."

"Okay," said Rachel. "I'm here to work." Suddenly nerves began to surface. She was about to begin her first film! Admitting the fact to David hadn't made its impact. Now, the prospect excited her, but at the same time, she wondered if Howard had been mistaken. What if she fell flat on her face?

She didn't have the luxury to think about Jamie. She had a full, sun-drenched schedule ahead of her. She was relieved to find the air quite dry, though, in comparison with Tel Aviv.

Fortunately, the revised scenes involving Rachel had been rewritten shorter, rather than longer. The weather complied and they were ready to leave for Tel Aviv once again by midday on Tuesday.

On the fourth day of filming in Tel Aviv, Jamie visited the set. Although membership in Screen Actors Guild wasn't necessary as far from New York as Israel, Rachel had thought there might be a small part for Jamie on the picture. She had mentioned this to Tom, and he made the suggestion that Rachel invite him to the set, which was at the end of the extensive beachfront, past the Hilton Hotel.

Rachel hadn't expected him to arrive with company.

Jamie alighted from the taxi first. He withdrew a pair of crutches from the backseat, and then, very slowly, the other passenger emerged.

She was a woman of an age somewhere between sixty and seventy-five; her afflictions made a more accurate estimate impossible. The temperature was around ninety degrees Fahrenheit, but she wore heavy gray woolen trousers and a matching woolen sweater. Her hair was short and cropped, brownish flecked with gray, and the knobby, perhaps once-strong fingers now made an attempt to arrange her coiffure in a more presentable fashion. Her feet were covered in bulky orthopedic shoes, and as Rachel came forward, she realized that the woman could not straighten up without Jamie's assistance. She was obviously in agonizing pain as she adjusted her arms on the crutches. When one slipped, she banged her leg with angry force. "Damn!" she snapped.

Rachel was certain she'd heard a hollow, knocking sound.

"Don't worry," cautioned the woman, apparently sensing Rachel's concern, "it's made of wood. It doesn't *feel*."

Jamie's guest spoke English with an Eastern European accent. "Come here and let me look you over. My eyes do not permit the luxury of casual observation."

Jamie said, "Rachel, this is my inspiration, Annie Singer. Otherwise known as the rock of Gibraltar."

"The so-called rock has been sinking for some time." said Annie. "Your friend Apollo was good enough to rescue me today. I trust he is forgiven this intrusion?"

They were joined then by Tom Jarrod. Rachel didn't know whether to introduce Jamie with the name by which she knew him or by that in the *Fiddler* program. She certainly couldn't give his name as Apollo. But apparently the two had met.

"Nice to see you again—when Rachel mentioned an old friend from the States, I had no idea—"

"She didn't give me your name either!"

Tom explained that he and Jamie had met at a performance of the Bat Dor Dance Company shortly after Tom's arrival in Israel. While they caught up on recent news, Rachel helped Annie Singer into one of the few solid chairs on the set and seated herself on a folding canvas stool.

"You must wonder why Apollo brought me here," said the guest. "It was at my husband Georgie's insistence. He thinks the air"—she laughed, but it was neither a laugh of amusement or bitterness—"is good for me. But I think really it is because he wishes to play some of his more bombastic pieces, which he knows drive me insane." She peered up through thick, clouded eyeglass lenses and explained, "He is a musician."

"Oh . . ." Rachel was trying to find something interesting to say, but Annie Singer hadn't finished.

"Apollo tells me that you sing. You must come to visit us. We are only several blocks from the opera."

"That's very kind of you."

"It is not kindness. We have so few guests anymore. If it were not for your Apollo"—she gestured toward the general area where Jamie and Tom stood talking—"both Georgie and I would be left alone most of the time. When my husband is away, our young friend is my salvation. You are very fortunate to be so close. Have you known each other long?"

"I . . . we're . . . very old friends." Had they really met less than two years before? Rachel wouldn't have believed it.

Just then, Jamie returned. Tom went back to his script to make some last-minute changes, and while Annie rested in her chair, Jamie and Rachel excused themselves. "We'll bring coffee for all three of us," offered Rachel.

"That will be very nice of you," answered Annie Singer.

As they made their way to the makeshift refreshment table, Rachel asked, "What's the matter with her? Does she really have a wooden leg?"

Jamie nodded. "Advanced diabetes. They had to amputate the left leg, and the right one isn't in the best of

293

shape. She's almost blind, too. Can't get around at all, except for the maestro—"

"And you, she told me," interrupted Rachel.

"It makes me feel needed," he said, "and I meant that about her being my inspiration. She's quite a lady."

Rachel had already gathered that.

When they returned with coffee and pastries, Rachel couldn't keep from studying Annie Singer's face. It struck her as remarkable; the skin was beige, not tan; taut and shiny, it resembled polished kidskin and was surprisingly free of wrinkles for one so racked with pain. Despite the bottlelike lenses concealing her eyes, Rachel had sensed immediately that Annie saw better than most.

Rachel had only five lines in that afternoon's scene. When Tom called it a wrap for the day, Annie turned and said, "Why not come back to the apartment now? Apollo arrived today with a basket of fresh fruit, and we have some wine, if Georgie has not finished it in our absence—"

"I'd love to," Rachel replied. She was tired from the heat and didn't feel up to a recital in Caesarea, where the rest of the cast and crew members were headed.

As one of Tom's assistants was helping Annie to the waiting taxi, Rachel asked Jamie, "Why does she call you Apollo? Is that Hebrew for Boris Bar-Lev? Or is Boris the translation of Jamie Morgan?"

He shook his head. "None of the above. Annie likes to rename people. You'll see. I'm sure she's cooking one up for you already. The name in the program—well, lots of new immigrants take Hebrew names. I figured it gave me a clean slate—you know, like starting from scratch. Jamie Morgan wasn't doing that much for me—and for a while it gave me a problem"—he laughed about it now—"and besides, Jamie Morgan isn't my name, either."

"It's not?"

"Nope. I was born Hyman Morganthal. That's great

for a doctor, but not for a singer. I changed Hymie—I hated the nickname!—to Jamie when I was ten. And I just shortened Morganthal." Then he surprised Rachel. "Apropos of name changes, will you be offended by a question?" Without waiting for an answer, he said, "Are you planning to change your name?"

"To what?"

"To Rathborne," he said.

But the taxi's horn obliterated any reply that Rachel might have offered.

The taxi stopped at Rehov Trumpledor. Jamie hopped out and paid the driver, then helped Annie, who suggested to Rachel, "Why don't you go up ahead of us? We might be a while. Just knock. It's the third floor."

Rachel could see that Annie was struggling with the crutches; she wondered how the woman would manage three flights, even with Jamie's support.

She entered the dark passageway and began climbing stairs. It was difficult to make her way on both legs in the pitch-darkness. She didn't know whether the light had burned out or if it had never existed.

When she reached what she hoped was the right floor, she knocked on the door. She heard a shuffle of slippers growing closer. Then several locks were unbolted and the heavy, creaky door swung open.

There stood the hunched-over, paunchy conductor Rachel had seen holding together the performance of *Fiddler* on the night of her arrival. "Come in, *shalom!*" he said, and Rachel entered the eclectic realm of George and Annie Singer.

The Singers' apartment was badly in need of repairs; Annie was undoubtedly too ill and the maestro, given what Rachel had gleaned from Jamie, was too preoccupied with his music.

295

"I see that you are curious," said Annie as she and Jamie entered the apartment. "Georgie, take our new friend for the tour." She laughed bitterly. "It is not much to look at, but we are old now. It is no longer important."

The maestro took Rachel by the hand. "Come with me. Our friend will visit with Annie. They always have so much to discuss." He led her down a small corridor. "Nothing of interest," he said, indicating the living room. "Ah, but *this*—he flung open a cracked glass door— "this is my studio!"

He bowed formally and beckoned Rachel to enter the room. She had never seen such a cluttered mess.

Buried beneath piles of yellowed scores and notebooks was an ancient grand piano, well camouflaged by a frayed piano throw and torn scarves. A bust of someone—Rachel knew only that it was *not* Mozart—leaned precariously against a corner shelf. A faded antimacassar hung haphazardly from one end of the Bösendorfer instrument, and countless books, which had come loose of their bindings, lay strewn about the floor as they probably had for decades.

The maestro beamed proudly. "I love this room! It is filled with memories. Memories from a better time."

He pointed to the walls, which were covered with framed, autographed letters and photographs. Rachel recognized the more familiar names: Rubinstein, Toscanini, Gershwin, Puccini. "I knew them all," he said. The joy with which he now shared his treasures seemed to remove, as if by magic, seventy of his seventy-five or more years. His boyish exuberance was contagious and it emboldened Rachel to speak freely.

"Maestro, forgive me, but I have to ask. Besides," she added with a mischievous grin, "I've been told that Israelis are very direct—"

"What do you want to know?"

296

"Well . . ." Suddenly she wondered if she would be invading his privacy. Nonetheless, she said, "What are you doing *here?* You could conduct anywhere. Why do you stay?"

He shrugged. "Life . . . Annie . . . I manage to conduct in Europe each year, just symphonies or concerts—there is less rehearsal time required, less time away from her. And I am neither as young nor as attractive as you. You know, we have an Indian leading the Philharmonic. Not a bad musician, but you see, he is very handsome and debonair. That helps, these days. I am just an old man." He spoke without regret. "Also, you may find this difficult to believe, but the orchestra at the opera? All those Russian violinists are learning to play Gershwin—*I* am teaching them how!"

He seated himself on the piano bench and lifted the lid to expose the chipped, yellowed keys. It was the first time Rachel had noticed his fingers; they were long, slim pianist's fingers. As he placed them on the keyboard and began to play, they seemed to belong to someone else, their elegance belying their owner and his surroundings.

He started with a medley of *Porgy and Bess*. When he came to the evocative opening of "Summertime," he looked up. "Do you sing?" he asked.

In reply, Rachel began Clara's beautiful lullaby. It felt so good! She hadn't sung in weeks—how she'd missed it! George Singer's accompaniment was like having her own, personal orchestra in attendance.

He didn't stop at the end of the song; instead, he nodded an opening cue and led her into the Bess-Porgy duet. He spoke the words—Rachel discovered that his singing voice was atrocious—until it was time for Bess's entrance. "Porgy, I's yo' woman now," she sang. "I is, I is," and on to the end of the line.

Suddenly, from across the street, came a glorious baritone voice in reply. "Bess, you is my woman now," he

297

sang—with decidedly Russian vowels. Rachel looked up, startled, but the maestro whispered, "Go on, sing it through with him!"

She obeyed, and as so often in the past, she found herself gradually transported by the music, despite the incongruity of her surroundings: the old man at the piano; her unknown Russian Porgy across the street; Bess, a role she would never be allowed to sing onstage. And Gershwin had brought them together!

When the duet ended, a burst of applause greeted her ears—not only from the parlor where Jamie and Annie were ensconced, but from balconies up and down the length of Rehov Trumpledor.

The maestro rose from the piano and took Rachel's hand. Together they stepped onto the balcony. "Bow," he whispered. "It's expected."

She bowed, feeling both ridiculous and elated at the same time.

"Shalom!" shouted the neighbors, waving frantically. Rachel and the maestro waved back.

When they had taken their improvised curtain call, Rachel and the maestro reentered the stuffy room. "Israelis may be very direct," he said, "but they are also very open. If they like something, they let you know." He giggled gleefully. "Once I auditioned a terrible singer. She had a huge wobble in her upper register—but who knew? When she finished, they threw tomatoes." Winking, he added, "That was why I asked *first* if you sing."

"I might have been terrible," she teased.

"I think you would have told me," he said.

Jamie was preparing fruit salad in the minuscule kitchen. The maestro spent two minutes with Annie and Rachel and then disappeared again into his studio. The two women were alone in the small parlor.

"You have a good voice," said Annie.

"Thank you. I . . . I hadn't warmed up. I didn't expect to do any singing during my stay here."

"Youth can accomplish anything. I sang once. I did many things. Now I barely survive. But"—she suddenly slapped her artificial leg—"it will all be over soon."

Rachel waited for her to explain.

"You know, when I had two strong legs of my own, I swam across a river—with Georgie—to escape the Nazis. We were so young, so full of life!" She spat. "Look at us now!" Then, recovering, she said, "I beg your pardon. There are also days when I am grateful to have even one left." She stroked the good leg affectionately. "There is one thing I know: that we are given choice—at least over some matters. For now, even with this wretched stump, I choose life. But if they must take the second leg, I shall choose death."

She paused to wipe her forehead with the back of her hand. Then she cleaned her eyeglass lenses with the border of her sweater and shook her head. "It is far easier to face when one becomes part of the choice."

Jamie reentered then with a bowl of colorful fruit chunks.

"Well, Annie, have you decided on a name for Rachel?" he asked.

"From what I recall in the Bible, Rachel was beautiful and good, and she was intelligent. I think perhaps your friend's name suits her." Looking up at Rachel, she added, "Just remember always to choose well, my young friend of Apollo."

Chapter Twenty-one

There was a message from Howard, who had telephoned from London. He expected the Malcolm Campbell tantrum to be ended and the matter resolved by Sunday, at which time he would fly to Israel. There was also a letter from Beth Burns, with news about *The Red Shoes*. I'll send her a telegram for opening night, Rachel decided. She wasn't up to a letter just yet.

She was tired. Her reunion with Jamie, the long days shooting in the sweltering heat, and her encounter with Annie Singer had added to new and strange sensations. Now, walking down a hot, deserted avenue in Tel Aviv with Jamie—who had accepted the resumption of their friendship as an everyday occurrence—she felt a resurgence of that same peculiar yet familiar bewilderment, as though she were again watching a film in which she played the starring role.

The detachment—for its very meaning—was unnerving. It brought to mind the astronaut in Kubrick's *2001*; there were times such as these when Rachel felt *she* had been hurled into space, into a sea of weightlessness, with no destination and, still worse, no possibility of turning back. It frightened her, because with it came the threat of apathy. Was Annie Singer right? Was it a matter of choice?

But even Annie had said *choice* wasn't available in all areas of life. What about those areas over which one had no control?

* * *

They had returned to the Dan Hotel and were stretched out across the length of the bed in Rachel's room. The air-conditioning was running at high cool. Jamie turned on the Jordan television station and pulled up a chair to watch a vintage British war movie. Since Jordan also provided viewers with polylingual subtitles, Rachel lay back on the bed and allowed the leading man's rich, resonant baritone to soothe and relax her. His voice reminded her of Howard's, although the actor's speech possessed none of Howard's humor, and physically, Rachel noted before closing her eyes, they were worlds apart.

Howard would arrive on Sunday. Despite indecision regarding their relationship, she was eager to see him. This forced separation had offered an opportunity to examine her feelings from a new perspective, but finding Jamie had reopened old, nagging questions that had to be addressed before change could occur. Even if some matters were out of anyone's control, Rachel knew that the matter of Jamie was not among them.

Perhaps her inner conflicts were no more than the result of recent hurts — she had pretended that losing *The Red Shoes* was not so important to her; that Beth *hadn't* disappointed her; that she understood completely about Lehman Stern's dilemma.

In truth, the expenditure in energy and effort had been enormous; that Rachel had been convincing indicated only her acting prowess.

By the time the movie was over, night had fallen. Rachel had dozed intermittently, while Jamie was stretched out along the foot of the bed. She observed his sleeping form, the blond hair falling over his closed eyes as it often did when he was awake; the double-thick, dark blond lashes, and the boyish innocence she had always found so . . . what? Seductive? Or elusive?

She restrained an urge to wrap her arms around him. There was so much about Jamie that she still didn't comprehend, so much he would never share with her. Paul had once speculated that Jamie might be incapable of love. But was it true about him—or about her?

Paul's words haunted Rachel as, propped on her elbow, she lay pondering the question.

Whatever the answer, Jamie didn't appear troubled by it. He slept peacefully, as children do, his breathing deep and steady, his body languid and free of tension. Instead of enabling Rachel to relax, it increased her restlessness. She wrote a note and placed it beside him so he'd see it when he awoke. Then, taking her room key, she slipped out the door.

The beachfront was deserted, yet it was safer than the crowded area around the opera house and Henri's café. Prostitutes obviously didn't find much business along the water's edge.

The moon was a crescent sliver of silver, casting a slim, undulating highlight across the indigo waters. Rachel looked up at the shape in the sky. As a child, she had believed her brothers' tale—that the round sphere was a man whose face was made of green cheese. Studies in school had quickly dispelled that myth, but somehow she had never fully abandoned her romantic notion about the force that controlled cycles and tides and, despite Shakespeare's negation, the inclinations of so many minds. Even with the astronauts' recent landing, despite "one giant step for mankind," the moon still held a mystical fascination.

Tonight it penetrated even deeper, as Rachel reflected on its oneness with humanity, with all life on the planet. This was the same moon shining over her family's home in Minnesota—most likely glimmering over a pre-

Thanksgiving snowfall. This was the same moon that hovered over London, where Howard was probably sitting before the cozy fireplace at William and Jennie's in Hertfordshire. And it was the same moon illuminating Shubert Alley and the theater where Beth Burns was about to open as Victoria Paige in *The Red Shoes*.

That last thought erased the romantic element from Rachel's thoughts, yet strangely drew her back to the poetry of Shakespeare. She gazed upward and said to the air, "He was right after all. The fault *isn't* in our stars." She didn't know why this should excite and exhilarate her so, but her breathing deepened suddenly and her energy soared, as though replenished by a life-giving source. Annie Singer *was* right—it *was* a matter of choice!

She couldn't wait to return to the hotel and tell Jamie!

He seemed somewhat unsettled when she reached the room.

"What's the matter?" asked Rachel when she saw his eyes avoiding hers.

"Howard called from London."

"Is he all right?" she asked, suddenly agitated.

"He was before he got me on the line," Jamie answered. "I guess he didn't expect to find me in your room."

"What do you mean? What did you say to each other?"

"Not a lot. He asked for you, and I said you were out. He said he was glad we've reestablished contact—or something like that—but that he just hoped it wasn't adding to your confusion."

"And what did you say?"

"That sometimes confusion becomes a convenient excuse."

"I don't understand that," said Rachel.

"I didn't think you would. But Howard seemed to."

"Would you care to explain what you're talking about?" She tossed her keys on the desk and took a seat in the easy chair.

"Well, I've done a lot of thinking over the past months, Rachel," he said. "And I've reached the conclusion that sitting on the fence is often no more than an excuse for procrastination. In my case, falling in love with you let me put off admitting to myself that I was gay—"

"You told me you'd admitted it long before—you just hadn't accepted it," she interjected.

"That's true. But it's one thing to accept a fact intellectually. Emotionally can take a lot longer."

"Okay, that was *your* fence. What about mine?" She sensed a defensive tone in her voice, but that wasn't within her control.

"For some reason, you haven't wanted to make a commitment to Howard. Staying confused about me is a noble excuse—"

"Now wait a minute—"

"No, Rachel, listen to me. Has Howard asked you to marry him?"

When she didn't answer, Jamie continued. "I thought so. He adores you."

"You don't seem upset about it," she said. "That's a first."

"I'd like to see you happy. And he's really not so bad."

"You've changed your opinion."

"About a lot of things. I think Howard and I could get along—except that he probably holds me responsible. Just as you do."

"Responsible for *what?*"

"For your indecision. He thinks you're still in love with me."

"He *said* that?"

"Not in so many words. But I heard it, just the same."

For a moment neither of them spoke. Then Jamie said softly, "Rachel . . . are you?"

Her eyes were not facing his, although she wasn't consciously avoiding him. "Am I what . . . ?"

"In love with me?"

She drew a deep breath, rose, and seated herself beside him at the very edge of the bed.

"I went for a walk on the beach while you were napping," she said. "I watched the moon for an hour. It was beautiful."

"Meaning?"

"It's always the same, and yet it's constantly changing. I guess I must feel that way about you. Just when I think I've discovered the answers, something new crops up to remind me that I don't really know a thing." Her earlier elation had been replaced by a dull, empty void.

"Welcome to the club. I'm a charter member." He took her hand and stroked her slim fingers. "I love you," he said. "I always will. But I've come to understand that it has to be a love that isn't any more or any less than just what it is."

"That sounds like Zen—"

"When the pupil is ready, the teacher appears."

"What?"

He smiled. "You'll understand. I think Howard does."

"But you said—"

"I said he wasn't thrilled to find me here. I wouldn't be either, if I were Howard."

"Well, I'm glad the two of you had a chance to visit," she said sarcastically. "It's nice to be discussed by both of you."

"Rachel—"

"Look, I'm tired. I have an early call tomorrow. And I'd like to call Howard back."

"You'd like me to go?"

305

She nodded. "I don't enjoy having my mind and my motivations analyzed as if I'm a specimen in a biology lab."

"We both love you," he said, shrugging.

"At times that can be suffocating, Jamie." She was aware as she spoke that her breath had crept higher and the gag reflex in her throat was strangely present.

"Can we have dinner tomorrow after you wrap? I promise to make myself scarce once Howard arrives—if that's what you want."

She accompanied him to the door. "If I knew what I wanted, this conversation would never have taken place, would it?"

She knew it was rhetorical, and he must have sensed her need for distance. When he bent to kiss her good night, she made the slightest involuntary physical retreat.

The switchboard had put through the call to London, but Howard was out. Rachel had the operator try both the house at Hertfordshire and the Savoy. The hotel hadn't seen him for two days, and there was no reply from William and Jennie's. Yawning repeatedly, Rachel undressed and went to bed.

In the morning new script changes, although minimal rewrites, required Rachel's full attention; she was secretly grateful.

During the lunch break, she received a message from the hotel. Howard had called again and had just missed her.

"How's he doing all alone in London?" asked Tom Jarrod.

"You can ask him that yourself," she said, pocketing the message slip. "He's flying in this afternoon."

"I thought he wasn't coming till Sunday."

"So did I, but I guess the business he had to take care

of was cleared up earlier than expected." She didn't tell Tom, but she wondered if Howard's conversation with Jamie had caused him to push his flight date ahead.

Jamie echoed her thoughts when he arrived at location to meet her and she told him the news. "Well, it may be adding insult to injury, but I'll be glad to drive you to Lod to pick him up. What time does his flight get in?"

"At five. But it may be better if I ask David Bar-El to drive me. We're not that far from the airport."

"It's up to you. I wish you'd believe me when I tell you I want you to be happy, Rachel."

She had forgiven him for the previous night. "I do," she said. "I always did."

They had one more sequence to shoot before the day's wrap. The dialogue again involved only four lines, but the wind had changed direction and was rapidly increasing to gust velocity. The cameras had to be moved and fastened down before they could continue.

"We'd better hurry," advised David as he rushed up to Tom and the crew. Rachel and Jamie were seated in canvas director chairs beside one of the equipment trucks, which served as protection from the blowing sands.

Rachel checked her wristwatch. It was going on five o'clock, but the upcoming scene could be shot in minutes. David seemed to be overreacting again.

But it wasn't because of the hour. "That wind," he explained, "is the onset of a *chamsin*. We can't work in it."

"Surely it isn't all that serious," joked Tom.

"It is that and more," said David.

Rachel didn't know whether to chide David for his extreme caution or to admonish Tom for taking his Israeli adviser too lightly.

Suddenly, she had energy to do neither. Without warning, the wind calmed to a deathly stillness. At once,

307

there was an eeriness of motion slowed, then stopped, as if by time-lapse photography. On film it was thrilling; but now, as Rachel fought an oncoming dizziness and then remembered David's advice of *not* trying to fight it, she realized that his description had omitted several sensations, one of which was the terrible feeling of sinking through sand to a bottomless pit.

At the moment she closed her eyes to keep from falling over in her chair, she was shaken by an incredible *boom!* Her eyes flashed open in time to see an explosion in the sky. The giant ball of fire, plummeting to the earth, left a jet stream of thick, black smoke in its wake.

Despite the heaviness in the air around them, Rachel pulled herself to a standing position as people crowded around Tom Jarrod and his portable radio.

Through the static came the words: *terrorists . . . bombing . . . London.* At first, Rachel thought it was a shortwave news report of an IRA bombing in Britain's capital. But suddenly it hit her with a force ten times stronger than that of the *chamsin.*

It was five o'clock. "Oh my God!" she cried. "Howard's flight!"

She thought they would never reach the airport. Fortunately, the *chamsin* slowing their movements also cleared the road of most traffic. The skies en route to Lod Airport became blacker. David was behind the wheel, while Jamie and Rachel were huddled together in the backseat, gripping each other's arms for support. The already stifling air now mingled with the acrid smells of burning metal and plastic. Smoke became so thick that David was forced to close the windows of the car; the heat inside was unbearable. Ambulance sirens screeched, then faded away or grew louder, depending upon their direction.

Just before reaching the airport entrance, David's car was stopped by an army guard. He spoke in English when David rolled the window down. "I am sorry, sir, there is danger of further explosion. You cannot drive the vehicle beyond this point."

Rachel insisted, "But I'm meeting someone! He was on the flight! I—" Her voice was choked.

The soldier said to David, "You will have to leave the car here and go on foot. The road must also remain clear to move the wounded to the hospital."

"What if he's already there?" Rachel cried suddenly. She refused to allow her mind to consider that Howard might be severely hurt—or worse. Nausea overwhelmed her as she struggled to submerge any but optimistic possibilities.

Before David or Jamie could stop her, she flung open the rear passenger door on her side of the car and began running in the direction of the terminal building. The plane had obviously exploded quite close to its landing strip.

Jamie tore after her and caught up easily; the *chamsin* and the smoke-filled air were making breathing difficult and calm impossible. When Rachel saw that Jamie was gasping for air, she realized that she had been hyperventilating since hearing the radio announcement.

With only adrenaline coming to her rescue, she rushed into the swarm of airport and hospital personnel. Wounded passengers lay on makeshift cots. Some moaned, others were unconscious. Plastic body bags and blood-soaked sheets covered lifeless forms. Rachel's stomach churned and the room began to sway as her mind registered the numbing images.

Where was Howard? Face after face, none of them his. Relief, coupled with a growing panic.

Spotting a woman with a clipboard and a walkie-talkie, Rachel, followed by Jamie, pushed through the crowd until they reached her. "How can I find a passenger from the—the London—flight?" Rachel gasped.

The woman held a pen and, using it as a pointer, indicated several areas. "The serious casualties are over there, awaiting hospital transport. Those with minor wounds are in the office." She nodded toward a door. Then, with a chilling matter-of-factness, she added, "The dead are in that corner. Other bodies have yet to be recovered from the debris."

Rachel's knees buckled, but Jamie caught her.

As fear edged closer toward hysteria, Rachel and Jamie made their way through the chaos until they reached what looked to be the center of control.

Approaching the man in charge, Rachel opened her mouth to speak. No sound was forthcoming. It wasn't the smoke; she was aphonous. Jamie gave Howard's name to the official.

The man read dispassionately through a long list.

"These are names of survivors. The bodies of the deceased have not yet been identified." When he reached the bottom of the second sheet of paper, he looked up and said, "No passenger named Rathborne is on my list." Then he must have seen Rachel's pallor. "Look," he said, "I have only names of some who escaped with minor injury. But I have not all the names—"

"Y-yes . . . t-thank you," stammered Rachel as Jamie led her away from a gurney carrying a screaming woman and her baby.

As Rachel looked down at the tiny infant's scratched face and minuscule, defiant fists, Jamie ordered, "Lean over."

"W-what?"

"Your face is too white. Bend your head over to get the blood circulating again. I'll be right back."

"Where are you going?" she asked. "Don't leave me here!"

"I'll find something to keep you from passing out on me," he said, hurrying back into the confusion.

She obeyed; David Bar-El found Rachel seated on a bench with her head on her knees. "I have checked the outside area, but so far . . . I have learned nothing. I was told, though, that more wounded are still being brought in from the wreckage. Apparently, the bomb went off in the toilet, but the entire plane did not explode."

Rachel lifted her head to better comprehend his meaning.

"If it had been more centrally placed," explained David, "there would have been . . . no survivors."

Fortunately, Jamie returned with a cupful of ice at that moment; otherwise, David's attempt at tact would have had the opposite effect: she would have fainted.

The ice's shock to her nervous system provided temporary relief and allowed her senses to subside. Logic was needed here, not emotion. Perhaps that was why the officials in charge seemed so unfeeling, she reasoned. Her vision began to clear as a small cube melted under her tongue and she swallowed the cool liquid.

But David said, "If your questions have met with little compassion, Rachel, you must understand that such occurrences are nothing new to us. These are facts with which we must live every day."

His remark shocked her into reality as quickly as had the ice.

For the next hour Rachel and Jamie asked one passenger after another if anyone had seen or sat beside a tall, distinguished Englishman with graying hair and deep blue eyes. David telephoned the hospitals that were receiving the wounded, but he did not find Howard among them.

Finally, the one official who had earlier shown empathy approached. "Excuse me, but you were looking for one of the passengers?" he asked.

"Yes!" Rachel jumped to her feet. "Have you . . . have you found him?"

"No, but they have just freed several more people from the wreckage."

"Where! Please, where . . . ?"

"Out there," he said, pointing. "But be careful. The plane crashed into one of the old buildings. Do not go inside. There is fear that it may collapse."

Rachel thanked him and grabbed Jamie's wrist. Together they raced through the exit door to the direction they had been given. A slight wind had come up.

"Thank God for small favors," said Jamie. "The *chamsin* is lifting!"

But Rachel didn't hear him. She was rushing toward what remained of the plane. It looked as though it had been cut in half, and its nose was smashed, the latter probably from its impact with the two-story cement and wood structure into which it had rammed.

There were six passengers lying just free of the wreckage. Their faces were covered with blood and soot. Two of the wounded were women. Hurrying past them toward the four men, Rachel called out frantically to each of them, "Howard! Howard!"

But none of them responded.

"Lady!" cried one of the six. *"Look out!"*

Before Rachel could get out of its way, a wooden beam from the rickety roof of the building came crashing toward her.

A split-second later, everything went black.

Rachel knew she was in a hospital; she could tell from the antiseptic smells and the whispers all around. Her eyes were closed and she feared opening them. In the illogic of sedation, a surreal voice told her that if she kept her eyes closed, she might avoid whatever truth awaited her. Once she opened them, there would be no turning back.

She ached. Or felt numb. She wasn't sure which. She moved one hand, then the other. They weren't attached to any hospital apparatus; that meant she wasn't on an IV. But oh, how her head throbbed!

Then she heard a nurse talking in low tones and realized that she was the subject under discussion. "She's been asking for you. All through the night, even in her sleep."

Rachel tried to speak, but she felt as though her mind were weighted. She couldn't form words through the fog.

"She goes in and out, but it's the medication. She'll be all right in a few days. It's just a concussion. But try not to tire her. She's had quite an emotional shock."

Rachel heard the click of heels as the nurse retreated.

Then a hand touched hers.

Tears welled up inside her as he gently squeezed her fingers. Somehow she found the strength to return the pressure. And then, she slowly opened her eyes.

"Oh, Howard!" she whispered. "Is it really you?"

"Yes, my love," he said, brushing away her tears.

"But . . . we looked . . . everywhere . . ."

"I wasn't on the plane. I had a last-minute delay."

"You . . . you did?" Was it possible? Was she awake and was he really sitting beside her?

His kiss settled all doubts.

She lifted the hand closest to him and stroked his cheek. His face was lined with strain and he needed a shave. "But how . . . did you . . . ?"

"Jamie got hold of a passenger list and found out I wasn't aboard. He rang me in London and I took the next flight here." He smoothed her damp hair and said gently, "The nurse says you've been asking for me."

"Oh, Howard . . ." She looked up into the depths of his blue eyes. "I . . . I've been meaning to tell you something . . ."

"Have you?" he asked, kissing her brow.

"Howard . . . I wanted to tell you sooner, but I . . . I didn't know it before."

"You mustn't tire yourself," he said softly. "I promised the nurse."

"I love you," she whispered, startled by the burst of energy suddenly ignited by her own words. "I've loved you for so long, but I didn't recognize it until I thought—" She was unable to voice what she had feared most.

Their hands were intertwined now, and she saw tears in his eyes. However, when he spoke, his voice was low and gently teasing. "There's one matter still to be settled, you know."

"There is?" She loved him—what could stand between them now?

"Yes," he said. "It's about the pewter mug—"

She felt a smile forming at the corners of her mouth. "Is there time to engrave it with . . . with the letter *R?*"

Howard's laugh betrayed traces of the past day's emotional toll, but it was a laugh, nonetheless. "Is that . . . a proposition?"

She shook her head, despite the dull, insistent ache. "No . . . it's a proposal."

He took her face in his hands and placed another tender kiss on her lips. "In that case, my darling, I accept." To the air, he sighed and added, "I thought she'd never ask."

BOOK TWO

Chapter Twenty-two

October 1975

It was more like a cottage, not in the least pretentious, a place where Rachel and Howard could escape the pressures of her highly visible career and her husband's management of it. Having William and Jennie as neighbors was an added inducement, but what had sold the couple was the white picket fence. It was so different from their apartment on Fifth Avenue; indeed, it was different from any house they had occupied in almost six years of marriage. Nonetheless, the moment they had seen the TO LET OR TO BUY sign on the way to the pub, they knew the house was meant to be theirs.

As the movers deposited carton after carton in the front entrance hall and living room, Rachel wondered how it was possible to have accumulated so many *things*.

"Nomads aren't supposed to be acquisitive," she mused aloud.

"What's that, mum?" asked one of the workmen.

"Nothing," she answered. "I was just talking to myself."

"Oh, well, me wife does it all the time, but I tell 'er it's all right as long as she knows she's doin' it." He set down two large boxes. "This where you want 'em, mum?"

Rachel nodded. For the moment, one place was as good as another. Time to start unpacking, so the house would be livable by the time Howard returned from New

York the following week.

She rolled up the sleeves of her blue work shirt and tucked the shirttails into her jeans. Then she opened one of the cartons marked: FRAGILE: HANDLE WITH CARE. That would contain either the Waterford crystal, the Wedgwood china, or framed photographs; neither she nor Howard collected knickknacks.

But it was her awards "collection." At the top, cushioned for traveling with layers of foam, was her framed gold record for the single of "My Light Through the Trees"; the hit song from *Robin Hood* was now considered such a standard that no one could enter an elevator in America or a lift in England without hearing the Muzak rendition. She smiled at the memory of the excitement, the nervous anticipation with which she had first sung the song that launched her career, a career so spectacular that it had now gone even beyond her wildest girlhood dreams.

Further evidence of her fame and artistry lay carefully wrapped in the financial section of *The New York Times*. She unrolled the sheets of newsprint that protected her Best Supporting Actress Award for *The Sixth Day*—an Oscar for her first film. So long ago, she reflected, thinking back to those brief weeks on location in Israel, as she unwrapped George Singer's tattered score of *Porgy and Bess*. Jamie had sent it after the maestro's death. "He would have wanted you to have it," he'd written. Rachel's eyes misted as she fondly recalled Annie. The woman had kept her word; with the other leg taken, she had made her choice. Now the couple were both gone from the cramped, dilapidated apartment on Trumpledor Street; the great musician who had known the masters had been relegated to a single paragraph on the obituary page, and all that remained of his artistry was a dog-eared copy of Gershwin's opera with ink scratches in both Georges' hands. Even less remained of

Annie, who had only outlived her adopted country's most recent war by a matter of months.

So much has changed! thought Rachel. Does it, as Annie said, *always* come down to choice? She reflected on Watergate, and politics led her mind to other forms in which that word was applied. She laughed aloud as she fingered the edges of her Tony Award for *Robin Hood*. How naïve I was then! she said to herself. I really thought I'd won because of *talent!* She was still less than pleased with the publicity campaigning both the Tony and Oscar awards had required. Mina MacDonald and Howard had assured her that if *she* hadn't capitalized on the nominations, some other actress would have—and some other actress would have won.

"My God," she said aloud, "the public never knows, does it?"

"What's that, mum?" asked the mover, balancing a large carton piggyback. "Did'ja say somethin' about the pub?"

Rachel glanced at her wristwatch. "Oh . . . yes . . . why don't you and the other men take a break and go down to the pub? I'll try and clear some of this stuff to make room for the rest by the time you get back."

She didn't have to repeat the suggestion.

It felt good to be alone in the house for an hour. Rachel rose and stretched her arms above her head. Then she put a cassette of a Bach violin concerto into her small portable Sony recorder; the richer, fuller sounds would have to wait until Howard's arrival—she had no idea how to connect the amplifier's power system. She turned the volume higher, and as Itzhak Perlman compensated for the thinness of sound coming from the tiny internal speaker, she again toured the house that she and Howard had fondly christened Rathborne Cottage.

There were two bedrooms at the top of the mahogany staircase, which was flanked by a newly refinished banis-

319

ter and ornately carved newel post. The third "floor" contained only a small attic. Every room boasted dark, beamed ceilings and leaded casement windows, giving the house a cozy Tudor appearance, although Howard had seen to it that the bathroom—only one, between the two second-floor bedrooms—was equipped with modern plumbing and all new appointments. The shower was glass encased, and a deep, inviting, extra-long tub, although resembling the ancient relic in Jamie's Fifth Street kitchen, was gleaming with shiny porcelain and polished brass spigots. It occupied an entire wall and stood on four feet; Rachel hadn't decided whether they looked more like the paws of a lion or the claws of an eagle.

The master bedroom peered out over a small vegetable and flower garden, and before leaving for New York, Howard had engaged a handyman named Owen to tend both garden and shrubbery. So far he had trimmed only the hedges, but he was probably waiting for the owners to settle in.

Rachel placed the awards—her personal souvenirs, not for public display—on the floor in the corner of the attic, which she planned to transform into her studio. She and Howard had agreed to keep the furnishings of their living quarters free of professional adornments. She might, however, leave the *Porgy* score on the piano, which was yet to be delivered. The instrument itself would have to remain in the living room; the attic was too small for even a spinet. But this little upstairs garret space would be Rachel's domain; she had fallen in love immediately with its turretlike separation from the rest of the house.

"You have your office-den in New York," she'd told Howard. "This will be *mine*." Even if it served only as a place for reading or studying scripts, she enjoyed the idea of a secret hideaway. It recalled the tree house that her brothers had built years before. "It's our private place, and only those who know the password will be admitted," they'd said. But they had never shared the password, and she had not gained entry.

Only the living room, the staircase, and the bathroom had thus far been renovated; the downstairs guest room and dining area would need considerable work, and the kitchen was, in a word, primitive. The small gas stove was new, but the refrigerator, old and only shoulder-height, was the single electrical appliance in sight. The sink was low and made of stone. No visible presence of modern technology: not a Mr. Coffee, Cuisinart, or microwave to consume counter space—which, empty, was less spacious than the wooden cutting board in a tiny corner of their New York kitchen. Thank God I learned how to cook in small spaces! thought Rachel.

She wandered back to the guest room and made a mental note to ask Owen if he'd ever stripped and refinished wood. She'd try her hand at the task, but this was going to require help.

At last the movers had unloaded all the cartons, trunks, and furniture. Dusk was settling quietly over Hertfordshire. William and Jennie would be back from London tomorrow, and they'd already invited her to dinner. Tired but nonetheless relaxed, Rachel unpacked the other electrical "appliance" that didn't need Howard's expertise: his portable electric typewriter. Then, hoping it wouldn't cause a power blackout, she connected the adaptor and plugged it into the socket. She held her breath. Nothing exploded, so she pressed the ON key. A little light blinked, and a soft whirring sound began. "We're in business," said Rachel. She propped the machine on top of an unpacked crate and, seating herself on a cushion on the floor, began a letter to Jamie.

By the time Howard arrived at Rathborne Cottage, Rachel had learned the art of wood finishing. She marveled at the pleasure derived from accomplishing such simple, everyday chores. If a stranger had wandered past the open doors and spotted the lady of the house in her cutoff jeans, T-shirt, and sneakers as she applied thick varnish remover to doorframes and floor moldings, a dirty canvas glove holding the sticky, dripping brush, while the free hand tried to keep stray wisps of hair in her ponytail, that stranger would never have taken her for the internationally acclaimed singing and acting "sensation," Rachel Allenby Rathborne. *Stars* simply didn't do this kind of work!

Howard assumed at first that a team of craftsmen had performed the transformation, since he found Rachel in black silk lounging pajamas, and her hair was no longer in a ponytail but hung long and full around her shoulders. The ruby and diamond earrings he had given her for *Robin Hood* dangled from their platinum posts—Rachel's ears had finally been pierced—and she had poached a salmon to Voisin perfection. Howard's favorite Meursault was chilling in the newly scrubbed refrigerator, and although Rachel hadn't gone so far as to master a sewing machine, she had purchased in town dotted-swiss curtains that now framed each window and added a homey, lived-in touch. At an antiques auction, she had found and framed small prints of the English countryside; Rathborne Cottage was not the setting for Howard's French Impressionists.

"So Owen has been a help, after all," said Howard, surveying his wife's handiwork. "I was worried that he seemed lazy and a bit surly."

"I haven't seen him all week," Rachel answered. "And that's just as well. I've had a marvelous time." She kissed him tenderly; his embrace made the long hours of sand-

ing, rubbing, and polishing more than worth the effort.
"Welcome home, darling."

He tossed his briefcase to the chair beside his suitcase
and took her in his arms. "You look wonderful," he
said. "The 'rustic' life suits you."

They laughed, sharing the joke. How, she wondered,
could this man ever have been married to a woman like
Cecily Wilton? It doesn't matter, she reflected as he
kissed her again. *I'm* married to him now.

A month had passed, four weeks in which Howard
had shown his own prowess with hammer and nails. He
had installed the stereo system, replete with speakers in
every room. The central terminal, in the living room, ran
along an entire wall. It had taken Rachel an afternoon to
master the various red, green, and yellow buttons on the
display panel. When she finally found the right balance,
the blinking lights held steady and reminded her of a
Christmas tree.

Howard had spent the week in London, this time for
pleasure as well as business. This evening he would
collect Lehman Stern and a guest—Lehman's guest—at
Heathrow, and the three would drive back to Hertfordshire together. The prospect delighted Rachel; she
hadn't seen the conductor-turned-director in months. His
schedule was as active as hers, but most of his work was
confined to the Broadway and London stage, while Rachel's recent activity had taken her as far away as Japan
and Russia on goodwill singing tours. She and Lehman
hadn't done a show together in two years. Or was it
three?

She was pleased that his vacation plans and the "resto-
ration" of Rathborne Cottage had coincided; she was
eager to see him again and curious about the guest he
was bringing. Lehman had never traveled with a compan-

ion, yet this was someone he was bringing all the way from New York. Rachel had heard enough rumors—and had seen him years before with Paul—to know that his general behavior was part of a life separate and quite different from his professional milieu.

They would dine at a small country inn after stopping for drinks at The King's Ransom, where Rachel's engraved pewter mug now occupied a place beside Howard's and the other regulars'. Lehman was as much an Anglophile as she, and a quiet dinner at Rathborne Cottage, while holding its appeal for the masters of the house, would not "entertain" Lehman. He loved to be fawned over in public. Although neither Mike at the pub nor any of the staff at The Hearthside would pander to anyone less English than Lord Olivier himself, patrons were served royally, in a manner that neither Rachel was prepared, nor the cottage was equipped, to handle.

She glanced at her wristwatch. It was early, just past five. Lehman's plane was due at six, and the drive to Hertfordshire would take longer than usual tonight in the light rain. The pendulum of the antique clock beat a slow rhythm, not unlike the ticking of a metronome. Outside, the steady, gentle downpour seemed to join in harmony with the crackling of the fire in the hearth and created a counterpoint duet. Simple, almost music in itself, like a piece by Satie or Debussy.

Rachel poured herself a sherry and leaned over the stereo to make a selection. She set the speaker button for "Bath," but then decided against a recording; she wanted a good, long soak in a mountain of bubbles—not the kind of bath that would end by the time a record needed flipping. She pushed "Tuner" and the soothing voice of a BBC announcer came into the room and broke the peaceful silence.

The tub was full, the mirrors fogged over with steam. Rachel's hair was piled on top of her head and tied with a ribbon. She sank halfway into the bubbles, to which she had added a generous capful of Halston perfume, and lay back against the cushion as the radio announcer gave the title of the next piece—Castelnuovo-Tedesco's Concerto in D for guitar and orchestra. The composer's name was familiar, but unlike Howard, she could never remember the individual opus numbers or the keys in which they were written.

The concerto began and Rachel luxuriated in both the happiness of the music and the bubble bath, its mist rising and dampening her hair. She reached for the towel and dried one hand, with which she retrieved the copy of *Time* magazine from the wicker rack adjacent to the tub. A broad grin crept over her face as Beth Burns's face beamed out from the cover.

Rachel had tried to phone Beth in New York as soon as she'd seen the issue, but Beth's maid had told her that "Miss Burns is singing at the White House and will be in Washington through the weekend."

Now, opening the magazine, Rachel turned to the cover story on page forty-three. Eight pages, with a dozen photographs of her friend.

Rachel was as thrilled for Beth as she had been to see herself on the cover the year before. Still, she couldn't help wondering at what price, despite considerable talent, her friend had obtained such stardom.

Rachel was holding the magazine with her right hand; now she blew a handful of bubbles with her left. One large sphere held its own prism for several moments, then burst. It made Rachel laugh at the analogy between bubbles and fame. "Neither to be taken too seriously," she chided herself—and the *Time* cover—aloud.

So Beth was at the White House, too. Rachel recalled her own "command performance" with the First Family and reflected on the contrasts between her first and second visits to the nation's capital; the first, as a last-minute replacement in *Arrowhead* when she'd met Lehman and Howard and endured Gloria Doro's wrath; then, more recently, an invitation, sent months in advance, to a small dinner party with the President's more intimate friends. Was that, she wondered, so the other guests would assume that she, too, was an "intimate friend"? Or were they, not unlike Rachel and Howard, merely acquaintances designed to "dress" the White House setting?

Theater. Washington, New York, Hollywood. Shakespeare and his "all the world's a stage," thought Rachel, reading Beth's "history" with growing amusement. "Well, it's good fiction, anyway," she said aloud to the dissipating bubbles. About one-fourth of the article bore a resemblance to truth.

The second movement of the concerto had begun, and the simple, almost humble notes of the guitar strings reminded Rachel of the last time she'd heard the Castelnuovo-Tedesco. It had been at Lehman's weekend house in Nyack, New York, after an evening with his neighbor, Helen Hayes. Lehman had such marvelous taste in music. And friends.

Again, her thoughts turned to his taste in men. "I'm bringing someone special," he'd said. "A young man with great promise." But Paul's comments of the past had hinted that the director's patronage was seldom of a strictly professional nature. This "someone special" must be a musical genius — or else Lehman had finally fallen in love.

She hoped for her friend's sake it was the latter. She hoped that Lehman had found the peace, the love, the wonder that she shared with Howard, a fulfillment that no award or magazine cover — or presidential invitation — could equal. She felt a rush of warmth, the kind she always felt when her thoughts went to Howard, and breathed deeply. Then, as invisible fingers plucked the last five notes of the second movement on the strings of the guitar, Rachel closed her eyes and gave herself to the poignant beauty of the music, which was the closest joy she knew to that of love.

The music had ended, and the BBC weather forecast promised a clear evening with a beautiful day to follow.

Rachel would have liked for the rain to continue. She enjoyed the gentle showers that were only somewhat heavier than a mist. Moreover, rain tonight would have solved any indecision concerning wardrobe. Her closets here and in New York now fairly bulged with clothes. Good clothes. But when she wanted to be relaxed and comfortable, a sweater and jeans, with broken-in boots, were still her preference. True, the sweaters were now made of cashmere, and the boots bore Magli or Ferragamo labels; however, despite several suits and dresses by Calvin Klein, her jeans still carried a leather patch that read Lee or Levis.

Levis would have suited this evening, were it not for Lehman's impending visit. It had always pleased him to see his former discovery "well turned out," as he termed it, looking every inch the star. Probably because he took pride in knowing that he had figured importantly in the creation of this "star," mused Rachel. Well, all right. For Lehman, she would greet him "well turned out." But for drinks at the pub and dinner in the village, even silk would be overdoing it. She would strike a happy medium between comfort and glamour. Maybe it was better, after all, that the rain had ended. Rain was murder on suede.

The wheels of the car made a crunching sound over

the gravel in the driveway just as Rachel tucked the shirttails of her ivory crepe shirt into the beige suede slacks and pulled on the matching bolero jacket. Her hair was pulled straight back and arranged in a large bun at the base of her neck. Having taken extra care with her makeup, she now inspected her reflection in the mirror.

"Spanish," she said aloud. No doubt influenced by the concerto during her bath. Pleasing, if a bit severe. But the starkness would appeal to Lehman.

She opened the armoire door and pulled out her trenchcoat. Then she flicked off the bedroom light switch and reached the foot of the stairs just as she heard the doors of the car slamming shut.

Chapter Twenty-three

The scene, when Rachel opened the front door, struck her as comical. Howard, Lehman, and Owen, the always-absent handyman, were struggling with enough luggage for a month's change of wardrobe. Lehman was coming for the week.

His traveling companion stood facing the men, with his back to Rachel. She heard him say, "Please, I can carry *something*." But Lehman and Howard insisted that three of them could handle everything.

Rachel didn't understand why they wouldn't allow Lehman's guest to help. She didn't appreciate Howard's lifting heavy suitcases; he'd been having trouble with his back, which was one of the reasons they'd hired Owen in the first place: so that Howard wouldn't be tempted to do exactly what he was doing now.

The small caravan marched single file up the path. As soon as he was inside the entrance hall, Lehman dropped his bags to the floor with a loud thud, spread his arms wide in Broadway tradition, and cried, "Rachel, *darling!*" They embraced, and she laughed at the fierce hug. Then Lehman released her and stood back, holding her at arm's length. "Let me look at you!" His assessment covered her from head to foot. "Fabulous! Casual elegance. I hope this ensemble is for my benefit."

"It is," she assured him, grinning.

The door slammed from behind. Owen stood awkwardly, his fists tightened around the handle of each large suitcase. He was obviously uncomfortable, and his eyes betrayed a wariness of Lehman's "grand manner."

"Shall I take these upstairs, mum?" he asked in his cockney accent.

"No thanks, Owen," Howard answered for Rachel. "We'll move these into the downstairs guest room later. If you'll just park the car in the garage, we'll not need you again for the evening."

"I thought you was goin' t' town, sir. I can drop you off on me way 'ome. 'Course, me own car hain't no limo, but it'll get ye there."

"Thanks, Owen, but I'll drive us in the Mercedes."

Owen nodded, casting a suspicious glance at Lehman, who waited until Owen's departure and then said, "The gamekeeper, Lady Chatterley?"

"Hardly," answered Rachel, laughing. "He's a bit sinister-looking for my taste. Besides," she added, with a wink to Howard, "I like mature men. Owen's too young for me."

"Well, good," said Lehman, "since he's too *old* for me . . . which reminds me. Rachel, this is Eric."

His guest had remained in the shadows of a corner, and now Lehman took him by the arm and led him to the center of the hall beneath the overhead light fixture. The older man's face appeared transported, beatific. Lehman was obviously smitten. Rachel noted that this was not so much an introduction as it was a presentation. He helped Eric out of a coat as though unveiling a fabulous jewel. And Rachel immediately saw why.

Eric was exquisite. His brown hair glistened with golden highlights. Dark brows and lashes accentuated pale blue eyes. His skin was smooth, his cheeks blushed with color from the chill in the damp night air. No late-day stubble dotted his strong, clean jaw or his dimpled chin. Rachel wondered if this was due to a very close shave, or whether he even *had* a beard. His body was slim and long, and he seemed to possess a curious androgeny, the kind of human physical perfection with which Thomas Mann had endowed the young boy in *Death in Venice*.

But it wasn't his beauty that disturbed Rachel; it was his youth.

"Come, let's have a drink," Howard suggested, leading the way to the liquor cabinet in the living room. "You both must be tired."

"And hungry," said Eric, following Howard. "The portions on the plane were so *small!*"

When she was certain Eric was out of earshot, Rachel put her arm through Lehman's and asked quietly, "Tell me . . . how *old* is he?"

"Umm . . . around twenty . . . I think. Why?"

Rachel raised an eyebrow. "In that case, he's remarkably well preserved."

Lehman laughed loudly, and eventually, Rachel's own observation brought a smile to her lips. But she hadn't meant the question to be amusing.

Howard called from the living room, "What's so funny, you two?"

"Life, my dear Howard!" exclaimed Lehman, clapping his hands. "Life is funny. As is love!"

When they entered The King's Ransom, Rachel and Howard were greeted by James; it was Mike's night off. The "regulars" lifted their pewter tankards in welcome, and one of the older men—John or Don, Rachel could never remember—tipped his hat and called, "Evenin', Missus R."

She liked that. The local patrons no longer fell into a hush when she made an appearance; there had been some initial shyness on their part—not when she'd first come to Hertfordshire with Howard, but once she had achieved stardom. They had finally relaxed when it became clear that Rachel had no wish for "special" treatment. Hence, she was regarded with friendly deference. If anything, she knew their familiarity was a form of acceptance, and this she treasured highly. It was mutual; the customers knew that an evening's drinking wouldn't be hampered by the presence of "fame."

Over dinner, Eric spoke a little—very little—about himself. His shyness hindered any ability at easy conversation. It was also quite evident that he was famished; what talking did occur was only between mouthfuls. Lehman's constant interruptions added to the boy's halting manner; the end result was a very sketchy portrait, gleaned from unconnected bits of information that, food and Lehman notwithstanding, had somehow managed to surface. The only certainty in Rachel's mind was that Eric was well under twenty and that Lehman worshippd him. If any doubts remained, the after-dinner brandies erased them.

"I'd like to hear what you and Rachel think of Eric's voice," Lehman said to Howard.

"Voice?" asked Rachel, turning to Eric and adding, "I didn't know you're a singer." She managed to hide her surprise.

"Well," he replied sheepishly, "it's something I've always wanted to do. And I've studied a little."

"Eric's a great admirer of yours, darling," said Lehman. While the boy blushed, his patron continued. "He was nervous about meeting you—especially when I promised to ask you a favor."

Rachel sensed that she was about to be put on the spot. She smiled politely, but didn't take the bait.

So Lehman said, "I'd like Eric to sing for you and Howard. Just an informal audition."

"The piano's just arrived, Lehman," said Rachel. "It still hasn't been tuned." She hated when anyone asked her to listen to—and pass judgment on—someone else's talent. Lehman knew her well enough to be aware of her aversion. It didn't seem to matter. His infatuation was beyond awareness.

"Oh, I'm sure the piano will do—whatever shape it's in," he said.

Rachel drew a breath. She'd make one more attempt. Howard would back her up.

"Lehman, it's late. I'd hate to disturb the neighbors."

Howard nodded, adding, "And I've had too much brandy. If you'd mentioned it earlier in the evening—"

"Oh, I didn't mean tonight!" The conductor-director patted Eric on a very flushed cheek and said, "We'll do it tomorrow afternoon."

At 2 P.M. the next day, they gathered for Eric's "audition." Lehman tested the keyboard, while commenting to himself, "Not in bad shape at all. Perfect . . ." There was nothing for Rachel and Howard to do but to make themselves as comfortable as possible on the loveseat.

Eric took his place in the curve of the piano, cleared his throat, and began.

After thirty seconds, the truth was apparent: Eric had no singing voice. Rachel knew by the hard pressure of Howard's hand on hers that they were in total agreement. She almost winced at the stiffness of his phrasing—and Howard's squeeze made the diamond on her ring finger almost cut into her pinky.

What will we say? she wondered. How do we tell a dear friend that his . . . protégee . . . is devoid of talent? How to gently advise the boy to seek other pursuits—that singing was for him a waste of time, studying a waste of money? And even if they could "cushion the blow," did she and Howard have the right to discourage him? Certainly many untalented but ambitious performers had carved out successful careers. Ambition often counted far more than talent.

Rachel sneaked a glance at Eric, who seemed oblivious to her scrutiny. No, she thought, I'm looking for the logic that *I've* always sworn doesn't exist. Even *ordinary* performers had to possess *something* besides ambition and drive, some indefinable spark that transcended mediocrity. Eric had none.

Am I being too critical? Rachel asked herself. Has he some quality that I'm just not seeing?

But as Eric sang the final notes of the song—one she'd never heard before, so there was no possibility of subconscious comparison with another singer—she could tell from the set of Howard's jaw that they were of one opinion.

The door chimes saved them all. It was only Owen, with a telegram for Howard, but—at least for the moment—they were off the hook.

The message had required immediate long-distance attention, and Rachel escaped on some urgent excuse—what it was, she promptly forgot—but it precluded any "judgment" before dinner. When she came downstairs after her bath, Howard and Lehman were talking in the garden; Eric had gone for a walk.

Rachel was searching for a tactful entrée to the subject once they were settled into the car, but Lehman unwittingly saved her. Clasping Eric's hands, he said, "Rachel, darling, I appreciate your kindness in listening to Eric this afternoon. So does he."

"I . . . I know we haven't had time to . . . to . . ." But words failed her.

"Everything's taken care of, darling. Howard and I had a good, long chat while you were upstairs. Eric is going to be just fine."

The boy certainly didn't *look* as though his dreams

had crumbled. Maybe, thought Rachel, he has more backbone than any of us realized. She was impressed by the boy's spirit, considering what Howard must have said; no matter how tactful, rejection was still rejection.

But she was mistaken. After they had returned from the cello recital, Howard and Rachel declined a nightcap and went upstairs. It was their first moment alone since Eric's "audition" that afternoon. Howard waited until he had closed the bedroom door and then said, "I'm signing the boy to the roster."

"You're *what?*" Rachel lowered her voice; their room was directly above Lehman and Eric's. "Howard, are you *serious?*"

Howard stifled a yawn as he unbuttoned his shirt. At last he said, "Yes, I am."

Rachel seated herself on the edge of the bed and lifted her feet. From habit, Howard pulled off each of her boots and let them fall to the rug.

"Thank you," she said. Then, "Howard, Eric is very sweet, but . . . well, he's so young, and . . ."

"And so ordinary? I know, Rachel. I'm doing this more for Lehman than for the boy."

"But what about you? People will hear him sing and think you've lost your mind."

He was emptying the contents of his pants pockets onto the dresser. "I'll take the chance. Besides, he's very handsome. I can find him work that doesn't require him to sing."

"That's assuming he can act," she said.

"Look, he doesn't need to *act*. He'll be perfect for soaps, commercials . . . maybe a television movie."

Rachel hadn't removed any of her clothing except for the boots; she still sat, staring at her stockinged feet, even when Howard said, "I wouldn't do it if it were that much of a risk."

She nodded but remained silent.

"What's the matter, darling?" he asked.

She hesitated and turned her eyes toward him. "All right. I grant you he's gorgeous. But I keep thinking of all the *talented* singers and actors who can't even find a *lousy* agent, much less one like you."

"Rachel," he replied, "I've been worried about Lehman for quite some time. Now that he's found someone, I'm concerned in a different way."

"What way?" she asked.

"His obvious . . . obsession. Eric seems to mean everything to him. I've never seen Lehman like this. I don't know how he'd take it if he lost the boy."

"Howard, Eric is at least twenty-five years younger than Lehman. It *will* end. You know that." She rose and unfastened one earring as she crossed to her dressing table.

"You're probably right," Howard answered. "But *I* won't be one of the reasons it ends. I want to see Lehman happy for as long as he can be."

"I see," she said. "Someone lands one of the best agents in the world by sleeping with that agent's client."

Howard came closer and leaned against the back of her chair. "Rachel, you're no longer naïve. You've been in the business too long for that."

Her mind formed an image of Beth Burns. But *Beth* had talent. And so did Jamie, with his acting and singing ability and good looks, but whose career was languishing while Eric—this boy—was having it handed to him on the proverbial silver platter.

"I know you're right," she answered at length. "And I hate it."

"Nonetheless, it's true. Darling, when is your hyperactive sense of justice going to relax?"

Rachel thought for a moment. Then, glancing up at his reflection in her dressing table mirror, she replied, "Never, I hope."

She was relieved when Lehman and Eric left. The furtive, intimate glances that passed between the older man and the boy had Rachel feeling as though she were a voyeur in her own home. That, in addition to Howard's contract with Eric, made her resent the very visit that she had anticipated for so long.

At the same time, Owen's surreptitious watchfulness contributed to Rachel's fishbowl sensations and eliminated the very privacy that had sold Howard and her on Rathborne Cottage in the first place.

"He's just shy," said Howard. "And he's somewhat intimidated by Lehman and Eric."

"So am I," she confessed, "but I haven't been lurking around in the shadows like something out of a BBC thriller. He seems to pop up when he isn't needed and then disappears into the woodwork when I could really use his help."

"Well, I agree that he's not exactly addicted to work." She laughed wryly at the understatement.

Each month, postcards arrived from the glamour capitals. In December, Lehman and Eric were "having a fabulous time in Paris"; in January, "an incredible experience" in Venice; February and March brought Rome, "to be remembered eternally," followed by "a dream come true" in Rio. Finally, after "playing for a few days in Acapulco," they were homeward bound.

Rachel was more amazed with each newly arrived card. Lehman had never been parsimonious about money, but the vast sums he seemed to be lavishing upon his "protégé" exceeded even *his* reputation for extravagance. "Perhaps it's all that money amassed from never shopping retail all these years," she mused aloud.

337

"Hmm?" Howard was leafing through a stack of papers.

"Oh, nothing. I was just thinking . . . maybe this is Lehman's way of saving the world from Eric. If they travel forever, he'll never have a chance to display his other . . . talents."

Howard glanced up and removed his reading glasses. "If that's a joke . . ."

"No," she said, not wanting to rekindle the subject of Eric's audition or the resulting contract with Howard. "It wasn't funny."

In May, Cecil Beaton photographed Rachel for *Vogue* in clothes by her favorite designers. When the contact prints were ready, she couldn't decide which were best; all were wonderful. Beaton's mastery over blacks, grays, and whites—with myriad and subtle gradations among the tints of even those three tones—was nothing short of inspired. The textures of her Halston wool crepe, the Oscar de la Renta taffeta, her Givenchy bouclé, and the Bob Mackie wisp of gossamer chiffon covered with glittering jet bugle beads made Rachel's head spin. Despite her glamorous outward appearance at galas and premieres, she was still amazed to see her own image, frozen in magazine photographs or given life onscreen, rendered so splendidly—as yet without the need of filters to veil any lines or wrinkles. She could sympathize with aging Hollywood beauty queens, and was grateful to be blessed with a voice and acting ability; in ten or fifteen years those would save her from obscurity.

Which returned her mind to Eric. Devoid of talent and personality, what would happen to him? Or would the boy's aging matter to Lehman?

The telephone interrupted her thoughts. It was Mina MacDonald, calling from New York and bubbling with excitement.

". . . and all they need from you is a *yes*. Isn't that marvelous?"

Rachel was trying to absorb Mina's news. "Wait a minute. I'm a singer. An actress. Why would anyone in the world want to read *my* autobiography? Henry Kissinger's, sure. Any of the Kennedys. But *me?* And more to the point, *what* publisher in his right mind would suggest that *I* write it? All I've ever written is letters — and movie reviews for my high school paper!"

"Darling," reasoned Mina, "it's simple on both counts. One, you're famous. The world glorifies, deifies, *worships* fame. Two, they've offered you a choice — several, in fact: they can supply a ghost writer —"

"Never!" said Rachel adamantly.

"I said as much. So they mentioned an as-told-to collaboration. Lots of stars opt for that."

"Stars who can't read or write, I'd imagine."

Mina laughed into the phone. "I had a hunch that'd be your reaction. So did Vera Garland."

"Who is Vera Garland?"

"Your prospective editor. Nice gal. We've had lunch."

"I take it I was the main course."

"We saved you for dessert. Anyway, Vera thinks you have enough of a head on those shoulders to handle the project yourself — and she'll be there to help, of course."

"Of course." Rachel's inner monologue was racing faster than Mina's "sales pitch." A tragic story of a star — a Marilyn Monroe or a Jean Harlow — was one thing, but . . .

"Look," said Mina, "they're willing to pay you a fortune —"

"I don't need the money."

"You can donate it to charity," said her publicist.

At this, Rachel laughed heartily. "Mina, you're so gung-ho on this, why don't *you* write it?"

"Because, love, like you, I don't believe in 'ghosts.' "

By the end of their conversation, Rachel had agreed to meet with Vera Garland in early June, when she and Howard would be in New York for the Tony Awards.

Vera Garland, Rachel later reflected, was charming and very persuasive. "Just not persuasive enough," she told her publicist as they left the restaurant.

"I still think her offer is too good to turn down," said Mina.

"Look, I haven't slammed the door shut. I just can't snap my fingers, say 'presto,' and have an instant 'past.' Mine isn't that exciting *or* scandalous —"

"Well," observed Mina with her customary pragmatism, "remember what Vera said."

"I've already forgotten, but I'm sure *you* haven't."

"Vera said if that should change — if life becomes either or both of the above — her offer is still good."

Rachel smiled and shook her head. "Exciting or scandalous. Thanks for reminding me. You're a big help."

"That's what you're paying me for, love."

Rachel's lunch with Vera Garland was not her only restaurant meeting that week. Jamie called, and they made a date at Gleason's, a New York–style Irish pub near the Museum of Natural History. It was a crosstown taxi ride for Rachel and only minutes from Jamie's new apartment on Manhattan's Upper West Side.

"I wanted to feel you out about something," he said when they'd settled into a booth.

"That seems to be the definition of lunch these days," she said, smiling. "You're not by any chance working for a publisher, are you?"

He laughed; she'd told him over the phone about the

340

book offer. Then, simply, he said, "Paul and I are back together."

Rachel was surprised—not by his news, but by her own reaction. She was happy about it. "Jamie . . . when?"

"Coincidentally, I went to read for a commercial and his agent had sent him up for it, too." His eyes twinkled. "It's the same old story. I'm blond, he's dark, the ad agency has no idea of what they want, so every male actor in the city—there were even some black guys and some Asians reading the same copy—gets submitted. But that's not important. Paul and I went out for a drink and talked for three hours."

"And?"

"I think it can work, this time." His smoky blue eyes were calm, and his hands reached across the table to hers.

She squeezed them. "I'm glad, Jamie. You know, I've never believed in coincidence."

"Neither have I, really. If you like, we can stop back at the apartment—Paul would love to see you."

She nodded. "I'd love to see him, too."

During lunch they spoke on many subjects; Rachel's career was public domain, so they talked of Jamie, of Paul, of changes in their lives and in themselves.

"And I'm already exploring nontheatrical avenues," said Jamie, concluding a summary of his singing and acting inactivity since returning to the States.

"You don't sound upset about the prospect of doing something else," she said.

"It's been a long time coming, Rachel, but at a certain moment the rejection reaches a boiling point—I don't know what else to call it—and then, when I see casting directors who look half my age, maybe with a B.A. from the Yale Drama School or Juilliard to give them 'credibil-

341

ity' in the business, I think, 'Hey, what am I doing this for? It isn't fun anymore.' When I started out, I took it too seriously. Now maybe I don't take it seriously enough." He shrugged his shoulders and sipped his beer. "Whatever, I'm a lot more relaxed about everything. Life is more important than the next audition."

"It really is a crap shoot. You said so years ago."

"I talk a good seduction. I should have listened to what I was saying."

She noticed an absence of bitterness in his voice. Maybe that was why Howard's offers to help Jamie had been refused. At one time, his help would have been resented; now, perhaps it was too late. Whatever, Rachel sensed that the changes in Jamie were all to the good.

They finished their meal, then walked the four blocks to his apartment on Seventy-fifth Street between Central Park West and Columbus Avenue.

It was a far cry from the quarters Rachel and Jamie had shared on East Fifth Street between Avenues A and B. While not a luxury building with fountains and a marble foyer, the brownstone was completely renovated, with rich claret carpeting in the polished parquet wood hallways. Brass fixtures and plants adorned each floor landing, and the atmosphere was one of solid elegance.

The apartment itself was an enormous studio, with an eat-in kitchen and a huge bay window facing the street. It was on the top floor and offered a peek at the park.

"Jamie, this is lovely," said Rachel, entering the spacious foyer.

"I was sold the second I saw it," he said, adding, "thank God for rent control."

"Where's Paul?" she asked, leaning against the forest green velvet sofa.

"Voilà, madame," said the dark-haired dancer, entering through a doorway that Rachel had assumed to be a closet. They embraced warmly. "You're looking magnifi-

342

cent! I'm so glad that nowadays stars don't have to peroxide their hair and cap their teeth, et cetera." He swirled her around and started humming, "I love you just the way you are."

"You look terrific, too," she said. "I envy you dancers. The rest of us have to diet and exercise, and—"

Paul shook his head. "Jamie didn't tell you? I haven't danced in ages."

Jamie smiled sheepishly. "We had a lot to catch up on."

Paul nodded. To Rachel, he said, "I decided there's more money—regular pay, that is—and more control in choreography. Oh, I still do a commercial now and then—our combined residuals bought half the stuff in this room. But I don't like being ordered around like a puppet." He laughed. "I never did, but when you're twenty, you have a lot more resiliency. Suddenly I decided it was enough! And I tossed my tap shoes out the window."

"Actually," intervened Jamie, "it was out the door. And they tumbled down three flights of stairs."

"They wouldn't stop," Paul put in. "Just like the story of the red shoes—" He stopped himself.

But Rachel said, "Oh, please, that was centuries ago. I like us all better now."

"So do we," said Paul. "I'll fix us drinks so we can toast that."

Afternoon turned into evening as the three reminisced. "Your friend Beth Burns has taken this town by storm. You should have seen her last season—dancing, singing, acting in a tour de force like I haven't seen since Merman in *Gypsy*," said Paul. "Everyone's wondering what she'll do for an encore. You know, where do you go from the top?" He paused, then added, "Of course, you really *do*

343

know what I mean. Are you in town to do a show?"

Jamie touched her arm and teased, "Or to write a book?"

"Maybe to do a show. We'll see. I'm looking around."

Paul grinned. "Well, speaking of mutual acquaintances, I ran into dear old Lehman Stern the other day."

"*He's* got it bad," said Jamie. "I met him at a party. It's as if Lehman has stopped worrying about his reputation, the way he falls all over that kid—I forget his name, but Christ—"

"Eric," Rachel supplied. "They spent a week with us in England."

"I've met the boy," said Paul. "I wonder what your neighbors thought."

"Well, I'll tell you what *I* think," offered Jamie. "I think Lehman Stern has lost either his mind or his head. Maybe both. That kid only *looks* like Little Orphan Annie. He'd sell his grandma—if she hasn't been sold already."

"You both surprise me," said Rachel. "Eric is shy. And I admit he's not scintillating company. But he doesn't have a mean bone in his body. We saw him day and night for a week—"

"Maybe he's a good actor," interjected Jamie.

"No," said Rachel. "He's beautiful, but he doesn't have an ounce of talent."

"Maybe he's just hiding it," Jamie said jokingly.

"For what?" asked Paul.

"For the right moment."

Howard was home from the office by the time Rachel returned to the apartment. She found him reading in the den.

"Hi," she said, leaning over to kiss him.

"Mmm, that's nice," he said. "And your hair smells of

sunshine." He ran his fingers through her long waves. "Did you and Jamie have a good visit?"

She nodded and plopped down beside him. "He and Paul are back together. We had a regular reunion." Kicking off her shoes, she summarized their afternoon, adding, "You know, one thing I like about this city is the anonymity—if you stay in the neighborhood, that is. I was worried that we wouldn't have any privacy—and I wasn't sure how that would affect Jamie—but it was just a matter of a few people nodding when I walked into the restaurant. Not so different from Mike and the 'gang' at the pub."

"Surprised by that?" asked Howard.

She shrugged. "Well, I remember lunch with Drew Colton when we were rehearsing *Robin Hood*. I mean, by the time lunch was over, I'm sure the whole place was convinced we were having an affair."

Howard's arm went around her and he pulled her to him. "Darling, Drew Colton seeks that kind of attention. And he probably spent the entire time—what's that awful expression?—coming on to you."

"You knew?" she asked.

"I'd have been deaf and blind to miss it. Besides, I know the animal." He folded the newspaper and pushed it aside. Then, lightly, he added, "I've never been sure he didn't take Cecily to bed."

"But I thought she ran off with some Italian director—"

"That was later. She and Drew had more than a few lunches while he was still my client. At the time, his career needed whatever boost he could muster. Or at least he thought so. 'Insurance' is probably the way he looked at it."

"Did you ever confront Cecily about it?"

"What was the point? The marriage was crumbling by then. And Drew Colton loves to step in and pick up the pieces. Gives him a sense of power."

"That's heinous."

"So is trying to steal his leading lady's solo number, don't you think?"

Rachel emitted a lengthy sigh as she leaned her head against Howard's shoulder. "Doesn't anyone ever make it to the top on talent alone?"

"Well, darling, you have . . ."

"Thanks to *you*," she said. "If I hadn't met you, I might be where Jamie is—changing careers—or where Paul is"—here she laughed; choreographing was *not* where she'd be without Howard—"and then I think of people like Beth Burns. And Eric—"

"Beth is your friend, isn't she?"

"Yes, but it doesn't mean we see eye to eye on everything. And Eric," she repeated. "Something about him bothers me."

"My helping him, you mean?"

She shook her head, but the words didn't form; it was only a feeling. "No, Howard. Something else."

"What then?"

She paused, but still it remained no more than instinct. "I wish I knew," she said at last.

Chapter Twenty-four

June 1976

Rachel straightened the skirt of her linen suit as the elevator doors slid open. Robert, the new doorman, offered a polite "Good afternoon," then asked, "Cab, ma'am?"

She nodded, crossing the marble lobby to him.

"You might want to wait inside, Mrs. Rathborne. It's awfully hot out there."

"Thanks, Robert, but I'd just as soon get some air."

He pulled open the street door and followed her out onto Fifth Avenue. Immediately, Rachel realized the wisdom of Robert's suggestion; the air was very hot, heavy, and damp. It felt like a sauna—but one didn't wear linen inside a sauna.

While Robert stepped into the street to hail a cab, Rachel leaned against the building, grateful for the shelter of the canopy overhead.

Although she and Howard spent more time in New York than anywhere else, this kind of weather still surprised her. With the city surrounded by water, the humidity became almost tropical, and it wasn't helped by the heat trapped between the buildings that reached to the sky. This afternoon was particularly unpleasant, with a polluted haze and no breeze to cut through the stagnant air. One could almost taste it.

Rachel had luxuriated in air-conditioned comfort all

morning as she'd leafed through new scripts. A cool penthouse made one forget about the weather. She nodded to herself at the reminder of Jamie's unbearably stifling apartment on East Fifth Street so long ago; New York was far easier on residents with money.

A taxi finally pulled up alongside the curb and Rachel quickly got in. "It's air-conditioned," said Robert, closing the door.

She smiled in thanks and instructed the driver, "Shubert Alley, please." Between Beth Burns's schedule and her own, it had taken nearly a month to find a mutually convenient afternoon to lunch together.

Her friend had only an hour's break. She was in rehearsal for a new show, which according to Beth, was having book problems. Rachel in a way envied her friend these problems; she hadn't appeared on Broadway in a while, and the "itch" was badly in need of a "scratch." She'd been reading scripts for two months, but so far not one had captured her imagination.

The taxi entered the theater district and swung west off Fifth Avenue on Forty-third. When they stopped for a red light at the corner of Seventh Avenue, Rachel grinned. Just to the left was Nathan's, where she had often taken advantage of their two-for-one hotdog coupons. Uptown to her right had once been the hotel where playwright Eugene O'Neill was born. Beyond, the marquee of the National Theater obliterated a view of the Coca Cola billboard over the Castro showroom.

Rachel alighted at Forty-fourth Street and Eighth Avenue. The heat was even more intense now, and she hurried to the cool, dark vestibule inside the stage entrance. The doorman recognized her at once.

"Miss Burns said to go right up to her dressing room," he said, beginning to point out the direction.

"I know the way," she called, running up the stairs. Rachel had never played this theater but had visited

348

enough colleagues in the "star" dressing room to know its location.

She knocked, but there was no answer. She tried the knob, turned it, and the door swung open. "Honestly, Beth," she muttered with a smile. Her friend still hadn't learned to lock the door when she left the room.

Closing it behind her, Rachel glanced around at the sparse furnishings. A large clothes rack held only Beth's umbrella. The table was empty. A script lay open on an ice blue satin chaise longue in the corner. The producer of Beth's show also owned the theater, so the production enjoyed the luxury of rehearsing onstage for a full month before the first preview. Within weeks, Rachel knew, the room would be crammed with costumes, makeup housed in fishing tackle boxes, flowers, telegrams, and theatrical paraphernalia. But for now, it had an abandoned look.

She sat down on the chaise and absently picked up the script. On the title page was typed the name of the show: *One Night Only*. In blue ink at the top of the page the name *Tyler Beekman* was handwritten. Ah, yes, Rachel recalled. Tyler Beekman is directing Beth's show. They'd never met, but his reputation as a brilliant director was growing. *One Night Only* was his third Broadway play, and the two preceding had been huge successes, still running after a full season. Rachel tried to remember where she'd read that Beekman had emerged from the stable of new directors at Joseph Papp's Public Theater.

She flipped through the pages of the script while speaking a few lines aloud, "trying them on." They felt good. From just scanning a few scenes, she could see that the play was well written. One scene in particular drew her in so that she was barely aware of muffled voices in the hallway outside Beth's door. She was startled, then, by three quick raps, after which the door swung wide open.

Rachel looked up into the face of one of the handsomest men she had seen outside of Hollywood.

"Oh," he said in a deep voice. "Sorry. I thought Beth would be here."

"No," answered Rachel. "I'm waiting for her."

"Well" — he held up a script — "I think we got these mixed up. This is Beth's copy."

Rachel closed the black leatherette cover. "Then this is yours — if you're Tyler Beekman."

"I am," he replied, giving a short, comic bow. "Thanks."

They exchanged scripts. "I'll give this to Beth," Rachel said.

"Good. She's probably hunting all over for it right now."

He turned to leave, then looked back. His dark brown eyes sparkled, and wavy black hair fell over his brow. A thick mustache accented the white of his teeth, and though his cheeks and jaw were clean, he needed a shave. Rachel hadn't realized that she was studying him until he said, "Excuse me . . . but you're Rachel Allenby, aren't you?"

She nodded and felt color warming her face. She hadn't blushed in a long time and was surprised at her physical reaction, one that threatened her with a stammer if she spoke.

"I admire your work," he continued, offering a handshake.

"I've . . . heard good things about you, too," she said.

"I hope we can . . . do a show together . . . one day," he said haltingly, his eyes still on her. "In fact, I've got a new script I'd . . . love for you to read."

Rachel removed her hand from his. "Fine. I'm looking for a good play . . . My agent is —"

"Howard Rathborne . . . your husband," he said. "I'll leave a copy of the script at his office." The intensity of his eyes hinted at a hidden subtext to his offer, although he seemed as shyly surprised by his responses as Rachel was by hers.

"Ty!" Beth Burns appeared in the doorway. "I've been looking everywhere, and I can't find—"

"Miss Allenby has your script—and . . . I've got mine," he said, breaking his gaze away from Rachel.

"That's a relief! So the two of you have met?"

"Yes." Turning again, he said, "Enjoy . . . your lunch, Miss Allen—"

"It's Rachel. . . . And thank you . . . Ty?"

He nodded, dug one hand into the pocket of his blue jeans, and waving *One Night Only* with the other, said, "Thank *you*."

Beth closed the door and leaned against it. Staring at Rachel, she asked, "Now is that gorgeous or what?"

Rachel laughed to cover her nervousness. "That's gorgeous."

"Don't be embarrassed—I'm not sleeping with him, if that's what's got you jittery."

"I'm not jittery—or embarrassed, Beth."

"Well, it's not that *I* wouldn't—but *he* hasn't asked—he's so damned professional! C'mon, let's get something to eat. Thinking about sex makes me ravenous!"

They greeted acquaintances as they were shown to their table at Joe Allen's. The brick walls were covered with framed Broadway show posters. "I'm glad none of *ours* have landed on these hallowed walls," Beth joked. Only "flops" qualified for the coveted space in the theatrical hangout.

She ordered an enormous lunch and gulped every morsel. Rachel was surprised; Beth's appetite dwarfed her own. It amazed her, though; her friend seemed slimmer than the last time they'd seen each other.

Over coffee, Beth checked her wristwatch. "Still plenty

of time for a chat. Sorry I rushed with lunch, but these rehearsals keep me exhausted *and* starving. I need all the fuel I can get."

"I looked through the script," said Rachel. "You didn't tell me it's a *dual* role."

"Yeah." Beth nodded, sighing. "I play both the wife *and* the mistress. God, I'm nervous!"

"You're terrific, and the script is—"

"I know, I know. I mean . . . well, thanks . . . but I *need* this to be a success, Rachel. I can't afford a flop. I've got to prove that last year with the Tony and all wasn't just a flash in the pan."

"You'll be fine. Don't worry about it."

"Rachel," Beth insisted, "I don't *sing* in this one. Not a note. No dancing, either. That's got me worried, too."

"You'll pull it off. You might even make a bigger impact as a dramatic actress."

Beth shrugged. "I don't know . . . *You* did it, but sometimes I worry that people will find me out."

"Find you out?"

"I'm good, Rachel, but"—she lowered her voice—"I wonder if I'm as good as everyone thinks I am. I mean . . . *I* know I got here on my back—"

Rachel interrupted quietly. "You can't win a Tony Award by sleeping for it."

"Wanna bet?"

"What?" exclaimed Rachel in a shocked stage whisper.

But Beth squeezed her hand and laughed. "No, no— I'm kidding! They really thought I deserved the Tony!"

Rachel looked directly at her friend. "Don't you think so?"

"Oh, sure. But now that I'm where I want to be, I've got to show the ones I *did* schtupp that I've got what it takes to stay here."

Just then, Ty Beekman stopped at their table. His eyes on Rachel again, he said, "I would have asked you to join me, but it looked as if you two were ensconced."

"Women's talk," said Rachel, smiling and trying not to let him affect her a second time.

"I understand. Listen, Beth, when you get back to the theater, I'd like to talk over the second scene in Act One. I've got an idea. Meet me in the orchestra in, say, twenty minutes."

When he was gone, Beth said, "See what I meant? He's gorgeous, and brilliant, *and* he runs a rehearsal like Hitler."

"C'mon, Beth," said Rachel. "You're used to that. Lehman must have been just as demanding during *Red Shoes,* wasn't he?"

At the mention of Lehman Stern's name, Beth's face seemed to pale. She took a sip of her coffee, as if stalling for time. Then, slowly, she answered, "Well, Lehman may have had other reasons for being hard on me during *Red Shoes.*"

"Meaning?"

"Oh . . . nothing." After another hesitation, Beth asked, "Have you heard from him lately?"

Rachel told her about Lehman and Eric's visit. "It was the same week you were at the White House."

"Did my name come up?" Beth asked.

"Nobody's name came up all week, other than Eric's."

"I've seen that kid before. He learns fast."

"You're the second person who's said that. What do you know about him?"

"Nothing," answered Beth. "But even if he's just a kid, I think he and I are cut from the same cloth. Except that he's worse."

"You're right," said Rachel. *"You* can *sing."* And they both laughed.

They walked together back to the theater. When they

reached the stage door, Beth looked at her watch again and cried, "Oh, God, I'm late—he'll kill me!" She gave Rachel a quick peck on the cheek and ran inside.

Rachel felt like walking, but it was too hot. The black street paving had softened, and she had to step carefully to avoid sinking her heels into the tar. She didn't feel ready to return home for another afternoon of reading scripts, but as she glanced up Broadway at the movie marquees, none of the titles appealed to her. It wasn't Wednesday, so she couldn't take in a matinee. And the thought of shopping bored her.

It's restlessness, she thought, as the taxi turned into Central Park. Well, maybe there'll be one decent script among the latest submissions. That's what I need. A show. Musical or not. Ty Beekman had mentioned a play he wanted her to read. If he was as brilliant as everyone claimed, working with him might be exciting. She hoped he'd remember to leave the script at Howard's office.

She napped for an hour, then bathed and dressed. Thank God they were staying home tonight; it was too hot to go anywhere.

Rachel prepared a seafood salad; even with the air-conditioning running at high-cool, the penthouse would have heated up if she had opted to use the stove.

She and Howard took their coffee into the den and talked for a while, until their conversation grew into tender fondling and caressing. They made love, then went to bed and drifted to sleep in each other's arms.

Rachel awoke with a start, every nerve in her body tensed. She felt as if someone had slapped her into consciousness. What *is* it? she wondered. Then, the ringing of the telephone registered in her brain; its jangling as frantic as her pulse.

She drew a deep breath and waited for the answering

service to pick up. When it didn't, she fumbled about the night table for her reading glasses and checked the clock. Two A.M.! Who in his right mind would be calling at this hour?

She tried reaching across Howard for the phone, which was on his night table, but in her semi-asleep state, she kept falling backward. "God, I hate telephones!" she whispered aloud, marveling that Howard could sleep through the noise. She was just about to get up and walk around the bed, when Howard's hand appeared from beneath the sheet and, with groping attempts, finally lifted the receiver. Rachel flopped back into her pillows as Howard's voice said groggily, "Hello?"

Then, suddenly, he was sitting upright. *"What!"* His bedside lamp flashed on. Rachel averted her eyes from the glare as Howard said, "How bad is it? . . . Is he still breathing? . . . Bend down and check his pulse. . . . Good. Now get hold of yourself! All right. . . . Have you rung the doctor? . . . Why *not,* for God's sake? What? . . . I can't hear you . . . all right, all right. Don't touch anything. Take a Valium. Only *one.* I'm on my way over."

Howard replaced the receiver and rose from the bed. "Christ," he muttered, running hands through his hair.

"What's happened?" she asked softly.

"Lehman . . ." he began.

"Oh no! He's hurt? Howard!"

"No." He turned and, with a deep sigh, said, "It's Eric. There's been an accident."

The next fifteen minutes passed as if in a fog. Rachel and Howard moved through them quickly, automatically. She made coffee. He dressed.

At first she insisted upon going with him, but he vetoed that. After initial resistance, she relented. Then she assailed him with questions. "I don't know" or "I'm not sure" were the only answers he gave her. When she pressed further, Howard's voice rose. "Rachel, I don't know! I won't know until I get there!"

He seldom lost his temper with anyone, especially with her. But they were both upset, and he would have to handle whatever awaited him at Lehman's. It was better not to contribute to his upcoming ordeal.

"I'll call you from his flat," said Howard. It was 2:20 A.M. when he closed the door.

Going back to bed was impossible. Rachel poured her second cup of coffee and seated herself at the breakfast counter. Below, the city was almost soundless. She glanced out the window. The few street lamps along the paths in Central Park seemed hardly sufficient to fend off the eerie darkness. Only now and then did a pair of headlights snake through the streets. A hundred strange, frightening thoughts plagued her. Had someone broken into Lehman's apartment? Had Eric taken drugs? Poison?

Speculation increased her nerves, so Rachel tried to concentrate on logic. The clock read 3 A.M. Howard had left at 2:20. Assuming that he'd found a cab immediately, he'd have reached Lehman's by 2:30. Given time to assess the situation and call whomever—the doctor, an ambulance, the police—shouldn't Howard have phoned her by now?

She had moved to the den and was seated with the phone beside her. Ring! she almost said aloud. But silence filled the room. Her hand reached out for the receiver, and she began to dial Lehman's number. No, she decided, hanging up. No sense in aggravating the situation. If Howard hadn't called, there must be a reason. But *what* reason? Was Howard all right?

I can't stand this! she thought. I can't sit here alone, waiting. She felt powerless, helpless over events she didn't even know about.

She picked up the receiver again and dialed. After five rings, a sleepy voice answered. "Hello?"

"Jamie . . . ?" she began.

Rachel's major fear was that Howard had tried to call while she'd been on the phone with Jamie. They'd spoken for fewer than two minutes, but still, the line had been engaged.

At three-thirty, the house phone rang. Its bell made Rachel jump from the sofa. It was Dominick, the night doorman. Jamie and Paul were in the lobby.

"Send them up!" Then she ran to the foyer to meet them.

They had talked on and on, dozing intermittently. When Rachel opened her eyes, she found Jamie still curled up in Howard's leather easy chair, while Paul was stretched out on the rectangular rug on the floor. Rachel had fallen asleep on her arm at one end of the sofa, and now her shoulder was stiff from the position.

Gray light filtered in through the slit in the draperies; it must be close to dawn, she thought. Had Howard returned and gone to bed? But she knew he would have awakened her. That meant he was still at Lehman's. She glanced at the clock, but the hour and minute hands were not luminous dials, and the light from outside was insufficient for reading the time.

Rachel's mind was filled with unconnected meanderings. What in God's name had happened to be keeping Howard this long?

Just then, she heard—or thought she heard—a key

fumbling with the lock. Why should Howard be having difficulty with it?

Suddenly she was alarmed: what if it wasn't Howard? Quickly, she whispered, "Jamie! Paul! Wake up!"

As they did so, she heard the door in the outer foyer click shut. Then Howard's familiar steps approached on the parquet floor of the hall leading to the den.

His walk was slow, weary. Rachel jumped up, all at once alert and wide awake. Howard entered the den, and his tired eyes blinked with surprise at the sight of Jamie and Paul.

As if in reply to a question, Rachel said, "I . . . I had to call someone. . . . I couldn't stand sitting here, waiting. . . ." Then, when he nodded but didn't answer, she said, "Howard, tell us what's happened—is Lehman all right? It's been hours, and—"

"Eric is dead," he said without expression.

"He's . . . *what?*"

Howard shook his head. By now, Jamie and Paul were on their feet. "It was an accident. . . . Lehman found him going through his jewelry and private papers . . . they quarreled . . . Eric pulled a knife, and . . ."

"And what?" It was Jamie who spoke.

Howard crossed to the bar and reached for the brandy decanter as he answered. "They struggled. Lehman picked up the first thing he saw . . . and struck him on the head. Eric fell . . ."

"He must have fallen pretty hard if it killed him," said Paul bluntly. "What did Lehman hit him with—a crowbar?"

Howard lifted the crystal stopper and poured several inches' worth of the brandy into a glass. He took a quick swig and replied, "There was a brass candlestick beside the bed. . . ."

Paul nodded. "I remember. There used to be two of them."

358

Jamie glanced at him but said nothing.

Indicating the decanter, Howard asked, "Anyone else?"

Paul declined; Jamie moved to the bar, while Rachel said, "Yes, thanks. I think I could use one." She closed her eyes, recalling conversations with the three of them—Howard, Jamie, and Paul—about Eric. They'd all known it couldn't last. But she doubted any of them had expected it to end in this manner.

As Howard handed her a glass, she asked, "How is Lehman taking it? Is he all right?" She was surprised at her own reaction—feeling more concern over the man who had killed Eric than for his victim. But apparently *Lehman* had been the victim—in more ways than one.

"Did he phone the police?" asked Jamie.

"I did," said Howard. Turning to Rachel, he explained, "That's why I couldn't ring you. The police arrived almost immediately, armed with God-knows-what kinds of questions—"

He stopped short, but Paul said, "Howard, you can speak freely in front of Jamie and me. You mean 'questions as to the nature of their relationship,' don't you?"

Howard took another sip of his brandy and nodded. "Yes. . . . They wanted to know if Lehman and Eric engaged in . . . sadomasochism, rituals, that sort of thing. I guess they expected to find whips and chains in the closet, the way they went about checking Lehman's things, poor chap."

"What *did* they find?" asked Paul.

Rachel found Paul's detachment fascinating and marveled again at her own dichotomous reactions, one on a purely conscious level, the other far beneath it.

"They found Eric's suitjacket pockets filled with Lehman's jewelry—diamond cufflinks, gold rings and shirt studs, his platinum watch, cash. . . ."

"I can't believe it," said Rachel. "I just can't picture Eric—" This time she was the one who stopped in mid-sentence; was this the facet of the boy that had puzzled and disturbed her? Aloud she asked, "Lehman hasn't been arrested, has he? I mean, what happens now?"

"No, he hasn't been arrested. It's a clear case of self-defense. Eric's knife was lying on the floor beside him."

The whole episode seemed like some horrible nightmare. But the night was gone, and the sun now cast its steady beam through the parted draperies. No, reasoned Rachel. Lehman's nightmare has just begun. "He probably shouldn't be alone," she said.

"His brother was called," said Howard. "I left shortly after he arrived."

Rachel was still numb with disbelief. Perhaps Eric *had* taken advantage of Lehman's infatuation; perhaps he *had* encouraged the older man's generosity and hoped to profit from the director's connections. But he had been a guest at Rathborne Cottage for a week, with free access to the jewelry collection in the unlocked velvet chest on Rachel's dressing table. He had seen her wearing diamonds and gold and hadn't seemed to notice. It prompted one fact to loom strong in Rachel's mind: whatever Eric's motivations, the boy was *not* a thief.

Chapter Twenty-five

The front pages of the city's two major tabloids carried the headline on page one. Two photographs, one of Lehman, the other of Eric, accompanied the banner. The lettering was almost as large as when the Mets had won the World Series seven years before. Baseball, Rachel mused, took precedence—if type size held any importance—over all matters excepting presidential assassinations. She recalled that even the picture of Jamie and the Stonewall riots had been smaller than the banner and photo of the Mets' win in the fall of that year.

Eric, with his matinee-idol face and a past thus far unknown, occupied the larger picture space; Lehman, because of the Stern family's prominence in New York and his own in the theatrical world, boasted the bigger caption. Everyone, Rachel reflected, would scramble to read the "dirt." What troubled her was the missing story between the lines. The *Post* and *News* merely hinted at or implied "untold truths"; the *Times* ignored the more salient aspects altogether and reported only the facts—on page twenty-two. Rachel surmised that *Times* sales that day would suffer; the public wanted sensationalism, and the other two dailies were willing and ready. Both, with Eric's headshot, would sell millions of copies.

By midweek, a stack of each day's newspapers had accumulated on the coffee table in the den. They had all been read and deposited there haphazardly. Rachel's part-time maid was ill with the flu, and somehow Rachel was drained of energy; she hoped she wasn't coming down with the virus.

She glanced at the headlines staring up at her from the marble table surface. LOVE DUET ENDS IN DEATH read one; GAY SCENE SOURS read another. Beneath it, in smaller—but still highly visible—type, was the subheading: *He offered everything—and it wasn't enough.*

That made Rachel nauseous. She had learned from Howard that Lehman was not in jail; his family's battery of lawyers had taken care of the legal details. The director had moved temporarily from his own apartment on Park Avenue to his family's "fortress" on a quiet street in the East Sixties, between Madison and Park. The exact address remained undisclosed, since reporters had been camping in his Park Avenue lobby since the morning after the incident.

Rachel noticed that the media were extremely cautious with their wording. "Incident" or "accident" were the terms chosen, even in the scandal sheets.

"Is that to avoid a libel case?" she asked Howard.

"Well," he replied, "that and the fact that two of Lehman's brothers—Mortimer and Francis, I believe—own a fair share of stock in one of the dailies. And the *Times* isn't seeking to report speculation—"

"What kind of speculation?"

"Well . . . whether the boy was blackmailing Lehman, that sort of thing."

"Howard, about that . . ."

"About what?"

"All of it. Lehman's story about Eric's stealing from him. It doesn't ring true."

He looked up from his reading; his face wore a surprised expression. "Rachel, I was there. I saw what was in Eric's pockets. I saw the knife."

"It just strikes me as so . . ." But again, she was at a loss for words.

"Strikes you as so what?" Howard asked with a touch

362

of impatience.

She rose from the sofa. "It's so out of character! I mean . . . well, I *study* people, Howard. It's . . . it's part of an unconscious technique or something. And whatever you might say about Eric"—here she brushed her hand against one of the newspapers and it fell to the floor— "no matter what *they* say about him, he wasn't a thief!"

The paper in question had branded Eric—always with a question mark—as variously a hustler, pimp, possible dope addict, junkie, or both, certainly an opportunist, a "user" of people, a clever and devious "type."

"God!" Rachel said aloud. "You'd think the media knew him intimately—and not *one* of these people ever met him!"

"Darling," said Howard, rising and coming to her, "look, you're taking this harder than Lehman. Relax. He'll be all right. And"—he indicated the stack of crumpled papers on the floor—"whatever they say about Eric . . . well, I know it sounds callous, but . . . none of this can hurt him."

"That doesn't excuse it," she said. "And if Lehman adored him so, *he* ought to say something about it."

"He can't. His family is paying a small fortune to clear his name and calm the waters."

"At Eric's expense," she said curtly.

"Eric is dead. Nothing Lehman says or does can bring him back."

Suddenly the implications of Howard's words made impact. "Howard . . . are you telling me that Lehman's family is paying to . . . to have *good* things written about him?"

He shrugged wearily, and she knew that badgering him wouldn't help to alleviate the stress of his ordeal at Lehman's a few short nights ago. But she couldn't help it. Something seemed so unfair, so *unclean*.

"Rachel," Howard said slowly, "there are times when

363

one pays to get something *into* print, just as there are times when one pays to keep something *out* of print. You know that—Mina does it for you all the time."

"Howard, that's different! We're talking about career publicity—a new recording, a show, or film—we're *not* talking about life and death!"

"We're speaking of exactly that," said Howard, crossing to the bar and pouring a brandy. "We're speaking of Lehman's life—and his career. If Mina doesn't 'soften' his image in the press until this all subsides—Lehman's career will be as good as dead."

He had spoken with such emphasis that for a moment, Rachel couldn't reply. It wasn't fair—it was damned *un*fair—but professionally, Howard had a point.

He offered her a brandy and she nodded. Reaching for the glass, she said, "I just don't see where Mina's dragging Eric through the mud will help Lehman—or his career—survive."

"Well, put your mind at ease on that," he said. "Mina had nothing to do with any of the Eric copy. *I* wouldn't ask that of her. Besides, even if I had, *she* would have refused to do it."

Rachel let the brandy warm her and took a deep, long breath before she said, "I'm glad to know that, Howard. About both of you."

The heat lingered on into late summer. After the initial front-page scandal, the case received barely a mention in the newspapers. The public attention it had attracted began to wane, resurfacing only once to announce: GRAND JURY CLEARS STERN. A determination of self-defense had been handed down, and the case was closed.

Rachel folded the newspaper and took a sip of her coffee. So, that's all there is to it, she thought. Neatly tied up with skill and efficiency. Mina buries the publicity, and the Stern family's money sees to the rest; the law and media are satisfied, and everyone goes home.

She glanced out the window. The effects of a rainless summer were already dotting the foliage along Fifth Avenue with shriveled, yellowing leaves. Rachel was eager for this summer to end. Be done with it! she said to herself. Move on. Allow the change to happen, and let's put this in the past where it belongs. As of today.

She knew it wouldn't be easy—*shouldn't* be easy. To occupy her mind, she had accepted a "cameo" role, a guest shot in a film shooting in New York. Hardly taxing—or inspiring—but it would keep her busy.

The wall clock read 6 A.M. Howard was still asleep, and the apartment was quiet, except for the muted sounds of traffic from so many floors below. By 6:15, she'd have to shower; the studio limousine would be picking her up at 6:45. The day's shooting script lay beside the newspaper. She would be singing the title song on the "nightclub" set. Not a very good song, but she'd been assured of its "push" onto the charts. Later she would record the single, which was scheduled for release in conjunction with the film.

A stack of manuscripts still sat on the desk in the den. Not the *same* stack; the titles changed as the plays were read; Howard returned the rejects to the office in exchange for new ones he brought home at night. In three weeks, Rachel hadn't touched them, and they were mounting up. A rueful smile crossed her lips. A month ago, finding a script had been a priority. Now it seemed hardly important at all. Besides, appearing in the film consumed the time and energy that otherwise would have been devoted to reading.

But the film isn't important either, she thought. It entailed no work on her character, no exercise of her skill and technique as singer or actress. The greatest demand it made was her rising at the first light of the day.

And it was getting late—time to dress and look the way she didn't feel at all.

Could It Be You? was the picture's title, stenciled on a card to the left of the entrance to the soundstage. The building itself had once housed Fox Movietone News, but now it hosted local or visiting film companies and "became" whatever interior was needed. Today, it was an elegant nightclub.

Beyond the set was a labyrinth of dressing rooms situated off the winding staircases and corridors. Rachel's hair and makeup had been done hurriedly, and as she rushed down the stairs in her long gown and spike heels, she was glad her own dressing room was only one flight up—less distance to cover between takes.

The car had arrived late to pick her up, and traffic had been heavy en route to the studio. Now, stepping onto the set, she saw that there had been no reason to rush; the "nightclub" was still being dressed, lights in need of adjustment. She was annoyed that no one had told her they were running behind schedule; it looked like another hurry-up-and-wait morning. The piano accompanist was being made up, and a run-through of the song would be impossible until the first rehearsal of the scene. Worse, the piano was four feet too far from the camera and no one had moved it closer.

Rachel's spirits brightened, though, when suddenly she looked up and saw Norma Kendall. She waved as the secretary came toward her. "Careful," she warned as Norma was almost tripped by a coiled length of cable on the cement floor.

"Thought you might need this," she said, pulling Rachel's script from her oversized totebag.

"I didn't even miss it," answered Rachel, beckoning Norma to a canvas chair beside hers. "Where did I leave it?"

"Howard said it was on the breakfast table. He brought it with him to the office."

Forgetfulness further annoyed Rachel; she never neglected important things. Well, she mused, that's just it; this script isn't really important. Aloud she asked, "Why didn't Howard drop by with it? He loves to visit movie sets and see what goes on behind the scenes."

"No time, so I volunteered. Got me out of the office for a while. Howard's been on the phone all morning. Whoever said summer is slow? By the way, Lehman called. Sends his love. Says he's got quite a tan." Rachel thought she had misheard. "Did you say . . . tan?"

Norma nodded. "He's rented Noel's old house in Jamaica."

"Howard must have been surprised—we thought he was at his place in Nyack."

"Oh . . ." Norma tried to cover, but she was blushing as she fumbled with some papers in her bag.

"Norma, what is it?"

"Nothing," she said. "I . . . just assumed you knew where Lehman had gone . . ."

"You mean . . . Howard *did* know?"

Norma was visibly embarrassed. "Me and my big mouth. I made the travel arrangements for him . . . last week. Listen—Howard probably just didn't want to bring up his name right now . . ."

"Yes . . . of course," said Rachel, finding her mood worsening. It wasn't like Howard to keep news from her, and he certainly hadn't forgotten. She didn't want to ask him about it—he was leaving for the West Coast in the morning, and Rachel didn't want them to spend *another* evening talking about Lehman.

But why, she wondered, didn't he tell me?

* * *

367

"I simply thought that with Lehman out of town for a week, all our lives might return to normal."

"So you purposely didn't mention it?" asked Rachel.

"That's right," Howard answered, easing himself into the deep chair beside the fireplace.

"Howard . . . before this . . . happened . . . you wouldn't have lied to me. How can our lives 'return to normal' if—"

"Rachel, it was hardly a lie. Anyway, *why* is it so important that you know where Lehman is?"

She put her hands on the arms of the chair and leaned in closer to him. "It's not Lehman's whereabouts. I felt like a fool hearing it from Norma, that's all. She was embarassed, too. I'm your wife, Howard. I shouldn't have had to hear it from your secretary."

"Darling," he said softly, "I'm leaving for L.A. in the morning . . ."

"Which is why I almost said nothing. But you should have told me. Didn't you think I might ask about him—or try to call him in Nyack?" She sank to her knees on the rug, suddenly tired.

Howard reached down and took her hand. "Frankly, I was under the impression that your feelings for Lehman had changed," he said.

"They have. Or I think they have. I don't know, Howard, I'm confused. He's a wonderful artist, gifted and kind—at least I'd always thought so. But now he's run off to an island paradise to ease his conscience, while *we're* here, left . . . with . . . with . . ."

"With what, Rachel? *You* aren't responsible for any of this."

"I'm responsible to myself! I may have questioned Eric's motives, yes, but for everyone to imply that he was some sort of prostitute—"

"Rachel, this isn't really about my not telling you that Lehman's in Jamaica, is it? This is about *your* conscience. And I don't see why. You're entirely blameless—"

"But Howard, is Lehman blameless? The press may have said so, but that was all *paid* for by Lehman, his family, Mina—" She stopped herself before finishing the sentence.

"And me?" Howard asked.

There were tears in Rachel's eyes when she looked up at him. "I'm sorry. I didn't mean . . ."

"Darling," he murmured, his palm smoothing her hair, "please. You have to put this to rest. For your sake—and ours."

He joined her on the rug and with his index finger wiped away a tear.

"I will," she whispered, moving closer to him. "I love you, Howard. So very much."

His jaw seemed less tight as his arms enfolded her. "My dearest. I love you, too. You know that."

She nodded, leaning against him. "I know. Just hold me for a while. Just hold me."

Rachel worked the following day. At a break in the shooting, she glanced at the clock. Ten already. Howard's flight had left fifteen minutes before.

He'd been asleep when the limo arrived for her. She'd kissed him gently and whispered, "Have a safe trip," and then left for the studio.

Since their marriage, he'd traveled less frequently on business unless Rachel had been free to accompany him. But this time she had to stay, and the contract he was negotiating couldn't be relegated to an assistant; Hollywood moguls liked to be coddled, and only Howard in person would do.

Rachel silently cursed the film that was separating them for three days. Now, perhaps more than ever, it was

369

important for them to be together. It was impossible to express the fear that had recently gripped her. She would miss Howard—she always did, even when the trip was only an overnight jaunt—but this time there was more to it. Some unidentifiable sensation made her view these next three days with . . . what? Apprehension? She was filled with it and didn't know why.

"Miss Allenby!" the A.D. called.

Just get through the day, she told herself as she took her place in the curve of the piano for what seemed the hundredth time since dawn. Sing this idiotic song for this moron of a director. Do whatever he wants, exactly the way he wants it. Don't argue, even if you know it's wrong. Just do it. Get out of here as early as possible. You'll be safe at home.

Jamie and Paul were coming by. At least she could look forward to that.

"Oh, God, it's good to see you two!" she said, entering the living room.

They came to her and all three embraced at once.

Katrina, the part-time maid, cleared her throat. "Dinner's in the oven, ma'am."

Rachel was grateful that the woman, who seldom showed up at the appointed day or time, was on this occasion leaving. She wrote out a check and handed it, together with a ten-dollar bill, to Katrina. "In case you want to take a taxi," she said. The maid pocketed both and was gone.

Paul had mixed their drinks while Rachel accompanied Katrina to the door.

Over dinner, Jamie brought up *One Night Only.* "We went to see the show last week. Beth is really good in it."

Paul agreed. "I was surprised. Not that many singer-dancers can really act. She's grown a lot."

"Did you stop backstage afterward?" Rachel asked.

"No," said Jamie. "We tried, but there was a mob."

"I'm having dinner with her Monday night," Rachel said. "I'll tell her you liked it. She needs all the encouragement she can get."

"Is she *still* insecure?" asked Paul. "Christ, her *mother* could have written the reviews—they were that good. Beth's turned into one hell of an actress."

"True," agreed Jamie, "but Ty Beekman's direction had a lot to do with it.

"What did you think?" Paul asked Rachel.

She shrugged and sipped the last of her wine. "Howard and I went to the opening. I guess I ought to see the play again when I can give it my full attention. I wasn't exactly concentrating that night. But I'm happy for Beth."

For a moment, neither Paul nor Jamie spoke. No one needed a reminder that Beth's show had opened only a few days after Eric's death. Then, in an obvious attempt to change the mood, Paul said, "Look, I'll clear the dishes if one of you will pour me a brandy."

But despite the brandy, the mood *had* changed.

The two men tried small talk, and Rachel could see that it was for her benefit. Paul mentioned a backer's audition he'd seen. "It's almost a carbon copy of *Robin Hood,*" he said. Then he realized his gaffe and added, "Sorry, I didn't mean—"

"It's okay," offered Rachel. "We can't spend the whole evening avoiding topics that involve Lehman Stern."

"You're still taking this pretty hard, aren't you?" Jamie asked.

"I guess so. It's very odd. It didn't happen to me—it happened to Lehman and to Eric. But I feel somehow . . . guilty."

"Guilty?" Jamie asked incredulously.

She nodded. "That . . . or like a traitor. I find myself

actually disliking him for something *everyone* tells me wasn't his fault. I mean, I know—or have an idea—of what he must be going through. But . . . I can't get it out of my head that he . . . killed someone. A kid."

"He did, Rachel," said Paul matter-of-factly.

"All right, he did, but he was also the first person in the business to show faith in me. He got me my first job. He introduced me to Howard. I wouldn't be where I am now if it weren't for *Robin Hood*—he got me that job, too!"

Tears filled her eyes again, and Jamie leaned across the sofa to put an arm around her.

"First, Rachel, nobody got you that job except *you*. Second, you wouldn't be where you are now if you didn't have the *talent*."

"Oh please," she said, shrugging herself free of his shoulder. "We all know how unimportant *that* is."

"Well, two of us do," Paul said quietly. "You seem to have lost sight of it, though."

She turned to him. "Touché."

"You know," said Jamie, "I'll grant you that Lehman gave you enormous help, but he's not the goody-two-shoes you want to make him into."

"Oh, it's not that . . ."

"I know, I know . . ."

"Rachel," Paul said, leaning toward her as he spoke, "is it possible you don't know about Lehman's 'scene' after all this time?"

The word took her by surprise. "Scene? Like what? I remember you once said . . . wasn't *bizarre* the word you used?"

"It was that, all right," he answered.

Jamie looked up. "What d'you mean? I knew you'd had a fling with him—when we broke up—but you never mentioned anything . . . kinky." There was no anger in his voice or manner, merely curiosity.

372

"That was one of the reasons I got out," said Paul. "Lehman's tastes are pretty widely known."

"Apparently not to everyone," said Jamie. "Not to me."

"Nor to me," Rachel added. "Paul, what are you getting at?"

He looked from her to Jamie. "This is going to be a long night."

Chapter Twenty-six

Paul ran a hand through his dark hair and downed his brandy. "I could use another of these."

"Talk. I'll get it," said Jamie. Quickly he brought the crystal decanter to the table. He refilled all three glasses and Paul began:

"Well, you both have to understand that Lehman and I were only together for a couple of weeks. I'm not usually into older men—then or now." He glanced at Jamie and a half-smile formed. "But Lehman had . . . charm. A way of making someone feel special—for as long as he cared to anyway." He took a sip of brandy.

"Somewhere during the first week, he'd had too much to drink one night . . . and started getting argumentative. I couldn't figure it out—there didn't seem to be any reason. He kept badgering, really *at* me, y'know? He pushed me, and I pushed him back. It got worse, and . . . I raised my hand to strike him. All of a sudden, he ran into the bedroom. Then he came back into the den holding a pair of handcuffs out to me. . . . He started saying stuff. . . . That's when I knew he'd been provoking me into treating him roughly. He . . . wanted to be punished for wanting me . . . a fantasy wherein I'd force him to do . . . things . . . to me. Things he wanted to do but needed to be 'disciplined' into doing." He took several swallows more of brandy and added, "Read *Justine* or *The Story of O* for details."

"Christ!" Jamie said quietly.

"It gets better . . . or worse," said Paul.

"There's *more?*" asked Rachel.

Paul nodded. "Oh yes. Remember, I didn't leave till the

following week."

Suddenly Rachel recalled the bruise on Lehman's cheek when he'd arrived late for the first rehearsal of *Robin Hood*. "Go on, Paul," she said.

"I managed to calm him down—and sober him up—whatever. And nothing unusual happened until one night when I got home from the theater later than usual. When I let myself in, I could hear soft music. The lights were low. There was a fog of smoke—pot—in the apartment. Lehman smoked—"

"So do you and I, sometimes," interrupted Jamie.

"No . . . not like this, Jamie. Not five joints apiece—and not every night. Anyway, I walked into the living room, and there was . . . this . . . kid. Stark naked, just sitting there. Lehman came out of the john. He was naked, too. Said to me he'd 'brought someone home for us to enjoy.' " He paused for a moment, then added, "This wasn't *just* a threesome. The kid couldn't have been more than fourteen years old."

"My God . . ." Rachel murmured under her breath.

"There'd been gossip—backstage stuff—about Lehman's eye for 'chicken.' But I never took it seriously. No one had actually *seen* him with kids, and there were no magazines or porno around his place to hint at it . . . at least none that I ever found."

"What did you do that night?" asked Rachel.

"I threw the few things I'd been keeping there in a bag and left. He called me the next day . . . begged me to meet him for a drink so he could explain. I went. Christ, he told me he'd always been into kids—the younger the better. Said he'd even had a few scrapes with the law in Virginia and Boston, but his producers always kept it out of the papers. It's also why he liked to find runaways. Most of them were hustlers, even that young, kids with no family to be paid off if he got caught.

"Lehman began to cry. He was almost hysterical. I had

to get him out of the bar. He was helpless, really. Obsessed."

Rachel was sitting still, completely stunned. After a silence, Jamie said, "But Paul . . . *you're* not a boy. And the others we've seen him with . . . they weren't kids."

"No. Kids weren't his exclusive scene. Besides, he couldn't be seen in public with any of them, could he?"

"I guess not."

Paul finished his brandy and said, "I was with him the night he met Eric."

Rachel had been staring at the well of brandy at the bottom of her glass. Now her head darted up at the sound of Eric's name.

"I told you both I'd met him once. It was late summer, I think. Despite everything, Lehman and I kept in touch—we know so many of the same people, and I was in one of his shows. Then he called, asked if I'd like to have a drink. He sounded lonely, so I said okay. We met in a bar, and he kept staring at this young guy who sat there, staring back. Lehman started talking to him and offered to buy him a drink."

"So he *was* a hustler?" asked Rachel.

"No," Paul said, "Just a runaway. All he talked about that night was singing, acting . . . show business. Real starry-eyed. I'm not even sure he had any idea who Lehman was. But it was obvious Lehman was taken with him. Probably would have invited him home that night, except he knew it was too soon to spring that on him— and too late to try it again with me. I don't think Eric would have gone, anyway. I don't know how they got together later. Maybe Lehman gave Eric his phone number while I was in the john. But I am sure of one thing. The papers gave Eric's age as twenty."

"That's how old Lehman said he was when we met him," said Rachel.

Paul shook his head. "That night, I remember Eric

376

said he was almost sixteen. He looked older—otherwise the bar wouldn't have served him. But he was just a kid."

Paul seemed to have finished speaking. His face was strained and his eyes were tired.

"So," said Jamie, "everything in the papers . . . was a lie?"

"Well, all the stuff about Eric's background, yes. As for what really happened that night . . . nobody knows. Except Lehman."

Rachel had the weekend off. She wouldn't have minded working, even if she was totally bored with the film itself. A free weekend left her with too much time for thinking.

Howard called each night, but Rachel reported to him only the mundane occurrences of her days on the set. She missed him, but there was no point in relating Paul's conversation.

Too, a seed of doubt had been planted. If Lehman's producers had been involved with keeping his predilictions from the public, had Howard, Lehman's agent, played a part in covering up? Could Lehman have brushed so closely with scandal without Howard's knowledge of it? He knew of Rachel's fondness for the director. But would he have ignored such behavior just to preserve Rachel's image of her mentor?

She thought over Lehman's claim—that Eric had attacked him. Yet what if Eric had purposely been provoked—as Paul had? Had it gotten out of hand and gone too far?

No matter the truth, Rachel had already begun to alter her thinking. Where earlier she had perceived Lehman as the victim, she now saw clearly that he was not. The victim was dead.

* * *

Dinner with Beth Burns would be relief after a listless weekend. Rachel hadn't even read the entire theater section of the Sunday *Times*. On Monday, she filmed one short scene and had the rest of the day "at liberty." So did the two other actors in the sequence just shot, but they weren't people with whom she could relax and talk freely. Beth always lifted Rachel's spirits and made her laugh. She needed to laugh. She couldn't wait until seven.

Rachel managed to disguise the signs of emotional fatigue, and by the time she rang Beth's bell, despite the humidity still hovering over the city, she felt refreshed at the prospect of an evening of theater gossip with her friend. She had used makeup and clothes to perk up her mood, and they seemed to have done the job.

Beth's apartment was a surprise; she had moved several times since Rachel had last been to dinner at the brownstone in Chelsea. Beth's new quarters, just off Central Park West on Sixty-second Street, revealed a side of her personality unseen by the theatergoing world.

Blues, pinks, and beiges combined with ruffles and frills to create a dollhouse effect. Hardly to Rachel's taste, its ultrafemininity bespoke nothing of the brash, outspoken New Yorker that was Beth's trademark and style.

They hugged, and Beth put a vodka tonic in Rachel's hand before she had even taken a seat.

"Christ, it's hot, huh? I had shopping to do today. Thought I'd pass out! I'll never get used to having just one day off a week. So much to do, you can't enjoy it. How's the flick going?"

Beth had spoken an entire paragraph in one breath, at her usual breakneck speed.

"I worked this morning," said Rachel, "and I have a six-thirty call tomorrow. I'm glad it's a small role—excuse

378

me, 'cameo'—the picture is going to be awful."

"Damn! I thought we could stay up and talk all night."

"Sorry. But it's early—we have loads of time." Rachel kicked off her shoes and curled her legs under her on Beth's shell pink sofa. "You look great," she said.

"And thin! Thanks. Dinner's almost ready. Hungry? I cooked it myself—well, I defrosted it myself and stuck it in the oven, anyway."

"You cook? What happened, did you fire your maid?" Rachel had teased Beth in the past about "going Hollywood," since Beth had hired a full-time, live-in maid the moment she'd begun making money.

"I think the bitch was stealing." Then Beth slowed down and put her hand on the arm of the sofa. "So, how *are* you—and things?"

Rachel was touched by her friend's concern but was also determined not to permit its intrusion again this evening. "Oh, I'm okay, I guess. I've been overreacting about it, though, and that's senseless. I mean, you know Lehman, too."

"Yes . . ." said Beth, taking a long gulp of her drink. "But it's a rough break for you. Too bad he didn't phone someone else, instead of you and Howard."

Rachel formed a wry smile. "You know, in all this time, I never considered that."

"You're not as self-centered as I am, honey. Anyway, Lehman's been cleared. It should blow over soon." She patted Rachel's hand. "Listen, don't move. I don't feel like setting the table tonight. I'm just going to grab some plates and we can eat right here and catch up on everything."

They went through two liters of chilled white wine with dinner, and afterward, Beth called from the kitchen, "This is my day off, so the hell with diets. Wait'll you get

379

a load of this!"

She reentered the living room carrying a *dacquoise*. The mocha whipped cream was already drooping, despite the air-conditioning.

"Oh, Beth, I don't believe you!"

"It looked better when it was delivered, but Dumas is all the way uptown, and even *I'd* melt in this weather. Here—dig in!"

Rachel obeyed. She attacked her portion with gusto. Beth poured more wine and they began to laugh at the slightest cue.

"That was scrumptious!"

"Another piece?" offered Beth in a tempting voice.

"Well . . . sure. Why not?"

"Exactly. Why not?" Beth's second servings were larger than the first. "What are you going to do when you're an old broad and that metabolism starts slowing down?"

Rachel was chewing a mouthful of the hazelnut meringue. She swallowed and answered, "I'll call you to recommend a diet!"

It set them laughing again. Then, when the dessert was almost gone, Beth leaned her elbows on the back of the sofa. In a quiet voice, she asked, "How's Howard holding up right now?"

"Better than I am," Rachel admitted. "Even Lehman is."

"Baby," Beth said, "you're really still upset, aren't you?"

Rachel shrugged her shoulders. "More depressed than upset. I guess it might be different if I were really into the film I'm doing. But I'm not, and Howard won't be back until tomorrow, late, and . . . and—"

"You need to talk?" Beth interrupted. "Do it. I'm all ears." She reached for the brandy decanter and poured.

"This seems to be the mainstay of conversation lately," said Rachel. She took a sip and slowly began to relate all she'd learned from Paul three nights before.

". . . So you see," she concluded, "none of it is what we thought. I mean, even if the boy *was* some kind of opportunist, it wasn't for money—or jewelry—it was for a dream that he thought Lehman could fulfill. Eric wanted a career. To sing. The fact that he had no talent is beside the point. His motives weren't so different from yours or mine. He just went about it the wrong way."

Beth had listened intently. Nothing Rachel had said seemed to surprise her. Now, shaking her head, she spoke. "No, he and I went about it the same way . . . eventually. Eric just made the wrong choice. I guess kids of sixteen don't make the best character judgments."

"Or those of us past thirty, Beth. We *all* misjudged Eric."

Beth nodded. "But honey, *we're* not *dead*. I hate to be so blunt, but . . . this isn't going to bring him back."

Rachel felt a sudden anger, but she quelled it. "You sound like Howard."

"Well, Lehman has done a lot for you," Beth reminded her.

"Oh Beth, I *know* that. But even before . . . this . . . I've closed my eyes to *other* things he's done. I've tried to dismiss them with asinine philosophy like 'that's show biz' . . ."

"What *other* things? Is there anything else—something I missed?"

Rachel paused; Beth leaned over, took her glass, and refilled it. Handing it back, she said, "So?"

"I was never going to tell you this . . . maybe it's the brandy on top of all that wine. . . . But Lehman did hurt me once. Very badly, and with no apology. He even used Howard to tell me."

"Go on," Beth urged.

"God, it's a good thing I'm not Catholic. I hate confessions!" Rachel smiled, but her eyes had unexpectedly filled with tears. "All right . . . here goes." Looking straight at Beth, she said, "I had been told that I was going to star in *Red Shoes* almost from its inception. I was thrilled about it. Then they changed the concept and needed a dancer. I guess it was out of Lehman's control, but it took me a long time to get over it. I was out and . . . you were in. That was all there was to it. But God, Beth, it really hurt."

Beth brought both of her hands to her forehead and closed her eyes. Moments passed before she said, "Oh Rachel, you've lived with that all these years and never told me?"

"I didn't want it to . . . come between our friendship. After all, it wasn't your fault that you could dance and I couldn't."

Beth's eyes were open now, and she was staring at her clenched fists on her lap. Slowly, she said, "Jesus, Rachel . . ." She shook her head sadly. "I guess I've got a confession of my own."

"What do you mean?"

She paused, as if weighing each word. "There was a kid—a boy—with the *Camelot* tour. It was his first Equity contract. We were in Boston, his hometown. But he never got in touch with his parents. I didn't understand why. Well, we got drunk together one night, and he told me that two years before, when he was sixteen, he'd apprenticed at a regional theater in Massachusetts. Lehman was jobbed in as musical director for one show. He went after the kid . . . and got him. Even then, I guess Lehman played rough. The kid ended up with cuts and bruises he couldn't explain, got scared, and told his parents the whole story. Lehman paid them off and hot-tailed it back to New York, while the producers kept it out of the papers."

"What happened to the boy?" asked Rachel.

"He's still in the business. We keep in touch. His

382

parents wouldn't let him go near a theater for the rest of the time he lived at home. But acting was what he wanted. He came to New York on his eighteenth birthday. He hasn't spoken to Lehman, of course, and his parents don't speak to him, so . . . I play adopted mama to him."

"Then . . . you knew all along about Lehman."

"Yes, Rachel, I knew. But that's not what I'm ashamed of."

"Well?"

Beth kneaded her hands together, first averting her gaze from Rachel and then facing her directly. Finally, she said, "I didn't know until tonight that you were ever in the running for *Red Shoes*. You've *got* to believe that. I only knew that I was right for the role and wanted it more than anything. So I . . . I . . ." Tears began running down her cheeks. "I got in touch with Lehman and . . . I told him I wanted the role. I . . . said that if I didn't get it, I'd tell the whole Boston story to anyone who'd listen. The kid didn't have a career to ruin, so I knew *he* wouldn't care."

It was still sinking in. "You mean . . . you . . . *blackmailed* Lehman to get the role?"

Beth nodded as a sob broke forth. "Rachel, please . . . if I'd known what I was doing to *you*, I'd *never* have . . ."

"Oh God . . ." mumbled Rachel. Suddenly, so many realizations were dawning on her as she watched Beth weeping. The betrayal she had felt when Lehman had cast Beth as Victoria Paige. The "pressure brought to bear" that Howard had spoken about. But had he said from which quarter that pressure had come? And again, the gnawing doubt, the same question: *Had Howard known?*

"Drink this," said Rachel, handing Beth the glass of brandy she had been drinking.

Beth obeyed and then wiped her eyes. "What are you going to do?"

Rachel replied without emotion. "I can't answer that, Beth. To say nothing is getting more and more difficult. . . . It takes too much out of me . . . I . . ."

"Are we still . . . friends?" Beth asked with pleading in her voice.

"This will take me a little time . . . to think through. I'm feeling . . . stupid, as if I'm the only person in this goddammed business who doesn't know what's going on around me." She had slid into her shoes and was standing.

"Rachel . . ."

"It's late, Beth, and I have to be at the studio at six. . . . I'll . . . call you . . ."

The chauffeur nudged Rachel gently. "Miss Allenby, wake up. We're here."

She opened her eyes. Even at dawn, a small crowd was gathered around the limousine at Fifty-fourth Street and Tenth Avenue. As Rachel alighted from the car, fans moved in, shoving pens and pads at her. She signed her name at the same time she walked to the studio entrance. "Thank you," she said, and quickly went inside.

By the time she was dismissed for the day, she'd had words with the writer about one of her lines. He'd insisted on having it his way; she finally realized that it wasn't worth fighting over. Giving in was easier.

A larger group of fans awaited her exit. Already she was dreading the next day, when they'd be shooting outside. That meant more heat and more crowds.

She fell asleep on the sofa while awaiting Howard's return that night. His flight was late, and he arrived well past midnight. But at least he was home. There'd be time to talk, later. For now, it was enough that he was there beside her.

It had been a long day, first at the studio on West Fifty-fourth Street, then outside at the nearby Tenth Avenue location. The weather hadn't helped, and the air-conditioning in Rachel's trailer had worked only intermittently. The scene itself had to be shot and reshot at least twenty times, first because of overhead airplane noises, then because of onlookers barging past the sawhorse barricades, and finally, the actors, from heat, humidity, and sheer exhaustion, had begun to go up on their lines. When Rachel heard the words "It's a wrap," they were like sweet music. All she wanted was to climb into the backseat of the limousine and be whisked home to a quiet dinner with Howard.

The studio car was cool, fortunately, since they were wedged between sixteen-wheeler trucks and moving vans in bumper-to-bumper gridlock. Rachel glanced at her wristwatch. It was shortly before the evening rush hour; it might be an hour before she got home! She lay back against the gray velour cushion and closed her eyes, just as the rear end of the limo hit a pothole. If it weren't for the heat, she mused, I'd do better by walking!

Young boys, Spanish for the most part, lined the streets along Tenth Avenue; some played three-card monte, others made obscene remarks or gestures to the passing traffic. A good-looking blond boy—one who resembled Eric—walked past a corner and two toughs close to him in age began mincing behind him, while chanting *"Mira! Mira!"* loudly enough for Rachel to hear through the closed windows of the limousine.

The portfolio of dark, bumpy-grained leather in eleven-by-fourteen size told Rachel that the boy was probably an actor coming from or going to an audition at one of the West Side film studios. She watched as he tried to ignore the jeers, although his feet carried him across Fifty-seventh Street much faster than the weather would have prompted, had no one been following to harass him.

Once the car had passed Lincoln Center, the traffic seemed to clear. To the East Side through the park, and Rachel would be home in another five minutes. Well, that was one advantage to being "at liberty" from Broadway just now, she mused. I don't have to do a show tonight. Still. . . . That old feeling of summer inactivity began to make its way into her thoughts. A throwback to that very first summer, no doubt. God! How did I stand it? she wondered. Maybe Jamie and Paul were right; in one's twenties, *anything* can be endured. She hummed the melody to "What I Did for Love" and laughed under her breath. *A Chorus Line* remained vivid in her mind — a show she could never, ever do, given the dancing, yet most of the hoofers in it were their own counterparts, offstage: chorus gypsies. Paul had been one. They worked so hard — endlessly — and remained in the background. Essential to any musical, while the public paid to see the star. A Rachel Allenby, a Beth Burns. All right, she reasoned, it's true the star's responsibility is greater. But could anyone in show business believe that anything was fair?

And yet, a part of Rachel needed to believe it. If not to rationalize her fame, then to justify her existence.

Thoughts such as these were always accompanied by restlessness, unease. They were difficult enough to quell in spring. But now it was summer in New York and too damn hot to fight.

The limousine pulled up alongside the curb, and Robert quickly stepped from within the cool, dark lobby to help Rachel out.

" 'Night, Miss Allenby," said the chauffeur.

She nodded as the doorman closed the door to keep the heat from entering the car. "Radio says it topped one hundred this afternoon," he said.

"I'm not surprised," answered Rachel, entering the building. She smiled at Robert and went into the side room to check the mailbox. It was empty, which meant either there had been none for them today, which was unlikely, or that Howard had returned early from the office. He generally tried to do so during the summer months. "The only time an agent can pretend to be a banker," he'd once joked.

Rachel entered the elevator; even the ride to the penthouse seemed weighted, heavy with the dank air, despite the cool within the marble interior of the building. Instead of a smooth, quick ascent, it jerked its way to the top floor, raising her breath and turning it shallow and thin. Her ears popped.

She unlocked the door, and the moment it closed behind her, Rachel kicked off her high-healed sandals and tossed her straw totebag and script on the loveseat beside the umbrella stand.

Voices, low but distinct, were coming from the den. One belonged to Howard. The other was . . . Lehman's?

Rachel quickly slipped back into her shoes and made her way down the hallway. Her heartbeat quickened, although she had no idea why.

And then, quite suddenly and accidentally, she knew the reason. She knew from the words that reached her ears and froze Rachel where she stood.

Lehman was speaking. Softly, but audibly. "I didn't mean to do it," he said, "but Eric was going to leave me. I couldn't let him leave me, Howard."

And then Howard said, "But the jewelry . . . the money . . ."

Between muffled sobs, Lehman said, "I stuffed them

387

in his pockets . . . after I dressed him . . ."

Rachel wanted to clear her throat, to utter some sound that would make her presence known. But she was rooted to the spot and her vocal cords refused to give her speech.

Howard hadn't responded for several moments. Finally, he said, "Lehman . . . what about the knife . . . ?"

This time the director's voice was choked and he didn't — or couldn't — reply.

The pause freed Rachel and she entered the den.

Both men looked up, and Rachel was again bewildered by the duality of her reactions: shock and disbelief, coupled with detached observation; the agonized pallor of her husband's face; the deep, bronzed tan of his client. Killer and confessor, in the opposite order and of opposing complexions. Rachel felt oddly stirred more by this than from the admission she had just overheard. Howard should have had the healthy, rested tan; Lehman's faced deserved the strain. Or did deserving have no place here, as it seemed to have no place anywhere? Rachel's physical sensations were as strangely divided as were her emotions. She felt dizzy, yet knew she would not faint; nauseous, but she would not vomit. Nervous, to a point of calm.

"Lehman." It was all she said.

He looked up at her with vacancy in his eyes, two voids that had once sparkled with sensitivity and wit. He shook his head slowly, but Rachel couldn't discern whether it was because he had confessed, or because she had witnessed part of the confession. And somehow, his reaction didn't matter.

She crossed the room to the sofa where Howard sat opposite his client's chair, but she remained standing. The moment seemed unending.

At last, Lehman lifted his head and said to Howard, "I

388

know my curse is to live with this. To relive it every night. But I had to tell someone. You were *there,* Howard. I had to tell *you.*"

Rachel's adrenaline suddenly shot through her and formed the words. "You've made my husband an accessory, Lehman. An accessory to murder."

"No!" he cried out. "I didn't mean to do it! Rachel, you of all people know me well enough—"

She cut him off. "I don't know you at all, Lehman. I only thought so." She turned to Howard and said, "But Beth Burns knows Lehman. Very well."

Her hands began to tremble, shaking almost imperceptibly, but Rachel recognized it as a signal that she was on the verge of losing control. She drew a deep breath and said, "Lehman, I think you'd better leave."

"Rachel—"

"I'm sorry, Lehman, truly I am. But"—her voice held a slight quaver—"you'll have to go. I'll see you to the door."

She walked as steadily as her legs would carry her, and a pathetic, broken Lehman Stern followed. Rachel wasn't aware of whether any of them said good-bye.

When the door closed between them, Rachel leaned back against it as though its massive strength would support her emotional burden and at the same time shield them from the outside world. She was home, alone with Howard. Safe from harm.

But Howard, who stood near her in the foyer, said, "How could you just throw him out?"

"You sound as surprised by my action as I am by yours," she said quietly. "How could you let him stay?"

"Rachel, the man is destroyed—"

"For the moment," she said. "But now that he's 'shared' it all with you, he'll be fine. He'll find another young boy, one whose parents are willing to be bought off—unless he picks a runaway like Eric, who can't be traced—"

"My, God, what are you saying?"

"I'm saying that men like Lehman Stern should be locked away, Howard—away from young boys like Eric—and all those who came before but who got away without being murdered—"

"Rachel—it was an accident! You heard him!" Color had returned to Howard's face and now anger filled it.

They were under the archway to the living room. Rachel walked to the French windows and looked out at the haze settling over the city as twilight began to fall.

With her back to Howard, she asked, "What are you going to do?"

"About what?"

"About Lehman. About the lies he told you and the police."

"Rachel, it was still an accident. You didn't hear the whole story."

"I heard enough—"

"No. You didn't hear about the pain this has caused him. The torture he's endured." He came to her and placed his hands on her shoulders as he had the first time she had ever visited his apartment. So much had changed! she thought. She still wanted those hands to hold her, to enfold her and caress her. But involuntarily she moved away.

"Rachel . . . darling . . ."

"You haven't answered my question, Howard," she said. Couldn't he hear the pleading between her words? Oh Howard, they seemed to say. Don't let this come between us. Don't let this drive us apart. "Are you going to tell the police?" were the words she spoke.

Howard bent over and took a cigarette from the silver box on the coffee table. Usually these were reserved for guests; Howard had stopped smoking several years before. He lit it and dragged on the cigarette, then exhaled both smoke and much pent-up breath before saying, "It wouldn't do any good to tell the police."

She couldn't believe that Howard—the man who wanted nothing but honesty from her—was ready to cover up for someone who had killed.

"Howard—he made it appear as though Eric was a thief! He—he's his own accessory! Lehman's ego—"

"His *love,* Rachel. Obsession, if you like—"

"His ego! He couldn't accept the fact that Eric was going to leave him—so he killed him! And in case *that* wasn't enough, he made it *look* like self-defense, instead of an accident!"

"Rachel, the police agreed that the knife belonged to Eric—and had his fingerprints on it."

"Maybe Eric drew the knife to defend *himself*—unless Lehman added *that* 'prop' as well! Don't you see, Howard? Lehman couldn't stand the thought of losing Eric—he'd said so often enough, God knows! And everyone is convinced—because *we've* all helped to convince them—that *Eric* was the one who victimized *Lehman!* People believe what they see in print—and thanks to Lehman's family's money, God! The public's certainly having its reading matter spelled out!"

Rachel's voice had risen, and her throat was trying to close. She willed it to stay open. "I just wonder, Howard, what the papers would do with the *truth* for once! What would happen if Lehman Stern were exposed for exactly what he is!"

"Rachel!" The tone of his voice stopped her. "In God's name, what's got into you? Do you think Lehman's any worse than people like Gloria Doro or Drew Colton—or your friend Beth Burns? Or the other pimps and politicians in this or any other business? What do you expect—for them all to behave like you?"

"No!" she shouted back. "I just don't expect *you* to behave like any of *them!*" Now she was shaking with anger. Something inside had snapped, and she could no longer suppress the suffocating emotion of buried outrage. "Howard! You've *got* to do something! You can't just let it die!" Tears began to rise. "Howard, please—I'm begging you—don't turn your back on this! For *us* . . ."

"Rachel," he said wearily, his voice only slightly less strained, *"why* are you insisting? What has it got to do with us?"

"Everything, Howard," she said between sobs. "And it frightens me that you don't see it."

Howard followed her into the bedroom and stood in the doorway as she opened the closet and withdrew an overnight bag.

"What's that for?" he asked. "Rachel . . ."

"I have to . . . to get away for a while. I need time to . . ." Her sigh finished the sentence.

"Rachel, this is ridiculous. You're upset, so you're overreacting—"

"Don't analyze me, Howard! It *isn't* ridiculous! Maybe if I were calm, I wouldn't be reacting *enough!* I've become so—so *civilized*—so immune to the garbage that's strewn around this business day in and day out! Everybody keeps saying it has to change—but it *isn't* going to change, Howard, unless *somebody* is willing to take the risk to *make* it change! How long can we— you—*all* of us go on sweeping things under the rug, pretending they don't exist, rationalizing—"

"Rachel—"

"No! *Don't* tell me to look the other way, Howard, because I *can't!* I've already seen what's there! I've been practicing *not* seeing things the way they are, Howard, and it's been driving me blind! Maybe people like my parents are lucky—they believe what they read and hear—the things that the media is *paid* to make *sure* they see and hear—"

"But *we* know the truth, Rachel—"

"That's just it, Howard—*we've* lost sight of it! My parents are innocent, because they don't *know!* The guilty ones are those of us who know and try to *hide* the truth!"

"Rachel, I'm trying to tell you that this . . . mess . . . with Lehman doesn't alter the truth! What he did was in desperation! If he had told the police that he and Eric were in bed and had a lovers' quarrel, do you *really* think they'd have believed that Eric's death was an accident?"

"He made it *seem* to be an accident, Howard! He even lied to *you!*"

"Perhaps he wasn't sure that I'd believe the truth . . ."

She had been flinging clothing into her overnight case on the bed. Now she tossed in her makeup kit and slammed the lid shut. "Didn't Lehman know that you'd cover for him, Howard? The way you're covering for him now?"

"Rachel," he said, his anger returning, "I am *not* covering for him! Eric's death remains an accident, whether Lehman acted in poor judgment or not. His *failure*—or weakness—in a moment of crisis does *not* make him a murderer!"

"You just don't understand, do you?" she said, choking back tears as she rushed past him into the entrance foyer.

He hurried after her. "Rachel . . . you don't want to do anything that you may regret later."

Between sobs, she answered, "I already regret it, Howard. But it doesn't change the way things are."

Chapter Twenty-seven

Rachel spent the night on the sofa at Jamie and Paul's. She had one more day of shooting on the film. The following morning, she made an appointment to meet with Vera Garland to discuss the book.

"It may be more than just an autobiography," she told the editor over the phone.

"Your name means big sales, Rachel," Vera replied. "We'll publish anything you want to say in print."

"You may have a few lawsuits on your hands if you really mean that," she said.

"Well, when the legal department gets the manuscript, they'll handle that aspect. By the way, you'll be our lead book, so be prepared for the media blitz. Y'know, the promotion tour, the TV talk shows. We'll work around your schedule, but just be ready for very high visibility." Then Vera laughed. "Sorry, sometimes I forget I'm talking to someone who's accustomed to public exposure. Y'know, some of my biggest authors try to crawl into the woodwork and hide from the buying public once the book is written. They only come out again to start the next book — or when we're slow in royalty payments, which is always."

Rachel laughed with Vera; it was her first such release in more than a month, and she was grateful. Making a movie — even a "cameo" appearance — was boring, and reading on the set was constantly interrupted for endless makeup retouches and retakes. Writing a book — this particular book—would occupy her time *and* engage her mind.

That reminded her of the scripts Howard had brought home the day before; she'd seen new binders on the living room coffee table upon her return home. Howard had probably forgotten to take them to the den because of Lehman's visit, and afterward, scripts hadn't entered her thoughts for a moment. Perhaps she could ask Jamie—no! She wasn't going to stick her head in the sand like one of Vera's other authors; she had a book to write, but she also had to find a new script, musical or dramatic. She smiled ruefully as she mused aloud, "I'd better do a show soon. Once this book sees print, the name of Rachel Allenby may be blacklisted from coast to coast!"

She also needed a few sundries that her hasty packing had overlooked, her reading glasses among them. She had been wearing soft contact lenses since their inception, and the various paraphernalia—what Rachel called her lens-cooking equipment—always traveled in her makeup case. But she'd only been wearing reading glasses for several months, so they weren't yet second-nature-when-packing. "Besides, I hadn't really planned on going anywhere," she heard herself say.

"You're doing that again," said Jamie, entering the room.

"Doing what?"

"Talking to yourself."

"Better than to the walls, hmm?"

"Depends." He kissed her on the cheek. "What about Howard?"

She looked up questioningly.

"When are you going to sit down and talk to him?"

Rachel shook her head and answered, "That's just it, Jamie. Right now we can't seem to talk to each other."

"You always could," he said gently. "As easily as with me."

She took his hand. "There was a time when you and I didn't have much to say to each other."

"I was being pigheaded and stupid. Howard doesn't strike me as either of the above."

"That's the whole point. If he were, I could probably understand his attitude. But his awareness and intelligence just won't let me."

Jamie crossed to the air conditioner and turned it to low. The heat wave seemed to have broken during the night.

"Rachel, maybe you and Howard . . . well, you were both tired, and the weather and all . . ."

"Jamie, don't make excuses—"

"I'm not. I'm trying to look at this from both sides. It's the only way I can help."

She smiled, but the corners of her mouth were forced upward, and her acting didn't feel convincing when she said, "I appreciate the attempt, but please . . . *don't* help."

She did allow him to accompany her crosstown, however, to the apartment on Fifth Avenue. She didn't expect Howard to be at home—it was midday, which was why she chose that hour—but she hadn't anticipated his being there with Lehman the day before either, so she couldn't be sure. Jamie was providing a dual service; he was giving her the courage to enter her own home as well as catching her if Howard was there and Rachel's knees should suddenly go weak.

She thought she asked Robert casually if "Mr. Rathborne is home early," but Jamie told her she sounded tight-throated. "And your doorman was eyeing both of us suspiciously," he whispered as they stepped into the elevator.

"He probably thinks I'm bringing my lover upstairs for

an afternoon tryst. All the neighbors are doing it, according to Katrina."

"Your maid has a dirty mind."

"You're right. But she's efficient—*when* she shows up. Too bad what's-his-name went back to India." Then she remembered the circumstances under which Rha-ji had been hired—Jamie's arrest and subsequent disappearance—and added lightly, "I'd love to match Katrina with Owen, our handyman in Hertfordshire. They're perfect for each other."

But that only made Rachel think of the house she and Howard had so lovingly remodeled and furnished, and emotion began creeping back toward the surface.

"Rachel, you okay?" asked Jamie as the elevator stopped on the top floor. "I can pick up your things while you wait downstairs—"

"No," she said. "We're here. If I'm going to go through with this book, I can't be afraid of the dark."

She didn't know whether she was relieved or disappointed by Howard's absence. Suddenly thirsty, she went into the kitchen. A list of messages lay on the counter beside the phone. *Call Norma,* read one. *Majestic Theater, 8 P.M.,* was the second message in Howard's familiar handwriting. *R—Jamie?,* read the note scribbled at the bottom of the pad.

He read over her shoulder. "Does that mean to call you at my place—or is he guessing that's where you'll be?"

"I don't know," she said, pouring tap water, drinking, and depositing the glass in the dishwasher. Either Katrina had been and gone, or Howard had skipped both dinner and breakfast; no dirty dishes were in the machine, and nothing had been left out or in the sink. "I wonder if he's eating," she said.

"Rachel, you don't know how to stay angry, do you?" asked Jamie gently.

"I'll learn," she answered, leaving the kitchen and heading for the den.

The new scripts had been removed from the living room and now lay to the left of the stack of rejects already read; it was easy to tell by the bindings which had been opened and which were new. One in the "new" stack, however, had its binding cracked. Rachel was about to leave it with the others, assuming she'd already seen it, when her eyes caught the slip of paper sticking up like a bookmark. She pulled it free to read and exclaimed, "Oh, he remembered!"

"What?" asked Jamie. "Who?"

"Ty Beekman—Beth's director. He said he'd drop off a script at Howard's office—something he thinks I might be interested in—and I was certain he'd forgotten. One of those 'I'd love to direct a show with you' lines that everyone says when you're first introduced, y'know?"

"No," said Jamie. "I don't know."

"I'm sorry. I meant it as a figure of speech. Vera Garland punctuates her sentence with 'y'know,' and I'm afraid I've picked it up." She squeezed his arm. "I didn't realize it still hurts."

"Only sometimes," he said. "It won't when I find something to replace it."

"Want to help me with the book?" she asked lightly, trying not to weigh down the offer or the conversation.

"I thought *you* said no ghosting or as-told-to—"

"I'm not asking you to *write* it for me," she said. "But I'll need an objective pair of eyes."

"Does that mean I'll be the first to read it—hot off the typewriter?"

She smiled at that. "Even before my editor sees it. That's a promise."

He reached out and grabbed her hand. "Lady, you've got yourself a deal."

Just knowing he'd be there helped, but it didn't alleviate the loneliness she felt, especially when she went to the bathroom in search of her reading glasses. "I'm sure I left them here, beside the phone." She checked the drawer of the night table, but neither the glasses nor their snakeskin case were there.

And then she remembered. "They're in the closet, in the pocket of my robe!" She flung open the door, and the smells of Howard's after-shave, mingling with her own perfume, greeted her. She touched the silk sleeve of his paisley robe, wishing he were there, furious at herself for letting her love for him dictate her mood. She pushed the hanger aside and reached into the far pocket of her black velvet dressing gown. Sure enough, the roughness of the cobra eyeglass case could be felt.

"I don't know why I left them in a pocket," she said. Just as she spoke the words, she recalled the reason: She had been wearing the glasses when Howard had joined her in the den. He had taken the book she was reading and placed it on the table. Then he had removed her glasses and kissed her. She had slipped the glasses into their case—in the pocket of the black velvet—and then Howard had removed the dressing gown and they'd made love.

Suddenly a longing for him overwhelmed her. "Jamie, I've got to get out of here before my head becomes as muddled as Lehman's." No, she amended, not like Lehman's. He had killed for love. Instead, *she* felt like the one who was dying.

When they returned to Jamie's, Rachel went over the shooting script for her last scene in the film. But she found it difficult to concentrate, to shut out thoughts of Howard, of Lehman, of events. Instead of memorizing lines, Rachel's mind darted back and forth over the ways in which all their lives—Jamie's and Paul's, too—had become interwoven. Hiding at Jamie's could provide only temporary refuge; when the film wrapped tomorrow, she'd have to make decisions. She had made one: to write the book. But was it a wise decision—or was it a too-hasty, impulsive act of defiance? No, she thought. It's a matter of choice. It's the only way I can live with myself.

When she was able to still her mind sufficiently to stay in the moment of the scene she was studying, the telephone rang. Jamie had been running interference, telling Howard the first time that Rachel was lying down; the second call moved her to the studio; the third, to the bath. Finally, feeling cowardly for asking Jamie to invent excuses—and knowing Howard could undoubtedly see through them—Rachel closed the script and answered the fourth call.

But it wasn't Howard; Norma was phoning from the office. "Did you . . . receive the script from that gorgeous hunk?" asked Howard's secretary.

"Yes, Norma. Thanks." In spite of her mood, Rachel laughed at the word *hunk*.

"Good. I'll pretend that's why I'm calling."

"But it's not the reason."

"Of course not. My boss looks like hell today. His wife—my friend—has the answering service taking messages . . ."

"How did you know I was here?" asked Rachel. She didn't think Howard would have mentioned it.

"Remember a long time ago I told you I was great in a crisis?" asked Norma. "Well, what's the first thing someone does in a crisis?"

"You tell me . . ."

The secretary laughed. "We revert to nature. The only place you *could* be is at Jamie's. So it's your turn to tell me: what's going on?"

Rachel said, "I can't put it into words, Norma.

Howard and I have had a . . . a misunderstanding."

"You don't move out over a misunderstanding, Rachel."

"I . . . I haven't moved out. I just need some time." She heaved a deep sigh. "I don't like fighting with Howard, Norma, but . . ."

"But you're fighting with him, just the same."

Rachel nodded to herself and said into the phone, "I'm not so sure it's Howard I'm fighting."

"I don't promise not to tell him that, Rachel. He's coming down the hall. I'll call you later."

The next time Howard did call, Jamie didn't have to cover for her. Rachel had—truthfully—fallen asleep.

When she awoke and nervously dialed the number, Rachel was half wishing the service would answer and say that Mr. Rathborne was at the theater or dining with a client. But he was home, and the moment she heard his voice, she was filled with both hope and dread: hope that he had come around to her point of view, dread that he would stand firm. From the tone of his voice, she realized they were on common ground in a single area: he missed her as much as she missed him. For the rest, they were at an impasse.

"Then you're serious about writing this exposé," he said.

"It isn't an exposé, Howard. It's a book about what this business is *really* like—what people don't know." She hesitated and then added, "It's the truth—*not* what they read in the papers."

There was a pause on Howard's end of the line, after which he said, "What makes you think the public cares what goes on 'backstage'?"

"I don't know," Rachel admitted. "But *I* care, and it's a good feeling for a change, Howard. Maybe it'll make a

401

difference, if not for the 'civilian' world, then for the kids with talent—the ones who come to New York with stars in their eyes—if just a handful of them can see the business clearly, for what it really is—"

"Aren't you using that as a 'noble' excuse?" interrupted Howard.

"Noble! What about people like Paul and Jamie—half the city is filled with talented, hard-working performers who will never get anywhere because they don't have the connections or the money or"—momentarily she thought of Beth—"or the willingness to sleep around or . . . or use blackmail—"

"Rachel," said Howard, "you're not telling me anything I don't know. I'm just trying to remind you of the risk you're taking—"

"*Someone* has to!" Now her anger was returning. "Howard—I *have* to ask this—did you know all along about Lehman? I don't mean that he's gay—every member of Actors Equity knows that!—I mean about his . . . prediliction . . . ?"

He didn't reply, so she continued. "Did you know that he liked boys—*young* boys? Did you know that Eric was sixteen? That he was *fifteen* when they met? And did you know the rest?"

After a short pause, Howard said quietly, "I don't think I want to know the rest."

"That's just it! *Nobody* wants to know—so on and on it goes! It's like a wife who doesn't want to see that her husband is cheating on her—"

"Rachel . . . since nobody wants to know, you'll be writing these 'truths' for nothing. Risking your career, and for what?"

"For me," she answered in a small voice. "If for no one else, at least for me."

"Then I hope your publisher is paying you a fortune, because it will probably mean the end of your performing career. Even with my—excuse the word—*connections,* I doubt I'll be able to bail you out."

He'd spoken in an almost managerial tone, which infuriated Rachel further. "That's a chance I'll have to take. I met a woman in Israel—Annie Singer—who told me it all comes down to choice. She was very wise."

"Did she have so much at stake?"

"Only her life," Rachel said bitterly.

Howard paused again before he asked, "Have you thought about us?"

Rachel was suddenly choked by emotion and a tightness across her chest. "I love you," she said between tears. "But I have to do what's right, Howard. Otherwise I'd grow to resent you—and us. I . . . I was hoping you'd understand."

"I can empathize, Rachel, but even if I were to change my impression of Lehman Stern, he remains my client. What has happened is causing him immense grief—otherwise I doubt he'd have to come to me with . . . the truth." Howard hesitated and then added, "And you, Rachel, have no right to ruin his career. If you care nothing about yours, well, as you say, it's a matter of choice. But you'll be destroying a man who in many ways is already paying dearly for what he's done."

"I'm not writing a book about Lehman," she said. "I'm writing about *all* the Lehmans, the Drew Coltons, the Gloria Doros, even the Beth Burnses in the business." She took a deep breath and added, "And your clients' names will remain 'safe.' I'm not going for anyone's jugular, Howard. Just justice."

"Even justice seeks a balance, Rachel."

"*That's* why I'm going to write this book," she answered. "Because justice's scales have been loaded for far too long."

"Look, I'm not asking you to become a hypocrite, Rachel. I'm just alerting you to the risks."

403

"I'm aware of them, Howard."

"Of all of them?"

She tried to swallow the lump in her throat. "Yes," she answered, fighting new tears, "of all of them."

"Do you . . . plan to do your writing . . . here?" he asked quietly. "Or are you . . . more comfortable . . . at Jamie's?"

She hadn't given it much thought, but now the prospect of writing at either place seemed impossible. She heard herself say, "I may get away for a while. Perhaps the cottage. I . . . I need a change. I . . ." Her voice broke at the image of Hertfordshire without Howard. "I'll . . . I'll write you from there."

She wanted to say more, but uncertainty stopped her.

Howard sounded as tentative, as emotionally spent as Rachel felt. "Safe trip, then . . ." was all he said.

It had been their first phone conversation in years that hadn't ended with "I love you."

Chapter Twenty-eight

October 1976

Several passengers aboard the jet asked for Rachel's autograph; she complied mechanically, remembering back to the little French bistro in New York, where she'd asked Drew Colton what fame was like. He'd predicted correctly—she *had* come to know, soon enough. No thanks to him, she reminded herself. That brought a small grin to the corners of her mouth.

She hadn't alerted Jennie or William of her imminent arrival in Hertfordshire. Only Owen knew; she wasn't in the mood to go from Heathrow to King's Cross Station, there to stand around waiting for the train. If Owen did nothing during the months in which Rathborne Cottage remained unoccupied, at least he could be of use as Rachel's driver. She laughed wryly; most of the people in her business—particularly people who were stars—would have referred to Owen as the *chauffeur*. Lehman always had.

Rachel had seen the film that was showing in-flight, so when she realized that the passengers seeking autographs had already approached her—a feigned seven-hour nap wouldn't be necessary—Rachel ordered a glass of wine and leafed through the current copy of *Vogue*. Damn, she thought. I've read this issue. I should have taken time at the airport to buy a book. Nothing heavy, just a good read—a few hours' escape.

She reached down beneath the seat and retrieved her totebag. In it she had stuffed the unread scripts collected from Howard's desk; she had packed lightly, but still her bulging suitcases had permitted nothing more, and she hadn't wanted to leave the plays behind.

Christina's World was typed in capital letters on the title page of the script with the cracked binding. In the upper-right-hand corner was a familiar name, written in a handwriting she recognized; Rachel had seen both inside the script of *One Night Only* in Beth Burns's dressing room on the afternoon they'd met for lunch. This had to be the play that Ty Beekman had dropped off for her, the script with Ty's note inside.

If this is a story about Andrew Wyeth's famous painting, she mused, it can't hold much promise. She did notice, however, a penciled question mark beside the title. Maybe, like *Knights in Nottingham,* the name was just a working title—which meant it was subject to change.

She leaned back and turned to page one. Even if it turned out to be a total waste of time, what else was there to do until the plane landed?

Christina's World wasn't remotely related to Wyeth, nor had the plot anything to do with the world of painting. Moreover, to Rachel's surprise, *Christina's World* was a musical. Why, Rachel wondered, is Ty Beekman interested in a musical—drama or comedy? Directors of his reputation usually dismissed musicals as "fluff"—even if musicals *did* support an otherwise dying Broadway. Peter Hall had moved from drama to opera, but would *he* ever think of directing "fluff"?

Nonetheless, as she read, Rachel gradually began to understand exactly not only why Ty Beekman wanted to direct this show, but why he wanted *her* to play Christina. It was as though the role had been written with Rachel in mind.

Although their lives and experiences were dissimilar, Rachel and Christina shared a common bond; both were sensitive, vulnerable idealists. Christina, however, was highly neurotic with deep-rooted inner conflicts; in the end, she found escape in death. Nonetheless, Rachel could empathize with a character unable to accept the dark side of her nature. She was more fortunate than Christina, whose inner light was gone. Edgar Cornwall's protagonist was indeed a tragic heroine, seeing the truth in everyone but herself. A parallel to Cassandra? Rachel wondered. During the course of two acts, Christina would open more than just Pandora's box. In the hands of a pedantic director, *Christina's World* might risk becoming more melodramatic than second-rate Puccini; but with Ty Beekman at the helm, the role might be just what she'd been looking for.

Rachel found herself eager for the plane to land so that she could contact the director. She hadn't felt this enthusiastic over a script since—my God, she thought—since *Robin Hood!*

At Heathrow, there was the usual fanfare that greeted Rachel upon her arrival in any public place. In London, admirers were only somewhat more respectful of her privacy than elsewhere; still, she spent the time in the customs line signing one autograph after another. She smiled wearily as she handed back what seemed to be the last felt-tipped pen of the lot. Instead of learning speed typing, she mused, I ought to have become ambidextrous!

But that reminded her of Howard's electric typewriter, sitting on the tiny desk in her attic studio at Hertfordshire. She hoped in her absence there had been no power failure; she hadn't thought to bring a manual portable machine, just in case.

Vera and she had agreed upon a deadline for her book. A year certainly seemed sufficient time in which to write the words that were already forming long paragraphs and chapters in her head. All she had to do was find the "hook."

Owen spotted her before she saw him; celebrity, she mused, did have its advantages. He found her at the center of more fans. He seemed completely unimpressed until a young girl asked him, "Are—*you* with *'er?*"

He nodded in his customary surly manner and went off to collect her two suitcases.

She didn't know what answer to give, should Owen ask about Howard. But as the car passed Eaton Square and the taciturn handyman still hadn't spoken two words, Rachel settled back against the soft velour seat, closed her eyes, and didn't reopen them until she heard the familiar crunching of gravel beneath the car tires. They had reached Rathborne Cottage.

The weather was damp after a late-evening drizzle, but Owen had built a fire in the hearth, and except for white sheets covering the furniture—a practice Rachel hated, since it made her think of funerals—the house was as cozy as when she and Howard had last been there.

Howard. Shouldn't she call to let him know she had arrived safely? Something held her back, and it was more than Owen, who stood awkwardly in the hallway waiting, it seemed, to either be invited in or dismissed.

"Thank you, Owen," said Rachel. "I won't keep you. It's late."

He gave a half-nod, mumbled "G'nite, then," and disappeared through the kitchen entrance.

The telephone rang. Rachel picked up the receiver expecting to hear Howard's voice. But it was Jennie.

"Welcome, luv," she said. "We saw Owen opening up the place this morning, so we asked and he said you were coming this evening. Why didn't you let us know? How are you and Howard?"

She hadn't told Owen that she was arriving alone, so Jennie's question wasn't meant to pry.

"We're . . . fine, Jennie. And we . . . I . . . this was sort of spur-of-the-moment." She paused and then added, "Howard's in New York. He couldn't get away just now."

"You mean you're here by yourself? Oh, luv, that won't do! You'll come to dinner tomorrow night—no excuses, right?"

"Well, I . . ."

"You'll have tomorrow to unpack. Look, I know you must be tired from the flight. I only called this late because I've been trying all evening and you still weren't here. William and I just wanted to know you'd got here safe and sound."

"That's very kind—"

"Nonsense. You're *family.* Now you get a good night's rest and I'll drive over to collect you myself—that way you won't have to rely on Owen, and if William's held up at the hospital, you won't be stranded."

"Thanks, Jennie."

"How's six-ish, then?"

"Fine."

"Right," said Jennie. "We can't wait to see you and hear all the news!"

Rachel hung up and glanced out the window. It was a moonless night, and suddenly, although her body was still on New York time, she felt exhausted. It was her first conscious encounter with jetlag upon coming "home" to England. Then she realized that her tiredness wasn't jet lag at all; it was because she wasn't accustomed to England without Howard.

* * *

Nor was she accustomed to sleeping alone in the king-size bed upstairs. When they had first bought Rathborne Cottage, while awaiting Howard's arrival, Rachel had spent the nights curled up on the flowered sofa in the living room, with a knitted afghan wrapped around her. The modest master bedroom seemed cavernous now, as Rachel unpacked aimlessly, every so often glancing toward the phone.

The stained-glass-colored afghan was folded neatly at the foot of the bed. Had Owen placed it there, or had she just removed it from the cedar chest? Rachel shook her head; she wasn't usually so disorganized.

She tried to put a call through to New York, but the circuits were busy. It was just as well; for the moment, what could she and Howard have said to each other? She washed her face with ice-cold tap water—she'd neglected to turn on the heater, and Owen hadn't bothered—and slid into a flannel granny gown left in the armoire for damp English autumn nights. Then she added a quilt atop the afghan, crawled into bed, and turned out the light.

Rachel was surprised at having slept soundly through the night, but Rathborne Cottage was so quiet! No overhead noises of airplanes, no screeching sirens or automobile horns—even in the Fifth Avenue penthouse, shrillness traveled on a high-enough frequency to penetrate the windows.

She hadn't called Howard, nor had he rung her. Glancing at the clock beside the bed, she saw that it was only 9 A.M. She could never remember whether the time differential between London and New York became six hours or five with the end of daylight saving time each fall. Whichever, it was the middle of the night across the Atlantic.

She'd try to reach him at the office, later. Several hours' respite would offer an opportunity to replenish her mental energies—at least for the duration of a telephone call.

Rachel dressed—the water was too cold for a bath—and went downstairs to make coffee.

She spent the morning arranging her "office" in the attic workspace. She found that the window light, which would be excellent for writing in the earlier part of the day, would create a glare by afternoon. First she repositioned the desk, but then realized that the cord from Howard's electric typewriter wouldn't reach all the way to the wall outlet. Perhaps she could ask Owen for an extension cord. "On second thought," she mused aloud, "if I wait for Owen, I won't start typing till Christmas!" She settled on a compromise: the adjacent wall, while a less attractive arrangement visually, would harness good enough working light in the morning and still be sufficient—without the glare—until three or four in the afternoon.

Next came writing materials. Rachel was surprised by this aspect of her personality. She was actually looking forward to the task of setting out typing paper and pencils, correction fluid, paper clips, and the rest of her supplies. She had forgotten carbon paper, but for now she'd only be composing notes. She withdrew a clipboard from the bottom drawer and set it to the left of the telephone.

She pressed the ON switch and the machine began to purr. Writing for the Excelsior High School paper years before, followed by all those temping assignments in New York, Rachel had learned to compose directly onto the typewriter. But the first item at hand—before any manuscript work—was a quick letter to Jamie and Paul. She positioned a sheet of stationery into the paper bail, rolled it, and began to type.

"Oh, Christ!" she exclaimed. "It needs a new ribbon!" She turned the machine to OFF and ran downstairs. There was a small street of local shops within fifteen minutes' walk. She'd bought writing supplies before, at the stationer's store next to the bakery.

She grabbed her trenchcoat and keys, then remembered to take an umbrella. The air was crisp and clean, but this was, nonetheless, England.

Owen was in the garden when Rachel returned an hour later with a half-dozen ribbons and some freshly baked rolls that had smelled too good to pass up. She had also purchased carbon paper, although the local stationer stocked only the old-fashioned kind that smudged everything it touched. She'd remind herself to buy the newer, cleaner kind when she went up to London.

"Mr. Rathborne rung while ye was out," said Owen.

Rachel checked her wristwatch. Eleven-thirty, English time. Howard must have an early day, she thought. "Thank you, Owen. Was there a message?"

"Just that 'e wanted to know if ye'd arrived."

"Will he be ringing back?" she asked.

" 'ow do I know, mum?"

He's not being insolent, Rachel said to herself; it's just Owen's way. Still, she had been ready to offer him a brioche, and now his manner changed her mind. He might expect a cup of tea with it, and she wasn't up to feigned politeness or pretense. That wasn't why she had come to Hertfordshire; it was why she had left New York.

Dinner that evening with William and Jennie, though pleasant, was nonetheless an ordeal, since Rachel wasn't ready to discuss her personal quandary with Howard's family. He hadn't called again before Jennie came to collect her, and something kept her from trying to call him back. Using jet lag as an excuse, Rachel was home at the cottage before eleven.

In the morning, she rose early, and by eight-thirty she had bathed—the water was steaming hot now—and eaten the remaining, slightly stale brioche of the day before. Nine o'clock found her in the attic studio seated beside the typewriter and wondering where to begin.

By midafternoon, she had written several letters, tended to chores, taken an hour's walk, and jotted notes for the forthcoming book. The days began to take on a routine, not unlike the more disciplined life to which she was accustomed in New York.

The only variation was the telephone call from Howard on the second evening. She couldn't recall afterward exactly what they had said; she had been more conscious of emotions than of words. He seemed to understand her need for temporary distance, however, and the calls came only twice a week. They generally ended with his "I miss you" and her uncertain "I know . . ." And they prompted restless nights.

Seated at the keyboard with a blank sheet of paper in the typewriter bail, Rachel was posed with a problem. Thinking back over the past proved curious. It wasn't disturbing; if anything, she worried that her past was too bland. An *Oliver Twist* childhood would make better reading, she mused. But hers had been an average, ordinary, middle-class upbringing. She had hoped to record any incidents that had shaped her character into the person she was now, but the most dramatic event had been exclusion from her brothers' treehouse.

She had sent a list of questions to her parents: the color of a certain dress, the age of a disliked uncle, the

413

married name of a favorite teacher. Her mother's detailed answer lay on blue deckle-edged stationery beside the clipboard. Its only effect was a strange one: some events she'd remembered as fact hadn't happened—at least, not the way in which she'd recalled them.

Her mother's letter also provided an unexpected bonus: although thousands of miles away, Rachel felt closer to her parents than she had while living under their roof. It wouldn't be difficult to portray them as loving and caring. The thought warmed her as she sipped her tepid coffee. Then she heard the telephone.

It beeped three times in the way of British phones—short, low-pitched double beeps.

"Damn!" she said aloud as she scrambled down the narrow attic stairs. She couldn't trust Owen to answer calls or take messages correctly. Besides, he hadn't shown up that morning.

She reached the receiver as the tenth set of beeps sounded. "Hello?" she said.

There was a pause, then a crackling noise on the line that told her it must be long distance. It was too early for Howard to be calling, even earlier for her parents' time zone.

"Rachel?"

The connection was poor, and she couldn't place the man's voice. "Yes . . ." She hoped it wasn't an emergency call.

"Ty Beekman here."

Relieved, she said, "My God—where *are* you?"

"In New York," he answered. "I got your note—and I'm thrilled."

"Thanks. I'm excited about the project, too. But Ty, I wrote—"

"I know. But as it turns out, we can discuss the show next week—in London—if you wouldn't mind going into the city."

414

"Of course not. But you're not coming all the way here to talk to me about *Christina's World?*"

"No. I'm staging *One Night Only* for the West End. I'll be in London for a month."

"Wonderful. Is Beth coming with the show?"

"No. She's staying with it in New York. She'll probably take over the London company later on—assuming we have a run."

"Oh you will. They'll love the play over here." She found herself almost hoarse from shouting into the phone.

"I hope you're right," he yelled back. "Listen, I get in next Tuesday. Can you meet me at the Park Lane for lunch on Wednesday? My schedule gets tight after that, and I'd like to talk with you while I have the chance."

"I'll be there. What time?"

"Let's say twelve-thirty."

"Fine." She paused, then added, "Ty . . . I'm very flattered."

"Don't be," he said. "You're the only person to play and sing Christina." Then he seemed to pause. "Rachel . . . I won't be horning in on your privacy, will I? Your . . . agent's . . . secretary gave me this number and said it was okay to call."

She appreciated his carefulness with the word *agent*. "Norma was right—it was okay."

"Good. See you next week."

She hung up, aware that her spirits had lifted. Her book, and now the prospect of the show, were exciting changes. New choices, made without Howard's guidance, were admittedly frightening. But if they proved successful, the wisdom of such decisions would be her own.

Rachel went back to the attic and leafed through the few pages she had typed. What wasn't right? she asked herself. The newfound ability to write phrases and paragraphs with style and ease delighted her, but the content of those paragraphs seemed . . . what? Somehow off-target. Every word appeared to skirt genuine issues.

And then she realized that the slant was all wrong. This wasn't the book she wanted—needed—to write. Her girlhood was irrelevant here. The journey of an aspiring singer and her arrival at the top of her profession were important. "Get to the point!" she commanded aloud.

With renewed vigor, she rolled a clean sheet of typing paper into the machine and began:

"Chapter One. I arrived in New York thinking artistry and stardom were synonymous. . . ."

Rachel hadn't known that Owen owned full livery. She would have regarded his uniform as ludicrous, even if it had been cleaned and pressed. Instead, as he stood holding open the rear door of the Mercedes, Owen looked as if he'd been caught in torrential rains. Rather than question his motivation, she stepped into the car—but it was difficult to suppress a smile.

The drive to London was uneventful and, as usual, without conversation from the driver's seat. Rachel occupied her time by reading once more through the script of *Christina's World*.

Owen deposited her at the entrance to the Park Lane Hotel.

"I should be at least an hour," said Rachel, opening the car door before he had time to do so for her.

Ty Beekman was waiting beside the main desk. As Rachel crossed the lobby, she was aware of stares following her and whispers of "Isn't that Rachel Allenby?" She was also aware of the same nervousness that had accompanied her first meeting with the director in Beth's dressing room.

He came forward to greet her. "You're prompt. Thank you."

"Thank *you*," she replied.

His arm encircled her waist as he steered her to a more secluded spot; now guests were openly eyeing them both.

"I have two hours before my production meeting. Do you mind if we eat here at the hotel, though? I'm still finding my bearings in this town."

"Here's fine," she said.

"Good." His mustache curled into a warm smile.

As lunch progressed, Ty gave her Christina's sheet music and a cassette of the entire show. "A few musical friends insisted I sing on it, too," he said. "So please forgive my voice."

She laughed. "I'm sure I've heard worse."

"Well, I'd like you to call me when you've played it through. I want to know everything you think about it, good and bad. There are a few awkward moments we'll have to work out—"

"I've already spotted one or two in the script," she said.

"And I bet I know what they are already. In the first act . . ."

He continued with his ideas, and Rachel was caught up in his enthusiasm. There was a boyishness about his earnest desire to make the show the best it could be.

"How's your schedule for early next year?" he asked. "Say January?"

Four months, she thought, answering with hesitation. "Well . . . I *am* working on . . . something. But I think I could probably do both."

Ty looked surprised. *"Two* shows at once? Rachel, *Christina* alone will be very demanding, and—"

"No, no!" She laughed, patting his hands reassuringly. "It's not a play, Ty. I'll explain . . . another time. Forgive me for being so cryptic. Actually, unless I have a booking that I don't know about, January's fine. In New York?"

417

He nodded. "I'll clear the dates with your . . . agent."

She noted again his word choice for Howard, but he had smiled and didn't seem to be prying.

"I'm going to like working with you," she said.

"Good," he answered. "I like it already."

A shadow fell across the table then as a woman's voice said, "Well . . . the world *does* grow smaller, doesn't it? I *thought* it was you."

Rachel looked up into the perfectly made-up face of Cecily Wilton, whose stare was directed at Rachel's hands. They were still covering Ty's. Color began to rise as she realized that removing her hands from Ty's now would seem an admission of Cecily's implication; at the same time, *not* to move them might be even more misleading—possibly to Ty as well.

However, Ty solved the dilemma by standing and offering Cecily his hand. "You're Cecily Wilton. I saw you in *Kismet*. You were wonderful."

"You must have been in diapers, but thank you."

Rachel quickly introduced them—too quickly, she sensed—and explained briefly about *Christina's World*.

"Well, good luck, then," said Cecily in her sweet-cream voice. "I'd heard you'd left New York . . . alone."

"Howard . . . couldn't get away just now," said Rachel uncomfortably.

Cecily gave a short laugh. "So . . . soon?" She smoothed her coiffure and said, "I really must dash. I'll be in New York next week, by the way. Can I give anyone your regards?"

"I don't think so," said Rachel. "But thanks just the same."

"Well," chimed Cecily, "I'll be *sure* to mention that I saw you." Then, with a glance at Ty, she added, "Both of you." With a theatrical wave of a gloved hand, she was gone.

Ty seemed confused. "A . . . friend?"

418

Rachel shook her head. "The former Mrs. Rathborne. And now, I'm sure, a harbinger of news."

She walked with Ty to his meeting a few blocks from the hotel. It was a warm day for an English autumn. Several passersby nodded in recognition, but she and Ty were left alone to enjoy a leisurely stroll.

"I hope whatever she spreads around doesn't hurt you," said Ty. "Or your husband."

"Oh, she'll be certain it gets back to him. But Howard will consider the source."

"Listen . . . since we're talking . . . she seemed to imply something . . . about your being here without him."

"We've . . . hit a little snag," she said. "I'm just giving both of us some space, Ty. That's all."

"Absence makes the heart grown fonder?"

"It does, you know. Anyway, let's just leave it at that, all right?"

"I didn't mean to pry."

"I know—and I appreciate it. Thank you."

He seemed lost in thought, and they walked in silence for a while. At last, Rachel asked, "What about you?"

"Me?" He turned to look at her.

"Anyone Cecily's rumors might hurt?"

Ty shook his head. "No. There was. She left me last summer."

"Oh . . . I'm sorry."

"I don't know why I . . . told you that."

"I'm glad you did."

He stopped in front of a large, imposing building surrounded by a wrought-iron gate and grillwork. "Well, we're here. My meeting's inside."

Rachel checked her wristwatch. "You're almost late. Thanks for lunch." For some reason, she wasn't eager to say good-bye.

"My pleasure . . ." He seemed as reluctant as she.

"So . . . we'll be in touch . . . about the show?" said Rachel.

"I'll get things moving as soon as I can. I'll be pretty busy till *One Night Only* opens."

"I understand. So will I, actually."

"I mean . . . it won't be until the end of next month."

"Ty, I *do* understand. Really."

"No, I'd like to . . . talk with you . . . before that. Listen, can you bear to sit through a rehearsal? We've changed the second act since the New York opening, and — well, maybe an objective view could give me some pointers, just about now." He paused, then added, "That's if you're not too busy."

When she hesitated, he said quickly, "I didn't mean to impose. I just thought . . . if it's convenient, that is, I'd like to hear what you think."

She nodded. "Fine. Give me a call."

"Thanks." With a smile, he added, "And good luck on your secret project."

"It's not such a secret, Ty. It's a book."

"Ah!" he exclaimed. "A novel?"

"I hope not," she answered. Impulsively, she squeezed his arm. "Listen, I'd love to see a rehearsal of the show."

His face lit up, and the smile spread into a wide, happy grin. "All right!" He waved and went inside the gate.

Rachel walked slowly back to the hotel entrance, where Owen was waiting with the car. She'd enjoyed the afternoon. Lunch had been excellent, Ty was good company, and the weather had cooperated. The single flaw had been Cecily Wilton.

Chapter Twenty-nine

Norma called from New York. Rachel hadn't had time for lengthy explanations before her departure. Now, hearing the secretary's voice, she realized that she missed their lunches together.

"How's it going?" asked Norma.

"I'm on Chapter Two."

"I . . . didn't mean the book."

"Oh. Well, it's . . . strange."

"Here, too." She paused. "So . . . you've decided to do *Christina?*"

"Mr. Beekman called?"

"Yes. I've mailed you a copy of the contract. Very nice deal. Percentage against salary. Call me—or get in touch with the London office—if you have any questions. By the way . . . Howard likes the script."

"I knew he would. It's good," said Rachel. "Is he there?"

"No . . . honest . . . he just stepped out."

"How is he, Norma?"

"Misses you. Smoking again. . . . You sure *you're* okay?"

"Yes."

"Listen, Rachel . . . word's out about this book you're writing. It may be none of my business, but people are already getting worried. Be careful."

"I will, Norma."

Another pause, this time making Rachel wonder if they'd been cut off. But then Norma said, "There's something else."

"What?"

"Well . . . it's a blind item in Rona's column this morning. About you. *And* Ty Beekman. And . . . lunch at a London hotel."

"Damn!" said Rachel. "Is Cecily Wilton still in town?"

"Oh, I'm glad *you* said that instead of me! Yes, she is. And she's been talking."

"Norma, that day at the Park Lane was only the second time I'd ever seen Ty!" Why then, she wondered, was her breathing suddenly shallow as she spoke? She was telling the truth.

"Look, you don't owe me an explanation. I just thought you should know what's been going on over here."

"Norma, does . . . ?"

"Not *yet*. He doesn't read Rona."

"I don't either, so I . . . appreciate your calling."

"It's a tough break. Remember, if you need me, yell."

During the next two days, Rachel received telephone calls from others who had heard the rumors. Beth Burns, Jamie, and Mina MacDonald each expressed deep concern. Vera Garland, on the other hand, was delighted—the gossip would boost book sales.

By week's end came the inevitable call from Ty Beekman.

"I guess we're an item, aren't we?"

Rachel laughed nervously. "I guess we are."

"Rachel . . . listen, we're going into our last week of rehearsal. I'd still like you to take a look at it. But . . . under the circumstances, I'll understand if you say no."

"Thanks, Ty, but we'll be working together soon, anyway. And besides, no matter what we do, people will say whatever they want to."

"Then you'll come?"

"I've been cooped up and chained to a typewriter for

three weeks. I'm looking forward to seeing what you've done with the show."

On Tuesday morning—the day of the rehearsal to which Ty had invited her—Owen conveniently came down with a cold. Little wonder, mused Rachel. After the last trip, he had grumbled and complained so long about noise and traffic that she'd regretted not having taken the train. For this occasion, then, a local taxi transported her to the station, where she purchased a first-class ticket and, sunglasses and slouch hat hiding her face, she stepped aboard the train to London.

When she arrived, the stage door was locked. She banged on it until the doorman opened it. Immediately, the familiar odors, dimly lit stairways, and hushed voices of backstage life enveloped her. The sweet nostalgia reinforced her excitement at the prospect of doing another show.

"They've just begun," said the doorman, pointing the way for her. She smiled at the prototype of every stage doorman she'd ever seen; they never varied—always ancient, white-haired, and graciously gruff.

Rachel made her way out into the house. She found Ty Beekman seated alone in the fifth row of the darkened theater. Wearing a black turtleneck and with his feet propped up on the back of the seat in front of him, he presented the stereotypical definition of a director. That he was scribbling on a pad of yellow legal paper only completed the cliché.

The rehearsal had begun. Quietly, Rachel settled in beside him. "My train was late," she apologized in a whisper.

He squeezed her arm and answered softly, "I'm just glad you're here." Then he turned his attention to the stage.

Although the set was only partially "dressed" and the cast members were still wearing their own clothes, it was already apparent that the show was very different from the production Rachel had seen in New York. Halfway through Act One, Rachel whispered, "You've made cuts—and they work." Ty nodded, deep in concentration.

The role originated by Beth Burns was now essayed by a British actress, and although her American Midwestern accent was more than adequate, the woman lacked the power of Beth's stage personality.

During the break, Ty introduced Rachel to the cast. Their collective reaction made her wonder if Ty had been wise to bring her among them. Everyone was cordial—in some cases deferential—but Rachel sensed a nervousness, especially in Celeste Farrar, the leading lady. Perhaps they interpreted her presence as judgmental. And since it seemed that both Ty and his star were aware of weaknesses in her performance, it might explain the tense atmosphere. If Farrar feared her job was in jeopardy, she might assume that Rachel was there to replace her in the role.

Rachel noticed that the play's author wasn't present. But Ty Beekman wouldn't make script cuts on his own; he was too much a professional to overstep such boundaries. "Where's the playwright?" she asked.

"He'll be back tomorrow. I've got *him* chained to a typewriter for revisions."

She laughed, and they took their seats for Act Two. There were fewer changes in the second half of the play, but again, Rachel couldn't help making a subconscious comparison of Celeste Farrar with Beth Burns, and still, Beth's talent shone brighter. Rachel was secretly pleased to feel this way—objectively—about Beth. She was even more pleased to have written Beth and to have received an immediate reply. They had cleared the earlier air of summer.

424

Rachel liked the newer, tighter version of the play. But what impressed her most was Ty's direction, seamless and fluid. At the end of the run-through, she remained in the background and listened to forty-five minutes of Ty's notes to the actors. Most directors' notes were negative. However, Ty Beekman emphasized not only what was wrong but also what was right.

Rachel mentioned this to him when they'd reached the lobby.

Helping her into her coat, he answered, "I used to be an actor. Performers need to be told when they're good."

They discussed the play as they exited the theater. As Ty opened the outer lobby door, the cold, damp wintry chill assaulted them. Rachel pulled her fur collar high around her neck. Just then, a gust of wind snatched her hat and carried it away. At the same moment a man, standing at the head of the alleyway leading to the stage door, shouted, "They came out the front entrance!"

Seconds later, a battery of reporters and photographers came running and surrounded Rachel and Ty before they could escape. Flashbulbs popped in rapid succession as the reporters fired questions.

"Where's the love nest—London or Hertfordshire?" asked one.

"How's your hubby taking it, Miss Allenby?" said another.

"Are you two getting a divorce?" asked the first.

"You two planning to marry?"

Rachel shut her eyes to stave off rising fury.

"Hey, Ty, what does Chrissy think of all of this?"

At the name *Chrissy*, Ty turned on the photographer with rage. He ripped the camera from the man's hands and threw it to the pavement, where it smashed into pieces. One of the reporters grabbed at Rachel's scarf, and several strands of fringe were pulled from it. Voices rose, the photographer began hurling expletives at Ty, and before the man could duck, Ty drove a fist into his face as more flashbulbs exploded with blinding light.

"Ty!" Rachel screamed, tugging at his sleeve. "Ty, come on!"

With one hand hooked around his elbow, Rachel began pushing at everyone in her way. Ty's arm went around her, and he too shoved the newsmen until a path of escape was forced open. Once free, they ran together down the street, while a gathering crowd of curious spectators called Rachel's name.

Two blocks later, fairly certain to have eluded their pursuers, Ty and Rachel slowed. They were breathless and cold. Ty glanced up at a sign over a doorway of the adjacent building.

"A pub!" he said.

"Thank God!" exclaimed Rachel, as they both hurried inside.

Ty had washed the bruise on his cheek, and Rachel had brushed her wind-tousled hair and examined the damage done to her scarf. They ordered Scotch.

"To survival," Ty toasted, clinking his glass to hers. Rachel took a healthy swallow. The smooth burn of the liquor felt good.

"I shouldn't have swung at him," said Ty.

"No, but it's done. And obviously he knew what would set you off."

"Meaning?"

"I guess it's my turn to pry," said Rachel. "Is Chrissy the person who Cecily's rumors can't hurt?"

"You don't miss a trick, do you?" But he didn't seem to mind.

She smiled. "I'm a quick study. Also undemanding, so don't say a word if you don't feel like it."

"No . . . it's okay. I've never talked much about her.

426

Maybe I should. And you're the first woman I've—" He stopped and inadvertently touched his bruised cheek. Rachel could see that he winced, and her own hand pushed his fingers away from his face.

"Tell me about Chrissy."

Ty shrugged. "She's an actress. Not famous. Nobody's really heard of her—I don't know how that guy even knew her name. Or why he brought it up."

"They dig and find things out just to provoke the kind of reaction you gave him," said Rachel. "It used to amaze me, once." She took another sip of her drink. "Please go on."

"Well . . . we met in school. Lived together after that. While I was still struggling, things were great. Then I started moving up—and she didn't. She got pregnant. Wouldn't marry me. Decided to have the baby, though. She wanted to act, but she gave it up—supposedly for our son. Anyway, she took him and left last summer, when he was six months old. She blamed me—and my success—for ruining her chances." He drained the rest of his glass. "Funny, I thought when things started to happen for me, everything would be better."

"We all think that," said Rachel. "But sometimes success changes *other* people."

He nodded. "I guess 'celebrity status' takes some getting used to, doesn't it?"

She gave a little laugh. " 'Lonely at the top'?"

"*Thirsty* at the top. Will you have another, too?"

They sat at the table until almost ten o'clock. Dinner didn't seem important, so they ordered sandwiches from the bar. Rachel sipped her drinks slowly; Ty was managing two for each one of hers. But his usual shyness and reserve had broken, and although they had joked about his loneliness, the events of Rachel's past several months evoked genuine empathy for his situation. She was also aware of a growing attraction between them—something

427

she wasn't about to encourage.

At the pub's closing time, she walked him back to the Park Lane. The night had grown bitter cold, and crowds huddled together on street corners.

"*I'm* the gentleman," Ty slurred. "*I* should see *you* to the train station."

"*I'm* sober," she said with a grin.

A block from the hotel, he stopped abruptly.

"What it is?" asked Rachel.

"I guess the booze loosened me up. I wanted to thank you—before we get to the lobby and go on public display." He put his hand on her shoulder and squeezed it. "You're a good listener."

"You're a good listener, too, Ty."

He laughed. "You know, this is the nicest affair I've never had." Looking glassily into her eyes, he added, "Not that I wouldn't like to . . ."

She didn't reply, although she could feel the tightening of his grip around her fingers as they continued hand-in-hand to his hotel. Once there, he said quietly, "Nightcap?"

Gently she touched his bruised cheek. "I . . . don't think it's a good idea."

He nodded, but his arms suddenly enveloped her, and his kiss was far more than a friendly good night. Rachel was the one to pull away at last, surprised by her own lips' lingering response. A cab had stopped beside them on the curb.

"Sure you won't come up?" asked Ty.

Opening the rear door of the taxi and still glowing from the warmth of his arms, the tenderness of his kiss, she said, "I almost changed my mind, Ty. Now . . . I don't dare . . ."

She had told Howard's cousins about the book; every

428

time Jennie stopped by the house, she found Rachel upstairs in the attic seated at the typewriter. Fortunately, Jennie was as discreet as on their first meeting eight Christmases before; she didn't ask for details after Rachel had explained that the subject was theater and it was a very personal story.

Rachel was amazed at how smoothly she was able to put her thoughts to paper, now that she had the right "slant" to the book. It seemed as though the first sentence—which for days had plagued her with indecision—had sparked a transformation. Once she had seen the line at the beginning of Chapter One, an unseen editorial eye seemed to have perched itself on her shoulder. Instinct guided her, and the appropriate words found their way from her head, through her fingers, and finally to the growing stack of paper-clipped chapters in the box on her desk.

She marveled over the mounting accumulation; at the outset of the project, she had feared never going beyond page fifty. Now, as she completed Chapter Five, she felt a sense of accomplishment, less ephemeral than a voice on a record or an image onscreen; and if she happened to experience a moment of doubt, she had the rising pile of typed manuscript as proof. She read and reread each new chapter with the same objectivity and commitment she employed onstage in a long-running hit or in a filmed sequence undergoing its fortieth take. Each time was "new" to her. And each new page of the book made her more and more confident that she was doing the right thing *and* doing it *well*.

During the evenings, she listened to chamber music on the stereo and studied *Christina's World*. She'd be off-book, with her entire role memorized, by the time they reached the first rehearsal in New York.

Howard continued to telephone from New York or California on a regular, twice-weekly basis. Occasionally he asked, in a casual voice that Rachel knew was practiced, "How's your writing coming along?" And each time, Rachel answered, "Fine." It was usually followed by a pause at both ends of the line.

She dined with William and Jennie on Saturdays. The rest of the time, she luxuriated in her privacy, which she sensed would be nonexistent as soon as *Christina's World* got under way. She didn't allow herself to think of the "visibility" her book would garner; Vera had amply warned her to be ready for anything—and the editor had yet to read the "indictment."

Rachel was looking forward to another month in the peaceful Hertfordshire cottage. Once she returned to New York, despite a May deadline for the finished manuscript and almost a year after that until the book's release, she sensed that her anxiety would increase daily as the publication date grew near. At least she'd have Vera there to offer help and encouragement.

She recalled her promise to Jamie—that he'd see the book prior to Rachel's handing it over to her editor. But she would keep her word; every page was typed in triplicate: one for Vera, one for Rachel, and a third for Jamie to read the moment she reached the last page.

Nonetheless, in spite of her confidence over the book and her newfound ability to write it, there were mornings, especially when it rained, when Rachel looked at the manuscript box and wondered if she'd ever get the whole thing done. Not because the task was overwhelming, but because there was so much to tell.

Rachel had debated over whether to spend the upcoming Christmas holidays in Hertfordshire, when Howard telephoned. He didn't mention Cecily or the rumors she'd been spreading, but Rachel wondered later if his decision to visit had anything to do with the gossip

430

surrounding Ty and her. Howard's only intimation was in his remark that he didn't relish spending holidays alone and recalled her similar dislike.

In most ways, she was relieved; Christmases in Hertfordshire, followed by New Year's Eve in New York, had become a pleasant tradition over the past several years.

Rachel wasn't thinking as far into the future as New Year's. She wasn't even going to plan ahead for Howard's arrival. That was still a week away, and rehearsing what they would say to each other or how they would be with one another was an exercise in futility.

She was learning to take each day as it came; writing was teaching her that. If she began the day—or the page—thinking ahead to its effect, her efforts became a waste of time. Staying in the moment—which she had always done so easily onstage—was as essential to her writing as she was finding it to be in life. Howard won't believe it, she mused, but I can't sleep past seven!

By seven-thirty each morning, she'd already revised the previous day's rough draft and retyped clean copy. She didn't shower and dress until eleven, when she took a twenty-minute break. Any other mundane chores neglected by Owen were attended to during "afternoon tea"—which for Rachel consisted of a cup of steaming cappuccino and the second half of whatever pastry she'd begun to eat at breakfast.

She was fascinated by the shadings of the words such as *habit* and *routine*. In school, at temp jobs, at anything she had ever disliked, the words held a pejorative meaning. But for theater, even rehearsing all night, the words meant discipline, professionalism. As with writing, she discovered. And it had nothing whatever to do with "keeping busy" or "occupying her mind." She was totally committed to the project.

* * *

Rachel's schedule was so well organized that she managed to include time off for holiday shopping. Two days before Howard's arrival, she and Jennie took the train to London, then a taxi to Knightsbridge, where they spent almost the entire day inside Harrods. "We'll buy out the Food Hall yet," Jennie said, scooping up boxes of biscuits and tins of caviar. They lunched at a nearby pub, stopped at the Reject China Shop, where Jennie replaced a set of demitasse cups and saucers and bought several serving platters with festive holiday designs. They exited the small store loaded down with carefully wrapped porcelain in two enormous shopping bags.

"I know this must be a bore for you, luv," said Jennie. "But I really do enjoy a bargain."

"It may surprise you," answered Rachel, "but so do I." The half-dozen packages of smoked Scottish salmon had been anything *but* a bargain; nonetheless, she would treat herself to very expensive sandwiches for the next week's lunches: slices of the exquisite coral-colored fish on fresh black bread with chopped egg and onion. Her mouth watered at the prospect.

"I'm awfully glad to have your company," said Jennie as they waited on the train platform at King's Cross Station. "Of course, I'm sorry Howard's been so busy in New York, but William and I often remark on how pleased we are to have you in the neighborhood."

If she noticed Rachel's discomfort, she didn't let on, and Rachel was able to say, "I'm grateful to both of you, too."

It was true; Jennie never intruded on her in-law's privacy. Rachel didn't know whether it was typical British reserve, or if Jennie was unusually perceptive—and tactful.

Both women were exhausted by the time they reached Hertfordshire. Jennie had wisely left her car at the train station. "I've no love for Owen's reliability either," she

432

said as they piled their packages into the backseat.

Rathborne Cottage was only ten minutes' drive. As Jennie swerved into the gravel driveway, she asked, "What about dinner? I can bring you home after we've had a spot of something to eat."

"Thanks, Jennie, but let me take a raincheck. I haven't the energy for anything except a hot soak and"—she laughed—"maybe an entire tinful of shortbread." The thought of gorging herself on the buttery cookies and washing them down with chilled white wine conjured an image of utter decadence. *That* would be a first!

There was a message pinned to the corkboard on the wall beside the kitchen telephone. Owen's almost illegible hand had scrawled, "Ty Beekman. Ticket for opening." Ty's hotel number was written beneath it. Rachel glanced at her wristwatch. It was past eight o'clock. Ty would be at the theater already; she'd call him in the morning.

The only other message was from Norma in New York, with the flight number and scheduled time of Howard's arrival. Well, thought Rachel, this is one time I'll have to rely on Owen; I've never learned to drive!

The white wine, she reflected, was better suited to the salmon. Smiling, she piled four slices of the aromatic fish onto thick black bread slathered with dill mustard. Then she poured a generous glassful of Muscadet and went up to the attic to review Chapter Six of *Inner Voices*.

Howard's flight was on time, despite holiday air traffic, and Owen, for once, was civilly pleasant as he departed for Heathrow. Rachel had prepared a cold platter in case Howard was hungry after his trip. It had also served to occupy the evening, once it had grown too dark outside for work. She had added ten pages to the manuscript, and eight o'clock found her curled up on the sofa

433

in front of the fireplace, rereading several chapters to see if they maintained continuity as well as interest.

Rachel was noting a typo in the margin of page 78 when the car pulled into the driveway. Inadvertently, she covered the manuscript with the knitted afghan and went to open the door.

She was relieved that Owen did not accompany Howard inside; she had remained true to her promise and had not rehearsed her response to his "entrance." But that produced its own qualms; she had no idea how she would react.

However, the moment Howard stepped into the hall-way, instinct took over, and their arms went around each other. She felt hesitation in his embrace, as he certainly had to feel in hers, but there was tenderness as well, and it was so good to see him! She wondered if his heart was pounding as hard and fast as hers—she couldn't tell through his heavy trenchcoat.

"I've missed you," he said, not releasing her.

"Oh, Howard . . ." She lifted her mouth to meet his kiss, and his eyes were warm and inviting.

"Hungry?" she asked when their lips parted.

He shook his head. "You?"

She smiled. "No. But . . . I've fixed a late supper."

"Fine. We can eat . . . later."

His inflection on the word *later* made Rachel's legs tremble. Her temples began to ache, but this was no tension headache. She had tried to ignore the longing for six weeks, six weeks without Howard's holding her, loving her. Now, despite the reasons for their separation, she wanted only to be in his arms.

Howard obviously felt the same. He threw off his coat and tossed it onto the sofa. Then he lifted Rachel and carried her up the stairs. She wouldn't have had the strength to refuse—if such had been her inclination.

She was still in his arms as he put her down gently on

the bed. He removed his tie and slid out of his shoes. Rachel lay against the pillow watching as Howard unbuttoned his shirt and joined her on the bed—the bed that, for the first time since Rachel's arrival, was the right width.

The fingers of his right hand began to stroke her temples, then her long, slim neck, and downward, first to the task of her blouse's buttons, then to the zipper of her slacks. All the while, she lay still, studying his eyes, which were studying her. Rachel's nipples grew taut as the silk fabric fell away, and she heard herself moan quietly as Howard's hand dipped between her legs.

He helped her to wriggle free of the soft velvet pants and the lace briefs beneath them. His strong fingers were also gentle as they teased again and again, then eased themselves inside her. Rachel soon found her hand moving to his hardened, full erection.

"My God, Rachel," Howard whispered, as his lips surrounded one of her nipples. "How I've missed you." His tongue brushed featherlight strokes back and forth across her breasts, while his fingers made her wet inside and sent chills of tension shooting through her entire body.

He lifted his mouth only long enough to take the other nipple.

She moaned from the sensation of flaming heat rising within her. Despite the emotional torture of the past months, her body responded to his touch as it always had; she wanted him now more than ever, and her conditioned reflexes, together with the urgent coaxing of Howard's fingers, brought her again and again to the edge of orgasm. Now his fingers were working harder, faster, and she gasped with pleasure. She pulled his head up to hers and kissed him deeply, then slid her lips from his mouth, down his chest, until she reached his penis. First she kissed its tip, then took it in her mouth and began moving up and down until he groaned and cried, "Rachel!"

Both of them seemed to recognize that this was not an occasion of languid lovemaking, nor a time to luxuriate in lingering, playful teasing. As much as they wanted each other, they *needed* each other.

Howard grabbed Rachel and held her so closely that she could barely breathe. Her mouth left his penis and her arms went around him. Quickly, he moved astride and entered her.

She gasped with pleasure at every thrust. Powerful sensation gripped her as she reached each newer, deeper orgasm and surrendered herself to unconscious abandon. They climaxed together in a frenzied burst of passion, the wavelike spasms still throbbing inside her, even after their emotions were spent.

Afterward, they clung to each other with desperate force, as though each feared that in letting go, one of them might vanish into the night.

Chapter Thirty

For breakfast the next morning, they feasted on the delicacies from Rachel's shopping spree. "I've never drunk wine for breakfast," she said, sipping.

"Well," Howard answered, "we're even. I never drank coffee in the morning until I met you."

She laughed and reached for another slice of salmon. "Oh, we're invited to the opening of *One Night Only*," she said.

Howard's eyes darted to the corkboard beside the telephone. "Ah . . . *that's* why he called."

It wasn't necessary for him to explain who "he" was. Rachel was surprised Howard had even noticed the message.

"Look, I . . ." But what should she say? "Howard, I had lunch with Ty Beekman . . . to discuss *Christina's World* . . . and we . . . ran into Cecily."

"I know," he said. "There've been rumors."

She reached for his hand. "They're only rumors, Howard."

"I assumed as much." He squeezed her fingers. "Even before last night."

The memory of their lovemaking still warmed her. "Let's make it an early evening at William and Jennie's, shall we?"

He nodded and helped himself to more salmon.

Rachel hadn't bought Christmas trimmings — she

hadn't known what to expect after Howard's arrival, and she knew that Jennie was going "all out." They drank hot, mulled cider while they adorned the tree with antique ornaments, some of which Rachel remembered from previous holidays spent with the Sterlings.

She and Howard returned to the cottage early—around midnight—and exchanged gifts. She had bought him a lizard briefcase to replace his worn one. He had bought her a familiar-looking box. Not familiar for its contents, but because it matched the Cartier box that had held the diamond and ruby earrings he'd given her for the opening of *Robin Hood*. She opened the lid. "Oh my! Howard . . ." A band of diamonds and rubies twinkled in the light.

"It's an anniversary ring," he said.

Her eyes glanced up questioningly, and he explained, "It's eight Christmases since our first together." He lifted her hand. "Let's see how it fits."

She slid her ring finger into the delicate gold setting. "Perfect! I feel like Cinderella with her glass slipper!"

"She and her prince lived happily ever after, if I remember correctly," said Howard, taking her in his arms.

"So they did," she replied, leading him to the staircase.

On the night after Boxing Day, Rachel and Howard drove up to London for the West End opening of *One Night Only*. Ty Beekman greeted them in the lobby. In addition to her own self-consciousness upon seeing him, Rachel sensed tentativeness in both Howard and Ty when she introduced the director to her husband. It wasn't from anything said by either of them, but she distinctly felt a polite detachment emanating from both men.

Ty handed them the tickets and said, "I'll see you both at intermission. Enjoy the show."

"Seems like a nice young man," Howard observed as they took their seats.

"He is. And he's a brilliant director."

"So I've heard."

Several acquaintances were seated nearby, and Ty's name came up more than once before the curtain rose for Act One.

At the interval, Ty joined them at the pub next door for a pint of stout. He seemed more relaxed as he and Rachel talked to Howard about *Christina's World*. Nonetheless, Rachel found herself simultaneously listening to Ty and studying Howard.

When they returned to the theater and Ty went backstage, Rachel said, "I hope we didn't monopolize the conversation, with all our talk about the show. It's just that Ty's enthusiasm—"

"Is contagious," said Howard. "And it's reassuring, too."

"It is?" she asked.

He smiled. "I don't believe rumors, but I'm not immune to them."

"I don't understand . . ."

"Well, granted he was a bit nervous at first. But if Cecily's little 'news releases' held any water, you and Mr. Beekman would hardly have been so friendly in front of me. You'd be avoiding each other like the plague."

Rachel gave a short laugh. "That's very astute. I never thought of it."

Howard said, "You're not the only one who studies people, darling. It's part of my business, too." He squeezed her hand—the one wearing the anniversary ring. Rachel linked her fingers with his; maybe the ugliness of the past months was over; perhaps it had been a nightmare, and they were finally awakening from it.

* * *

But the nightmare hadn't ended. It resurfaced the following morning. Since Howard's arrival in Hertfordshire, Rachel had slept an extra hour, until eight o'clock, while Howard prepared coffee and a light breakfast, a habit he'd adopted from living so long in New York.

When Rachel came downstairs, she found a tray on the captain's table. On it were the pot of steaming coffee, another of hot milk, and two warmed, buttered scones. Howard was seated on the sofa beside the fireplace. He was wearing his reading glasses, and a stack of papers lay to the left of his lap.

At first, Rachel assumed that he was leafing through business correspondence. But as she came closer, she saw that the lines were double-spaced, with one-inch margins on all four sides. In the upper-left-hand corner was a page number. She didn't need to read the name beside it. Suddenly she knew: Howard had been reading her manuscript.

He looked up and said, "Coffee's still hot."

She glanced at his half-empty cup. "Yours seems to have gone cold." Her voice had an edge to it as she added, "Must be interesting reading. . . ."

"I wasn't snooping," he said. "It was lying here, under the afghan, and I—"

"That's my oversight," she interrupted, mentally kicking herself for having left the chapters downstairs instead of in the privacy of her attic.

"Actually, it's probably a good thing." He paused to add hot espresso to the tepid cappuccino in his cup. "Rachel, you can't publish what you've written in these pages."

She felt the barrier returning again. "Howard, I have a contract—and a publication date."

"I'm not talking about *any* book. I'm referring to *this* book. To the chapters I've just read."

"They weren't intended for reading—yet."

"Rachel, they were *here*. And the point is, I *have* read them."

She noticed that he still wasn't drinking his refilled coffee, despite constant pauses in their conversation. They were awkward pauses, not of contemplation but, she sensed, of strategy. And she wasn't in the mood. *She* wanted a quiet breakfast. She bent to the table and tore the pastry into several pieces.

"Howard," she said, pouring her own coffee and placing a section of the bun on her saucer, "you've been doing the equivalent of eavesdropping, and if you don't mind, I'd like to let my editor be the judge of what can or can't be published."

"Oh, your publisher—and the public—will *love* what's in here. Hollywood will undoubtedly want to film it. That's not the issue."

"No," she said, "and neither is your opinion, as combative as that may sound. It's *my* book, Howard, and I'm rather pleased with the way it's coming along. I'm not about to allow anyone—even the man I love—to erect a stumbling block."

She was surprised at the calm in her voice. Perhaps it's because I'm right, she reflected.

"I thought . . . these past few days . . ."

"Howard, I *love* you. That didn't stop when I came here six weeks ago. But it has nothing to do with my book. In a way, I'm writing this *because* of love—"

"Are you certain it isn't because of guilt?" Howard asked.

"Guilt?" She couldn't believe his words. "Guilt about what?"

"I'm not sure . . . Somehow I have the impression that you don't think you *deserve* your success—"

"You're not making sense, Howard. We've had this conversation before—deserving has *nothing* to do with success. *That's* what the book's about—"

441

"All the same, there's part of you that isn't convinced. Otherwise you wouldn't *need* to write it." He handed her the paper-clipped chapters. "There's some tiny part of you that still thinks talent and hard work are enough. And for some ungodly reason, you really don't feel that your talent would have been sufficient without—" He cut himself off.

"Without your help? That's what you were going to say, isn't it?"

When he didn't reply, she insisted. "Tell me—isn't it?"

He crossed to the telephone. "The amazing part is you *are* that talented and *you* don't see it. You would have made it with or without me, but you won't allow yourself to believe it. Perhaps because you'd have to admit that other people—people whom you've always championed—weren't that talented and *wouldn't* have made it." He shrugged and reached for the receiver. "I don't understand, Rachel. It's too complex for me. The only talent *I* possess is a sense of other people's ability. I recognized the moment I saw you onstage that you had a rare gift. Eight years have passed, and *you* still don't trust it."

He shook his head. "Maybe insecurity goes with the territory. Olivier has never trusted his gifts either." Howard reached into his pocket, withdrew a small piece of paper, and began dialing a telephone number.

"Who are you calling?" she asked.

"Heathrow. I'm confirming my flight to New York. I have to be back in time for New Year's Eve." Looking directly at her, he said, "I had hoped you'd attend the parties with me."

She knew his words held far more than an invitation to the holiday celebrations. But she also knew the only answer she could give him.

"I can't, Howard. I'll be in New York at the end of January to start rehearsals for *Christina's World*. But for the moment, I think it's better for me to stay on here

442

and work on my book."

Rachel felt as strong a heartache when the car pulled out of the driveway as when she and Howard had separated in New York less than two months before. Briefly, she pondered over all he'd said. Was it possible that she was so insecure? And that influenced her decision to write the book?

Well, she thought. I may be confused about my feelings, but I *am* going to finish it — *and* publish!

The telephone rang. Maybe Howard had come to his senses and wanted to let her know.

"Hello!" she said breathlessly, grabbing the receiver.

"Hi!" came Ty Beekman's familiar voice. "I'm glad I caught you before you and Howard left."

"Howard left a few minutes ago," she answered, suddenly deflated. "I'm staying awhile longer."

"You sound like I feel," he said quietly.

"What's the matter?"

"Holiday blues, I guess. My first Christmas and New Year's without Christina in five years. Every time I look at the script, I get a little jabbing reminder."

"I can relate to that," said Rachel. Already, the house seemed cold and forlorn.

"I've got an idea," said Ty. "Everybody says misery loves company. We could drown our sorrows together in a few pints."

Their conversations about theater generally did infuse each other with energy. As long as he didn't get drunk — and as long as she didn't allow his good looks or her own loneliness to complicate matters — it was certainly preferable to sitting home by herself. After all, they'd be working together in another month; may as well start developing an "immunity" to his charms before then. "Sure," she answered. "I like the idea."

After a pause, Ty said, "I've got an even better one."

"What's that?"

"An old song title. 'What are you doing New Year's Eve'?"

Rachel and Ty shared December 31 in public, first by sitting through that evening's performance of *One Night Only,* then by attending a party given by one of the stars in the all-British cast. The two Americans seemed even more isolated during the festivities. Ty's usual cheerfulness was absent, and Rachel knew that her own mood was one of forced gaiety — another "performance." It might have quelled some of the rumors surrounding Ty and her, had the stroke of twelve not found them in each other's arms. To explain that Ty was no doubt thinking about Chrissy — as Rachel was thinking about Howard — would not have satisfied the scandal mongers. That neither she nor Ty displayed any shame was probably the most shocking aspect of all. Rachel almost laughed at the irony: the *lack* of shame was because they *weren't* lovers — but try telling *that* to people like Cecily Wilton!

When Rachel telephoned William and Jennie to wish them Happy New Year, they sounded surprised to find her still in England. Jennie mentioned Howard's call from the airport but didn't disclose whether he had told his cousin he was leaving alone. Rachel almost wished Jennie could be less tactful, not quite so ladylike; she needed someone in whom to confide. Beth and Norma were her only women friends, and they were in New York. So were Jamie and Paul.

"Everyone's in New York!" she said aloud to the typewriter.

She glanced at the manuscript sheet in the machine and the chapter just finished — a chapter about fairness.

She rolled the typed paper up and out of the bail, then

carried it, together with two dozen or more pages, to the window, where she proofread the entire lot. She sat down to jot a list of typos and eventual revisions; the ideas were clear, the phrasing precise, and actual changes would be minimal. "At least I know where I am on paper," she commented to the air. The book was good—from the heart—and it was honest.

Howard's words still echoed in her ears. *Guilt about not deserving.* Was he right? Could there be an ounce of truth to what he'd said? She'd always considered her attitude toward her talent as a healthy sign—disciplined, pragmatic, no exhibitionist tendencies, no egomaniacal drive or narcissistic craving always to be the center of attention. She recalled a book she'd read in college. An Englishwoman psychologist had written about the actor's "child within," the self whose desperate need to perform superseded disappointment, heartache, rejection. The *compulsion* to act had been broadly analyzed in the book, and deserving—as well as guilt—had been covered in depth. It hadn't rung any bells, then.

And, Rachel realized as she concluded revisions of Chapter Nine, it didn't ring any bells now either.

Interesting theory, she said silently, placing the pages in the box with the preceding eight chapters. "Very interesting. But wrong. Absolutely dead wrong."

She turned off the attic desk lamp and went downstairs, where it was warmer, to restudy the second act of *Christina's World.*

Beth Burns telephoned with her good news. "I'm in love! Can you believe it, Rachel? I met him three weeks ago, and I feel as if I'm sixteen again!"

"That's wonderful, Beth," answered Rachel over the crackling long-distance line.

"Is this a lousy connection, or are you less than ecstatic for me?" shouted Beth.

Rachel didn't feel up to explaining her mood at a yell-level across the ocean, so she said, "Listen, it's terrific, and I'm thrilled. But your voice sounds as though you're speaking into a bottle."

"Haven't touched anything but champagne since I met Gregory. Rachel, he thinks I'm divine—smart guy, huh?—and he wants me to move into his entire top floor penthouse on Central Park South—it's just his little pied-à-terre when he's in town on business, and—"

"Beth, I've never heard you so excited. That's great."

"It's more than great, honey. He's gorgeous, *un*married, and worth millions. He's from Houston—owns half of it, I think! I mean, who would've thought, l'il old me . . . ?"

"I don't want to sound like your mother, but are you two . . . serious?"

"Are we getting married? Well, he's proposed. . . . I've convinced him that we shouldn't rush into anything. But I am moving in—after all, I've never lived with a man before."

Beth's seeming innocence was amusing—and it was the truth; her friend had had countless lovers, but this "arrangement" would be a first.

It prompted an idea. "Beth, what are you doing with your apartment? Subletting?"

"I guess. I hadn't thought about it. Why?"

"What about me?"

There was a sigh from Beth's end of the receiver. "Then . . . you know?"

"Know what?"

"Christ, baby, why do *I* always have to deliver the bad news?"

"Beth, what on earth are you talking about?"

"Well . . . you haven't seen the latest issue of *Beautiful People?*"

446

"I've never even heard of it."

"I didn't know England was above such things," said Beth. "Anyway, it's a reincarnation of *Modern Screen, Photoplay,* et cetera. And honey, they *have* heard of you."

"Beth, get to the *point?*"

There was a trans-Atlantic pause, after which Beth said, "Two photos and two captions. One shows you and Ty—which I admit surprised the hell out of me!—and the other is with Howard . . . and . . . your publicity lady."

"Mina MacDonald?" asked Rachel incredulously.

"The same. And underneath is a bitchy little blurb that even *I* couldn't have dreamed up."

"What does it say?"

"Well, I don't have it in front of me, but something about 'Howard's work taking him to the best restaurants with attractive associates—while Ty Beekman and his new leading lady rehearse overtime for their new production.' You know the kind of dirt, Rachel. It's always the same—only the names change."

Beth paused again, then said, "But if you *didn't* know . . . why ask about my apartment?"

Rachel's head was spinning as she answered, "The original reason was so I could finish my book. Now . . ."

"Darling, don't do anything rash like filing for divorce or legal separation, or—"

"Beth . . . just tell me—can I sublet your place?"

"Sure—God, I'd trust *you* with my things before I'd hand over the keys to a stranger! How soon will you be back?"

Rachel had planned to stay in Hertfordshire until the start of rehearsals for *Christina's World.* Now that had changed. "I'll be home at the end of the week," she shouted into the phone, just to make certain Beth could hear her correctly.

Beth had stocked her refrigerator with sinful-looking pastries and bottles of chilling champagne. There was a fresh tin of Beluga caviar, a jar of sun-dried tomatoes, a tin of imported pâté, a container of macadamia nuts, and a jar of honey mustard. Rachel marveled at Beth's idea of a "standard diet," but then found a card beside the telephone. It read: *Order the staples from Gristede's around the corner — these are for a one-woman welcome-home pig-out. Love, Beth.*

She laughed. Beth had always managed to make Rachel laugh — except for the last time they'd "pigged out" together.

Beth had thought of everything; fresh linens, cut flowers, a down comforter at the foot of the bed. Only one essential was missing: a typewriter.

Rachel unpacked, called Norma — without asking for Howard — and left a message for Jamie and Paul with their answering service. Then she went out in search of an office appliance store. One thing at a time, in order of priority.

The gutters along West Sixty-second Street were slushy from a recent snowfall; areas of unshoveled pavement had frozen over into a slippery sheet of ice. The seemingly simple task of walking around the corner to Broadway and Sixty-first became a hazardous, twenty-minute ordeal. By the time she reached the store, her suede boots were white-stained with salt.

She selected the smallest electric portable typewriter in stock and handed the salesclerk her credit card and a ten-dollar bill. "That's to ensure immediate delivery."

"Half an hour," said the impish, older man. Then, adjusting his bifocals, he smiled. "Actually, Miss Allenby,

448

I'm a fan of yours. If I can have your autograph, I'll guarantee the typewriter arrives at your apartment before you do."

She smiled back. "Do you have a pen?"

Rachel hadn't expected Norma to withhold Beth's number if Howard asked for it; still, when she heard his voice, she didn't know how to react. She felt her defenses rising before he'd finished his first sentence. "I've tried to ignore the rumors, Rachel," he said.

And immediately she replied, "Which rumors, Howard? Those concerning you—or me?"

"Concerning *me?*" He sounded genuinely surprised.

"Concerning you . . . and Mina MacDonald."

For a moment Howard didn't answer. Then he said, "Rachel, she's a business associate. *Your* publicist—"

"And *your* dinner companion lately."

"That's *all* there is to it," he said. "But . . . I *would* like to know if you and Tyler Beekman are . . . seeing each other?"

"Howard, we're doing a *show* together."

"If there's nothing more, then why are you staying at Beth Burns's flat instead of ours?"

She wasn't sure whether his voice betrayed a tone of accusation. "I need time, Howard. Time to think, and . . . time to finish my book."

He paused again, then said, "I hope that's the only reason, Rachel. I'd hate to think it was so you could be alone with Tyler Beekman, especially after all the rumors I've been forced to deny."

"Don't believe everything you hear—or read," she said, wondering if she could follow her own advice the next time she saw an item pairing Howard with Mina MacDonald.

By week's end, Rachel had completed two more chapters of *Inner Voices,* and carbon copies of the book's first half had been given to Jamie and to Vera Garland. The editor was delighted. "You could do this full-time, y'know," she said after reading the opening pages.

"That's what I *have* been doing, Vera," Rachel answered. She hoped to keep up her schedule once rehearsals for the show began.

"I don't mean just time-wise, y'know. I'm saying that you write *well*."

"You sound surprised," said Rachel. "I think I ought to be offended."

"No, no, c'mon. Look, most celebs—especially singers and actors—are into me-me-me. No objectivity. I'll admit it, I'm impressed."

"Thanks. Um, any problem with . . . content?"

"Should there be?"

"I mean, is it . . . all right?"

"I'll say!" Vera exclaimed. "It's dynamite! Is it all *true?"*

Now Rachel *was* offended. "Vera, this *isn't* fiction—"

"Okay, okay. Look, it's sensational—I love it! Everybody will love it!"

Unintentionally, Rachel said, "My husband doesn't love it."

"Well, honey, look at it this way—he's an *agent.* Y'know, bottom line is we've got to consider our risks."

Yes, thought Rachel. She had just begun to consider hers.

"Rachel," said Jamie, "your editor's right—this *is* dynamite! It could blow the lid off this whole business—become a Watergate of Broadway—and your objectivity is the key." Impulsively, he kissed her cheek. "I'm so proud of you!"

"I'm glad," she said. "In some ways, I was more concerned with your reaction than I was about Vera's."

"Well, I'd offer to carry your luggage," he joked, "but I've just taken a job."

He hadn't mentioned it over the phone. "What kind of job?"

"A teaching position at Rutgers. I'll be conducting acting classes for singers. I know there'll only be one in fifty with any kind of talent, but—"

"But talent has nothing to do with it," she finished for him.

"Right. Still, I'm hoping to impart some practical 'philosophy' to these kids, so they won't be sitting ducks when they go out and start auditioning in the 'real' world. I want to help them find their 'centers'—to have enough belief in themselves to handle the rejection without falling apart. If I can get through to just *one* of them—"

Rachel interrupted again, this time with a laugh. "You and I *do* share the same ideals." She was pleased for him; Jamie hadn't seemed so enthusiastic about nontheatrical work in the almost nine years she'd known him.

"What's going to happen with you and Howard?" he asked suddenly.

Rachel bit her lip. "I don't know, Jamie. I'd like to believe that he isn't . . . involved . . . with Mina. I wish I could say it'll all be fine once the book sees print, but . . . it may be just the opposite."

"Would you change your mind about publishing—if you and Howard are at stake?"

Slowly she shook her head. "I can't, Jamie. Besides, there's no guarantee that *not* publishing would . . . bring us back together. If I were to change my mind—just to placate Howard—I couldn't live with myself. Or with him. Regardless of Mina . . . or anyone else."

451

Rachel's words were a sad reminder that she and Howard, despite the bonds uniting them, were not as alike as she and Jamie. She was also reminded of Annie Singer's advice. And, no matter the outcome, she had made her choice.

Chapter Thirty-one

February had never been Rachel's favorite time of year, and the second month of 1977 was proving to be unusually unpleasant. The constant snow, sleet, or rain, together with too little sleep, brought on a cold, and although it was a mild virus, work on the book and *Christina's World* seemed more taxing than ever.

Photographs of Ty and Rachel continued to appear in the columns, although Howard and Mina seemed to have been abandoned by the media. Jamie commented that it was undoubtedly due to Rachel and Ty's celebrity status; publicity personnel or agents—even "name" agents like Howard—only attracted the press as long as they were linked to famous people. If the world believed that Rachel had a lover, it no longer had need of her husband for "embellishment."

The Allenby-Beekman "affair" was official—captured in print—and everyone, including most people in the business, gave credence to the stories. Only intimate friends and members of *Christina's* cast knew the truth was just the opposite.

Rachel began to ignore passing remarks and innuendoes. Howard's suspicions had hardened her attitude toward the publicity. While it still infuriated Ty, Rachel grew increasingly detached, bored by the lies. It made her feel older, almost wizened, by comparison, although she was only a year or two Ty's senior.

The same protective shell, however, while helping her to remain impervious to slander, began to hinder her work in rehearsal. Alone while writing, she could let down her guard, allow her vulnerability to surface. But at rehearsal, her feelings were submerged, as if she were hiding behind a mask. Christina was a complex role, and to bring her alive, Rachel required full use of her emotional tools, tools she was finding difficult to employ. Her technique was now so well honed that a good performance was still possible. But unless she could permit truth to emerge, the result would be merely imitation.

It was a problem she could share with Jamie. Only another artist could understand the creative process in depth; Howard, even before their separation, could only fathom the process up to a point. But on the nights when technique and "presence" carried the performance, an artist knew, no matter how many curtain calls and *bravo*s. Maybe, thought Rachel, that's *why* Olivier is never satisfied; he knows it can always be *better*.

And she felt that Christina *wasn't* getting better; the role was growing *more* elusive. It had never happened to Rachel before, and it frightened her.

"No one can blame you for being a little gun-shy," said Jamie as he settled onto the sofa at Beth's apartment.

"Gun-shy?" she asked.

"Sort of. It's as if you're wearing armor."

The words struck her with impact. Suddenly, Lehman Stern's council of almost a decade before came to her. Had Rachel's hide toughened so much that the soul of the angel could no longer emerge? She recalled her answer to the conductor's warning at the cast party for *Arrowhead:* "I'd quit singing first," she had said. The words chilled her now.

"It's *not* that," she said, replying to herself as much as to Jamie. "It's as if I'm numb. Pretending emotion.

I'm acting *at* it, Jamie. The only time I seem able to express what I really feel is when I'm working on the book. It's been a real struggle, dredging up so much stuff, but now that I've learned how to do that on paper, it's as though I'm drained by it—emptied out, so there's nothing left to draw upon for Christina."

Jamie's eyes glanced across the room to the plain white manuscript box on the desk in the corner.

"What I've read so far explains some of that, Rachel. How much more do you have to write before it's done?"

"I'm past the halfway mark. Why?"

"Finish the book."

"I'm trying to," she said in a defeated voice.

"I know. But you can't give everything you've got to both the book *and* the show."

Funny, she thought. Ty had said as much to her in London when she'd first mentioned her other "project." It was too late now to give up one or the other.

"Jamie, the point is, they *both* demand it all. And I'm just not sure I'm strong enough to give them equal time."

"Rachel"—he leaned in closer for emphasis—*"finish* the book."

Jamie was right. When she was able to think more clearly, Rachel realized that the book had become uppermost in importance. Until she finished it, *Christina* would be relegated to second place.

Nonetheless, rehearsals continued, and with them, the fight to maintain her self-esteem as an artist.

Subletting Beth's apartment was a help. Surroundings that were someone else's belongings allowed better concentration for her writing. The atmosphere was comfortable, and she'd grown fond of the little secretary desk in the corner where she worked at night.

But she was aware of the strain on her nerves. Actors in the cast asked about her health; she looked tired most of the time. Edgar Cornwall took her to dinner and spent the evening making a transparent show of good faith. Her friendship with Ty, coupled with his sensitive yet firm direction, gave her needed support and understanding. Still, she could sense a palpable tension in the air as March arrived. Final rehearsals were set to begin within a week.

Rachel entered the apartment to find the telephone ringing. "I've got news!" Beth exclaimed. "Mind if I stop by to pick up some warm-weather clothes? I'll tell you all about it!"

"My God!" said Beth as she swept into the living room. "What hit *you?*"

"It shows, doesn't it?"

"Honey, you look like hell. Just let me throw some things in a bag and I'll fix us both a drink."

She disappeared into the bedroom, then emerged minutes later with two suitcases. The drinks materialized almost as quickly.

Rachel related only some of what was on her mind. Beth listened intently at first, but her contrasting buoyancy made Rachel only more aware of just how tired she was. Beth had gained weight for the first time since the two women had known each other, but it was becoming; she seemed healthier—and happier—than Rachel had ever seen her. While incapable of totally lifting Rachel's spirits, Beth's mood was effective in taking her friend's mind off matters at hand.

"So," Beth was saying, chewing on an ice cube,

"maybe it's time to rethink priorities, honey."

"No maybe about it. Does that have anything to do with your news?"

Beth grinned mysteriously. "I'm getting . . . married!"

"Oh Beth!" said Rachel, hugging her.

"I can hardly believe it myself. But in all the time I've been living at his place, we've only had one fight. So . . . I said yes." She swallowed the ice cube and added, "I'll retire for a couple of years, and then I'll make a dramatic comeback!"

Rachel laughed, despite her earlier mood. "I'm not sure I'm hearing you—you were always so . . . ambitious!"

"Listen, remember *All About Eve?* Well, at heart, I've never been much more than a bus and truck Eve Harrington. This star stuff . . . it wears thin after a while. I'm moving to Texas."

"Texas? Beth—are you certain?"

"What *is* certain?" She turned now, and her usual brassy facade disappeared as Beth, nodding toward the mantelpiece over the fireplace, said, "See the framed cover of *Time?* And my Tony? I've made a lot of money. I'm famous. *That's* what's certain."

"But it's what you've always wanted."

"I know. But I've *gotten* it. Understand? I did what I set out to do, Rachel." She paused reflectively, then said, "I need a new dream."

"You put that nicely," said Rachel. "Still, you're giving up a lot."

"Greg didn't ask me to, honey. It's my decision. Besides . . . life at the top isn't everything it's cracked up to be—*you* found that out."

The words stung, although Rachel knew Beth hadn't meant to hurt her.

"When are you leaving—for Texas?" she asked.

"In three weeks—right after my last performance. I won't be here for the Tony awards . . . but smart money's on me for a win." Beth opened her purse and withdrew an envelope, which she handed to Rachel. "This is my acceptance speech when you pick it up for me. Don't open it till they call my name."

Rachel nodded. "When will you be back?"

"I don't know, hon. Maybe never. You'll have to come for a visit."

Beth breezed out of the apartment leaving Rachel with a deeper, lingering depression. Why? she wondered. I ought to be thrilled for her—shouldn't I?

The next day was the most difficult rehearsal since work on the show had begun. At the end of the second act, Christina's heart-wrenching, vocally demanding final song was followed by her suicide. Rachel had sung much of the music at half-voice, marking so as not to tire her throat. However, she had to sing "Finding Answers" full-out at each rehearsal, to "put it into her throat." Today, as she reached for the last high note, tears suddenly welled up inside her and overflowed. She felt her throat close, and the note cracked wide open. Rachel broke down in sobs and fled the room.

In the ladies' lounge, she surrendered herself to the pent-up emotions and anguish of the past months. Tears erupted into convulsive sobs, and she was helpless to stop them. As they trickled down her cheeks, her image in the bathroom mirror reflected the irony of her situation. All at once she understood why Beth's news had only added to her burden. Her friend's ambition had led her to extremes—even to committing blackmail; yet Beth was prepared to abandon fame for love. Rachel, by standing up for the ideals in which she believed, was on the verge of losing her marriage—and possibly her career—in the process.

The irony stopped her crying. She wiped away the tears and splashed cold water on her face. She patted her cheeks dry while addressing the mirror with a long, steady stare. "All right," she said aloud, smoothing her hair and dabbing a touch of powder on her nose.

The outburst had been a catharsis, and although nothing had visibly altered, she returned to the rehearsal room and asked to take her scene from the top.

"If you're tired, we can work around you," Ty offered. "Some sleep would do you good."

"No," she said. "I'll be fine. Let's go on."

"Okay," he said reluctantly. Then, turning to the stage manager, he said, "Five minutes. Then we'll run Scene Four."

By the end of the day, she was grateful to have stayed. The effect of her breaking-down had triggered a breaking-*through*. It had freed her of an inner barrier and enabled Rachel, for the first time in weeks, to give life to the role of Christina. It meshed during the late-afternoon repetition of the final scene in the show. The truth was no longer blocked, she was connected to her voice, and somehow, her soul once more inhabited her body.

That weekend, she finished the book.

During the third week of March, both Jamie and Vera Garland read the second half of *Inner Voices*.

"Wow! Very steamy!" said the editor. "We'll make a bundle. I've just got a few requests for revisions, and—"

"Is something wrong with it?" asked Rachel.

"No—it's standard stuff. Pacing can use some goosing here and there, y'know? My notes are quite specific. I've put them in the mail this morning."

At first, the thought of revisions had annoyed Rachel. She was eager to be done with the project that had become so arduous. But when Vera's letter arrived, Rachel found herself in agreement with the suggestions, and by month's end the revised manuscript of The Broude Press's lead nonfiction release for April 1978 was in Vera Garland's hands. Rachel would next see it when the book reached the galley stage. As for its actual arrival on nationwide bookstore shelves, she would have almost a year's wait.

The relief of completion was accompanied by another, surprising sensation. Despite the book's emotional toll on its author, Rachel was sorry that the process of writing it was finished. She missed it as if it were a child—one who no longer needed its mother. Perhaps the feeling was no more than a dormant maternal instinct channeled into a different kind of creativity. Whatever, the book was "born" and independent of her.

But *Christina's World* was not. Rachel gave herself over totally to the last week of rehearsals. It was a time of finding her role's center and infusing it with life. Not so different from writing, after all, she mused each time she entered the theater. Unlike *Inner Voices,* however, *Christina's World* continued to be cut, rewritten, and reblocked, straight through the week of previews. Each night, Rachel dragged herself to Beth's apartment to memorize new lines—and to forget others—in time for the next evening's performance.

Following the Tuesday preview, Rachel sat at her dressing table replacing cut pages in the script with the latest revisions. It had become a routine, one in which

Christina's old world lay crumpled in the wastepaper basket, while new facets of her character joined the dog-eared, note-covered scenes in the leatherette binder. Rachel closed the cracked, worn cover and smiled wanly; whenever a script reached this sorry state, the show's official opening was never more than a few days off.

Not unlike Christina, Rachel felt split in half; there seemed to be two nights to each day: the first, lived in the theater, where she commandeered her energies for each preview audience; later, a second, longer night, spent in the loneliness of Beth's apartment. Rachel's immersion into the onstage life of Christina permitted time for little else. Two hours with a single intermission flew by. If only the second half of the night could pass as quickly!

Tuesday had been particularly difficult. Although the latest changes improved Act Two and strengthened the entire show, the afternoon's rehearsal hadn't gone well. A much-needed confrontation scene between Christina and her lover had been added, then worked and re-worked before that night's preview. Rachel's leading man, Gavin Atwood, was a fine actor—so fine that the truth of his performance was intimidating.

In the past, Rachel had found her own acting greatly enhanced by the quality of the actors playing opposite her. But that evening's show hadn't improved upon the afternoon's rehearsal, and afterward, Ty's notes touched upon the very fact that Rachel had sensed: she was holding back. Despite her recent breakthrough in the role, she was—in this single scene—shying away from total commitment.

She would think about it in the taxi on her way to Beth's apartment. The nightly ride from the theater would again bridge a passage of unoccupied time, a

461

silent journey spanning the reality of Rachel's life with that of Christina's, thereby separating the two.

She had just placed the script inside her totebag when there was a knock on her dressing room door.

"It's Ty. Can I see you?"

A chill swept through to the base of her spine; she knew he'd want to talk further about the new scene, and she still hadn't found its key.

"Rachel?"

She realized she hadn't replied. "Yes . . . c'mon in."

Ty entered the room and closed the door behind him. He was carrying his leather jacket over one shoulder; his other hand carried his own tote, with his rolled-up script protruding from one of the side pockets of the bag. He put the bag down and ran his fingers through his hair as if searching for a way to begin.

"What's wrong?" asked Rachel.

He leaned back against the door. "That's what I was going to ask you."

She rose and crossed to the coat rack. Reaching for her mink, she said, "Ty, I'm very tired. I took down all your notes, and I'll think them through tonight."

"I know you're working hard, Rachel," he said. "I just wish sometimes that I could . . . crawl inside you and . . . pull out the performance I *know* is in there."

Her hands had begun to tremble, and she feared her voice might, too. She slipped into her coat and went back to the makeup table, where she pretended to be looking for something—anything to avoid his gaze. Keeping her eyes from his image in the mirror, she said, "My brain can't handle anything more tonight, Ty. Sometimes I think more clearly when I get away from the theater."

When he didn't speak, she turned to look directly at him. He was staring at her, his eyes studying her face, her body. She could just hear the soft intake of his breath. The room was suddenly too hot, and with her coat on, she wasn't able to tell if the heat generated was from the radiator—or from Ty's effect upon her.

"Then let's go for a drink," said Ty finally. "We should talk."

"Please, Ty, let me run the scene with Gavin tomorrow. It's been too much for one day."

"Maybe it is. But . . . I had a thought that might help."

"What?"

He came closer to her and said, "I've asked Gavin to play the scene with more . . . urgency. Impatience. He'll be a bit more aggressive toward Christina. And . . . you can give some thought to the way . . . Christina might react."

"I . . . I know how she'd react."

Ty brushed his hand over the soft, dark fur on the shoulder of her coat. "How . . . would she react?"

"She'd be . . . pleased. Flattered that he still . . . wants her . . ."

"But?"

He was close enough to touch, and Rachel's body began to tremble as her hands had moments before. I can step backward and stop the way I'm feeling, she told herself. Instead, she glanced up at his face. Tiny beads of perspiration glistened across Ty's forehead. His lips were partially opened, and she could feel his warm breath on her cheek. Her throat was parched when at last she answered, "But Christina . . . is married."

"She and her husband . . . are separated. It's been . . . a long time . . ."

"Yes . . ." she replied shakily. They were looking into each other's eyes now, their mouths only inches apart.

"Too long," he whispered.

463

Rachel nodded, and as once before in London, Ty's arms went around her. But tonight he wasn't drunk. Tonight he was triggering the very reason why the core of the new scene—its hook—had eluded her: she was fighting her feelings.

She didn't fight his kiss. While a silent voice demanded that she pull herself away, her lips opened to his, and they held each other until her head was spinning, spinning as it had on a windy streetcorner in London. That night the arrival of a taxi had saved her. Saved me from what? she asked as the thought flashed through her mind.

But she knew the answer, and with the absence of a taxi, it was up to Rachel.

Gently, reluctantly, she withdrew from his embrace, while trying to appear calmer than she felt. But her knees betrayed her, and she had to reach out to Ty to steady her and keep her from falling.

"You okay?" he asked, his arms this time providing support.

"Y-yes. I . . . think so."

"Maybe I should be sorry," he said. "But . . . I'm not."

"Neither am I, Ty," she admitted. "Confused, yes. And tired. Rushed, perhaps . . ."

"I'm going as slowly as I can."

"I know. Look, I don't mean to act like some schoolgirl about it, but . . ."

"You're not." He dropped his arms from hers and, with a smile, kissed her gently on the cheek. Then he walked to the door and picked up his bag. Before leaving, he said, "Take your time. Christina . . . will be fine."

* * *

Ty was right about Christina, Rachel reflected later that night. As he was right about her. He hadn't voiced the words between the lines, but she recognized that their attraction to one another was far more than professional, just as she recognized his awareness of the fact. Running from the truth would harm both women—Christina onstage, Rachel in life. Nonetheless, for the moment, complications were definitely not desirable, and Rachel carefully outlined her own mental rehearsals: a way in which to work closely with Ty— while staying out of his arms.

The opening arrived. April had always been important to Rachel, who viewed her birthday month not only as a time for reflection but of looking ahead. Now, with the premiere of *Christina's World,* April acquired an added significance.

Howard had not attended any of the rehearsals; Rachel had often found herself peering out front into the dark, empty theater, where she half expected to see him seated in the last row of the house. She missed his presence as much as his objectivity, and she couldn't help wondering what Howard would think of her work—if indeed he would be there to see it.

Despite almost a decade of stardom, Rachel had never become immune to the impact of applause. Nor had she come to take it for granted. On opening night of *Christina's World,* she sang her final song with the same commitment she had employed in *Robin Hood* nine years before. By the time Christina's "poison" took effect and she lay "dying" at the foot of her bed, Rachel was bathed in perspiration. When her hand went

465

limp—on the musical cue—she could hear quiet sobs out front from members of the audience. At her solo curtain call, the now-familiar wall of sound thrilled her as it always had.

She drank in the adulation and bowed deeply for the final time that night. Exiting offstage right, she saw Ty, standing in the wings, applauding wildly and with tears in his eyes. Beside the director stood Edgar Cornwall, his hands in a thumbs-up sign. Ty stepped forward and threw his arms around Rachel. "Thanks for a beautiful job," he whispered. Then he held her at arm's length.

"I'm soaked!" she said, laughing. "Let me get out of these things. I'll be showered and changed in ten minutes."

By the time she reached her dressing room, a small crowd had already gathered outside the door. They parted as she thanked them and kissed old friends, colleagues, and cast members who passed by. At last she saw, closest to the door, Howard and Norma. Rachel's heart gave a little tug at the sight of him as she said, "Come in."

Norma kissed her quickly and said, "I'll wait out here and keep the wolves at bay."

It was the first time they'd seen each other since Christmas at the cottage, the first time they'd spoken since Howard's telephone call to her at Beth's apartment.

He stood just inside the door and said quietly, "I wanted to offer my congratulations. Your performance was . . . astonishing."

His voice had faltered, but Rachel found her own totally aphonous. Tears welled in her eyes and began running down her cheeks. She tried to quell a sob, but emotion choked her as she made another attempt at speech. How she missed him, longed to rush into his arms! Couldn't they erase the barriers between them? Wasn't their being together all that mattered?

But it wasn't all that mattered, and the realization held her back. "You're . . . with Norma," she said at last.

He managed a weak grin, although she could see strain in the lines around his eyes. "She and I will probably be in all the columns tomorrow."

A tiny, sad laugh escaped Rachel's throat. Her heightened opening-night adrenaline, combined with Howard's physical presence in the room, had overwhelmed her.

"I'm afraid my being here . . . isn't helping," he said.

Yes it is! she wanted to cry. He was the most important person in her life—how could they remain apart?

"I'm glad you came," she managed. "Maybe we can talk . . . at the party."

He moved back to the door. "I'm not going to the party," he said slowly. "It's your night, and . . . Tyler Beekman's."

"Howard," she said, her eyes filled with pleading, "this could be *our* night—if only you'll believe that Ty and I—" But her voice broke at the sudden memory of the week just past. How could she say to Howard that *he* was the only reason she *hadn't* been to bed with Ty? The answer was simple: She couldn't tell him.

"Rachel," he said, absentmindedly fingering the velvet collar of his coat, "Sitting out front tonight, I was . . . in awe of you. You enthralled me—everyone—with your performance. That's why I came backstage. That . . . and the fact that I—"

He stopped short, seemingly to clear his throat, and when he continued, it was with a different tone. "I'm still against the publication of your book. That hasn't

467

changed. I . . . admire your courage, but you're making a mistake." His hand reached for the doorknob. "Nonetheless, tonight you made me feel very . . . tall."

Then he left and closed the door behind him.

She was quiet in the limousine. At last, Jamie asked, "How do you feel? Something the matter?"

"You know me so well," she said. "It's . . . nothing."

"Don't tell me that. I *do* know you. So?"

"All right." She let out a profound sigh. "It's Howard."

"You'll work it out."

"I used to think so. But I don't know anymore."

They sat in silence as the car continued uptown. Then she said, "I thought Paul would be here."

"He got a call to choreograph *Mame*. He left for Florida this morning. In all the excitement, I forgot to tell you. But he sent love—I'll call him later and let him know how great you were."

"Maybe I'll call him," she said listlessly. "I don't think I'll stay long at the party."

"Rachel, this shindig is in your honor."

"Partly. It's the whole cast's. And Ty's." She yawned, then said, "I'm sorry, I'm just tired. Who was out front tonight anyway?"

Jamie ran down a list of the luminaries who had attended the opening. "Oh, and Lehman was there, too."

Her heart sank. "You . . . don't think he'll be at the party, do you?"

"He was brazen enough to show up at all, but I doubt he'd push his luck *that* far."

She hoped Jamie was right. One performance was enough for tonight.

Rachel's black-beaded gown caught the light as they entered to a standing ovation at Tavern on the Green. She nodded, feeling ridiculous, as she waved. Everyone responded as though she were their queen and they, her subjects.

The seating arrangement placed her between Jamie and Ty.

"You look fabulous!" said Ty.

"So do you," she returned.

That Ty had had several drinks was evident in his relaxed manner. But as the reviews came in—rave upon rave—and applause broke out after each was read aloud. Rachel noticed that Ty seemed somewhat ill at ease. By the time it was announced that *Christina's World* was a solid hit, Ty was beginning to stammer nervously. It had nothing to do with drinking—his speech wasn't slurred, but rather hesitant and clumsy. Each new stream of compliments seemed to add to his discomfort.

"How are you holding up?" Rachel whispered to him.

"Not too well. It's that obvious?"

She smiled gently.

"I . . . I thought this would be more . . . fun," he said.

"Well, you've put in the required time. It's okay if you leave now."

"Boy, would I love to!" he said.

"Then do it."

Ty hesitated. "You staying?"

"I—" she began, then stopped herself. I don't really want to be here any more than he does, she thought. "Wait a second," she said, and turned to whisper in Jamie's ear.

"Sure," he said. "Let's go. I've got an early class tomorrow morning. I just hope some of my neighbors are still up so they can see me arrive home in a limo!"

They said their good nights, and Rachel made her exit, accompanied by a man on each arm. They smiled for photographers as a flurry of whispers erupted from surrounding tables. "Well, gentlemen, by morning, our affair will have become a ménage à trois," she commented with a grin.

They dropped Jamie off first. She kissed him and said, "Thanks for being there."

"Anytime," he replied, hugging her.

When the car pulled away from the curb, Ty said, "You two . . . you're very close."

"He's very special to me. To my life."

"I envy you."

"Well, you have friends—I've met some of them."

He shook his head. "Not that close. Not the way Chrissy and I were close. I think that's why tonight was such a . . . letdown."

"Because she wasn't there?"

"No," he said slowly. "Because tonight I realized that it's over. I mean, it's been over for months, and I accepted it, but tonight . . . it didn't *hurt*. It's as if a part of my past is dead, and I'm feeling relieved—but sad—at the same time. As if I've been in mourning and just taken off the armband."

She didn't reply, and he took her hand. *"You're* a good friend," he said, stroking her long, slim fingers. "Listen, I apologize. I didn't mean to put a damper on the evening."

"You haven't, Ty," she answered softly.

They both seemed to be waiting for the other to

speak as the car stopped in front of Beth's apartment.

"Do you feel like being alone?" he asked.

"No," she admitted. "Would you like some coffee?"

"We could . . . get into trouble," he said lightly, grinning.

"I've left Christina at the theater, Ty," she answered. "The invitation is for *coffee*."

Ty had removed his tux jacket, tie, and cummerbund, and Rachel had prepared espresso. Now she kicked off her high-heeled shoes and joined him on the sofa. She purposely avoided lighting the fireplace or putting music on the stereo—all the while aware that Ty could probably read—and interpret—her motives as though he were directing a scene onstage.

"God, I'm glad the show is over," she said in an attempt to set a casual, friendly, shop-talk mood.

"You've been through more opening nights than I have," he answered, "but you don't sound used to it."

"Oh, I'm used to it, Ty. One *gets* used to it. It's part of the act. I don't mean the performance—it's the show *after* the performance that wears me down."

She closed her eyes, breathed in slowly, and exhaled. Leaning her head against the back of the sofa, she said, "I tend to lose perspective about it . . . without Howard."

She felt Ty's hand fold over her own. "I know."

He did seem to know, and the gentleness of his touch moved her to the brink of tears. "Oh God," she said, trying to force a laugh, "I'm going to cry." Her hands came up to cover her face.

Ty drew her close and whispered, "Let it out. It'll help."

As she did, his hand stroked her hair. The tears

471

gradually subsided, and she laid her head against his shoulder. They sat silently, their breathing the only sound in the room.

His fingers tilted her jaw upward, then kissed her forehead, her eyelids, her lips. Her mouth opened to his tongue, and she didn't pull away this time when she felt her body responding to his touch. As his hands moved slowly downward to her breasts, momentarily she tensed. She had never been unfaithful to Howard . . . she'd resisted Ty before. . . .

But his kiss continued, arousing desires born of aching need and heightened by her previous abstinence.

His fingers were caressing her through the cold, slippery beads of the gown. Her own hands undid his buttons and slid inside his shirt. Gently she ran her fingers through the hair on his chest and felt the ever-increasing rhythm of his heartbeat.

Without speaking, Ty rose and held out his hand. He pulled her up from the sofa, and together they walked down the hall to the darkened bedroom.

In the faint light from the living room Rachel could see Ty's eyes; they glistened with wonder. Slowly, they undressed each other. Even more slowly, they lay down on the bed and clung silently to one another. He kissed the nipple of each breast, and in turn her mouth explored his chest. She could feel his growing excitement mingling with her own, and it seemed only natural that when his hands moved between her legs, she should open to him. He entered her, and Rachel raised herself to each of his deeper thrusts; she wanted to share with him the closeness, the sweetness, and the tenderness she felt.

His movements inside her were strong, and although their union signified a special bond between them, a bond of love, of trust, of friendship, too, there was, in

472

addition, a need to satisfy the passionate longing denied by each since their first meeting. Denied because of Chrissy. Because of Howard.

When Rachel and Ty had climaxed together, they gazed into each other's eyes and realized only then that both of them were weeping.

With the opening of *Christina's World,* Ty's directing assignment was over. Gossip columns questioned, "Is *Christina's* affair ending its run?" They laughed at the irony: Accused of an indiscretion *before* it had happened, they were being "acquitted" *after* the fact. Jamie was right—there was no logic in the world!

When he and Ty took Rachel out to celebrate her birthday, she wasn't seeking logic. She was with two of the three people she loved most dearly. Despite Howard's absence and the growing uncertainty of their future together, Rachel had stopped questioning tomorrow.

It had taken nine years in New York—thirty-one years of age—to realize that questioning tomorrow would only diminish the importance of today.

Chapter Thirty-two

June 1977

Beth Burns won the Tony Award for *One Night Only*. Rachel squeezed Ty's hand and leapt from her seat, while trying not to trip over the hem of her gown as she hurried toward the stage.

"Accepting for Miss Burns will be Rachel Allenby, star of *Christina's World*," said Yul Brynner as Rachel reached the top of the stairs.

Stepping up to the podium, she opened her evening purse and withdrew the still-sealed envelope Beth had given her months before. Rachel had kept her promise and hadn't peeked at the contents, so she also took out her reading glasses.

Brynner handed her the award, and she tore open the envelope. Removing the folded paper, she said into the microphone, "Beth asked me to read this acceptance for her." She lowered her eyes to scan the typewritten paragraph before reading it aloud.

SINCE I DIDN'T SLEEP FOR THIS JOB, THANKS FOR REALLY LIKING ME. TO ANYONE WHO DIDN'T VOTE FOR ME, YOU SHOULD HAVE BEEN IN LINE FIVE YEARS AGO. TIMING, DARLINGS, IS EVERYTHING!

In black ink at the bottom of the page were scrawled the words, "Rachel . . . I *dare* you! Love, Beth."

I'll kill her! thought Rachel. She raised her eyes once again and looked out at the audience. She smiled nervously, clearing her throat to stall for time while her brain raced to find a "substitute" speech. *I can't say I left my glasses home, dammit—I've already put them on!* Into the mike, still trying to cover the delay, she said, "Forgive me. . . . I *know* Beth is watching this on TV tonight, and I want to be sure to get it right."

The audience chuckled. The stage floor-manager signaled her that she had twenty seconds before the cut to a commercial. At last she bent her head and, pretending to read from Beth's note, said, "The only thing that's nicer than winning a Tony—is winning *two*. Special thanks to my director, Tyler Beekman, for having believed in me, and to all of you for your continued faith."

Rachel folded the paper and looked directly into the lens of the camera. "Beth, congratulations. I'll drop this off—personally . . ." *On your head,* she added silently as the awards presentation went to the break.

Backstage, she was photographed holding Beth's award. She remained there for interviews and more pictures with subsequent winners coming offstage from their wins. Ty won the Best Director, and this time, he was genuinely excited. When Rachel showed him the actual contents of Beth's acceptance speech, he laughed.

"Tell her you're going to keep it—as an award for *your* performance, *tonight!*"

The party was held at Windows on the World, and the guests glittered as brightly as the city a hundred floors below. A waiter popped the cork on the first champagne bottle at their table and said, "I'm Joseph, Miss Allenby. And I hope *you* win next year. I've seen *Christina* twice. You're wonderful."

She thanked him and was about to offer Joseph house seats—if he could sit through the show a third time—when he asked, "Miss Allenby, I was wondering . . ."

She reached for a pen.

But he wasn't asking for her autograph. "We . . . we watched the telecast on the TV in the kitchen. Do you think"—he lowered his voice—"maybe I could *see* the award?"

"Well, Joseph," Rachel answered, "I'd be glad to show it to you, but . . . I don't have it."

"You don't?" he asked.

"No. Only one Tony is used at the ceremonies. After I was photographed with the award, it was presented to the next winner, who was photographed with it, and so on. Now it'll be reproduced, the winners' names will be engraved, and each actor will get his." The aptness of her phrasing—after Beth's note—made her smile.

"I never would have guessed that," said Joseph.

"Well, at one time, neither would I. When I won for *Robin Hood,* I was shocked—I thought they'd changed their minds and wanted it back!" She laughed at the memory.

Joseph's face expressed disappointment. "It seems so . . ."

"Cheap?" Rachel prompted.

He shrugged, but a nod escaped.

"Joseph," she whispered, "I think it is, too."

He refilled her glass, and Rachel glanced around the room. Certain luminaries, to her relief, were absent,

476

among them Lehman Stern, Arnold Gold, and Gloria Doro, none of whom had been reperstened on Broadway that year.

But people she loved were missing, too; Howard had not attended the festivities, and Jamie was out of town, with Paul. Only Ty was there with her.

Over the summer, while she continued her eight performances a week in *Christina's World,* she worked on a forthcoming album and caught up on her reading.

Vera Garland had urged her to keep a clear schedule for late winter of the forthcoming year. The editor was less than pleased to learn that Rachel would open in the London production of *Christina's World* the following December.

"You'll be out of the country when the book is due?" Vera asked.

"No, Vera. I'm only contracted for three months."

"That's March! I need you here in time for publication!"

"Vera, England is a very literate country. The British read even more than we do. And the book will be distributed in the U.K., won't it?"

"Well, of course, but . . ."

"Don't worry. I've agreed to sing at the Gala of Stars Benefit for World Hunger. That's in April. I've *got* to be back for that."

"Fabulous—that's the gala set for the Music Hall?"

"Originally. It's been changed to the Morosco. They've upped the seat prices to make up for what they'll lose in ticket volume at the box office."

"But the date is still the same—in April?"

"Yes."

"April what?"

"April tenth. It's a Monday. Why?"

"Rachel! Y'know, there's *no* such thing as coincidence! Your book is scheduled to hit the stores the same week—that morning, if deliveries are on time! All the extra, *free* publicity—I love it, don't you?"

In mid-September, Rachel gave her final New York performance as Christina. Rather than a lavish farewell party, she preferred drinks and dinner after the show with Ty, Edgar Cornwall, and a few members of the cast and production staff. This time, Jamie and Paul were present.

They lifted their glasses to toast her.

She thanked them all and then said, "I'd like to add my own toast." She nodded in Paul's direction. "Mr. Jacobi is about to begin choreographing his first New York production next week. I'd like to wish him the very best of luck."

A smattering of applause greeted the news. Paul blew her a kiss and Jamie mouthed the words "thank you" from across the table.

"We'll miss you," Ty said later. "I'll miss you."

"Not for long. I'll see you in London about six weeks from now." She squeezed his hand. "But I'll miss you, too."

"Give my love to Beth."

"Oh, I'll give her that—and more. She may be *wearing* her Tony before I've finished my visit!"

Jamie and Paul escorted her home and stayed for cognac. Their separation would be longer—six months instead of weeks.

"By the time I get back here," she said to Paul with

·tears in her eyes, "I want you to be giving Bob Fosse a run for his money."

"I'll give it my best shot," he promised.

Rachel was exhausted from the nightly routine of a role that had grown stronger and more intense with each performance. She found relief in the temporary respite from such an emotionally demanding part. Within weeks, she would be in England again—a month at Hertfordshire, then back to the "boards" for resumption of still another rigorous rehearsal schedule and a pre-Christmas opening of her limited run in the London production of *Christina's World*.

But first, she would deliver Beth's Tony Award and spend a week at Gregory John Kelly's ranch outside of Houston. She had received countless letters describing the Kelly-Bar Ranch, which Beth explained as having been named for the 1880s mahogany and brass bar that Greg had rescued from a Texas saloon before its demolition. Greg had bought the property—and the surrounding neighborhood—because he had fallen in love with the bar. Now the site was occupied by another of the Kelly glass towers rising into Houston skies. "You'll have to see it to believe it," Beth had written.

Rachel decided that her friend—and the Kelly-Bar Ranch—would be good for her. The visit might distract her thoughts from Ty—and Howard. She had continued to experience momentary twinges of guilt whenever Ty stayed the night, but she also treasured the time they spent together. And the next time wouldn't be for six weeks.

* * *

A stretch limousine awaited her at the airport in Houston. Beth, every inch "gone Western" in boots, denim, and fringe, alighted from the luxury automobile and waved, as a perfectly liveried chauffeur—a far cry from Owen—stood at attention.

"Rachel, *honey!*" she cooed.

My God, thought Rachel, she's even adopted a drawl! She turned and ran toward her friend, realizing only when they embraced that Beth had let herself go in more ways than locale. She was getting fat!

"Honey, Greg's off somewhere at an oil meeting or somethin' like that, but he sends his dearest love and says he'll be back by supper. That'll give us time to catch up!" She gripped Rachel's arm, and no reporters—if they had been present—would have *dared* cross their path to the car.

Rachel wasn't aware of how bright the Houston sun could be until they stepped out of the tinted-windowed limo and onto the portico to the grandest "ranch" Rachel had ever envisioned in her mind. Beth had written about its "hacienda splendor." However, since Beth's descriptions often ran to exaggeration, Rachel hadn't known what to expect.

"But nothing like this!" she said aloud, entering the spacious foyer that might have been transported stone by stone and plank by plank from Spain.

"Isn't it fun?" Beth gushed, squeezing Rachel's arm again.

Fun wasn't exactly the word Rachel would have used; *staggeringly severe,* perhaps. All the wood was massive and dark. Enormous black wrought-iron chandeliers hung from evil-looking chains that rose to the two-story-high beamed ceiling. The floor was inlaid with stone. Savonarola chairs flanked long side-buffet tables, and the cabinet work, while ornately carved and oiled to a mirrorlike patina, gave Rachel the impression that bodies remained hidden within, perhaps skeletons from the Inquisition.

"Jus' wait'll you see *your* room!" exclaimed Beth.

"I can hardly wait," said Rachel.

"Well, you'll have to! We're gonna sit and play ladies of leisure before we do a thing." She reached for a tapestry bellpull—which Rachel had thought to be merely ornamental—and as if by magic, a servant appeared. "Juan," said Beth, "we'll have margaritas on the veranda."

"You really sound like a transplanted Scarlett O'Hara," Rachel observed.

Ignoring the remark, Beth called after Juan, "And some guacamole and tortilla chips. Maybe some nachos, too!"

"Beth—I can't believe it's *you!*" said Rachel.

"Honey, believe it! Ol' Beth baby is going to pot." She patted her stomach. "Besides—" She hesitated, then said, "Ever see opera singers or ballet dancers when *they* retire? *They* get *fat!*"

Rachel observed her friend's profile but didn't comment; Beth seemed radiant.

They settled on the veranda—an enclosed area that ran the length of the house—and sipped their cold drinks. Only the sound of the wind and the buzzing of an occasional fly intruded on the peaceful quiet.

"Does it ever get *too* quiet?" asked Rachel.

Beth shook her head. "Spoken like a true New Yorker. Nope. I admit, I worried about that at first, but honey, you'd be amazed—I mean, this is how people *should* be able to live, not covering their ears all day to shut out the sirens and horns in the city. Of course, Houston's somethin' else—you'll see, we'll go shopping—but even *that* is a tomb compared with Manhattan."

"And the 'tomb' agrees with you, doesn't it?" Even with her excess poundage, Beth was beaming with health.

They talked on into dusk, Rachel sipping a second drink while Beth nibbled at everything on Juan's sumptuous platter. They brought each other up-to-date on *Christina's World,* the book, Beth and Greg's forthcoming, planned elopement.

"We want to keep it simple, and in Houston, nobody does *anything* simple. So we're flying to Las Vegas in Greg's l'il Lear, and by the time we get back, it'll be old news. Wanna be my matron of honor?"

"Sure. When?"

"Well, maybe this weekend, depending on Greg's business appointments. I mean, I'm in no rush, but y'know somethin', Rachel? I've discovered that after all I've said and done, there's a part o' me that's still old-fashioned. I think that a woman should get married—and *then* have the baby . . ." She looked up at Rachel with a mischievous grin and winked.

"Beth! You're not—" But she stopped herself. *That* explained the protruding belly.

Beth seemed to have read Rachel's mind. "I'll bet you thought it's all these nachos! Hell, honey, ever since we found out, I've been eating everything in sight! And guess what? Greg says he likes me better with 'a little extra meat'!"

Beth hadn't disappointed Rachel; she never failed to come up with new surprises.

"Are you happy about it?" asked Rachel. "The baby I mean."

"Happy? Honey, I'm in heaven! We both are!" She leaned closer and lowered her voice. "Y'know, there's that li'l matter of the biological clock ticking away, day after day. In a way, it's now—or never." She paused for a moment, then said, "This is none of my business, Rachel, but . . . well, even with the years I've got on you, it's time you gave it a thought."

She didn't answer, so Beth said, "Or have you? Did you and Ty ever get around to living the legend?"

Rachel felt her cheeks beginning to warm. Ty was the single subject she hadn't discussed with her friend.

"Sorry," said Beth. "I do tend to talk too much. I just figured, with Howard out of the picture . . . or is he?"

Beth's question had turned Rachel's mood to one of seriousness. "I don't know anymore, Beth. I still love him, if that's what you mean."

"It's only part of what I mean, honey," said Beth more gently. "In short, once the book is out, what then?"

Rachel shrugged. "Oh, I'm singing in the Gala of Stars benefit next spring—actually, about the same time the book comes out."

"That'll be interesting!" She patted her stomach. "I turned down the invitation to sing in the gala—Junior here'll be making his debut around a week or so before. But if he behaves and arrives on time, I'll fly in for the show just to see the fireworks!" Apparently she saw the distressed expression on her friend's face, because she said, "Rachel, you mean you hadn't stopped to think about that? God, I'd have figured you *planned* the timing with your publisher!"

"No," answered Rachel quietly. "I didn't."

"Well, you still haven't answered my question—and

now it's more pertinent than ever. What about it?"

"What about what?" Rachel's mind had wandered off.

"What about your *life?*"

Rachel felt a sudden return of the gag reflex that had choked her during rehearsal for *Christina's World* only eight months before.

"I don't know, Beth," she answered, "but I guess I'm going to find out."

In the evening, she discovered why Beth was so happy. Greg Kelly—Gregory J. Kelly, III—was all that Beth had made him out to be. Charming, affable, attractive, a perfect host, and utterly devoted to Beth. Since he knew that she and Rachel were best friends, he welcomed her immediately into "the li'l ol' Kelly clan."

They were joined at dinner on Thursday by Joe Tompkins, a banker and Greg's closest ally in what he termed a "backbiting business that would make *theatuh* people blush."

Rachel didn't argue, but she hardly thought that possible.

On Monday of the following week, shortly after dawn, Greg and Beth, with Joe and Rachel as their best man and matron of honor, flew to Las Vegas in one of Greg's private planes.

Five hours later, in an atmosphere of pastel-colored plastic flowers and taped organ music, bride and groom were pronounced man and wife.

No reporters were present; it was a hot, bright September day in Nevada, and no passersby could think it unusual that four members of a particular bridal party all wore dark glasses and hats that came down low over their faces. Both provided excellent shields from the glare of the sun.

"I can't wait till Rona sees the papers tomorrow," said Beth happily as they emerged from the pink and blue stucco chapel.

"I thought you were keeping this a secret," said Rachel.

"From Rona, hon. But I did drop a telegram to Liz. She ought to be reading it—right about now." She laughed merrily at her mischievousness, and the quartet set out for a proper champagne wedding breakfast.

Rachel spent a second week with the "honeymoon couple" before leaving for England. William and Jennie were on holiday in Greece, so she could relax at Hertfordshire without socializing or having to explain Howard's absence. When rehearsals began in November, she would move to the Park Lane to avoid the long daily commute up to London and back. In addition, Ty would be there. Whatever turn their relationship might take, Rachel would have somewhat more privacy in the bustling city than at a cottage in the country. That the cottage remained empty—Howard was unlikely to spend Christmas in England this year—made Rachel doubly eager to stay in town. It seemed as though whatever matters came to be resolved, others emerged to take their place. And Ty was only part of it.

Her forthcoming schedule promised to fill a void, while moving her into 1978. Celeste Farrar had been signed to replace her in the title role at the end of March, when Rachel would return to New York for the talk-show circuit to plug *Inner Voices*.

Upon her arrival in London, Rachel learned that

Mina MacDonald had resigned. Citing "a conflict of interests," she would no longer handle Rachel's publicity or Howard's agency. It served to rekindle speculation as to the nature of those "conflicting interests." But what right had Rachel, in view of her own affair with Ty, to question Howard? No right, she reminded herself. Then why should the thought disturb her so?

Norma wrote that Brian Xaviar would now work with Vera Garland to coordinate Rachel's book tour and television appearances on the *Tonight Show, Dick Cavett,* and *Merv Griffin* with the rehearsal schedule for the Gala of Stars.

Rachel felt a sudden twinge whenever her thoughts included Beth's prediction of the outcome. *Fireworks—* really, Beth! she mused. Her friend certainly wasn't lacking for imagination!

Preparations for *Christina's World* were no less demanding than those of the preceding winter. As he had done with the West End production of *One Night Only,* Ty experimented, adding or cutting wherever the show might benefit from either. He worked and reworked a scene here, a bit of business there. Rachel, too, was approaching her role as one she had never before acted or sung. As a result, rehearsals were again chances to explore and "stretch," rather than merely repeat and stagnate. She had finally learned to leave Christina at the theater at the end of each day. Perhaps she was adjusting to her current situation. Or it might be her success in the role; success enabled her to risk, where before she had feared.

Success also enabled Rachel to reach a long-postponed decision regarding her offstage relationship with

Ty. The only way in which she could sort out the various priorities in her life was by eliminating her own "conflicts of interest."

Ty didn't try to dissuade her; his understanding assured Rachel that their friendship would remain intact. Rehearsals continued as intensely as before, the challenge of discovery no less exciting simply because they returned to separate rooms at night.

Rachel reflected on the unusual ease into which she and Ty were able to settle. Any lingering gossip no longer affected either of them, and when they were together, which was constantly, there was never a need for explanation; they had developed the kind of intimacy that Rachel had always sensed possible between men and women not seeking to control one another. Their physical bond had served to deepen, not threaten, their closeness. And, strangely, it had deepened her love for Howard.

The West End production of *Christina's World* opened the week before Christmas. The reviews and public response were as unanimously vociferous as in New York's season just past. Rachel was again singled out for overwhelming praise; her name was ensured a place among the greats of musical theater: Gertrude Lawrence, Mary Martin, Ethel Merman, and more recently, Beth Burns. Moreover, noted each critic, Rachel stood alone as a singing *actress,* since *Christina's World* was a musical *drama* and not comedy. One reviewer went so far as to compare the show with opera and Rachel's interpretation with that of Maria Callas's caliber.

Rachel was deeply flattered, but Ty commented,

487

"Christ, that could *kill* us at the box office!" As a result, Rachel's favorite review was excluded from advertising promotions that quoted blurbs from the press.

With the show open, Ty left to attend a film festival, and Rachel was free to preside over several charity functions, give a series of master classes at the Royal Academy of Dramatic Arts, and take part in televised panel discussions for the BBC. She granted magazine interviews and, despite misgivings, agreed to appear, in February, on a local BBC-2 program hosted by Amory Evans. The misgivings were due to his weekly boast of "the most revealing half hour on television." She had already been filmed for *60 Minutes* two years earlier, but that was before so much controversy had begun to surround her name. Now she feared that Amory Evans might ask probing questions related to her marriage—or to her "alleged" affair with Ty Beekman.

However, when she was assured by a studio spokesman that neither subject would be broached, she relented. The show would fill an empty spot on her calendar. "And," she told Ty, who had returned to London in time for the cast's New Year's Eve party, "the show is taped. If Evans throws me any kind of curve, it can be edited out."

"Get that in writing. I don't trust interviewers."

"Neither do I. It's been added to the contract."

"Good," he said, guiding her toward the balcony of the apartment in which the party was being held. I boasted a spectacular view of the Thames.

"This is lovely," said Rachel. "It's almost the same view as the one from the Savoy."

"Howard?" asked Ty.

She nodded. "Our first trip to London together. I was very . . . special." She paused, not really feeling sorry for herself, yet missing him.

He squeezed her arm and together they looked silently out over the river.

"What are you thinking?" she asked at last.

Slowly, Ty shook his head. "I, well, I . . ."

Rachel glanced up at his hesitation. Intuitively, she asked, "Ty . . . have you met someone?"

His once-awkward shyness seemed to have returned. "I . . . this isn't . . . I mean, the timing . . ."

But Rachel felt no twinges. "Ty—where is she? *Who* is she?"

"You're sure . . . you don't . . ."

"Ty, you'll have me stammering, too. *Tell* me."

"She isn't an actress, isn't in theater at all. She's a journalist, would you believe it? *Not* a reporter—I really *don't* trust them—Joan writes about foreign relations, the government, that kind of thing. She's still on assignment in Paris—that's where we met." He paused to look deeply into Rachel's eyes. "I swear I didn't mean to spring it on you like this—on New Year's Eve—but everything's happened so fast, and I—"

"Ty," said Rachel, smiling, "you have to stop trying to 'protect' me from what you think me hurt me. Otherwise, *that* in itself could hurt." She kissed his cheek. "I'm thrilled for you. And you'd better believe me."

"Okay," he promised, his hands on her shoulders. "I believe you. But God, it's scary!"

"What is?"

"Being in love again. I've never been so nervous!"

In the background, a champagne cork popped and a clock struck twelve. As the other guests began singing "Auld Lang Syne," Rachel kissed Ty gently on the mouth and said, "Happy New Year, Ty. And don't be nervous about it. Be happy."

489

They welcomed 1978 standing together, champagne in hand, watching fireworks shoot over the Thames.

Ty left to join Joan in Paris, and Rachel continued her eight weekly performances in *Christina's World*. On her day off, she sometimes went to Hertfordshire, where she had finally apprised William and Jennie of her separation from Howard; the disclosure became inevitable after he had remained in New York for Christmas. Jennie had reacted in character—no questions, not a hint of curiosity. But she did offer, "Luv, if something's meant to be, it will, despite you and me and the Almighty, Himself. Just trust in that."

Rachel was trying, but she wasn't sure just what was meant to be.

The second week in February, the spokesman from Amory Evans's BBC program telephoned to remind Rachel of the taping. She would be collected at the Park Lane at seven-thirty on Thursday morning. Eight o'clock makeup call, nine A.M. on set. The taping would probably take two hours, from which thirty minutes would be extracted, edited, and televised later in the month.

It rained heavily through the night, and Rachel awoke at six in the morning with a sinus headache and a crick in her neck. It didn't help to alleviate her foreboding. As she showered and let the hot water play against the point of tension just above her shoulder, she kept reminding herself that this wouldn't be a *live* interview; there was nothing to fear from a *taping*.

The limousine arrived punctually, and at eight o'clock

Rachel was seated in the dentist-style makeup chair as a studio technician studied her and said, "A bit more color, I think. You really do have an English complexion, Miss Allenby. Peaches and cream—terrible for the tube!" He laughed as the makeup artist, Tony, applied a darker base.

The humidity had added a stubborn wave to her hair, but Tony sprayed and brushed, and at last Rachel didn't look at all as though she'd risen at the crack of dawn and still had a splitting headache and a stiff neck.

She glanced at the overhead clock. Tony had worked his magic in record time; she had twenty minutes to spare.

As if reading her mind, he said, "Why don't you have a seat in the green room? Someone will come for you when we're ready to go. In the meantime, maybe you'd like some tea?"

"Is it possible to have coffee?" asked Rachel, rising from the chair. She'd cut her caffeine intake lately, but the stimulant might help rid her of the headache this morning.

"Sure thing. Just make yourself comfortable. It's down the hall to your left. I'll bring the coffee to you there."

Rachel's adrenaline began to rise as she walked the few steps to the door that read GREEN ROOM. My God, she thought as her hand reached the knob. Coffee nerves *before* I drink it? Or stage fright? After all these—

The thought cut off abruptly as she swung open the door and saw Amory Evans's other guest seated on the sofa.

It was Lehman Stern.

* * *

491

He seemed as stunned as she. Involuntarily, he rose. The two of them were rooted, staring at each other as though each had seen a ghost.

Lehman spoke first. "I didn't expect to find you here—or I wouldn't have come."

Rachel couldn't connect with her voice.

"I *thought* I'd been invited to talk about my new show," he said. "I can see now that Amory has other plans." When she still didn't speak, he continued. "Were you aware of Amory's little surprise, Rachel? Am I the reason you're here?"

Regaining her poise, Rachel answered, "Hardly, Lehman."

He reached for the cigarette lighter on the table beside him and began to flick the striking wheel back and forth. Rachel noticed from the clean ashtray, however, that he hadn't been smoking.

"What are you and Amory planning to discuss?" asked Lehman. *"Christina's World?* You're very good in the role."

"Thank you," she replied, aware that he hadn't taken his eyes from her. "I don't know what Mr. Evans has in mind, but I doubt it has anything to do with the show."

"Not controversial enough?" asked Lehman.

She thought a note of edginess had crept into his voice.

"You'd have to ask him, Lehman."

"I will—the minute we get onto the set." His eyes traveled around the small room before returning to her again. "Speaking of controversial, I don't suppose you'll want to say much about this little book you've been writing . . ."

"I—"

"Or have you thought better about it and decided not to publish?"

She paused before answering and then said, "Actually, I've thought better about it and decided *to* publish."

"I didn't know that was ever in doubt," he said.

"For longer than you can imagine, Lehman. I don't enjoy hurting people."

"Really? That's not what I've read in the papers lately." He was still playing with the lighter. The constant clicking sound was beginning to annoy Rachel—almost as much as being trapped in the green room with him.

"Don't believe everything you read in the papers, Lehman. *You* of all people ought to know that."

"Rachel, darling, how you've changed! I hardly recognize you. You were so guileless . . . once."

"I didn't see what was right before my eyes . . . once."

His features seemed to grow narrower like those of a predatory bird. "You don't practice what you preach, Rachel. And you *do* know the old saying about people in glass houses . . ."

"You're hardly the one to tell me that—"

"Oh, you ought to see *yourself,* Rachel! You've become like all the rest of us—another Gloria Doro—and *you* once told me you'd stop singing before you'd become like her!" He set the lighter back on the table with a pronounced thud. "You'll stop *yourself* from singing, darling—you won't need an Arnold Gold or a Gloria Doro—or me—to stop you. You'll do it to yourself with this damn-fool crusade of yours! When this little book of lies hits the streets—"

"Lies!" She was trying to keep her voice from rising.

493

"You amaze me, Lehman. You really believe your own publicity. You see yourself as a victim—an innocent!"

She could see Lehman's futile attempt to hide his mounting anger. "Oh come on, Rachel!" he said, his face reddening. "Why don't you admit that this book of yours is just one big publicity stunt! Who gives a damn about what you've written, anyway? The whole world makes trade-offs—that's nothing new!"

She was thinking, *The whole world doesn't commit murder,* but she caught herself and said instead, "Some trade-offs are more costly than others, Lehman."

Shrugging, he said. "Well, whatever gets you through the night." He picked up his cup and saucer from the table. Rachel noticed that despite the calm of his *non sequitur,* his hands were trembling; the teacup's rattle betrayed him.

Tony arrived then with Rachel's coffee. "Why don't you sit down, Miss Allenby?" he asked. She had remained standing inside the doorway. "We still have about fifteen minutes."

"Thank you, Tony," she answered, "but I won't be staying for the taping."

"Not staying?" Tony looked at her quizzically.

"No," she replied. "You can tell Mr. Evans that his brand of surprise is not my sense of humor. Live or taped."

As she turned to go, Lehman asked, "How *is* Ty Beekman these days?"

Whirling around to face him, she said, "He's *alive,* Lehman—why don't you discuss *that* with Amory Evans!" She brushed past Tony so fast that the cup and saucer in his hands went flying. The makeup man jumped out of the way as hot coffee splashed everywhere. Rachel didn't stop. She ran through the hall to

494

her dressing room, grabbed her coat and umbrella, and was out of the studio and down the street before anyone could detain her.

Even after she was safely back in her hotel room, where she could be alone with her anger, Lehman's words rang in her ears. She *wasn't* like Gloria Doro. That hadn't caused her rage. Nor had the intimation about Ty. It was Lehman's own self-righteousness!

Several hours later, Rachel realized that, in a very bizarre way, Lehman Stern had done her a favor.

Whatever misgivings she had nurtured over the forthcoming publication of *Inner Voices,* that morning's encounter with her former mentor had, once and for all, silenced them.

Chapter Thirty-three

April 1978

Years before, Rachel had met Jamie for cocktails in the lounge of the Algonquin Hotel. Then, it had been a special occasion and an expensive treat. She had almost envied the famous guests strolling past in the lobby. It hadn't occurred to her that, celebrated or not, people only stayed at hotels if they had nowhere else to stay.

Now, however, it was Rachel who was the object of attention as the doorman bowed and she strode across the deep-piled carpeting to the registration desk. A bellhop and Garrett Simone, of the Gala of Stars' production staff, attended to Rachel's luggage while she checked in. The clerk handed her a sealed envelope and a small stack of messages, but she stuffed them all into her totebag without looking at them. There was plenty of time for business matters. An entire week.

The bellhop deposited her suitcases and drew open the draperies while Rachel read the cards attached to several large bouquets. The greetings brightened her spirits as the flowers did the room. Multicolored tulips from the producers of the gala, white and yellow orchids from The Broude Press, her publisher, and a stoneware bowl with a spray of deep red roses from Jamie and Paul. Their card read: "Happy birthday in advance, dinner to follow." Beside it was a bottle of champagne, compliments of the management.

Garrett tipped the bellhop and handed Rachel another envelope. "This is the rehearsal schedule for the gala and the lineup for the actual performance. Norma Kendall said to call her at home if you have any questions. The limousine and driver are at your disposal."

"I don't think I'll need the car, Garrett. I can walk to the theater, and a taxi will be fine for anything else. Thanks."

"My pleasure, Miss Allenby. Oh . . . and good luck."

He didn't say whether the wish was for the gala or for her book.

The book, however, was uppermost in Rachel's mind. She opened the champagne and curled up on the sofa to read through her messages: Ty, Vera Garland, Jamie and Paul. She opened the Gala of Stars envelope. It outlined what she already knew—that the evening would be a live telecast—and listed the rehearsal schedule: twenty minutes with orchestra to go over her material, and a camera run-through of the same. Thankfully, Rachel wasn't slated as one of the speakers, so she wouldn't have to spend more then an hour at the theater, all told, before the actual performance.

She picked up the phone and dialed.

"Welcome home!" said Norma. "How are you?"

"Fine, so far. I just got in."

"Did you get all the info?"

"Yes—except for what I'm singing."

"It's a medley. Your choice, but they did say they'd like your biggest songs—'My Light Through the Trees,' 'Finding Answers,' 'Could It Be You?'—"

Rachel interrupted, wincing. "Not *that,* Norma. I know the record was a hit, but I hated the song—I still do—and the movie was filmed at . . . well, at a low point in my life."

"Say no more. I'll call the production office in the morning."

"Tomorrow's Sunday."

"They'll be open because of the tight schedule—some of the stars have to fly to the Coast for the Oscars."

"When are they?"

"Hon, where have you been? April third. Monday's Oscar night."

"Is Howard . . . in California?" Rachel asked.

"No, he's"—she hesitated—"in London."

Rachel felt her heart sink. "How long has he been there?"

"Well . . . four days . . ."

They'd been in the same city for four days and he hadn't attempted to call. Rachel tried to hide the hurt from her voice as she asked, "When's he due back?"

"He didn't say. It's some problem with Malcolm Campbell's new show. Look, Rachel . . ."

"Never mind. If he calls, tell him . . ."

Tell him what? she asked herself. That *Inner Voices* is about to make its debut and I'm scared to death of the outcome? But Howard knew the publication date; it wasn't a secret. His silence spoke louder than any rebuff.

Norma seemed to feel the awkwardness. "Listen, hon, I hate to see you at a hotel, even if the ghosts of the Barrymores *are* there to keep you company."

"Well, Beth sublet her apartment while I was in London. Besides, I'm planning to let room service wait on me hand and foot." She laughed lightly and added, "If I run into a crisis, I'll call you."

"Do. And . . . stick close to your friends. *Real* close."

"Norma . . . what are you trying to tell me with that subtlety of yours?"

"Only that I've read an advance copy of the book. *I* think it's terrific. But if *I've* read it, so have other people . . people who will be at the gala. Some of them are *in* the gala. Take my advice and watch where you step."

"Thanks, Norma . . . I think."

Her engagement calendar filled quickly. Among appearances on the *Today Show* Wednesday morning, *Dick Cavett* on Thursday, and *The New York Times* interview scheduled for after—or was it before?—that, Rachel managed to squeeze in an afternoon and evening with Jamie and Paul and dinner with Ty Beekman and Joan.

She liked Joan at once and was glad for Ty; their apartment, with Ty's theater memorabilia and Joan's journalism souvenirs, expressed the individuality of each of them. The mixture was one of harmony rather than of conflict, and reminded Rachel of the same balance she and Howard had achieved at Rathborne Cottage. It also emphasized her presence as a third person and the fact that she was alone. Still, their company was treasured in a week crammed with professional appointments.

It was a short walk from the Algonquin to the Morosco. Rachel noticed that in her few months' absence, new buildings had appeared, and older ones were gone. Theater marquees displayed new titles, some with old stars, others with names Rachel had never seen before. *Hello, Dolly!* was back again, this run at the Lunt-Fontanne, instead of the St. James.

The marquee of the Morosco advertised a new play entitled *Da,* due to open the following month. The showcase windows, however, displayed posters for the Gala of Stars' single performance. Rachel saw her name near the top of the alphabetical list. It was just beneath Alan Alda's. Farther down she noticed the names of Drew Colton and Gloria Doro. Small wonder Norma had said to watch her step.

She went in through the stage entrance. The doorman's vestibule cage was deserted; indeed the entire wing area seemed abandoned. Inside, however, she heard sounds of life, sounds of heavy equipment being moved and of musicians tuning up.

In an eeriness of time suspended, Rachel recalled the radio interview for the New Stars auditions. She'd met Norma that same day. And first seen Jamie, in a mirrored reflection. Stepping to the right of the stage manager's desk, she realized that Jamie's first words to her —*break a leg*— had been spoken on the very spot where she now stood. Full circle? she mused, wondering what had become of the blonde girl who had won—or to Pink Tulle, who *should* have won. Ghosts of Aprils past . . .

She was summoned to the present by a familiar voice onstage. Gloria Doro was rehearsing her number for the gala. From the corner where she stood, Rachel could see the red-orange hair of the older, heavier star.

"You're on time," whispered the stage manager, "but *we're* running late, thanks to Miss Doro. We had hoped to keep each star to twenty minutes' rehearsal time, but that doesn't seem important to *her*."

Rachel nodded and leaned closer to hear the verbal exchange onstage.

"Miss Doro," the conductor was saying, "can we take this section a little *faster?* You're behind."

"Listen," Gloria called out, "this song was written *for* me, and in *this* tempo. So *you* slow down!"

The stage manager shrugged, but Rachel smiled. Despite her feelings toward Gloria Doro, her own decade of performing experience had taught her to protect herself. Doro was doing that now. It *was* her "signature" song, it *had* been written for her, and the orchestra *was* taking the song too fast. I'd have insisted about the tempo too, thought Rachel.

Nonetheless, Rachel was relieved that she was standing in the wings stage *right* and that Gloria Doro exited to the wings stage *left*. Surely Doro had glanced at *Inner Voices* by now. No point in looking for trouble.

Rachel's own run-through required only ten minutes; she and the conductor were together all the way. Anita Oate applauded as she approached. "You look and sound marvelous, darling!"

"Thanks, Anita. You too."

"Listen, I've got an adorable little dance trio in mind for you and Julie and Angela—"

"Anita," Rachel interrupted, "this is a cue for 'I Won't Dance, Don't Ask Me.' You do remember *Robin Hood?*"

"How could I forget? But darling, *this* will be *simple* —"

"So was *Robin Hood*. No, Anita. Stick me in a kick line for the finale if you have to, but my feet still can't do what *you* want them to."

"Okay . . . there *is* a kick line for the finale — and I'll hold you to that promise!"

The camera run-through on the following Sunday went smoothly. Stars rushed in and out, sandwiching themselves among heavy schedules, some dashing to or from matinees. The backstage area traffic was so brisk that stars were allowed to enter and exit through the front lobby as well, to speed up the process. Rachel almost preferred the backstage confusion to the funereal atmosphere of a darkened auditorium, even with people milling about the lobby. She remained as unobtrusive as possible, and at least the unlit house provided the relative anonymity that the cramped backstage quarters wouldn't have offered.

Jamie picked her up on Monday afternoon and accompanied her to the executive offices of The Broude Press for *Inner Voices'* "debut" party.

The street-floor windows of the publishing firm were filled with copies of the book. They flanked an emormous life-size photograph of Rachel.

In the elevator, she grabbed Jamie's hand and held it tightly. "Just squeeze," she said. "Hard."

He did.

Applause broke out in the crowded room as Vera Garland escorted Rachel to the podium. Flashbulbs popped, and she smiled.

"Here she is!" exclaimed Vera. "Our star and author of the next number one best-seller!"

Enlargements of the more flattering reviews were

mounted on display boards, and most of the guests who approached Rachel had either read the book or heard enough about it to comment intelligently. She repeatedly heard phrases such as "beautifully written" or "deeply motivated" as she signed her name to copy after copy. Only occasionally did she hear a whispered "sour grapes" or "who cares" among the throng.

After an hour of cocktails and chatter, Rachel excused herself and said to Jamie, who was seated in a corner near the buffet table, "My smile muscles are aching as much as my writing hand. Get me out of here—please?"

He rose and took her hand. "The more things change. . . ?"

If Rachel had thought the Morosco was crowded during rehearsals for the gala, it was nothing compared with the confusion backstage on the actual night of the performance. From out front, the Morosco was one of the last Broadway bastions of "jewel-box" theaters to avoid the wrecker's ball; the area behind-the-scenes had never been spacious; on the evening of April tenth, the congestion was sufficient to present a fire hazard.

Rachel was carrying her garment bag over one arm. Inside it was the ice blue chiffon gown Zandra Rhodes had designed for her in London. Maid Marian's color, she had decided, since her runaway hit song from *Robin Hood* would wind up her medley.

As she stepped carefully over coiled cables just inside the entrance vestibule, an old man of seventy or more tapped her on the shoulder. "I always thought you should have won," he said in a scratchy voice.

"I beg your pardon?" she said, turning.

"The New Stars auditions—I was working in there"—he pointed his cane in the direction of the doorman's cage—"and you were terrific. But you made it, anyway. I'm glad

502

was right."

"I'm glad you were too. Thanks for the vote of confidence."

He grinned and said, "How's it feel to be back where you started?"

She realized he hadn't meant the question to sound the way it came out, but it made her smile. "The place seems . . . smaller, somehow." For the New Stars auditions, she had wondered how her voice would ever fill the theater.

"Could I ask you a favor?" he said. "A special autograph?"

"Sure . . . but I haven't any paper. . . ."

"Will this do?" He reached down behind his chair and produced a copy of *Inner Voices*. Opening the book to the inside cover, he handed it to Rachel. Then, taking a pen from his pocket, he said, "Just put *For Al, who was right*. Okay?"

She nodded and began to write.

"By the way, who is Annie Singer?" he asked.

Rachel finished Al's autograph and turned to the dedication page, where Annie's name was inscribed. "Well," she answered thoughtfully, "I guess you might call her a teacher. She was a great lady."

"You're doin' okay yourself," he said with a wink.

She returned the book and pen, then asked, "Al, where do I dress?" During their exchange, a steady stream of theater personnel, stagehands and crew, stars and chorus alike, had been filing in; other people on their way out of the building only added to the clutter and confusion.

Al consulted his clipboard. "I kept a copy of the dressing room assignments 'cause I figured some stars might miss the list on the callboard." His bifocal lenses scanned the page. "Sorry, it's not in alphabetical order."

Finally, he looked up and said, "Well, you're sharing—but everybody's got two or more to a room. You're one flight up, third door on the right." He patted the book. "I can't

503

wait to read this," he said.

"You're not alone, Al," she said with a wave on her way up the staircase.

The first door had a notice that read:

Miss Channing

Miss Kitt

Miss Minnelli

Miss Moore

Rachel noted that for the actual dressing rooms, as with the listings outside the theater, strict alphabetical order was observed—probably to avoid ego tantrums over which stars received top "billing."

The door opposite also bore a sign that played no favorites:

Mr. Alda

Mr. Jourdan

Mr. Langella

Mr. Price

Several dancers wearing *Grease* T-shirts rushed past as Rachel checked door listings for the one to which Al had directed her. "Hey, Miss Allenby!" called a blond chorus boy. "I bought your book this morning—wow! You're a gutsy lady!"

"Yeah," said a redheaded girl in a silver bowling jacket. Its logo identified her as a cast member of *A Chorus Line.* "You've done something for all of us—thanks!"

But at that moment, another redhead—Gloria Doro- exited an adjacent dressing room. She was accompanied by Arnold Gold.

Doro's eyes traveled up and down Rachel as they had a decade earlier at the Capitol Theater in Washington, D.C.

"Well, you've got a pair of brass ones to show your face. If you're smart, you've brought some friends along." She paused for a beat, then said to Gold, "That's if she has an

504

friends left." She yanked her husband's arm and tore past Rachel.

Rachel was at a loss for words. When she heard Doro call out, "Drew! Darling!" she quickly ducked inside the dressing room to which Al had directed her and slammed the door shut. She didn't need a confrontation with Drew Colton to follow one with Gloria Doro.

The room assignments were also posted on small cards tucked into the corner of each mirror. She leaned closer and read:

Miss Allenby
Miss Bergman
Princess Grace

However, neither of her two childhood idols was present. Glancing at their dressing tables, then at the printed lineup schedule, she saw that both stars were on toward the beginning. Ingrid Bergman was scheduled to speak on world hunger, and Princess Grace was going to introduce Cary Grant.

In a way, Rachel was relieved; she felt vulnerable enough without having to share the intimate surroundings with two stars who had been "grown-up" for as long as she could remember. *She* felt anything *but* grown-up just now.

Turning up the volume on the squawk box, she listened to Liza Minnelli sing a rousing number from *The Act,* followed by Dorothy Loudon's big song from *Annie.*

Drew Colton didn't sing a number from *Robin Hood* — after all, Rachel's song was the single hit that had survived the long-running show. Instead, Drew joined in a duet with Gloria Doro. Birds of a feather, Rachel mused. Even their voices blended well together.

She heard gushy laughter from outside her dressing room while Stephanie Mills was onstage with *The Wiz.* At first, Rachel thought it was Carol Channing, whom she'd seen

505

joking with several friends on her way into the theater. Suddenly, the door was flung open, and Beth Burns—newly slim, *or* harnessed into her sequined gown—made her own *Hello, Dolly!* entrance.

"Rachel!" She threw her arms around her friend, and the two of them embraced fiercely.

"I didn't hear from you—I thought you weren't coming!"

Beth gave out a Phyllis Diller snort. "What, and miss the shoot-out? I just wanted to wait until La Bergman went onstage—I mean, I've been a fan of hers all my life. Mustn't let her see us carrying on like two silly asses!"

"Beth, you look wonderful!"

"You like the cotton candy hair? Greg calls it that—and little Junior *loves* tangling his teensy fingers in it!"

She dug through her sequined purse and pulled out a photograph. "Now, did you ever see *anything* so adorable?"

Rachel began to laugh. "He's bald!"

"Baby, he's *only* two weeks old!"

"He's beautiful, Beth, really he is. Congratulations."

"Likewise on your book. I though they'd lynch you on your way to the theater." She paused, then said, "Look, I hate coming backstage before a performance, but I've had my ears open out front, and I thought I ought to warn you."

"Warn me?" said Rachel. "Of what?"

"All anyone's talking about is your book, darlin'. That crowd may be out for blood."

"Beth, really—"

"Just don't be shocked if they wind up sitting on their hands tonight."

"*You're* a sure cure for stage nerves!" But she realized that Beth was only voicing her own qualms.

There was a knock at the door. "Miss Allenby. Places please."

"Cross your fingers?" she said to Beth.

"And my legs, honey, Give 'em hell."

506

She knew that Jamie and Paul were somewhere in the audience, but anticipating the backstage confusion, she had asked them not to come to her dressing room before the show. Now, as she stood in the wings offstage right and waited for her name to be announced, she wished she had remembered to ask their seating locations. With the spotlights and television cameras, she wouldn't be able to see them anyway, but at least it would have provided a mental point of concentration. Ty had said he and Joan would be at the rear of the house, but that, too, covered a wide expanse.

Rachel needed to even the "odds." She had sensed that *before* spying Lehman Stern standing opposite, offstage left. She couldn't see his eyes from that distance, but his face was fixed in her direction, and he was obviously staring at her. As if knowing he had captured her attention, Lehman dropped his cigarette and ground it out with his heel. Then he turned abruptly and walked away.

Why is he here? Rachel wondered as her palms grew moist. Could Beth be right about a conspiracy? Over the book?

Just then, Bennett Jerome touched the sleeve of her gown. "You look as beautiful as ever, as on the night your star began to rise." He brushed his fingers against the rubies and diamonds dangling from her ears. "Lovely. Just the right touch."

Howard had given her the earrings for the opening of *Robin Hood*—when her star had begun to rise. Maybe it was fitting that he not be here on the night her star might fall.

Bennett kissed her cheek. "Hang in there, darling. You've done the right thing. Remember, openings are all the same. Shows, books, you name it."

"Doesn't it ever get easier?"

"I don't know yet," he said. "I've only been in the business for thirty years."

507

Vincent Price announced Rachel's name, and she strode unsteadily to the center of the stage.

She was aware that her name drew no applause, but perhaps that was due to the time demands of television. At other televised galas, audiences were often asked to hold their applause until each artist had performed.

Rachel began with her old standby, Cole Porter's "In the Still of the Night." As the music soared—and her voice along with it—she recalled the April evening of ten years before, when she had sung these same, familiar lyrics on this same, then-unfamiliar stage. Tonight, though, instead of the solo piano accompaniment, she had the "cushioned" backing of a lush, full orchestra and the knowledge that she had made it to the top.

She closed her eyes and sang, "Do you love me, as I love you?" The words held many questions, but on this occasion, they were directed only to the person who mattered most. And he wasn't there.

She fought the division of her attention and followed the orchestra's segue into "Finding Answers," her tour de force finale from *Christina's World*. Bennett had wanted her to close with the showstopper, but she had insisted upon her personal favorite from *Robin Hood*. "My Light Through the Trees" marked a milestone in her career and in her life. The song ended on a note of hopeful optimism, as she wanted tonight to end: with acceptance of tomorrow, whatever that might bring, and the courage, born of love, to face the oncoming day.

Rachel found new meaning in the words as she thought of the "lights" in her life, the people and places who had all played their roles along the way.

She had rehearsed with the conductor and he had agreed to follow her last high note until it had faded into the softest *pianissimo*. The orchestra would continue to diminish its sound until Rachel closed her eyes and lowered her head.

Now, as the final phrase approached, she was swept into

the warmth of the music, the lyrics, the magic. She sang with the artistry for which she had become known. But tonight, she was singing with something more.

She was singing with total freedom. While conscious of technique and timing, she was simultaneously immersed in the immediacy of the moment. On another, deeper level, she was experiencing a sense of oneness. A great surge of loving energy swept over her; she felt as if at any instant she might float away.

She had never known such freedom, onstage or off.

The song came to its end, her high note faded into infinity, and Rachel slowly lowered her head.

There was silence throughout the theater. But it was not the kind of silence that had preceded her ovation on this stage ten years before. Her heart began to hammer. Was it a deliberate silence? Had it been *planned?*

The half-dozen seconds seemed an eternity.

Then, from the rear of the house, came the sounds of two solitary pairs of hands clapping.

Rachel lifted her eyes and looked out into the auditorium. Two men were standing. She could barely make out their faces, but she knew one of them was Jamie, and the other was Paul.

At the opposite end of the last row another man joined in, adding a cry of *"Bravo!"* to his applause.

He had only called a single word, but Rachel recognized the voice as Ty Beekman's.

Now she heard *"Bra-vo! Ra-chel!"* in Beth's grand-style Ethel Merman. More began to join in. Some rose, and others followed, until the entire audience was on its feet and cheering as one.

Rachel stood glued to the spot. She was stunned by both reactions — the shattering silence that had greeted her and now the pandemonium erupting throughout the theater.

She drew a deep breath, and remembering that the show hadn't ended — there was still Anita's kick-line finale — Rachel made her way to the wings.

Her eyes were blurred with tears, and at first she didn't see the man in the corner, offstage right, holding her garment bag and tote. He dropped them at his side as she came toward him. He was carrying a book.

Her book.

"Howard!" she cried, now running, flinging herself into his arms.

The audience was still clapping and yelling wildly. But Rachel heard only the pounding of Howard's heartbeat racing in her ear as she buried her head against his chest.

He tilted her tear-streaked face and, looking deeply into her eyes, said, "I've been wrong. It's your finest performance." He lifted *Inner Voices* from behind her back, where his arms had locked her in his embrace. "I love you, Rachel More than you can ever know."

"I love you, Howard," she said. "I always have."

The crowd inside hadn't stopped clapping or shouting Rachel's name as she and Howard collected her bags and headed for the exit. Only the stage doorman, seated in his vestibule cage, witnessed their kiss. He looked up from his reading and winked at the couple.

"You did win, after all," he said.

Rachel leaned in and give him a peck on the cheek. "For Al, who was right," she answered.

The applause continued to echo in her ears as Howard pushed open the stage door. For a fleeting instant, Rachel thoughts darted to Anita's kick-line finale.

But the moment passed, and she slipped an arm through Howard's. Then, together, they stepped into the still of the April night.

THE HAND OF LAZARUS (100-2, $4.50)
by Warren Murphy & Molly Cochran
The IRA's most bloodthirsty and elusive murderer has chosen the small Irish village of Ardath as the site for a supreme act of terror destined to rock the world: the brutal assassination of the Pope! From the bestselling authors of GRANDMASTER!

LAST JUDGMENT (114-2, $4.50)
by Richard Hugo
Only former S.A.S. agent James Ross can prevent a centuries-old vision of the Apocalypse from becoming reality . . . as the malevolent instrument of Adolf Hitler's ultimate revenge falls into the hands of the most fiendish assassin on Earth!
"RIVETING...A VERY FINE BOOK"
— *NEW YORK TIMES*

TRUK LAGOON (121-5, $3.95
Mitchell Sam Rossi
Two bizarre destinies inseparably linked over forty years unleash a savage storm of violence on a tropic island paradise — as the mos incredible covert operation in military history is about to be un covered at the bottom of TRUK LAGOON!

THE LINZ TESTAMENT (117-6, $4.50
Lewis Perdue
An ex-cop's search for his missing wife traps him a terrifying se cret war, as the deadliest organizations on Earth battle for posses sion of an ancient relic that could shatter the foundations c Western religion: the Shroud of Veronica, irrefutable evidence c a second Messiah!